THE NIGHT
BROTHER

Also by Rosie Garland

Vixen
The Palace of Curiosities

THE NIGHT BROTHER

BROTHER

ROSIE GARLAND

THE BOROUGH PRESS

The Borough Press
An imprint of HarperCollins*Publishers*
1 London Bridge Street
London SE1 9GF

www.harpercollins.co.uk

Published by HarperCollins*Publishers* 2017
1

Copyright © Rosie Garland 2017

Rosie Garland asserts the moral right to
be identified as the author of this work

A catalogue record for this book
is available from the British Library

ISBN: 978 0 00 816610 6

Jacket design Claire Ward © HarperCollins*Publishers* Ltd 2017
Illustration © Aitch

Set in Minion by Palimpsest Book Production Limited,
Falkirk, Stirlingshire

Printed and bound in Great Britain by
Clays Ltd, St Ives plc

MIX
Paper from
responsible sources
FSC   **FSC˚ C007454**
www.fsc.org

FSC™ is a non-profit international organisation established
to promote the responsible management of the world's forests.
Products carrying the FSC label are independently certified
to assure consumers that they come from forests that are managed
to meet the social, economic and ecological needs
of present and future generations,
and other controlled sources.

Find out more about HarperCollins and the environment at
www.harpercollins.co.uk/green

For Manchester
and all the wanderers who have found a home
in this Rainy City

All things must change to something new,
to something strange.

Henry Wadsworth Longfellow,
Kéramos

MANCHESTER
AUGUST 1894

My night brother is here.

Halfway between yesterday and tomorrow morning, he shakes my shoulder.

'I'm asleep, Gnome,' I grunt. 'Go away.'

I hug the blanket close. Sounds from the taproom steal through the floorboards: calls for mild and bitter, porter and stout; jokes and merriment to ease the day's care and pour forgetfulness upon the toil to come. The tide of voices rolls back and forth and swells into shouting. This is brief and all contention settles into a rumbling burr, laced with the toffee scent of malt, breathed-out beer, wet coats and wetter dogs. A bedtime story that rocks me back to sleep.

'"Boys and girls come out to play,"' he sings. 'Wake up.'

'Don't want to,' I mumble.

He claps his hands and I taste the tremble of his anticipation.

'Have you forgotten what's happening tonight?' he cries. 'It's Belle Vue fireworks!'

He yanks away the blanket and we begin our tug-of-war: me hanging on to one end, him the other. He wins. He always wins, for he bests me in strength as in everything else: bravery, brains, riot and loving kindness. The room swirls awake. One blink and I can make out the rectangle of the window. Two blinks, the door.

'Shake a leg,' he whispers.

I sit up and it sets off a yawn so wide it could swallow the mattress. He presses my lips together, shutting me up as tight as the bubbles in a crate of ginger beer.

'Don't give me that. You're not tired.'

I am, but I save my breath. He always gets his own way.

'We can't go without asking Ma,' I say.

'She won't miss us. What she doesn't see won't grieve her.'

'But I'm not allowed out in the dark.'

'I'll get you back before it's light.'

'But she'll see us come in.'

'Then we'll sneak through the window.'

'But she'll shout.'

'She won't.'

'But—'

'But but but! You don't half whine, Edie. We're going and that's that.'

I yield to the press of his authority. For all my protestations I am thrilled. For two weeks I have been breathless with hoping Ma might take me to the firework show, the street having spoken of little else. Even Miss Pannett's Sunday School voice brightened when she described last year's extravaganza. Excitement tingles down my arms, into my legs. I leap from the bed.

'Good,' he grunts. 'About time, silly girl.'

He speaks fondly and I am not hurt by the words. Ma says there's no money to squander on toys. I have Gnome. Better than a hundred dolls. Wherever I go he holds my hand. I watch him lay the bolster along the mattress and arrange the blanket on top of it.

'It doesn't look anything like me.'

4

'Who cares? It's not like Mam is going to come in and kiss you goodnight, is it?'

'She might,' I protest, voice as empty as my wishes. If Ma looks in at all, it is a swift open and shut of the door after she's cleared the bar at closing time.

'And I'm the king of . . .' Gnome mutters, fastening me into a pair of britches. He snaps braces over my shoulders to stop them falling down, for they are far too big.

'Why have I got to wear trousers?' I ask. 'I'm not a boy.'

'Hush your racket. It's easier to climb out of windows, and no one will remark upon— Oh, I haven't got time to explain, you little goose. We must go.'

He drags me towards the window.

'Wait,' I say.

'No waiting.'

'Wait!' I grab a handful of marbles from under the pillow: each one a prize hoarded from the cracked throat of a lemonade bottle. I shove them into my pocket and hear the reassuring clink. 'They're lucky,' I say.

He sighs. 'Are you ready? We must go. Now.'

He rolls up the sash and hauls me on to the sill. I blink at the long climb down the drainpipe.

'I'm afraid, Gnome.'

'It'll be worth it. Wait and see. Anyhow,' he adds with a twist. 'If there's an ounce of trouble, it'll be you that gets it in the neck. I'll be long gone by the time Mam gets her hands on you.'

A familiar feeling swirls in my chest, sick and uncomfortable. 'What do you mean?'

'Stop asking daft questions and get down this damned pipe.'

I am silenced by the coarse word and obey. He shows me

5

where to put my feet and fingers. My knees grind iron; rust stains my hands. We jump to the privy roof, which rattles beneath our feet, but holds steady. Then it's only a short drop to the ground and we melt into the dark of the yard. Through the gate we scuttle, over the chipped cobbles of the back alley and on to the street.

Gnome gallops ahead full tilt, wind lifting his curls, whooping loud as Buffalo Bill and all his Indians. I tumble after, puffing and panting with the effort of keeping up. He laughs between my hurtling breaths.

'You should come out and play more often, Edie,' he teases. 'It'll build you up strong and healthy.'

'I am going fast as I can, Gnome,' I wheeze. 'Ma says I should behave as befits a young lady.'

'Mam says this, Mam says that. Mam says rot,' he says dangerously, waiting for my shocked reaction. When it doesn't come, he grins. 'That's more like it. Who cares what she thinks.' He giggles. 'I suppose you are doing well. For a girl.'

I pinch his skinny ribs and he squeals with laughter. We leap puddles dark as porter, hopscotch from lamplit pool to lamplit pool of light, my hand in his and his in mine. The faster I run, the easier it becomes. I flap my arms, imagining them wings. I could run forever.

Gnome sings the praises of Belle Vue. What a fairyland it is: more fantastical than any I could dream up in a month of Sundays. He spins stories of Maharajah the elephant, Consul the intelligent chimpanzee, the crocodiles with gnashing jaws, the pythons that can squeeze the life out of a man. I'd be frightened out of my wits if I were not so over the moon.

We are not alone in our exhilaration. The closer we draw to our destination the busier the streets. Hyde Road is so thick with wagons and omnibuses that not one of them can advance more than an inch at a time. We weave through the throng, Gnome guiding us with his skilful feet and eyes.

'We're here,' he announces at last.

The entrance gate looms above our heads. Through its arch I spy an avenue lined with trees radiant with electric lights. It's only as we stand there gawping that I remember there's not so much as a halfpenny in my pocket. I grind the marbles and wish for a miracle.

'Watch and learn,' says Gnome and taps his nose.

He saunters across the road and I have little option but to follow, dodging carts and charabancs. We head for a roadside stall selling tea and fried potatoes. He slaps his grubby palms upon the counter.

'Begging your pardon, sir,' he chirps, and tugs the peak of his cap. 'The chaps in the lion house have a fearsome thirst on them and have sent me to fetch their tea.'

'Hah. Sharples again, is it?' growls the stallholder, who is a veritable mountain of a man. 'He's a cheeky sod, sending a lad your age to do his work.'

'I'm eight next birthday, sir!' says Gnome, cheerfully.

'Are you now?' replies the man. He hefts an enormous steel teapot and pours steaming liquid into four mugs, each bigger than our milk jug at home. He thumps them on to a tin tray and shoves it across the counter. The mugs jiggle perilously. 'Mind you don't spill them!'

'Not me, sir. Thank you, sir!' Gnome cheeps.

'Tell him he owes me sixpence!' yells the tea-man as we carry the tray away.

Gnome strides to the front of the line, chin up. I try to close my ears to the complaints of *cheeky lad, there's a queue here you know* and hug his side, close as his shirt. At the turnstile, a fellow in a dark blue uniform plants his hand in front of Gnome's face and we teeter to a halt.

'Watch it!' cries Gnome. 'I almost spilled this tea!'

The gatekeeper chews his moustache. 'A shilling after five o'clock,' he grunts.

'And if I don't get these to Mr Sharples at the lion enclosure in less than two minutes, he'll take more than a shilling out of my arse,' says Gnome, so loudly that the man behind us expels a cry of disgust.

'Good Lord!' exclaims the gent. 'That's hardly the sort of language ladies should hear.' His wife and children cluster at his coat-tails, scowling.

The ticket inspector raises his hat. 'I'm dreadfully sorry, sir! We offer our apologies that you have been so incommodicated. I do hope this won't spoil your enjoyment of this evening's entertainment.'

The gentleman is already bustling his brood forwards.

'Far more interested in getting a good view of the fireworks than any real argument,' murmurs Gnome in my ear.

The gatekeeper glares at us and jerks his thumb into the park. 'Shift it, you little blighter. Now. And don't think I won't be having a word with Fred Ruddy Sharples about the class of lad he gets to do his fetching and carrying these days.'

'Yes, sir!' cries Gnome smartly. 'I'll be sure and let him know!'

We click through the turnstile and melt into the crowd. As soon as we are out of sight, Gnome plonks the tray on to the ground and passes me one of the mugs. 'Go on. Get that down you. It'll warm your cockles.'

The tea is strong, hot and deliciously sweet.

'It's the best thing I ever drank,' I breathe.

'That's the ticket. Hits the very spot,' says Gnome. He takes a slurp himself and lets out a satisfied belch.

'You're a marvel, Gnome,' I say, in awe of my cunning brother. 'I didn't know a person could do anything half so sharp.'

'Here's the thing. If you act confidently, folk believe what they see and hear. Act nervous, like you don't belong in a place, and you'll stand out like a sore thumb.'

I take a long draught of tea. 'I wish I were a boy, Gnome. I'd be as smart as you. And I wouldn't have to stay at home with Ma and Nana.'

He shoots me a look. The light is not good, so it may be anger, it may be fear, it may be something else.

'Don't talk nonsense. You're not dim, so don't act it.'

'I don't mind being stupid. With you at my side, nothing can hurt me.'

'You don't know what's around the corner,' he sighs.

'I do,' I say. 'You are.'

'Oh, Edie,' he says. 'We can't live this way forever.' He lays a hand on my shoulder and squeezes. 'We're growing up. Jack and Jill have to come down the hill sooner or later.' He heaves a sigh at my uncomprehending stare. 'You don't have a clue what I'm talking about, do you?'

I shake my head.

'I don't mean it nastily,' he says, smiling again. 'It's just – ach. You'll understand one day.'

He drains his mug and shoves it under a bush, tray and all.

'Shouldn't we take them—'

'Shush. We'll collect them later,' he says.

I know he isn't telling the truth. He doesn't care for the cups now he has finished with them.

Gnome drags me past the animal enclosures and their rank scent of dung, meat and straw. I hear the grumblings of beasts who'll get no sleep tonight. It is hardly like night-time. Everywhere we walk, lights banish the dusk. At the Monkey

House, he bows his legs and hobbles from side to side, scratching his armpits, funnelling his lips and hooting. At the elephant house he swings his arm like a trunk, and trumpets; at the bear pit he growls; at the kangaroo house he hops. I can't catch my breath for laughing.

'Who needs the zoo when you have me?' he says.

He pushes on and I scramble in his wake. If I lost him in this strange place it would be awful. I'd be lost forever.

'Stop worrying, little sister. It's not possible,' he whispers, as though he has heard my thoughts.

I don't know how he can murmur in my ear and yet still be bounding ahead, but I'm far too excited to give it much thought. Besides, he is Gnome and he can do anything. He pauses at a confectioner's stand, produces a penny from his conjurer's store and buys a bag of cinder toffee. As we scoff it, we press on towards the Firework Lake.

'There won't be anywhere left to sit at this rate,' he grunts between mouthfuls. 'It's your fault for being so slow out of bed.'

'I can't go any faster.' I feel the tight clumping of tears in my chest.

'Don't cry! Not when we're so close.' His voice is so desperate that it swipes aside my plunge into self-pity. How funny he sounds. He is never usually so nice. 'I've always been nice to you, you ungrateful little brute,' he grumbles, although I can tell that he is relieved. 'Now, please let us hurry.'

A wooden scaffold has been constructed on the dancing platform, high as the Town Hall if not higher. Gnome tugs me underneath, into a jungle of posts and cross-beams. He slips between them as nimbly as one of the apes he so recently imitated, starts to climb and I clamber after, up the ranks of seats until he is satisfied with our vantage point. We squeeze through the thicket of skirts and trousers.

'I say!' exclaims a chap as we struggle between the legs of his brown-and-yellow tweed britches. 'Whatever are you doing down there!'

Gnome tips his cap. 'Bless you, sir!' he cries. 'Thought I was going to get squashed flat!' I pause to curtsey my thanks but he drags me down the walkway. 'He smelled of mothballs,' he hisses, and I giggle.

At the end of the bench are a spooning couple.

Gnome smiles angelically. In his politest voice he says, 'If you'd be so kind,' and they shuffle aside. There's only the tiniest squeeze of a space but we manage to fit somehow.

'You're getting fat. What's Mam feeding you, bricks?'

We laugh. No one ticks us off for making a noise. Indeed, we can hardly be heard over the commotion: shuffling of feet, rustling of petticoats, crunching of pork scratchings and gossiping about how grand the display was last time and how it can't possibly be as good tonight. I'm so a-jangle I'm going to burst.

'Stop wriggling,' he snaps. 'If you don't calm down I'll shove you under the bench and you'll see nothing.'

I am shocked into stone by the awful threat. My lip wobbles. 'For goodness' sake,' he sighs. 'I don't mean it. Shush. The show is about to start.'

Expectation ripples through the both of us. A trumpet blares and a hundred suns shine forth, illuminating a new world. There is a gasp from the entire company. Even Gnome lets out a whistle. Cries of wonder rumble in my ears: *Huzzah! Bravo! Best ever!* Heels stamp, so thunderous the planks shake. Before us stretches a strange city towering with castles, parapets and battlements. Not Manchester, but a fairyland better and brighter than any of the stories told by Nana when Ma spares her to sit with me.

11

'What's happening?' I whisper. 'Where are we?' I shrink into Gnome and he laughs.

'We're in Belle Vue!'

'We can't be. Look! When did they build all of that?'

'Build all of what?' says Gnome.

'The castles.'

'It's a painting.' He sniggers. 'A new one every year and this is the best yet. You *are* a dimwit.'

Now that I look more carefully I can see it is a canvas banner: taller than two houses one on top of the other, longer than our street and riotous with colour. I gawp open-mouthed, bursting with gratitude that Gnome did not leave me at home.

'As if I could,' he says gently. 'Anyway. Shut your trap. There's a train coming.'

There's a general shushing as a gaggle of men in scarlet uniforms charge across the platform, bayonets glinting in the torchlight. I can pick out the noble hero by his flamboyant gestures and clutching of his breast. His mouth opens. The wind is rather in the wrong direction, and I only catch the words *spirit* and *devour*, but no one minds terribly much and we applaud his brave speech all the same.

Cannons roar; mortars boom. Beams of electrical light fly back and forth, sharp as spears. Two vast ships heave into view, one from the right and one from the left. We cheer our jolly tars and boo the enemy, who are dressed as Turks. Their ship shatters like matchwood at the first assault and they pitch into the lake, yowling like cats. I watch them struggle to the shore and squelch up the bank, shivering. They'll catch a chill and Lord knows what else from that mucky water.

'Don't worry,' says Gnome. 'They have sandwiches waiting.'

'Is this the Relief of Mafeking or the Battle of the Nile?' asks the lady beside us.

'Who cares?' says her companion, tugging his side-whiskers with gusto. 'It's a right good show, that's what it is.' He sweeps off his hat and waves it around his head. 'Blow 'em to kingdom come!' he cries.

The crowd shriek like demons and the fireworks answer in hellish agreement. The night sky of Manchester is wallpapered with flame. Spinning cartwheels roll on roads of fire and set the lake ablaze. I spy serpents and stars, Catherine wheels and Roman fountains. Rockets burst and bloom like flowers hurled into the heavens and rain down silver dust.

I look around. Lit by the flicker of firecrackers we have been transformed into demons: eye sockets pierced deep as death's heads, black flared nostrils, teeth bared in rictus grins. The lady to our right moans and groans like a cow trying to give birth, or at least that's what Gnome whispers in my ear. I titter at his naughty joke. No one hears my little scrap of laughter over the din. No one wags their finger and tells me to be a good girl. The realisation of such delicious liberty occurs to us both at the same time. Gnome's eyes glitter, teeth sharp as a knife.

'Come on. Make a racket.'

'I can't.' He grabs the skin of my arm and twists. 'Ow!' I squeak. My skin burns as though he's stubbed out a cigar. 'Stop it, Gnome.'

'Not till you scream. No one can hear you.'

In agreement, a barricade of bangers is let off. My stomach pitches and rolls.

'Aah!' I try, hard as I can. All that comes out is a feeble mewing.

'Do you want me to pinch you black and blue?' Gnome growls.

'Aah!' I cry, a bit louder.

'More. Still can't hear you.'

I am struck by the realisation that tonight will never come again. I will not be able to claw back so much as one second.

'That's right,' says Gnome. 'Drink every drop. Live every minute. Yell!'

My voice breaks out of my throat. 'Aaaah!'

'Yes! Open your cake-hole and let rip!'

I stretch my lips wide and shriek. Gnome joins in and together, our shouts punch holes in the clouds and soar to the stars.

'Oh!' he cries. 'Wouldn't it be grand to grab the tail of a rocket and fly all the way to the moon and live there and never come back?'

I think of my warm bed, the comforting arms of my grandmother, kind-hearted Uncle Arthur on his monthly visits. The thought of losing them makes my heart slide sideways.

'Isn't the moon awfully cold?' I say nervously.

'Not a bit. Don't you ache to spread your wings?'

'Do I have to?'

He waggles his hands in frustration. 'Don't you ache to be free?'

'Free of what?'

'Just once, I wish you weren't such a stick-in-the-mud, Edie. I'm never able to do what I want. Always chained to you, shackled like a prisoner—'

The barrage of words finds its target and stings.

'Oh,' I say.

He frowns. 'Dash it all, Edie, I didn't mean it like that. Don't take on so.' But he does mean it, exactly like that. 'Forget I spoke. I should hold my tongue.'

He makes amends by sticking out his tongue and pinching it tight. I try to smile, but it is not easy. I don't understand how he can say such a cruel thing. I never demand that he come and play with me. I never force him to stay. If he finds me so tiresome, I don't know why he insists on my company. It is confusing.

Gnome piggy-backs me home. He does not grumble, not once.

'I thought you said I was as heavy as a hod of bricks,' I mumble.

'So you are. But I am strong as a bricklayer.'

I squeeze him so tight we can't breathe. 'Don't leave me, Gnome. Not ever.'

He doesn't answer; too busy hoisting me on to the roof of the outhouse, up the pipe and through the window. We tumble through, tickling each other and rolling on the floor like puppies.

'Get into bed,' chides Gnome, herding me towards the cot he hauled me out of such a short time before. 'It'll be light soon.'

I skip across the floor, ears buzzing, fingertips shooting sparks as though I've brought the fireworks home. 'No it won't.'

'It's usually you who is the sensible one.' He tries to be stern, but I can hear glee at the back of his words.

'How can I sleep after such an adventure? It is quite impossible.'

'No, *you* are quite impossible. Hurry up. Get out of these britches,' he says, fumbling with the buttons. I try to help but I'm all fingers and thumbs. 'Leave off,' he cries. 'I'll be quicker.'

He wrestles with the fly and wins. The trousers fall to my ankles. I take a step, trip and fall flat upon the mattress. Marbles scatter across the rug. He seizes his opportunity, pins me down and endeavours to drag the shirt over my head.

'We've got to fold the trousers and put them away tidily,' I mumble.

15

'No time,' he says with an odd urgency. He sounds an awfully long way off, as if he has turned into a gnat and is whining in my ear. I flap my hand but it is stuck half in and half out of the shirt. 'Stay still,' he says, so grave and unlike his usual self I can't help tittering.

All my clothes are off. The blanket is scratchy, coarse.

'Tell me a bedtime story, Gnome,' I say, halfway gone.

Breath close to my ear, hot and stifling. He folds his hand in mine. My hand in his. I think of Nana folding butter into flour. I flutter my fingers and hear Gnome giggle.

'That tickles.'

Perhaps I say it. Perhaps it is Gnome. I'm so sleepy I'm no longer sure where he ends and I begin. Nor does it matter: I have never known such bliss and I know he feels it also. I know everything he has ever known, feel everything he has ever felt. It is so simple. I did not realise—

The door flies open. Ma stands against the light, her candle shivering the walls with shadow.

'Come now, Edie,' she says. 'What's all this noise?'

'Ma!' I cheer, still fizzing with excitement. I reach for her to gather me into her arms.

'Why aren't you asleep?' She plonks down the candle, marches across the room and closes the window.

Shh, hisses Gnome. *Don't tell.*

The space between my ears is spinning with red and yellow lights; rockets are bouncing off the walls of my ribs. I can't help myself.

'I've been to the fireworks!' I crow. 'It was wonderf—'

'You naughty girl!' she exclaims, pushing aside my grasping hands. 'If I've told you once, I've told you a hundred times. You're too little to step out on your own.'

'I didn't. Gnome held my hand.'

16

Don't say my name! says Gnome. *Not to her.*

'What?' Ma swallows so heavily I see the muscles in her neck clump together. 'Who . . . ?'

'I told Gnome you'd be cross, but he wouldn't listen . . .'

'Gnome?' she gulps. 'No.'

Her eyes stretch so wide they look like they might pop out of her head. I hold my hand over my mouth to push the giggle back in.

That's torn it, says Gnome.

'No. No. No,' she mutters, over and over, shaking her head from side to side. 'I'll not have it. There's no such person.'

'There is! He's here every night.'

I don't know why Ma is being so silly. The candle flame wobbles. Her expression twists from disbelief to belief, belief to shame, shame to fear, fear to anger. She slaps the back of my legs. Not hard, but it stings.

'Ow! Ma, you're hurting.'

'Serves you right for telling lies.'

'I'm not. Gnome!' I cry. 'Come back and tell Ma!'

I can't see him. Maybe he's hiding under the bed. But Gnome doesn't need to hide. He's not afraid of anyone.

'Shut up!' Ma cuffs the side of my head. My ears whistle. 'He's not real. He can't be! When are you going to get it through that thick skull of yours?'

I shrink into the bed as far as I can, curl against the wall. There is no further I can go. I don't know why Ma is so furious. She is strict, but not like this: wild, white-faced. I want the mattress to open its mouth and gobble me up.

'It was all Gnome's idea!' I squeal. 'He made me go with him!'

It's a terrible lie. The air freezes, pushing ice so far down my throat I can't breathe. Ma seizes my shoulders and shakes me.

'He's not real! Say it!'

'No!' I wail.

'Say it!' she roars.

My head jerks back and forth, my neck as brittle as a bit of straw.

'Say it!'

Roaring in my ears. Dark, sucking.

'He's not real,' I moan.

'Louder!'

'He's not real!' I whimper, the thin squeal of a doll with a voice box in its chest.

'What's all this to-do?' booms Nana. She can barely fit into the tiny room beside Ma, but fit she does. She throws a quick glance the length of my body and turns to Ma. 'Well, Cissy?'

Ma's face contorts. 'Lies. Nightmares,' she spits. 'She says she's been to the fireworks. With – no. No! Her and her wretched imaginings. It's enough to try the patience of a saint.'

'Stuff and nonsense,' says Nana pertly. She lowers herself on to the mattress and huffs a sigh that matches the springs in weary music. She pats the blanket. 'Come here, Edie.'

I shake my head the smallest fraction and cling to the bedstead.

'No one is going to punish you.'

'I'll be the judge of that,' growls Ma.

'Pipe down,' snaps Nana, throwing her a glance that could burn toast. 'Now then, Edie,' she says very carefully. 'Why aren't you in your nightdress? You've not a stitch on.'

I shake my head again. It seems to be the only thing of which I am capable.

'Filthy little heathen,' says Ma.

Nana continues in her soft burr, coaxing me out of my funk. 'You'll catch your death. Here.' She plucks my nightdress out

18

of thin air, or so it seems to my fuddled brain. I clutch it to my chest. 'I think we could all do with some sleep,' she adds.

I nod. My head bounces, broken and empty. Nana turns to Ma and frowns.

'Look at her. She doesn't know whether she's coming or going. Be gentle with her. As I was with you.'

'Since when did any of that nonsense do any good? She's tapped. I'll have her taken away, I will.'

'Hush. You'll do no such thing. You're frightening the child. If you let her play out rather than keeping her cooped up, she wouldn't need to make up stories.'

'Who cares about her? What about *my* nerves?'

Nana ignores her and returns her attention to me. 'You're a good girl, aren't you, Edie love?'

'Yes?' I say uncertainly.

'So you haven't really been to the fireworks, have you?'

Ma glares over Nana's shoulder, eyes threatening dire punishment. I am afraid of lying, terrified of the truth. My heart gallops like a stampede of coal horses.

'No,' I squeak.

Ma smirks; Nana does not. I have satisfied one and not the other. I have no idea how to please them both.

'*Was* it a nightmare, Edie?' Nana purrs.

I can tell the truth, if that's what she wants. But I no longer know what anyone wants. 'Yes,' I lie.

'Well, then,' she says. 'You were dreaming. That's all.'

Ma storms out of the room, grumbling about my disobedience. Nana pauses, screws up her eyes until they are slits. I have the oddest notion she's trying to see through me and find Gnome. She leans close.

'Herbert?' she whispers.

'Shh,' I hiss. 'He hates that name.' She gives me a startled glance. 'I'm sorry, Nana. I didn't mean to be rude. But he likes to be called Gnome.'

She looks over her shoulder, as though worried Ma is watching. I did not think grandmothers were afraid of their own children.

'Quiet now,' she murmurs. She kisses my brow. 'Let's have no more of this talk. Not in front of your mother. You can see how it riles her.'

'But he's my brother.'

'No, he's not.' She rolls her eyes. 'I can't explain. You're too little. One day. Just don't say his name again. A quiet life. That's what we all want.'

'Can we run away, Nana?'

'Hush, my pet. Do you want your ma to come back in here?'

She pinches my cheek. It is affectionate, but her eyes are desperate. She slides away, taking the light of the candle with her. I lie in a darkness greater than the absence of flame. I'm afraid. If Nana is too, there's nowhere I can turn. Through the wall I hear them argue, voices muffled by brick.

'This wasn't supposed to happen,' wails Ma. 'She's ruined everything.'

'She's ruined nothing. She's the same as you and me, that's all.'

'That's *all*? I raised her to be normal.'

'Cissy, for goodness' sake . . .'

'It can't be true. I won't let it be.'

'You can't alter facts. We are what we are,' says Nana, over and over. 'We are what we are.'

I smell home in all its familiarity: a stew of spilt beer, pipe smoke and damp sawdust. And something else: my hair, reeking of gunpowder. I crawl out of bed. Underneath is a pair of britches, ghostly with warmth from the body that wore them. Beside them

20

are my boots, mud clumped under the heel. I press my finger to it: fresh, damp. Ma says I was lying. Nana says I was dreaming. If I didn't go out, I must be imagining this as well.

I tiptoe to the window. I can't be sure if I opened it or not. I peer through the glass. I would never be brave enough to climb down the drainpipe, not in a hundred years. My thoughts stumble, stop in their tracks.

'Where are you, Gnome?' I sob. 'I need you.'

However many times Ma's told me off, I've always been able to find his hand in the dark and hang on. He's always been there. But tonight, there's no answer. Something emptier than silence.

I try to make sense of the senseless. Ma says Gnome is all in my head – a nightmare. Nana says he isn't my brother, that he is imaginary. They would not lie to me. Grown-ups are always right. I am the one who is wrong. I am a naughty girl. I tell lies. I make things up.

I must have been asleep. I must have dreamed the whole thing. I will be a good girl. I will scrape his name from the slate of my memory. If I say what Ma wants then it will be the truth and she will be happy. She won't be cross any more.

I double over in agony, as though I have been split in half and my heart torn out. I squeeze my nightdress, expecting to find it soaked with blood. All is dry. In the faint light I examine my chest, searching for wounds. My skin is whole, undamaged. I am just a girl, on my own.

I throw the marbles out of the window; hear them click as they roll down the privy roof, and the fainter thud as they fall into the dirt. There is no such thing as luck.

'Gnome?' I say his name for the last time.

The sound echoes off the ceiling. I have lost him. I do not know how to get him back. If he was ever here. For the first time in my life, I am alone.

PART ONE
MANCHESTER
1897–1904

EDIE
1897–1899

Stroll through Hulme of an evening and you will be forgiven for imagining it a den of drunkards. Brave the labyrinth of streets, row upon row of brick-built dwellings black as burned toast, and there, upon each and every corner, you will find it: haven for the weary traveller, fountain for the thirsty man – the beerhouse.

Hulme boasts a hundred of them; a hundred more besides. There's the Dolphin, famed for its operatic landlord; the Duke of Brunswick with a ship's bell clanged at closing time; the Hussar and its sword swiped at Peterloo. If you can ignore their glittering siren song and press on, only then will you find us, breasting the tip of Renshaw Street like a light-ship.

The Comet.

Sparkling Ales is etched upon one frosted window, *Fine Stouts and Porter* upon the other. A board stretches the width of our wall, announcing *Empress Mild and Bitter Beer.* Above the door and brightest of all, the gilt scroll of my mother's name: *Cecily Margaret Latchford, Licensed to sell Beers and Stouts.* Come, it beckons. Enter, and be refreshed.

That is the full extent of our finery and flash. We are no glaring gin-palace for we boast neither piano room, spirit licence, nor free-and-easy on a Saturday night; we field no darts team, no skittle alley, no billiard table. You'd be forgiven for thinking us a temperance hall on account of the sober principles Ma polishes into the long oaken bar. We are so plain I scarcely understand why The Comet is full each evening; lunchtime too.

They said we'd not make a farthing, but Ma is forged of steely stuff and has proved them wrong. She gives neither short measure nor employs the long pull. A pint is a pint to the very drop. She never raises her voice, nor needs to. At closing time she glares at the clock. That's all it takes for every glass in the room to be raised, every mouthful drained. By ten past the hour she slides the door-bolts into place and turns down the gas, with not so much as the shadow of a dog remaining under the tables.

For all that Ma will have no truck with nonsense, the walls of The Comet bulge with mysteries. Some are simple to plumb. Ma refuses to speak about Papa, a moustachioed fellow who hangs above the bar in a picture frame, only pointing to the black riband looped around the corner. That, I understand. Some things are less easy to explain: why Ma takes to her bed three days in every month; why my beloved Uncle Arthur only drops by when she's laid up.

Then there are my nightmares. I can't understand why people talk of sleep as a welcome undoing of strife and woe. They must mean something else entirely. I am hag-ridden. I tell no one of the night-voice that shrieks so piercingly the whole street ought to hear. I dare not. I tell no one how I wake with finger-nails grimed as black as soot, knots in my hair and scraps of bacon rind wedged in my teeth. I dare not.

The only person with whom I share my stories is Papa, behind his glass. Sometimes I wish he'd speak one word, give one nod of encouragement, but his face is stiff. He keeps my secrets well.

At school, I hunger for mathematics and its security of

two-times-two-equals-four; prefer geography and the massive consistency of mountains. Even the most determined friend despairs of my inability to engage in games of make-believe and I am left to the click of my abacus. What they cannot know is that I cling to logic with the dogged desperation of one drowning. I strive to make Ma smile.

Every night she stares as I undress, as though searching for something she does not want to find. I wonder if the removal of my petticoat will reveal me to be a bat, ready to squeak and burst out of the window.

'Don't you stir,' she says.

'No, Ma.'

'You stay right there.'

'Yes, Ma.'

She sits on the bed, stands up, sits again. It makes me dizzier than physick. At last, she leans close and I thrill that tonight she may kiss me.

'I know you,' she whispers, the words crawling into my ear. 'You're waiting for me to look away for one minute, aren't you?'

'No, Ma,' I say.

'Liar,' she replies, exhaling heat upon my face. 'I know what you're thinking. Everything. Before you think it. I know you better than you know yourself.'

'Ma?' I don't understand. I never do.

'You can't fool me. Don't try,' she hisses.

'I won't,' I promise desperately. I close my eyes. Green lights dance behind my eyelids. The next time she speaks it is from further away.

'I am watching. Always.'

'Yes, Ma. Goodnight, Ma,' I mumble as drowsily as I can manage.

The door clicks shut. I shake my head from side to side, but her words stick fast and refuse to tumble out on to the pillow. I climb out of bed, kneel under the picture of Jesus and Mary and press my palms together. I beg them to send me to sleep and not wander in wild dreams. They look down at me with sad expressions, pointing at their fiery hearts, eyes reproachful. Their insides are burning too, but they don't complain. Not like me.

From below come the sounds of The Comet: clink of glass, rumble of voices, the percussion of Ma's footsteps drumming back and forth. I stare at the ceiling until my eyes grow used to the dark. Tonight, perhaps, I will be spared.

It begins small, as always, like a dray rumbling over cobbles three streets distant. Street by street the thunder draws closer, gathering speed and vigour. I clap my hands over my ears to stave off the din, but the commotion is from inside, not out. The shadows thicken and in their depths I spy the glint of monstrous eyes, the flash of leviathan teeth, ready to devour me.

Edie. I'm here, roars the fiend. *Let's go out to play.*

'No!' I howl, but the wail is trapped within the confines of my head. 'I can't hear you! I won't!'

I strain to get away. If I can stir so much as my little finger, I will win and the beast will be vanquished. But all that is Edie has shrunk into a marble, tiny and lost.

You used to be so much more fun. Don't you remember the fireworks?

'No.' It is a lie and I weep with the wickedness of telling it.

I can't waste time chatting. Time presses. Let me in.

I fight to stay awake. The creature surges forwards, opens its jaws. Claws drag me into darkness and I do not rise again.

The next morning I wake with a fog of unknowing between my ears. My first thought is: *Where am I?* The second: *Who am I?* Gradually, the room resumes its familiar shape. This is home and I am in it. I lie abed, half-breathless from last night's dream of bruised knees, slammed doors, thumped door-knockers and racing away. The curtain sways. The window stands half-open. Last night Ma closed it tight.

My hair is sticky with spiders' web and I'm wearing muddy boots and britches. I daren't let Ma see me like this. Before I go downstairs, I clean the boots and take the scrubbing brush to my hands. I stand before the mirror at the top of the stairs and rehearse my smile in preparation for breakfast. My face looks back, pallid and starved of sleep.

'Did you sleep well?' Ma asks as I pull my chair to the kitchen table.

'Yes, Ma,' I lisp and stretch my deceitful grin to the tips of my ears.

I am shepherding the last bit of porridge from bowl to mouth when Nana lays her hand on my forehead.

'You look a bit peaky,' she says.

I butt into the broad warmth of her palm. Half the porridge slips from the spoon back into the bowl. Her tenderness is my undoing.

'Yes, Nana.' I yawn. 'It was that dream again: where I jump out of the window and get into all sorts of naughtiness.'

Her hand makes peaceful circles across my brow. My eyelids droop.

'Dreams,' she murmurs, half-statement, half-question.

I am more than halfway back to sleep. 'I never know why I wake up with dirty hands and feet.' The delicious massage ceases abruptly. 'Nana?' I mumble.

I winch open my eyelids to see Ma shooting my grandmother a look of such blazing fury I am surprised she does not incinerate on the spot.

'Cissy,' says my grandmother in a soothing tone. 'It's only right. Let me tell—'

'Not a word,' rasps Ma, shaking her head. 'Unless you wish to look for alternate lodgings.'

'Cissy! I am your mother!'

'And as long as it is my name upon the licence, you will abide by my rules. Remember who does everything around here. Everything!'

My spoon hovers between dish and lips. What species of imp prompts the next words I do not know.

'Uncle Arthur,' I pipe.

'What?' growls Ma, her eyes wide as saucers.

'He helps.'

She lets loose a cry that could split firewood. 'He does nothing, do you hear?' she screams. 'I work my fingers to the bone and he swans in once a month!'

I bow my head and let the storm rage. I think her ungrateful, but I'll never be the one to say so. Uncle Arthur is a pearl of a man. Without him, who knows how we'd manage when Ma takes to her bed, regular and reliable as the full moon.

Life continues on its confusing path.

I grow into a swallowed voice of a girl. I speak when I am spoken to and often not even then. Ma says sufficient for the two of us, sharp as thistles and as bitter. I gulp down my words before they are born and they wedge in my throat like stones. If I lay my hand on my chest I feel them grinding together, locked up tight.

As soon as I'm old enough to stand without hanging on to the furniture Ma has me collecting glasses and washing them too, for she scorns the idea of squandering cash on a servant. I learn quick not to break one, having no desire to increase the number of times she takes out her wrath on my backside.

Year follows year until I reach my twelfth birthday. It is a

30

proud day indeed, for I carry a jug of beer from the cellar without spilling a drop. It makes Ma happy. And when Ma is happy, well, so is everybody else.

Our customers have their little ways. There's the temperance man who disappears for a fortnight at a time, only to reappear with a famished look, ready to spring to the defence of his porter at closing time. There's Old Tom, who takes the same seat by the fire and woe betide anyone who tries to purloin it. There are the pipe-smokers, teeth stained brown as the benches they sit upon. There's the bearded fellow, white stripes running from the corners of his mouth and lending him the appearance of a badger.

And there's the charming man.

The hair on his head is black, but his eyebrows and moustache are copper-red, adding a streak of spice to his features. I find it difficult to like a man whose head disagrees with his face. Whenever I pass through the bar on one errand or another, he grabs me around the waist and pulls me close, squeezing out what little breath I have to spare. Every time he does so Ma ticks me off.

'Stop annoying the customers,' she growls.

'She's not bothering me,' he replies.

One evening, after a particularly onerous spell of cuddles and pinches, I retreat to the privy. The night-soil collectors emptied the bucket the previous evening but it retains the fruity stink of human ordure. I consider the smell preferable to his unwanted attentions. There is no point in wasting a visit, so I hitch my skirt around my middle.

I hear a light cough, more of an apology.

The ginger-faced man slides into the doorway and hovers

31

there. I stretch out my hand to pull the door shut, but he braces his foot against it.

'I'll make sure no ill befalls you,' he says in his soft, polite way.

I want to tell him to turn around and leave, but something in the way he speaks smothers my protestations. I have the sensation of a pillow stuffed with goose down being held tenderly over my face.

I tug my skirt over my knees. It is tricky to keep my balance at the same time as preventing the hem from trailing in muck. My insides shrivel. I cannot go while he is watching. I pull up my drawers as modestly as I am able.

'I didn't hear you tinkle,' he says, the loveliest of smiles lighting up his face.

'I've changed my mind,' I whisper. 'I don't need to.'

'Oh, but you do,' he purrs. He doesn't shift aside to let me pass, nor does he lift his protective gaze from me for one instant.

'I *can't.*'

'But you must.' His voice is as sticky as barley malt. 'Ah!' he breathes. 'You're afraid someone will barge in, aren't you? I'll tell you what. Let your old friend help you. I'll fight off any rough fellows who come this way.'

I can neither move nor speak.

He waggles his fingers, fanning the sickly air. 'I'll be your lookout. Carry on.'

A cry for help twists my innards. 'No.' It is less than a squeak. Barely an exhalation.

'Do it,' he says, a fraction sharper. 'Now.'

I sit down so quickly I crack my tailbone on the seat. I watch him turn very slowly until he takes position with arms folded, gazing towards the beerhouse door. I raise my petticoats, lower my bloomers. My body clenches. I tuck my chin into my chest and stare at the ground between my knees in the hope that I can

32

block him out. I know he'll not release me until he is satisfied.

Whether it is my prayer or merely an urgent need to pass water, but liquid splashes into the bucket. I didn't know it is possible to feel such relief. It gushes on and on as though it'll never stop. I tear a scrap of paper from the string, wipe myself and rearrange my clothing. When I raise my head, he is staring right at me, beatific grin in place.

'That's better, isn't it? I took care of you, didn't I?'

I do not reply.

He stretches out a hand. 'Here, little miss. Ups-a-daisy. Don't want you falling in, do we now?' he says sweetly.

I struggle to my feet without the aid of his proffered hand. He chuckles at my refusal of help, shoves his fists into his pockets and saunters back to the bar, whistling. I trudge behind. I could have shouted for help. I could have screamed, *You lied! You looked!* A single word would have broken the spell. I stayed silent. I'm not sure why. What I am sure of is that this must be my fault.

It is impossible to speculate how long I might have continued in this muddled state.

Two weeks later, I traipse downstairs at breakfast-time to discover that Ma has retreated to her room, bedridden by her fearsome and unexplained women's ailments. At school, I daydream that luck will smile; that Arthur will come through the door at the very moment Ma is shouting at me. I picture him stepping into the fray and calming her wrath. She'll listen to her brother; she has to. She'll lay her head upon his shoulder and promise she'll never be angry, never again.

The moment the bell rings I race home. As soon as I open the door I know he is there. Some pleasurable tickle in the air betrays his presence. I dash into the kitchen and am swept into his arms.

'Princess!' he roars.

'Was ever a mother so blessed,' says Nana.

In feature and bearing Uncle Arthur and Ma are more alike than two bottles of beer set one next to the other. My mind supplies the unkind observation that one is bitter, one mild. I thrust the thought aside hastily.

'How about a stroll to pick blackberries?' says Arthur, kissing me till I giggle. 'If that doesn't strike you as the most boring idea in the world.'

'Never,' I gasp.

The waste ground between the tracks and the canal seethes with brambles.

'Keep an eye out for trains, eh?' he says. 'Let's get you home with both legs attached.'

We wave to the folk as they rattle past. Those in third class wave back. The grand folk in first class do not.

'They can sneer all they want,' says Uncle. 'They're not having blackberry pie for their supper.'

The first few berries explode under my fierce fingers.

'Pick them, don't throttle them,' he advises. 'They're not your enemy.'

After a while I manage better and show off the tin proudly for inspection. He nods approval each time. The berries tantalise me deeper into the bush, the next always better than the last: bigger, juicier, each drupelet as inviting as liquorice. My mouth waters.

'Can I eat any?' I ask shyly.

'Of course you can. Go for the ones that burst when you touch them. They'll go off before we can get them through the front door. But they're fine to eat now. How's that for a plan?'

We beam at each other. Brambles brush my face and snag

my pinafore. I yelp as I prick myself. He takes my hand to inspect the thorn.

'Close your teeth around the tip. Don't bite or it'll snap and you'll never get the blighter out.'

I do as instructed. It is like kissing my finger.

'Now, spit.'

Simple as that, it is gone.

I study my palm. 'It's not even bleeding.'

He smiles. 'They don't go deep. Only a problem if you leave them and they fester.'

Even with the handfuls I stuff into my mouth, the tin fills with remarkable alacrity.

'Done already?' asks Uncle, peering at my hoard. 'Let's be getting off, then.'

'We don't have to,' I say, stabbed with disappointment. 'There are thousands. Look, I can carry them in my apron.'

'They'll stain. Blackberry juice is the very devil to get out. Don't make work for your ma.'

We pick our way up the siding. In my mind's eye, Ma sits up in bed, remarking how much better she feels. Even though the sun beats down on my head, clouds may as well have pulled a curtain across the sky. I clutch Arthur's hand.

'Who'll make the pie?' I whisper. 'You or Ma?'

'You're stuck with me tonight, Edie,' he says. 'Though I'm sure your ma makes better pastry.'

'Mm,' I murmur, spilling some of the berries. They tumble across the pavement like soft marbles. 'They're dirty!' I sob.

Uncle kneels and begins to pick them up. 'Nothing a rinse under the tap won't sort out.'

'It's your fault!' I wail, far more upset than I should be.

'Ah well,' he says mildly.

He returns the rescued fruit to my tin. The kitchen is empty on our return and my spirits rally. Uncle gets started on the pastry, rolling a sheet so vast it swamps the dish. I glance at the door, afraid that Ma may clump into the kitchen and knock him out of the way. The afternoon ticks away. When the pie is slumbering in the oven, he sits beside the range and fills his pipe.

'You keep looking at the clock, Edie.'

'Do I?'

He pulls me close. 'My little pickle. I could gobble you right up.' He nuzzles my neck, presses his eye to my cheek and flutters the lashes. 'Here come the butterflies!'

'Don't! No!' I squeal.

He draws away. 'Want me to stop?'

'Never.'

I make a special effort to smile, which eases some of the clutching of my heart. He pats his knee.

'How about a story?' he asks.

'It's not bedtime.'

'Who knows what'll be afoot by then.'

I clamber on to his lap and cling to his arm, solid as oak beneath the shirtsleeve. 'A story, please. Yes. Now,' I gabble.

As he reads, I run my finger across his stubbled chin, revelling in his perfume of tobacco and fresh sweat. He smiles and on an impulse I throw my arms around his neck and squeeze.

'Careful, child,' he says. 'I can hardly breathe.'

'Yes you can,' I say. 'You're as strong as a bear. You can take any amount of hugging.'

I burrow into the broad sweep of his chest and imagine a home where he lives all of the time. A home where his shirt warms next to the hearth and a pipe of tobacco stands by. My throat tightens. Each mouthful of air has to negotiate its way past a stone lodged there.

'Uncle.' I press my ear to the slow thump of his heart. 'Don't

36

go,' I say, whispering the disloyal words. 'I wish you were my pa.'

If he hears, he shows no sign. The weight of his hand alights on the crown of my head and warmth seeps into my scalp, as though a night-cap has been laid there. 'Shush now, my pet,' he purrs.

Very gently, unnoticeably to begin with, he rocks backwards and forwards, cradling me in the safe sweep of his arm. It is a feather-light embrace, more precious than all the shillings in the till on a Saturday night. I steel myself not to cry. I am a grown-up girl. Besides, if I begin, I don't know if I'll be able to stop.

'Don't worry, Uncle,' I breathe, and manage to make the words sound level. 'I'm happy.'

It is not a lie. I am happy when he is in the house.

'I love you too, Edie,' he replies. 'Don't you forget it.'

'I won't.'

'Be brave. Chin up.'

'Yes, Uncle.'

The room sweetens with the scent of baking pastry. He drifts into sleep, head tipped back, mouth agape. I devour him with my eyes, as though by some trick of memory I can gorge myself on this moment and keep it forever; as though, by sheer force of childish possessiveness, I can hold him here.

Perhaps it is guilt at wanting him to stay that makes me do it. Perhaps it is curiosity. Perhaps I want to plumb the mystery of Ma's monthly troubles and discover what transforms her into a hermit. Perhaps Ma's sobriety is a lie and she spends three days as a dancer in a high-kicking line of women with frothy petticoats. Perhaps it is something for which I have no word.

I slip from my uncle's lap. He does not stir. His breath wheezes in and out, halfway to a snore. I pour a cup of tea and stir in an extra spoonful of sugar. Nana is always praising its powers. By taking a cup to my slumbering mother I shall prove I care for her.

I tiptoe up the stairs with such a pounding of the heart, I think it will pop out of my mouth. The cup shivers on its saucer in a sympathetic rhythm. I pause at the stairhead. Ma's door presents a blank face. I try the handle and nothing happens. I am surprised by how relieved I feel. I can slink downstairs, climb back on to my uncle's knee and chide myself for disobedience. He can drink the tea.

But the catch is merely stiff. I twist it fully and the chamber releases with a clank. The door swings open, hinges shrieking. The curtains block out the sunlight but I can make out the mound of Ma's body upon the bed, bundled up beneath the quilt. The noise is sure to have woken her. She does not move.

'Ma?' I whisper. 'Here's a lovely cup of tea.' I hold my offering at arm's length as if its perfume might steal into her nostrils and tempt her awake. 'It's nice and hot. Just as you like it.'

Nothing. My hand trembles. The china clinks.

'Ma?' I say, louder.

Outside, the rag and bone man yells *rag a' bo'aah!* loud enough to rouse a bear from hibernation. Ma does not budge.

'Ma!' I cry.

I run to her bedside. There is not so much as the gentlest snore to be heard, not a breath. I'm seized with panic. Have women's problems been the death of her? Hard on the heels of fear dawns the thought that if she is dead, Uncle Arthur can stay forever. I will be happy. I shove it away but it is too late: it is the worst thought I've ever had. Everything Ma says is true. She *does* know me better than I know myself. I am a horrible child.

'Ma?' I quaver. 'Please don't be dead. I love you.' I try to sound sincere, but quail with the knowledge that she'll know I'm lying. 'I don't want you to die!' I wail.

She does not answer. I don't deserve to have a mother. I

don't deserve anything. I reach out and grasp her shoulder. It is pliable to the touch. Hardly like bone.

'Ma?' I ask, withdrawing my hand.

There is no reply. I prod her with a timid finger. She gives way as though her body is the consistency of rag pudding. Some awful change has been wrought upon her. The ailments at which she hints so darkly are so ferocious they have rendered her boneless. Crazed with misery and terror, I shake her – hard. Something breaks off under the blankets. I freeze. The room is ghastly with silence.

'Ma!' I shriek. 'I've killed you!'

I hurl myself on to her prone form, hugging her so fiercely the headboard rattles. The cup of tea spills across the eiderdown. I must clean it right away or it will stain. I tear away the covers, revealing Ma's body. Except it is not Ma's body. I blink. It has to be, I tell myself. But, however many times I squeeze my eyes shut and open them, the truth is incontrovertible. Laid along the length of the mattress is a line of cushions.

My mind reels. Where has she gone?

I race downstairs to tell Uncle Arthur the terrible news. He nods in the chair, blanketed in the scent of baking. If I wake him, this moment will shatter as surely as if I threw a bucket of stones upon it. I dread what he may say: that Ma *is* a dancer in the halls, *does* make a spectacle of herself in a skirt of feathers and nothing else.

But that's not what I truly fear. I don't know why, but somehow I'll be the one to blame for Ma's absence. After all, I'm the one Ma never kisses. I'm the one Ma won't hug. If Ma goes away for three days, it's bound to be because of me.

I can't bear the thought of Uncle Arthur's face changing from love to coldness; can't bear the thought that today's hug may be the last. I tiptoe to my room, and do not speak a word: not to him, not to Nana, not even to the picture of Papa. If I don't tell, no one will know what I've discovered. If I pretend hard enough, maybe I can convince myself it didn't happen. Even if it's a lie, I'd rather have a happy lie than the agonising truth.

Two days later, Ma is in the kitchen when I come downstairs for breakfast. I run to her and bury my face into her apron.

'Don't cling,' she snaps. 'You're not a baby. I can't move for your mithering.'

'Where've you been?' I moan.

'In bed.'

I squeeze harder. She walks peg-leg across the kitchen, dragging me with her. I'm so relieved to see her that any determination to keep my secret disappears into thin air.

'No you weren't.'

She grinds to a halt and grasps my shoulders. 'What did you say?'

'I brought you a cup of tea,' I mumble. 'You weren't there.'

Her features twist. She looks like a dog backed into a corner. 'I told you never to disturb me!' she roars, giving me a furious shake. 'Spying on me, were you?'

'I was scared you'd gone forever!'

'Scared?' Her eyes shift from cornered to crafty. 'Yes, of course I'd gone. I can't stand being around you with your infernal snivelling and pawing.'

'Ma!' I wail.

'Don't you come crying to me. All you had to do was give me three days' peace. You've brought this on yourself.'

This is the secret Ma and Nana argue about. I should have guessed it. I am so unlovable my own mother has to escape from me each month. This is why she is always angry. I deserve it. I must do. Ma would never lie. Of all the tasks I set myself, it was to make Ma love me. I have failed.

40

GNOME
1899

Every night it's the same.

I come to, gasping, and I'm off that bed like it's on fire. I squint at the mirror but won't be convinced till I've run my hands the long and the short of what I see: head, fingers, knees and toes, ballocks and bumhole. It's only then I can breathe easy. I'm in one piece, all twelve fine upstanding years of me.

It's a crying shame to cover such a splendid specimen but I can't go outdoors in my birthday suit and that's a fact. Nor shall I wear out this night in self-admiration when there's adventure to be had. The moon doth shine as bright as day, et cetera, and I have merriment to attend to. A lad of my mettle can perish of cloistering cling and playlessness.

I drag my britches from underneath the mattress where they've been pressed a treat and tuck my hair under my cap. With my shirt half-buttoned I'm raring to be gone, but there's no point in doing so without a penny in my pocket. I tiptoe downstairs quieter than the mice worrying the walls and dig my hand into the sugar bowl on the mantel. If Mam will insist on stowing thruppences in such an obvious place it's her funeral if half go missing.

I avoid the front door. The shunt and rattle of those bolts

are enough to wake the dead and I'd get what for. Out of the bedroom window is my way, the best way. I creep back up without a squeak and pound the corner of the sash: three sharp punches and it slides up, wide enough to stick out my head. My left arm follows, then the right and to round it off I wriggle my hips clear. Watch a cat ooze under a door and you'll know how it's done.

I am free.

I swing off the ledge, ripping the seat of my trousers. I've no time to attend to such inconsequential matters. Mam will fix it. Down the fall-pipe, hit the ground and I run, savouring that first rush of delight, heady as a pint of best bitter downed in a single gulp.

I dance the tightrope of the pavement edge, dash between soot-faced terraces that squat low on their haunches. It matters not what I'm racing from or to; all I know is that I am alive. I am a mucker, a chancer, a chavvy, a cove. I grab life by the neck and squeeze every drop into my cup. If it's good, I'll take it by the barrel. If it's bad I'll do the same. I take it all: the world and his wife, the moon on a stick and the stars to sprinkle like salt on my potatoes. I hammer on doors for the thundering crash of it. Chuck stones at windows to hear the glass crack and the spluttering interrupted snores of those inside.

'Wake up!' I cry, windmilling my arms. 'Life's too short to spend it sleeping!'

I am the handspring of time between shut-eye and wake-up, the dream forgotten upon waking, the taste it leaves under the tongue. I am the crust of sleep in the eyes, the grit on the sheet. I am the yawning drag of Monday morning. You can keep the day with all its labour, misery and grime. I am King of the Night. I am Gnome.

I won't be here forever. I have plans. Away from cramped

windows, tiny doors, squeezed staircases; away from brick and cloud and rain-puddled gutters. I will go west. Not Liverpool, not Ireland – America. There's a dream of a place: men in broad-brimmed hats and fancy moustaches so long they can wrap them around their thumbs; cornfields that stretch forever with not a fence to bar the way; cattle herds that take a day to rumble by. That's where I'll go. See if I don't. It's a greater journey than I can make in one night. But a man must have dreams.

All in good time. Tonight, Shudehill Market will suffice. It's a fine place for a Saturday night's entertainment, or any night for that matter. The crowd is as thick as mustard. I spot Russians, Latvians, Italians, Syrians, Egyptians: men with faces dark as a japanned brougham. Their tongue-twister salutations call out to me like the very sirens and I am tugged into their wake.

I stroll through the jumble of stalls. The air is busy with Manchester aromas, surpassing all the perfumes of Arabia: treacle tarts rub up to meat puddings; tureens of pea soup steam alongside pyramids of oranges so vivid they sting your eyes; buns and barms are hawked cheap by the stale sackful. Butchers bawl their bargains. Despite the reek of meat left standing all day like a tart with no takers, there's still a pack of ravenous crones haggling over tongue and cow-heel, tripe and heart.

A pie stall tantalises. I'm hungry enough to eat a horse, which is as well for I bet my berries that's what's in them. I slap down tuppence and savour my supper under the stars, or the closest Manchester gets to them. I wolf it so fast a scrap of crust catches and I cough. My feet hiccup, the cobbles fly up to meet me and I sprawl, nose-down in muck and grease and God knows what else.

A hand grabs the back of my jacket and hauls me upright.

I wrap my hands around my head in case he's of a mind to clout me, but this stranger has come to my rescue.

'Careful, lad,' he roars. 'You nearly bought it there.'

He jerks his head at the wagon thundering past. It shows no sign of having slowed by so much as an inch to avoid crushing me into cag-mag.

'Thank you,' I say, spraying pastry.

My saviour laughs. 'Next time, save me a bit of pie.'

I lick my fingers. What a fine night this is turning out to be. The older lads and lasses pay me no mind, too busy with their rough flirtations. One girl pauses before the chap of her choice, plucks the flower from his buttonhole and bites off half the petals before crushing it back into its tiny hole. His chin hangs in a gawp as she struts away, earrings swaying, swinging her umbrella like a sword. Another pert miss, hat loaded with more fruit than a costermonger's barrow, swipes the tea mug from her beau and takes a good long draught before returning it, a crescent of scarlet greasing the rim.

I stick out my chest in the hope of gathering similar attentions. I might, you know. One day. For now, I loiter at the tea-stand, entertained by the music of coarse songs and coarser jokes. I chuckle at the half I understand, laugh louder at the half I do not. Not that it's only tea in those cups. *Tea and a bit* will get a fellow a splash from a mysterious jug kept beneath the counter and it certainly isn't water. I slap down a sixpence, wink knowingly.

'Hop it, short-arse,' growls my host. 'It's not for little boys.'

'Get knotted,' I retort. 'I'm fifteen!'

'My arse. When you're tall enough to see over the counter, then I'll serve you.'

I've a few inches to go. In this world you need to choose your battles, so I screw up the sodden bit of newspaper that held my pie and bounce it off the head of the nearest urchin. He spins about with a glare fit to take the head off a glass of porter, takes one look at the size of me and changes his mind. He rubs his noggin, contenting himself with a scowl. Not that I intend him any harm: it is exuberance, not meanness of the heart.

I'm still ravenous. Coins clink a reminder: *Don't let us go to waste!* I splash out on an ounce of cinder toffee. The taste spirits me away to a place of fireworks, a sweet yet bitter recollection and one I do not wish to have in my head. I spit out the muck and the memory with it, shove the remainder into the hands of the little lad. He unwraps the bag, stares at it in disbelief.

'Take it,' I grunt. 'No catch.'

He eyes me like I'm a god come down to earth with a fistful of miracles. In search of fresh diversion I walk on, my adoring acolyte dogging my shadow. Beggars clot shop doorways, hands outstretched, eyes as empty as winter windows. Women gaudy with rouge gear up for a night of horizontal wrestling. Carts are lined up beneath their lanterns, the drovers supping quarts of four-ale. Halfway along the wall, a puppet booth has been set up, ringed by a brood of grubby nose-pickers. Punch is battering Judy against a painted backdrop of pots and pans.

That's the way to do it, quacks Punch.

I elbow my pipsqueak friend and point at Punch's beaky nose. 'See that hooter?' I say. 'It's where he stores his sausages.'

I wait for him to laugh. His mouth hangs open, catching moths, still unable to believe that I gave him an ounce of toffee free, gratis and for nothing. My talents are sorely wasted on some fellows. The play proceeds with the usual thrashing and squawking of blue murder. Judy sprawls on the counter, staring at me with wooden eyes as Punch belabours her.

Take that you shitty-arsed cow! he screeches, employing words not in the regular repertoire. *Here's another, shit-faced old bag.*

My little pal tugs my sleeve. His lower lip is trembling. I take a moment to survey the sea of small children. Every last one of them is quivering on the verge of tears. I can't spot a single mother. They've all deserted their babes to go in search of a bottle of stout. It seems I have been left in charge of this ragged army. What a fine general I shall be. I rub my hands, take a deep breath and echo the puppeteer.

'Shitty-arsed cow!' I yell.

No one threatens to wash out my mouth with soap. The carters chuckle at my impertinence. I nudge my companion encouragingly. He combs grubby fingers through his hair so that it stands up in an exclamation mark, eyes wide with the realisation that no one's about to thump better manners into him either.

'Shitty-arsed cow,' he whispers all in a rush, in case time runs out on insolence and he is called to account.

The little 'uns screw their heads around from the marionettes and gawk at us.

'Go on,' I say, thumbing my lapels. 'You can shout as loud as you like.'

One girl shakes her head. She fusses with the hem of her pinafore, revealing stockings going weak at the knees. We don't need her. The rest take my lead, in cautious disbelief at first, then louder, till the whole cats' chorus are yowling: *Shitty-arsed cow, shitty-arsed cow.* I am their bandleader, stamping out the rhythm of the words as we parade in a circle. Some bang invisible drums, some clash cymbals, some thrust trombones out and in and out again, all to the tune of *shitty-arsed cow, shitty-arsed cow.* I am so swept up in the cavalcade that my devotee has to tug my sleeve three times before I take notice.

46

'Look,' he says, pointing.

'What? Don't stop now. We are having such larks.' I holler *shitty-arsed cow* for good measure.

'No, *look*,' he repeats.

The puppets have been joined by their master, a scrawny man with a nose the shape and size of a King Edward's, face curdled with bile. He rams Judy face down on to the shelf at the front of the booth and thrashes her with such force that plaster brains tumble like rice.

'Turd! Turd!' he shrieks, spittle flying from drawn-back lips.

'*Turd*,' I snicker. 'He said *turd*.'

Judy slumps, arms drooping over the cloth. Punch's red coat hangs in shreds, the whole of his hump and half his knobbled cap broken away. The backdrop tangles around the puppeteer's arm but he continues to whack the puppets against each other, screaming obscenity after obscenity.

'Look at the mess he's making,' gasps the boy. 'Shouldn't we tell somebody?'

I shrug. I don't care if he drags the whole tent around his ears. I don't care if he pulps the puppets into glue and the children bawl their eyes out. Mayhem is my meat and drink.

'Stop being such a little prig,' I snap. 'This is the most fun I've had in an age.'

It's only when every infant is wailing that the drovers put down their pipes and pile in. They cart off the puppet-master, still yelling filth. This must be the best, most roisterous, boisterous night known to man or boy.

I am encircled by dirty faces, agog for the next game. I am so engaged with racking my brains that I do not notice the bigger lads until I'm surrounded. One by one my midget congregation melt away, leaving me alone with this new gang. At first they ignore me, busy punching each other in a comradely

47

fashion, although one of them strikes with far more vicious intent than the others. I'm glad he's not whacking me. Though not the tallest, he carries the mantle of king upon his shoulders. He also wears a black eye like a campaign medal.

'That's some shiner you've got there, Reg,' says a lad with a face like a ferret and hair to match.

'It is indeed, Wilfred,' says Reg.

Quicker than a bolt of lightning, Reg thumps Wilfred in the guts. He doubles over, wheezing. No one dares go to their comrade's aid, for fear they'll be next in line for similar treatment.

Reg chuckles, the sound of a dog being strangled. 'You should see the other fellow.'

The gang snigger timidly and I join in. It is a mistake. Reg twists his head in my direction.

'Who are you, pipsqueak?' he says, legs apart, hands deep in his pockets and pushing out the front of his trousers.

'I'm Gnome, that's who I am,' I say with as much of a swagger as I can muster.

He grins, his teeth sharp and grimy. 'Where did you crawl in from? Never seen you before.'

'You have,' I snort. 'Here every night, so I am.'

'Are you now?' he replies. He turns to his companions, who form a circle. 'He says he's here every night.' They snicker, sharing the joke I am not privy to. The ring of bodies tightens. 'I'm in charge here,' Reg declares. 'Time for you to step away, and step lively.'

'Don't see why I should,' I reply, fists in my britches. He's not the only one who can thrust out his nackers.

Wilfred lurches forward. 'How dare you talk to Reg like that,' he snarls, still cringing from the blow he received from the man in question.

48

I wither him with a pitying glance. Poor sap, if he thinks having a pop at me will restore him to his master's good books. His face reddens.

'You little—' he growls, aiming a punch. 'Show some respect!'

I duck, quickly enough to avoid a broken nose, too slow to save my cap from being knocked off. Curls tumble as far as my shoulders. There's a pause. I retrieve my hat from the cobbles, shove it back on my head.

'My my,' says Wilfred, whistling appreciatively. 'What have we here?'

'Don't know what you mean,' I grunt, tucking away hanks of hair.

'You're a girl!' he hoots.

'Don't talk soft,' I reply with a snort of derision. I turn to Reg. 'Are all your lot this daft?'

It is another mistake.

'Wilf's got a point, for once,' says Reg. Wilfred preens in the glow of approval. 'Maybe you are a girl.'

'I'm bloody not.' I hawk and spit. My mouth is dry and I barely make a mark.

'Let's have a better look at you,' Reg murmurs, stepping close. I smell gin, so strong and thick you could wring him like a dishcloth straight into the bottle. He grabs one of my ringlets and rubs it between his fingers. 'I declare. You're a proper Bubbles.'

'Don't call me that.'

'Bubbles!' squawks Wilfred.

'Shut up!' I cry.

'I'll call you what I like,' leers Reg. 'You're a genuine, certified Pears advertisement.'

He circles his thumb and forefinger and blows through the hole. Another chap cracks the brim of his boater, conjuring it

49

into a makeshift bonnet and puckering his lips for a kiss. Another picks up the hem of an imaginary skirt and prances around me. One after the other, they join in the pantomime.

Bubbles!

Bubbles!

What a dainty little damsel, all sugar and spice.

Round and round they go, Reg chasing after and growling like a bear. If you can't beat 'em, join 'em, so I clap and cheer, loud as the rest. I'll show them I'm the kind of fellow who can laugh at himself. I'd be a welcome addition to their number. With the suddenness of a thunderclap, they stop. I stop also, but a second behind. They stare at me, chests heaving.

Reg draws his hand across his mouth. 'Who said you could laugh?'

'No one,' I mumble.

A chill crawls down my thighs, right to my boots. Reg pokes me in the chest.

'You're laughing at me, aren't you?'

'No sir!' I exclaim.

I stumble under the assault of his finger. Someone kicks my legs from under me and I drop to my knees, hard and heavy as a sack of turnips. Wilfred wrenches my arms behind my back and holds them tight. Reg presses his nose to mine. He has sharp eyes that see through me as easy as through a piece of glass, right to the other side.

'You little shit. Asking for trouble, aren't you, eh?'

'You tell him, Reg,' says Wilfred, his expression even more weasel-like, if that were possible. 'How about a new game?' he murmurs in Reg's ear. 'A man's game.'

The world breathes in, like that moment before a storm begins. I hold particularly still.

'There's a thought,' says Reg.

He unbuttons his fly with luxurious deliberation, licking his lips to ensure I am paying close attention, which I am. He slides his hand into the gap and draws out his porker. It's near long enough to tie a knot in. The other lads grin, their eyes slick with knowing.

'A proper man's pipe, that's what I've got. How'd you like to blow bubbles on this?'

I try not to breathe. I mustn't show I'm spooked. If he smells fear who knows where this may end?

'Even better, how about a ride on Jumbo?' he purrs. He tugs his pocket linings inside out. They look uncommonly like elephant ears. 'Little girls like a circus ride.'

His coven giggle, wheezing like witches. It takes every ounce of courage to affect an air of boredom. I roll my eyes lazily and shuffle away.

'Not so fast,' leers Wilfred.

He wraps his arm around my throat, shoving his nadger into my spine. It's rigid and I'm damned if I can understand why. I have no leisure to solve the conundrum, for I am far too exercised by having the life crushed out of me. Reg swings his hips from side to side and his sausage swings too. He takes a lumbering step forward.

'Come on,' he says. 'Only a penny a ride.'

'That's a bargain,' says Wilfred.

'Cheap at half the price,' quips another, until the whole nasty lot are egging him on.

'Put him down!' blares a woman in a hat as broad as a soup tureen. She waggles her finger in the direction of Reg's privates. 'You can put that away and all.'

'Says who?'

'Says me, Reginald Awkright. He's half your size.'

'We're only playing.'

'You're throttling him.'

Wilfred tightens his grip. 'Nah. Bit of rough and tumble, isn't it, Bubbles?'

'Tumble!' I squeak.

'See?' says Reg. 'He loves it, don't you?'

Wilfred squeezes again, like I'm a set of bagpipes.

'Yes!' I rasp.

'I said, leave the poor mite be,' she snaps. 'He can't hardly breathe. I know your sort, Reginald.'

He lets out a whickering laugh. 'I know your sort and all, Jessie, you wet-kneed slapper.'

The remainder of their banter is lost in the roaring between my ears. Reg and his rabble seem a long way off. Or rather my head seems a long way from them, detached from the neck and floating away. It is most peculiar, very like the feeling I get when I – she—

I splutter into myself. 'Get off me!' I shriek.

Whether it's the command in the woman's voice, or the shock of me fighting back, I've no idea, but Wilfred loosens his stranglehold. I tumble forwards, giving my elbow a blinder of a crack and half stagger, half crawl away as fast as I can. Jessie picks me up as easily as you might a dropped glove. I don't cling to her like a drowning man to a lifebelt. Not me, not by a long chalk. I just need to steady myself on her arm, that's all.

'There you go,' she says, setting me upright. She rounds on the gang. 'As for you lot, play nicely or bugger off.'

She commences patting dirt off my jacket. She smells of trapped violets.

'I'm all right. Don't need help,' I say half-heartedly.

'You tell her,' jeers Reg. 'See? He doesn't want you, you old whore.'

The boys snigger at the insult. I wait for the blubbing to

start. But she tips up her chin with something that looks uncommonly like pride.

'Don't you just wish you could get a morsel of what I've got to offer!' she hoots.

'As heck as like,' snarls Reg. I've never seen a man's eyes so famished. He points at me. 'I wouldn't touch you with his,' he declares.

Jessie furnishes us with a bray of merriment, turns with extravagant grace and promenades into the throng. I watch her go, mightily impressed. I've no idea why Reg called her old, either. She's as pretty as a picture. The sort of woman a chap would be proud to have on his arm. However, I have precious little opportunity for approbation.

'Just like a girl,' he growls. 'Ganging up on us.'

'I'm not a flaming girl,' I sigh with wearied emphasis. 'You blind or brainless?'

'You cheeky little sod. You are what I say you are.'

'That's right,' says Wilfred, still determined to get on the right side of Reg. He grinds his fist into his eye socket. 'Run to Mama,' he whines. 'Wah, wah, Mama!'

Reg twists his unpleasant attention from me to Wilfred. My face cools as the awful heat is taken away.

'Who are you calling Mama?' he says.

'I didn't mean you, Reg, old pal. I mean her.' He stabs a finger in the direction of Jessie. She's long gone and he is pointing at a vacancy.

'I don't see anyone.'

I concentrate on making myself unnoticeable. Things could still change in a heartbeat.

'It's a joke,' Wilfred blusters.

'I know what a joke is,' Reg says. 'You saying I don't?'

'No! Never!'

Reg inhales slowly and glances at me. I'm out of arm's reach. Wilfred isn't. 'You saying I'm like that old tart?'

'Yes,' I whisper. 'Sounds exactly like what he's saying.'

There's a horrified silence. No one drops so much as a giggle into it. Reg jabs a rigid finger into Wilfred's chest. He reels backwards like he's been hit with half a house brick.

'No!' he wails. 'It was a joke! I didn't mean you! We're chums, aren't we?'

Reg roars and at the signal the whole lot of them pile on to their new enemy. I don't hang about to see the outcome. My conscience pricks briefly about dropping Wilfred into it, but it was him or me. I show the cleanest pair of heels this side of the Mersey and run slap bang into the lady who saved me. Of course, she didn't exactly save me. I did that for myself.

'Mind where you're going!' she chirps. 'Oh, it's you. You all right?'

'Course I am,' I mumble. 'Why wouldn't I be?'

She ought to tell me to get lost and I don't know why she doesn't. She ruffles my hair. I rub my head against her hand like a cat that aches to be scratched. Her fingers comb through my curls.

'Bonny lad,' she purrs.

The words startle me back into my skin.

'Leave off!' I squeak. 'I'm no one's bonny anything!'

I untangle myself from her skirts and fire homewards like a rocket. The kitchen is busy: Grandma sucking on that disgusting pipe of hers and Mam waving her hand and muttering, *What a stink*. Not that Grandma takes a blind bit of notice. So much for the welcoming bosom. After the night I've had a smile wouldn't go amiss. I help myself to a slice of bread and dripping, plonk myself in front of the range and stare at the coals.

I can't go back to Shudehill. Reg will make my life a bloody misery. Where else can I go? What else do I have?

'Is all well?' asks Grandma, deigning to notice my presence. She taps her pipe on the edge of the table, to another complaint from Mam.

'Why shouldn't it be?' I grumble through a mouthful.

'Don't you give me any of your lip,' she replies.

'You leave him alone,' chips in Mam without looking at me. 'He's my special treat, so he is.'

'It wouldn't hurt to hear you saying that about Edie once in a while.'

Mam snorts. 'Her? I wish things were the other way around.'

'That's half-daft. How can you dote on one and not the other?'

'I'll do as I please, thank you very much. All any mother wants is an honest-to-goodness son to do her proud. If you don't like it, there's the door and remember to shut it behind you.'

I scoff my bread, looking from one to the other. Biddies. I'll never unravel the mare's nest between their ears. But what I do hear is an advantage I didn't know I had. I lick my fingers and leave them to it.

The bedroom sash is open. I clamber through the gap and ride the stone saddle of the windowsill, one foot in and one out. The sky is becoming pale as it considers the coming morning. I puff out my chest, draw the last scraps of night into my body until there's no telling us apart.

There was a time.

I've not forgotten that land of sweet content, bright as a favourite story told at bedtime. Things aren't the same since Edie got frozen into an obedience she imagines will thaw our flint-hearted mother into loving her. You may as well try to

55

fold gravy. Mam can't stand baa-lambs unless they come smothered in mint sauce.

Edie's worse than a mouse; at least mice chew the walls and confetti the floor with their tiny turds. Her goodness clings like quicksand. If I get sucked in, it'll be curtains. Every night I step close and try to take her hand, like we used to, but our fingers slide through each other. It's like she doesn't believe in me; like she thinks I'm not real. I don't know what more I can do.

My chest is hot and tight. I grind my teeth until the feeling passes. If you've been booted out of Eden, moping like a snot-nosed toddlekins won't bring it back. I will not think about things I can't have. Fairy tales are for the cradle and I left that a long while ago.

Living in a houseful of women has dragged me down to their simpering level. I must toughen up if I'm going to make my way in this wide world. I'm not a bad lad; not the type to tie cans to a cat's tail, string them up by their paws, set them on fire or any one of the bloody things boys do. But there's no point being soft. In this life, you're either a ginger tom swaggering the streets or a cowering kitten that gets trampled underfoot. I'll let tonight be a lesson. My fault for not standing my ground, for being caught unawares. God helps those who help themselves.

I'm not lonely. Not by a long chalk. I just need to meet the right fellows, that's all. The sort of pals who will stick by a chap through thick and thin. So what if I have to go to ground for a while? I've got tomorrow night, even if I have to steer clear of Shudehill. There's always another night. There has to be. A man must have dreams.

EDIE
1900–1901

I grow up with my ear to the floor, listening to Ma and Nana fight.

They argue about the beer, the takings, the sawdust, the spittoons, the weather, the dirt on the doorstep. If they chose the kitchen, I'd be none the wiser. But they go at it hammer and tongs in the scullery, beneath my room. Maybe they think I'm asleep; maybe they think me too much of a mouse to eavesdrop; maybe they don't care either way. It is such a habitual lullaby I learn to sleep through it, much in the way that folk who live next to the Liverpool line slumber through the rattle of trains.

So things continue. The old century tips into the new, not that it makes a scrap of difference to my days. My height belies my age. At thirteen I overtop every sixteen-year-old hereabouts: a gangling beanpole of a girl as graceful as a donkey with three legs.

Ma won't let me hide upstairs and read my schoolbooks, so I help out in The Comet. The customers make jokes at their plain Jane barmaid and I never master Ma's knack for laughing yet keeping them at arm's length at the same time. That's not to say they are wicked folk; they are our neighbours and a mild crew by and large. Night after night, month after month, I listen to the same conversations about dogs and wives; who's drowned in the Bridgewater; who's been flattened by a cart. I ache for something I cannot put my finger on. But there's no point wishing on half a wishbone, or setting my heart on stars when the likes of me won't climb higher than the chimney.

So I nod, smile, serve beer and dread Thursdays. It is the day the ginger-moustached groper drops in, regular as the man from the Pearl come for his penny. I grow cleverer at avoiding him, although nothing stops his gaze following me around the room and singeing holes in my apron.

One evening, as I'm drifting into the dark hole of sleep, I prick awake. At first I think it's the cold, for an icier February I never knew, but it is only Ma and Nana at loggerheads. I pull the blanket over my head.

My ears burn. There is an unaccountable magic wrought when one is the subject of conversation, some vibration of the ether that communicates itself directly to the person being talked about. I pick out my name, hissed over and over. They are arguing about me.

I can't hear precisely what they are saying. I need more. I creep out of bed, and, praying that the stairs do not squeak, tiptoe to the scullery door.

'She's starting to notice,' says my grandmother.

'Is she?' snorts Ma. 'She wouldn't notice a loaded dray if it drove over her, horse and all. She's as thick as a ditch.'

'She is not.'

'I can't do a thing with her,' says Ma. 'I set her to a simple task and she falls asleep with the broom in her hand. Lazy good-for-nothing.'

My throat tightens at the hurtful words.

58

'Exhaustion. It's not her fault. You know the cause as well as I.'

'I most certainly do not,' grunts Ma.

'Cissy. It is time to call a halt to silence.'

All hell breaks loose: the kettle clangs on to the range; pots bang and scrape and rattle.

'I will not have this subject discussed under my roof!' Ma roars, fit to burst the windows out of their frames. 'It's disgusting!'

'She's old enough to understand!' shouts Nana over the racket. 'If you won't tell her, let me.'

'What, so she can let it slip at school? In church? On the street?'

'She won't do that.'

'Won't she? She's addled enough. We'd be driven out. Don't you remember—'

'I do,' sighs Nana.

'Want that all over again?'

There's a pause. I want to scratch my nose. It seems to contain a beetle with barbed claws.

Nana lets out a heavy sigh. 'Of course not.'

'You see? We'd all be better off if she'd never been born.'

'Cissy! What a terrible thing to say.'

'Is it? Before she came along I had a fine man, so I did.'

'Fine? He was a work-shy, good-for-nothing—'

'How dare you speak ill of the dead!'

'Away with your nonsense, Cissy. Everyone knows he ran off with that baggage from—'

'Who can blame him?' Ma cries. 'I'd be away if I could, and all. No decent man would . . .' The pandemonium subsides. Through the crack in the door I see Nana cup her hand around Ma's cheek. 'Don't . . .' Ma says. It is a perilous sound such as a child might make and shocks me far more than any bellow.

'My kindness did you no harm, Cissy. Surely you can do the same for your own child.'

'Don't,' she replies in the same strangled squeak. 'Don't make me talk about this. I can't. We are shameful. We are cursed!'

'We are not cursed. I don't know why you insist on this idiocy. You know the truth, plain as your head and toes and everything that lies between.'

The truth? I tremble. My questions are about to be answered.

'Don't you dare speak to me and – and—'

Ma's words stutter to a halt. I see an impossible thing: Nana wraps her arms around my mother. She bears it a moment only. Like a fly trapped by a spider, she flails until she breaks free and dashes into the back yard, slamming the door behind her. I return to my bed and bury my head under the pillow. Awful words fill my head: *thick as a ditch, lazy, shameful, cursed.* Papa didn't die. He ran away.

Next morning, I wake with knots in my hair and dirt beneath my fingernails as usual. I can't go on like this. What's more, I shall not. This morning will be different, I tell myself bravely. I am almost fourteen and I need answers. I will have them, if it's the last thing I do. My hand trembles as I brush my hair. After tidying myself as best I can, I make my way downstairs.

Ma is out, as is Nana, which leaves me somewhat deflated. Lacking anything better with which to fill the time until they return, I peel potatoes for dinner. A while later, Ma comes in, knocking ice off her boots.

'It's coming on to snow,' she remarks, somewhat unnecessarily. She removes her hat and slaps away imaginary flakes, not that one would be so foolhardy as to settle. I continue peeling. The stubs drop into the bowl and pile up like wet leaves. I clear my throat. I don't know what to say, but I have to say something.

'Ma,' I begin.

'What?'

Words find my tongue and spill. 'I've heard you and Nana. Talking about me.'

'Had your ear against the wall, have you?' she spits. 'Sneaky little madam. If I've told you once I've told you a hundred times. Curiosity killed—'

'Listen to me, Ma.'

'Ma, Ma, Ma. You sound like a nanny goat.'

I pick up a potato and check for eyes. 'I don't know who I am. I just want to understand. It's all I've ever wanted.'

'No idea what you're on about,' she replies in the sort of voice that indicates she knows only too well.

I turn the potato in my hand, rubbing its face with my thumb. I dunk it, rinsing away the mud and find a wound in the flesh where it was caught by the spade. It is mouldy through and through. I won't be put off – not this time. I hurl the potato to the floor.

'Don't you go wasting food,' she mutters.

'It's rotten.'

'Don't get testy with me, young . . . lady,' she says with a pause before the word *lady*.

I toss the knife into the bucket of slops. Water splashes on to the floor.

'Then give me some answers!' I cry. It is a dangerous question, but silence never gave me anything. 'I don't know what you want from me.'

'I want nothing from you.' She grips my elbow and marches me across the room to the mirror. 'Look at yourself.'

I regard my reflection in the yellowed glass. I'm nowhere

close to prettiness, not by a country mile. 'Looks aren't everything,' I say uncertainly.

'What mother could love a face like that?' She shakes her head, the staccato gesture of someone bothered by flies. 'No one, that's who. It betrays everything about you that is unwholesome. Unnatural. I should have thrown you out with the rest of the rubbish.'

This is not going how I wanted. There has to be a key to unlock the door to Ma's spitefulness. If I can find the right words, I can speak them; the spell will be broken and she'll soften. She'll love me. Pathetic as it is, I still yearn for her affection.

'Ma. All my life I've tried but there's no pleasing you.'

'You could never please me,' she says, and stabs my chest with the point of her finger. Through the reddened skin the bone shows white. 'Never!'

'What did I ever do to make you so angry? Was it Papa running off?'

Her eyes stretch so wide open I can see the white around the iris.

'What?' she screams, shrill as a mill whistle. She jabs me with two fingers, then three, poking at my chest over and over, bunching her hand into a fist. I hold up my hands to shield myself from the blows. 'Want to know why we argue about you?' she cries. 'You want the truth? Here it is. I hate you. From the day you were born, you've blighted my life. I never wanted you.'

'Ma?' My voice trembles. 'You can't mean that.'

'Can't I?' she sneers. 'Want to know what's wrong with this family? You.'

'No,' I whisper.

She shakes my shoulder. 'I. Was. Cursed. With. You.'

'No, Ma.'

62

'Lord only knows I tried to get rid of you. Knitting needles didn't work. You were stuck fast like a pigeon up a chimney and I've had to put up with you ever since.'

'You're lying.'

'Am I? Ask your sainted grandmother.'

'What?'

'That's taken the wind out of your sails, hasn't it? Go on, if you're so clever. Run and complain how cruel I am. She only pretends to love you. She hates you too.'

And with that, she lets go of me. I crumple to the floor. She has said many things over the years and I've suffered her insults, borne her tirades. This is the first time she's used the word *hate*. Like a child who picks at a scab until it bleeds, I've provoked Ma into spewing out the truth. It has turned to ashes in my mouth. This is the mystery I sought to plumb: hatred, pure and simple.

By the time I raise my head, the room is empty. I remain curled on the rug. I try to imagine myself a cat: a beast with no worries other than to lick its paws and sleep. My stolid imagination fails me. I am a repulsive girl, unwanted by my mother. Neither use nor ornament.

I lie there a while longer. Some grain of hope remains that Ma may relent and return. The house is silent, as if holding its breath: no shouting, no pounding of her feet up and down the boards. I wonder what she is doing, or rather not doing. I scramble to my feet and press my ear to the wall. I take a glass from the dresser and return to my listening post. I hold the glass to the brick and listen. There is a faint whooshing, like wind through trees.

'I know you're listening!' Ma yells. I stagger backwards, dropping the glass with a crash. 'I hate you, do you hear? Get away from me!'

Very carefully, I gather up the fragments. I can hardly put them on the shelf: Ma might cut herself. I stow them in my pinafore pocket.

'I've broken a glass, Ma,' I say timidly. No answer. The hush is unnerving, far more so than the sound of complaints. 'The big one, with the blue ring around the top.'

I don't know what to do. I want her to come and tell me off. The glass is a favourite of hers. I can't remember a time when she did not have it. Gingerly, I shake the splinters on to the tabletop. If I can find some glue, I can mend it. But there don't seem to be enough pieces to make it whole again. I can't understand why the edges of each shard are red, until I look at my fingers and find the answer.

As I watch, a dreamlike sensation creeps over me. My finger-tips are oozing blood, but seem unconnected to the rest of my body. There is no pain. There is no sensation of any kind. It is not unpleasant. With the same cool detachment, I notice that my pinafore is stained crimson. I will have to use cold water when I scrub it. Hot water sets bloodstains hard.

Time slips through my fingers. I stand there for hours, or a few seconds. I have no idea how to keep track of the minutes, nor indeed the point of such measurements. Questions cluster at the fringes of my consciousness. Why does Ma hate me so much? Why can't I feel my fingers?

I glance at the half-completed jigsaw of glass, turn and leave the room. Walk down the corridor to the front door. Try to take my shawl from the peg. It snags on the hook, impossible to untangle. I step outdoors without it. I do not expect a stroll to solve any problem. I simply wish to remove myself from anguish.

I know it's a mistake the moment my foot strikes the kerb. I've never known it so cold. Slush the colour of pewter slops underfoot, turning my toes to stone. It is neither night nor day, rather a time balanced between the two. I glance over my shoulder. The windows of The Comet twinkle with a cheery welcome. It is false. I'd rather cut off my own nose than creep back in. I press my face into the shrill edge of the wind and set out, whither I neither know nor care. If I am missed, Ma will think it a cause for celebration rather than sorrow.

Hulme is the nearest thing to quiet I've ever heard. Snowflakes tumble from a leaden sky; spears of ice dangle from the gutters. Clouds roll overhead, slow and black as coal barges. I think of us beneath: twisting our light-blind eyes upwards, necks bent beneath iron rain, and the wind sharp enough to pierce you right through.

I pass a smattering of folk swathed in thick coats, scarves drawn tight under the chin, their breath steaming behind them in a foaming wake. No one gasps at my bloodstained apron, or remarks that I should get to the infirmary sharpish, that I'll catch my death. As I go, the sensation of cold lessens rather than intensifies. It is most curious. I wonder if I am truly walking down the street or if I'm dreaming the whole thing. Perhaps I am still at home, this very moment.

Home. I laugh out loud, to a flurry of turned heads. I no longer have a home; that has been made clear. I walk on through frigid sludge, numbness rising from my ankles to my knees. Gradually, the snowfall peters out and I find myself at the gate of Whitworth Park. I peer through the bars. The paths are streaked with ruts where mothers pushed perambulators earlier that afternoon. Snow cloaks the lawns and piles in heaps upon the bushes, transforming it into a strange, smothered landscape.

How I scale the locked gate I have no notion, but in the blink of an eye it is behind me. The clouds peel away, leaving the sky clear. I make my way into the park, ploughing through the drifts. I find myself lying down. I must have slipped and fallen. My shoulder and elbow shriek. It appears that I can feel pain, after all.

I struggle to my feet and continue walking, trailing my finger-tips along the hedges. Without any warning, I am on my knees. I must have fallen again. I don't remember. My memory is as full of holes as a tea strainer. I examine my arms, sleeves rolled to the elbow from when I peeled the potatoes. The flesh is bluish. There is no longer any sign of bleeding.

The snow is as thick as a mattress and as inviting. Without thinking overmuch about what I am doing, I lie down and sink into feather softness. I cannot recall ever feeling so content. I wonder if this is happiness. If so, it is very agreeable. I will stay here. There is no shouting. No loneliness. No confusion. No pain. No hate.

I close my eyes. A distant part of myself knows I ought to feel cold. If anything it is the opposite. Something that is not precisely warmth, but very much like it, steals through my limbs. It is unbearably sweet. Tears spring, forming icicles. My head draws away from my body, my limbs also. I lose sight of them. I do not care. I am at peace. It has all stopped. All of it. So simple.

My heart beats. The thumping grows in intensity until my body is shuddering. I am a door and someone is knocking so furiously I am being shifted off my hinges. I smile at the pecu-liar idea. In the thunder I hear a voice.

You! You! Get up!

'Leave me alone,' I mutter and stick my fingers into my ears. If I can't hear him, he'll have to go away. I'll be able to hide. I will, I will.

You can't do this! he yells. *Edie!*

All I want is to fall asleep. But this creature won't let me.

'Let me stay here,' I say.

Not a chance.

'I'm happy.'

You're not.

'Am so,' I whine. 'Just a little longer.'

Bloody get up! he screams. *We need each other.* There is a pause. *I need you, Edie.*

A longer silence follows, so profound I can sense each snow-flake in the quilt beneath which I lie.

It's not fair. You can't do this to me.

'You're not real,' I mumble.

I'm Gnome, you idiot. Have you forgotten?

A chill cuts to my core, far icier than the burrow in which I'm buried. I shake my head.

'No. You are all in my mind. Gnome is a bad memory. Ma says . . .'

My brain is being dragged awake. I try to ignore its spark and fizz, try to slip back into the delicious lassitude, but it nags and niggles and will not let me lie. I hardly know if I pull myself or am pulled out of the snowdrift, but emerge I do.

Now, I feel the bitterness of the weather and wish I didn't. I look over my shoulder at the soft bed I have just left, but the voice lays on the whip and drives me forward. Each step is like walking barefoot on broken glass. I stagger to the gate of the park and this time, climbing over is torture.

I lurch along the street, shivering. People throw sideways glances, wrinkling their lips at this guttersnipe straight from the pages of a cautionary tale told to warn girls of what they'll be reduced to if they stray.

There is nowhere for me to go but The Comet. It is not home, not in the way the world takes the word, but it is all I have. By the time I turn on to Renshaw Street it is past closing time and the windows are dark. My fingers are so stiff I can barely open the door. I cower in front of the kitchen range and listen to my teeth chatter, oddly loud in the quiet house.

The broken glass has been cleared away, the plates and cups on the shelf rearranged. There's no sign it was ever there. The only proof I left The Comet is my sodden pinafore. Did I really lie down in the snow? Was I really waiting for – wanting to – My mind gutters like a cheap candle.

I can't stay here for Ma to trip over me come morning. I tiptoe through the public bar. Papa observes me from behind his glass.

'Did you leave because of me?' I whisper. 'Who are you, really? Who am I?' He lifts a hairy eyebrow. I've always taken his expression to be sympathetic, but after this evening, nothing is certain. 'Why am I talking to you?' I sigh. 'You're a photograph.'

I climb the stairs. Nana calls out a sleepy greeting. I peel off my filthy clothes, promising whatever guardian angel is listening that I'll wash them tomorrow. I crawl into bed. Arguments rumble through the wall. The sound is almost comforting.

'Why me?' Ma whines. 'What did I ever do to deserve this?'

'You're a hard woman, Cissy. The child is going out of her mind.'

'So she should be.'

'A secret is one thing. Hatred is another.'

My door opens. I hear the smoky wheeze of Nana's breath. The mattress shifts as she lowers herself on to the end of the bed.

'You shouldn't rile your mother, child,' she sighs. 'She takes care of us all.'

She speaks carefully, and I know it is because Ma is eavesdropping.

'Yes, Nana,' I reply. I lower my voice. 'Why does Ma hate me?' I whisper.

'What sort of foolish notion is that?' she replies, but will not look me in the eye.

'Am I so horrible?' I say, words thick with misery.

'Lass. There is nothing horrible about you,' she replies with great tenderness.

'Then why . . .' I sob.

'Your mother has a difficult time of it,' she continues. 'She's not strong, not like you or me.'

I'm strong? It is a strange idea. Nana stretches out her arms, draws me into the safe harbour of her lap and begins to sing.

'See how she runs, she tumbles and falls,
She catches the sunbeams that come through the door.
Nobody knows how I adore
Nana's little girl.'

For the space of a song, I taste safety and it is delicious.

'Will I grow up like Ma?' I ask with a guilty blush I hope is obscured by the darkness of the room.

'I pray to all the saints in heaven that you don't,' she sighs. 'Enough. You might not need to sleep but I do. Goodnight.'

She presses dry lips to my brow. Her chin scratches. I think nothing of it, not till much later. I lie quietly, the warmth of my body soaking into the bed, and fall asleep.

The next morning, I wake up with not so much as a speck of dirt under my fingernails, nor one tangle in my hair. I regard myself in the mirror. Ugly as always, but miracles are not for the likes of me.

However, there has been a small miracle of sorts. The previous evening, I came close to extinguishing my life, and stayed my hand. I stumbled, but didn't fall – not all the way. My mother poured her whole store of bile upon me, all fourteen unlucky years of it. It should have destroyed me. It did not. I have not been vanquished.

If I can survive that, I say to myself, I can survive anything. Perhaps Nana is right, and I am stronger than I imagine. I may have nowhere to go, nor any hope of escape. Yet I sense a core of steel of which I was not previously aware. Even if Nana cannot – will not – stand up to Ma, affection is affection and I'm not such a fool as to spurn it. Things may not be different in my life, but they are in my heart. I pledge myself to the improvement of both.

I am to be tested far sooner than expected.

The Wednesday after, all is as usual in The Comet: the bar full to bursting and a scuffle to stand closest to the fireplace. Ma and I circle each other like warring cats. She plays the cheery landlady, acting as if no cruel words were ever spoken. I move through the crowd, offering pipes from the rack to those who desire them, when one of the customers yells across the din.

'Hey! What's the weather like up there with you, lass?'

Every eye swivels in my direction. It is an old joke and one I am well used to. I stretch my lips into a tolerable impersonation of a smile.

'How about a song, Lady Goliath?' he shouts, clearly not done with me.

'Her? She can't carry a tune in a bucket,' quips another toper.

'Shush now, you'll upset the wee creature. She can't help having cloth ears.'

'Wee? You blind all of a sudden?'

There ensues a general bout of mirth at my expense. I pick up a dirty glass.

'Now, let's have some respect.'

I throw a grateful glance at whoever has spoken in my defence and find myself eyeball to eyeball with the bane of my existence, copper eyebrows and all. I wasn't expecting him till tomorrow. He smoothes his hands up and down the front of his waistcoat and tugs at his cuffs. His shirtsleeves are uncrumpled, uncommonly fresh for this late in the day. I wonder how he keeps himself so clean. I'd bite off my own tongue rather than remark upon it.

'Give us a smile,' he leers, pinching my cheek. 'Anyone would think you weren't pleased to see your Uncle Bob.'

'You're not my uncle,' I reply as rudely as I can, which is not very.

'I declare. You've got a sight more zest these days. Then again, I like a lass with a bit of spunk in her.' He doffs his cap and rolls his eyes at Ma. 'What say you, Mrs Latchford?' he enquires, the soul of civility. 'A song from the lips of your charming daughter?'

Ma rams a cloth into the throat of a pint pot and sniffs. 'As you like it.'

'Positively Shakespearian,' he titters.

Ma shrugs and concentrates on pouring a precise measure of porter into the clean glass. The head is thick with cream. He returns his attention to me.

'I wager that you are a nightingale!' he trills. 'Furnish us with a song!'

I shake my head. 'I don't know any songs,' I mutter, worrying my apron into knots at the prospect of his slippery attentions twice a week rather than once.

'I bet you do,' says my tormentor cheerfully. 'Do not disappoint your impatient audience!'

The room takes up the cry, banging beer pots on the tables and stamping their feet. I am trapped. I wonder what it is about me that makes this scoundrel feel he has the right to pin me

71

to the spot. It's clear that peace will not be restored until I've placated the crowd with a song.

'"Father, O Father, come home to us now,"' I whisper.

'Speak up, love!' someone cries.

'Can't hear you!'

'Put some vim into it.'

I throw a pleading glance at Ma. She is looking in the opposite direction.

'Go on,' growls the gingery man. 'Sing.'

I place one hand flat against my stomach and hold up the other, pointing a finger at the ceiling. I clear my throat, gabble the verse and scuttle back to the safety of the bar.

'If you will parade yourself you deserve everything coming to you,' says Ma sourly enough to take the polish off a chapel pew.

'I did nothing!'

'Oh, hush your moaning and take this,' she snaps, shoving a platter of fried bread into my hands.

'But, Ma . . .' I whimper. I want to give that man a wide berth for the remainder of the evening. Indeed, for the rest of my life if I can help it.

'Move, girl, or I'll make you regret it.'

I squeeze between the tables. I've gone less than half a dozen paces when the pest grasps my arm and pulls me between his knees. He eyes the plate and smacks his lips.

'Bringing me a treat, are you?' he asks.

'It's for everyone.'

'Such ingratitude!' he chortles. 'Is this how you treat your knight in shining armour? I saved you from the rude and churlish ways of this rabble. How about a thank you?'

'I have to take the bread round.' I take a step backwards, but he hangs on to my arm.

'Go on. Give Uncle Bob first nibble,' he says, poking me in the stomach.

I hold the bowl out of reach, but Ma barks my name and I have little choice but to proffer it, however unwillingly. He takes a piece with a dainty gesture and places it between his lips.

'That's tasty,' he says, gaze swarming across my breasts.

I try to wriggle free. He presses his knees together like the jaws of a man-trap.

'Let me go. Everyone else wants a bit.'

'I'll bet they do.' He selects another piece of bread and slithers his tongue over it until it glistens with spittle. 'I'll bet you've got a queue of beaux lining up for what you've got.'

'I don't!' I try to sound outraged at such an indelicate suggestion, but it comes out as petulance.

'No?' He swallows the damp morsel with a gulp. 'Unplucked. How delectable.' He sucks grease off his fingers and wipes them on his spotless waistcoat. 'I must check such an assertion.'

As innocently as a man retrieving a dropped sixpence, he bends to the floor. Hidden by my petticoats, I feel his hand circle my ankle. I start away but am caught in the vice of his thighs. In a leisurely fashion, he draws himself upright and, as he does so, his fingers slide up my calf. I can't move, can't speak. He squeezes my knee.

Our eyes lock. He smiles with tender solicitation, as if it is the most natural thing in the world for a stranger to have his hand up a girl's skirt. I look at the other customers. They are ogling their glasses and joking with each other as if we are quite invisible. I cast a desperate look at Ma. She is busy washing glasses. I open my mouth to shout for her to come and rescue me.

The cry shrivels.

What can I say? What sort of girl allows a man to do such

a thing? The shame of it: I imagine every head in the room turning in my direction and seeing what is happening. I will bring ignominy on to Ma's head. I will cause The Comet to become known as a den of iniquity where such carryings-on take place. Ma's years of building up a respectable name dashed into smithereens in a moment.

His hand creeps an inch higher.

'What a pretty thing you are,' he says, tilting his head to one side. 'I believe this is going to become my favourite beerhouse from this moment on, if it has you to tempt me so. Wednesday night, Thursday night. Why, every night, I declare.'

His fingers continue their spider-climb under my skirt until they reach the tops of my stockings. He caresses the naked skin of my thigh. My breath bundles in my throat. With all my being I try to say *stop*. Such a short word, less than a breath, but it falters on my tongue, silenced by the lifetime of lessons drummed into me that children should be seen and not heard, and that good girls do what they're told.

I tremble so much that the bread dances in the dish. I dare not slap him away; indeed I cannot, for I'm holding on to the plate and if I let it fall I'll catch it off Ma. Besides, everyone will look to see what the noise is about and I'll die of mortification. When I think that I am about to burst, the strangest thing happens. I bend my head until my lips are on a level with his ear. A voice I do not recognise spills out of my mouth, quiet enough for him to hear, but none other.

'Get your filthy paws off me,' I growl. A confused look shadows his features. His hand freezes but does not withdraw. 'Right now.'

A smirk worms its way across his lips.

'Or what, my little pet?' he leers.

'Or what?' I fill my lungs with cleansing breath, and continue.

'Pin back your bloody ears and listen. I shall watch you, every moment of every day. I shall bide my time. One night, when you've dropped your guard, I'll take my knife, the one I use for chopping this bread so nice and neat, and I shall slide it between your ribs. And when you fall gasping to the floor I shall unbutton your greasy britches, grab your wizened meat and two veg and saw off the whole damned lot.'

I straighten up in a leisurely fashion. He draws his hand away from my leg and tucks it into his trouser pocket as if it has been there all evening. Around us, men sip beer. We stare at each other, blankly as strangers do. He swallows heavily, staggers to his feet, stutters an apology and hastens away, leaving tracks in the sawdust. I follow him to the door and watch him scurry down the street. He stops, slings a look over his shoulder and disappears around the corner.

'What's up with him?' asks Ma.

'Who?'

'You know very well who. You scaring off my customers?' she says.

I hitch my shoulders lazily. I carry the bread around the room, offering it with a perfect smile. When the plate is empty I return to the bar, where I set it down without so much as a rattle.

That night I stretch on my bed, staring into the shadows where the wall meets the ceiling. I've no idea who planted those words in my mouth. I've never spoken like that before. Yet tonight, I did. I answered back. I said no. Maybe this is the strength Nana spoke of.

GNOME
1901

At last. She is standing up for herself. Good thing too. I was beginning to think she was as much use as a dog with one leg. Of course, it took plenty of help from yours truly, but I'm not the boastful sort. Nor have I any desire to squander more brain matter than absolutely necessary upon my sister. There are more important things to worry about.

Top of the list is just how far Reg and his minions have put the wind up me. The last thing I want to admit is that I'm too scared to go to Shudehill, but facts are facts and I may as well swallow them, thorns and all. I stick close to home, prowling the confines of my neighbourhood. I tell myself I am still King of the Night, even if my kingdom has shrunk to the size of a postage stamp. Tell myself this is better than nothing at all, that I am biding my time before I return to the site of my defeat. No, not defeat. I'm simply a wise general who knows when to advance and when to retreat; when to strengthen home defences before venturing abroad on far-flung campaigns. I tell myself this is consolidation.

Weeks slide into months, which stretch into a year, and I wonder if I'm fated to spend my life pacing this grimy cage. No lion ever chafed so against his bars, or roared so disconsolately at the injustice of his imprisonment. I can't go on like this. A lad's needs are manifold and I itch to stretch my legs.

First off, this hair will have to go. I let Edie grow it long and look where it's landed me. This is what happens when you let kindness and consideration get the better of you. A little lad can get away with curls, but I'm fourteen and that's not little, not by a long chalk. We are growing up. Time to get shot of childish things.

The scissors swish as curls pile around my ankles. On my head they looked gold, but on the floor they are as tarnished as old leaves. It's a trick of the candlelight, a trick of the heart that sneaks in and whispers that I am cutting off more than hair. I grit my teeth and finish the job. With each snip, the true Gnome emerges, untrammelled by floppy fussiness. It's hard to shear a straight line and I look like a badly plucked goose when I'm done, but nothing can be allowed to stand in the way of progress. I feed the dead hair into the mouth of the range and savour the smell of burning.

The kitchen door swings and in stomps Mam, drawn by the stink. She's in her nightdress, face wrinkled from the pillow. She blinks a powerful number of times, like it's hard work to fit me in. I can't tell if she's going to chuck a saucepan or take me to her bosom.

'That'll put the cat amongst the pigeons,' she says, nodding at my haircut.

'Want me to look like a lass?'

She chews the inside of her cheek while she tries to work that one out. I break the silence before her eyes pop.

'How about you sit down. Let me make my dear mam a brew.' I slide the kettle on to the heat. 'Work your fingers to the bone, don't you?'

77

'Hmmph. Someone has noticed,' she says in a voice that splits down the middle like a bit of kindling. 'Finally.'

'Not right, is it?' I pour a cup and stir in a hill of sugar.

'No.'

'Good thing I'm here, isn't it?'

'Yes,' she mutters, and slurps the best cup of tea this side of the Pennines. 'No one knows how hard I slog.'

'Except for me.'

She gawps fondly. 'Except for you.'

'That Edie, eh?' I sigh.

'I'm a fool to myself,' she says, and gives me a soppy grin.

Now that I have her where I want her, I chatter how I barely get a minute to myself; how I'd love to step out; how lads need to stretch their legs or grow into wet nellies. Mam nods and shakes her head by turns.

'Ah,' I sigh. 'If only I had thruppence for a bag of sweets.'

That's all it takes for her to divvy up a handful of coins. I let her pinch and kiss my cheek, which is worth another handful, till my pockets are freighted with a small king's ransom.

'All I ever wanted was a good lad like you,' she snuffles.

Before she can blub her silly eyes out, I blow her a farewell kiss and take the first tram heading into the city. I've better things on which to spend the fare, so I travel in style, hanging on to the bars at the back. Sparks fly as steel grates against steel, fine as any firework show.

I pull faces through the window. The passengers do their damnedest to ignore me, burying their noses into the evening papers to blot out the scruffy tyke cadging a free ride. I've half a mind to squirm through the window and turn cartwheels, but I'd be out on my ear. There'll be plenty of time for hilarity when I get where I am going, I promise myself. As the tram slows for Shudehill, I leg it into the crowd.

I make a cautious tour of the aisles, cap pulled down to my chin. I've sprouted an inch and I bet I could take Reg on and trounce him good and proper. However, only a fool wastes his vigour on fisticuffs and I'm relieved to find neither hide nor hair of that particular gentleman. I take an invigorating breath and shove my cap to the back of my head.

This is where I should be: at the centre of things, where my ears din with clatter and clank. To my right, a raggle-taggle band blow trumpets, bang drums, scrape fiddles. To my left, an organ-grinder grinds. Straight ahead, the lads and lasses of the monkey-rank shout and laugh and waltz into taverns arm in arm. I am tugged this way and that, tempted by the barking of tripe-shop owners, fried-fish vendors and oyster-sellers. It's the bustling, clanging symphony of this city and I love it: the rub of tweed on wool, of silk on serge, and all of it scented with coal dust and horse-shit and pepper and sweat and oil and electricity.

I need no penny paper when I have this. Murder, highwaymen and horrors come a poor second to these wonders. I am on the brink of manhood, with a taste for the salty, the savoury, the spicy. I appreciate things my childish self could neither understand nor appreciate.

Now that I have established the coast is clear, it is time to find some folk to fall in with. I spy a knot of likely fellows at a fried-potato stand, all of them smaller than yours truly. I can read boys faster than my A, my B and my C and this lot are floundering at the periphery of the action, clearly in need of a commanding officer. I saunter to their rescue.

'Hey now!' I cry. 'You scrawny little shitwipes. I've not seen you in a donkey's age.'

Before they have a chance to scratch their verminous noggins and ask who I am, I dead-arm one of the shortest with a sly blow. We share a laugh at his expense, watching him pirouette, piping *ow ow* over and over and threatening all kinds of punishment he is unlikely to deliver.

'Coo,' declares one. 'That's a jolly jape.'

'You got Cyril good and proper,' chirps another.

Cyril rubs his funny bone and shoots me a murderous glance.

'That's just for starters,' I say. 'Plenty more where that came from.'

I glance about and my eye falls on an effete youth who looks like he's stepped off the wall of an art gallery. I imagine the picture: *Narcissus Clothed*, reclining on his elbow and regarding his fat face in the water. On his arm is a girl with skin as pale as that on a tapioca pudding.

'Look at him,' I jeer, jerking my thumb over my shoulder. 'Those trousers. So baggy he may as well be wearing a skirt.'

I wink at my new pals, sneak behind the milksop and punch his elbow. It is so easy that it hardly counts as sport.

'I say!' he quacks, inspecting the numb limb.

'Pansy!' I yell. 'Flapping about like a big girl's blouse!'

I wait for his face to fold, the tears to fall. He raises his uninjured hand to shoulder height and for the space of a breath I think he is going to slap me. But he sweeps his fingers under the flowing curtain of his hair, flips it back and stares at me down his long nose. His lips tweak in a half-smile and I hear his thoughts, clear as the cry of a coal-heaver.

You piece of dirt. When you leave here, you'll tramp to your broken home on your broken street in your broken boots to eat supper with your broken teeth. I shall hop into a brougham and be whisked away to a grand place you'll never know.

I hold my smile steady, but it is the greatest weight I've ever lifted and near breaks my chin to keep it there. I poke out my tongue and blow a raspberry. His lass sticks her nose in the air.

'What a low class of person frequents this place,' she declares.

'Oh, I don't know,' drawls the aesthete. 'Vulgar folk are so fascinating.'

She clings to her limp companion, devouring him with eyes so ravenous you'd think them organs of digestion.

'No point casting your hook at him, love,' I shout as they flounce off. 'Looks like he couldn't raise a smile.'

'I can never understand how these chaps have always got a pretty girl in tow,' grumbles one of my crew.

'Pretty?' I sneer. 'Peaky, more like,' I say. 'A skinny ghost in need of a plate of pie and peas.' They snigger, much cheered by my observation. I shall not let that flaccid flower-boy spoil the evening. 'As for him, what a wet herring!'

'Nah,' interrupts Cyril. 'Sprat, more like.'

Their attention swings away, towards him.

'Tiddler,' I respond, and have them back again.

'Stickleback,' he says firmly. 'Nothing smaller than a stickle-back.'

I rack my brains and, in the time it takes, I lose them. Cyril rattles off a list of fishy insults and they laugh like hyenas at his feeble efforts.

'Oh, stop it, Cyril,' wheezes one. 'I'll piss myself at this rate.'

'Too late. Already have done,' guffaws Cyril.

He makes a show of walking in bow-legged circles, kicking make-believe droplets off his clogs. He wears such a pained expression that the whole lot of them lean against each other, cackling. I don't know why everyone is paying him such mind. He's not that funny. Besides, Cyril is minced mutton of a name, in my opinion.

I point out an ice-cream cart and stand everyone a twist of hokey-pokey, with much flourishing of my largesse. It's a race to gobble the stuff before it soaks through the paper, and some of us are more proficient than others. Me, I like the sensation of ice trickling down my fingers. I draw out the eating of it to such a marvellous degree that I make a mess of my shirt from collar to cuffs. Cyril nods at me.

'You're going to cop it off your ma,' he observes.

'Take the broom to you, she will,' says another. 'That stuff's murder to get out.'

'You'll not sit down for a week.'

I shrug and wipe my lips on my sleeve for good measure. 'My mam does exactly what I tell her,' I reply with a haughty air. '*Mam! Scrub my cuffs!* That's what I say.'

'As heck as like,' scoffs Cyril.

'You don't know my mam. I shall stride in and declare, *Mother! I have a job for you! Wash my shirt!*' I hitch my thumbs behind my lapels and puff out my chest.

'What a windbag you are,' says Cyril.

'That's not the half of it,' I continue, rather wishing he'd button his lip. '*Be quick about it! Chop chop!*' I make a panto-mime of an old dame, one hand pressed to my back and tugging my forelock. '*Yes, Gnome!*' I squawk. '*As fast as ever I can, Gnome!*'

They giggle, as much out of nervousness as awe. I do not care if they take me for an empty-headed boy, all hot air and nothing else. I'll not be outdone by a midget like Cyril. There's room for only one Caesar and I wear those laurels.

We plough on, avoiding the slip and slide around the cow-heel stall. Drawn like wasps to jam, our promenade carries us past a confectionery stand. I eye the jars of wine gums, slab toffee, liquorice, Pontefract cakes and coltsfoot rock. The ground crunches with sugar. The girl weighing out the sweets has a starved look: chewed-down nails, hair draggled in sticky ringlets.

82

'How about a lollipop, miss?' says Cyril, poking his tongue against the inside of his cheek in a suggestive fashion.

I groan and roll my eyes. That's not how to get a handful of mint balls without paying. Her cheeks flush and she fiddles with the bun on the back of her head, where some tendrils of hair have worked loose.

'You look sweet,' I say. That's the way to do it.

Cyril throws me a pitying look. 'I've got a stick of rock if you fancy a gobble,' he adds, louder.

'Ooh,' says one of the younger boys.

'Now there's a thing,' says another.

'Hur, hur,' a third.

'You buying, or wasting my time?' the girl trills pertly. 'No money, no service.'

She serves half an ounce of coloured sugar to an urchin who looks too young to be out, and a quarter-pound of cough candy to a fellow in a leather apron who calls her Maggie.

Cyril makes a snorting noise. 'Name as plain as her face.'

'You'll get nothing if you talk to her like that,' I say.

'Who says I want to get my hands on her pear drops?' He shakes his head. 'You young 'uns don't know the first thing—'

'Young! I'm twice your age.'

'Nah,' he says with an appraising glance. 'You'll understand when your balls have dropped.'

'Better than being a short-arse.'

He yawns and stretches his arms. 'You lot can stay here and spoon with ugly lasses if you want. I'm getting bored.'

He saunters off, shooting a wily grin over his shoulder. His sheep follow, one by one. Maggie watches his cock-of-the-walk strut with something approaching wistfulness. The last lad to desert me tugs my arm.

'You coming?'

'I'll follow when I'm ready,' I declare.

I'll be damned if I'll be a rat trundling after that particular piper. I'll show him. I'll get half a pound of humbugs out of Maggie, so I will, and share it with them all, except ruddy Cyril. Then we'll see what's what and who's who. Maggie weighs out an ounce of monkey nuts for a pair of lovebirds. I take off my cap and, hugging it to my chest, furnish her with my nicest smile.

'What a rude boy,' I chirp with a virtuous expression that'd shame the angel Gabriel. 'I wouldn't address a young lady so.'

'You still here?' she says with a glare that could curdle milk.

It's Cyril she ought to be angry with, not me. Female thinking. It's got me stumped. I gear up to give her a piece of my mind when my eye is drawn to a lady hovering over the table.

It may have been months and months ago, but I recognise Jessie, the woman who tipped the scales in my favour over that nasty business with Reg. She's dressed in fusty taffeta and on her feet are velvet slippers trimmed with beads around the toe. They'll last a couple of weeks, I muse; if she steps into a puddle, a lot less.

I buck up considerably. I draw closer, full to bursting with tales of my new cronies, when I notice how queerly she is behaving. She points at a dish of treacle toffee, yet as soon as Maggie prepares to weigh a portion, she interrupts.

'No, not that!' she says. 'Here now!'

She indicates the sugared almonds, as if they're what she meant all along. When the jar is lifted for approval she shakes her head.

'Dear me, no,' she says. 'Not the *almonds*.'

She waggles her fingers in the direction of a canister of humbugs. As she does so, the long tippets of her muff dangle across the table and obscure what she's doing with her other hand. Calm as you like, she is plucking chocolates from the shelf and sliding them into the side of her skirt, secreting them in what must be a hidden pocket. With a grunt, Maggie hefts the humbugs.

'No, no!' pouts Jessie, tossing her head. The flowers on her hat tremble with indignation.

Now she wants the barley sugar. What a pretty glove she wears on her right hand: crimson leather with emerald stitching, bright as a banner. Only a philistine would pay attention to her light-fingered left hand when distracted by the display of the right.

Maggie scowls at this tiresome female who can't make up her mind. She remains polite, for the customer is always right, even if they spend an age choosing between an ounce of Everton mints and an ounce of liquorice. Jar after jar is proffered, to pretty shakes of the head. All the while, Jessie fills her pocket with steady grace, stealing the sweets as if she has a claim to them.

Finally, she decides upon the treacle toffee, the very thing she started with. While Maggie weighs out two ounces, Jessie extracts pennies from the embroidered purse hanging on her arm. She accepts the twist of paper and inclines her head in thanks before gliding away. She cocks her elbow and turns out her toes, kicking them to each side so that passers-by may glance down and remark on the trimness of her ankles. I follow her along the line of tables and draw up alongside.

'Give us a toffee, missus,' I say, just loud enough for her to hear.

She looks down her nose. 'In your dreams. Hop it, you little twerp.'

'Give us one of those chocolates, then.'

'What chocolates?' she says with a dangerous tilt of her eyebrow.

I slide closer and pat her skirt, which crackles with something very like brown paper. She must've lined the pocket.

'That's clever,' I say. 'So they don't melt.'

'Shut up,' she hisses.

'You must have quarter of a pound in there,' I continue. 'You won't miss one.' I jerk my chin in the direction of the confectionery stand. 'Maggie will, though. Sooner or later. Specially if I tell her.'

She looks me up and down, swinging her purse on its chain. 'You're a cheeky toad. I'll give you one and no more. Not here, though.'

'Course not,' I say with a grin. 'I'll stand you a cup of tea. Fair exchange is no robbery.'

She brays laughter. 'Charmed, sir. Quite charmed.'

I crook my elbow. She laughs again, gently this time, and places her scarlet glove upon my arm. As we proceed through the market hall I have the odd sensation of being a tugboat pulled up alongside a freighter. I spot Cyril and the lads, treat them to a roguish wink and am gratified to see their silly mouths flop open as they get an eyeful. I may only come to her shoulder, but I'm in the company of the finest lass in Shudehill and that trumps anything that Cyril can muster. No one's ever going to get the jump on me again. Never. And certainly not a worm like him.

At the tea-stand I order two cups and slap down sixpence, chest puffed up with pride. The tea-man leans across the counter and fills up our mugs.

'Got yourself a new bully, Jessie?' he says with a chuckle.

She barks a quick, businesslike laugh. 'Him? He's my bonny lad.'

She puts her arm around me and squeezes. I don't push her away; not this time. It's over as fast as a sneeze, so it's not like anyone notices. She shovels spoonful after spoonful of sugar into her cup.

'You'll suffocate that tea,' I say.

She takes an enthusiastic slurp. 'The cup that cheers,' she declares. 'Well, now. A gently brought-up lady such as myself ought to be formally introduced to a gentleman before she takes tea with him, don't you think?'

'Indubitably,' I reply, warming to the theme. 'Yet I see no appropriate soul upon whom I may call to accomplish such a task. Should I go? Must we part so soon?'

'That would be a pity,' she sighs.

With her index finger she taps her chest, as though sounding out the heart beneath the bodice. There's a light in her eye that suggests she's used to playing games, but rarely of this sort. I raise my cap.

'You have forgotten. We are already acquainted, fair damsel.'

'We are?' She looks me up and down, appraising me as keenly as she would a fur coat for moth-holes.

'You came to my aid, many moons ago, when I was sore affrighted and in need of succour.'

'Oh my Lord. You're that Little Lord Fauntleroy. You've had your hair cut. Aww, what a crying shame. I liked those curls.'

'Get away,' I grunt, but not harshly. I am having too much fun to be out of sorts. 'May I make so bold as to effect my own introduction?'

'How presumptuous,' she says with a grin, fanning her cheek with her glove. 'See my maidenly blushes.' Her face is unruffled.

'Madam, miss, my lady,' I say, doffing my cap. 'I am your humble servant, Gnome.'

'What sort of a name is that?'

'Mine, and none other.'

She laughs. It is a surprisingly delicate sound.

'Gnome it is. Charmed, Sir Gnome. And I am Jessie.'

'I know. It is my absolute favourite name for a lady. Now give me a ruddy sweet.'

'All in good time.'

'Now's a good time.'

She sets down her cup. 'You're a caution, that's for sure.'

'Sure as eggs is eggs.' She offers the bag of toffee and I shake my head. 'Not so fast. Don't give me second best. Chocolate, we said.'

'Chocolate, *you* said.'

'Chocolate!'

She rolls her eyes, slips a hand into the concealed pocket and draws out a paper bag. I make a grab for it but she holds it out of reach.

'Now, now,' she chides. 'Didn't your mother teach you how to behave?'

'What mother?'

She gives me a careful look, unscrews the mouth of the bag and with great reluctance hands one to me. I snatch it before she can change her mind and cram it into my mouth. Syrup laced with cherry liqueur oozes down my chin.

I shove out my hand. 'Go on,' I say stickily. 'Give us another.'

'Not on your life!' she says. 'I'm not wasting high-class confectionery on the likes of you. That went straight down without touching the sides.'

'So?'

'There are some things in life best served by taking your time.'

'Like what?'

She leans on her fist and grins. 'No, I don't think you're ready.'

'I am!'

'Really?'

'Really!' I cry.

'Be a good boy, then.' I nod furiously. She waggles her fingers like a magician, dips into the bag and draws out another chocolate. She waves it a tantalising inch in front of my mouth, little finger cocked. 'Open wide.' I stretch my lips to their fullest extent. She pops the confection inside. 'Slow down. No chewing.'

'How can I eat it without chewing?' I mumble.

'Leave it on your tongue. And wait. And if needs be, you wait a bit blinking longer.' She pauses, and stares at me dramatically. I hold still. 'Wait,' she says. The chocolate softens. 'Wait.'

I obey. The centre dissolves, flooding my mouth with violets. It is the most delicious thing I ever tasted.

'Oh, Jessie,' I say.

She tips back her head and guffaws. There's a band of dirt around her throat, but it's the prettiest throat I've ever set eyes on.

'Didn't I tell you? You can take your angels and your harps and you can stick them. If there's no chocolate in heaven then I'm stopping here.' She drains her mug and slaps it on the counter. 'I'm off,' she declares. 'It's been a pleasure, Sir Gnome.'

I scamper to her side. 'Wait,' I gasp. 'Let me walk you home. Go on.'

'Home? I should cocoa. I've got work to do.'

'Oh.'

Her gaze dances across my face, soft as feathers. 'Penny for them?' she says, peering down at me.

'Nothing important,' I mutter. A brainwave strikes. I turn out the contents of my pockets. The fortune glistens. 'I'll give you all of it. You don't need to work.'

She stretches her hand across the space between us. I think she's going to take the coins, but she runs her forefinger along the line of my cheek with a leisure that intimates she has all night to execute the gesture.

'Bonny lad,' she murmurs.

While I'm gulping air, she bids me a ladylike adieu and swirls away.

I sway home, head swimming like a chap with five pints of mild in him. I reflect on my new friends and it strikes me that of them all, the only name of which I am sure is Cyril. I push aside the uneasy thought and return to Jessie, a far more cheering proposition. There's a sparkle in my chest that wasn't there before. My shoulders prickle as though wings are budding, on the brink of breaking free. I'm growing into a man, so I am. What other reason could she have for supping tea with me?

There's a commotion up ahead and I fly in its direction, like iron shavings to a magnet. I'm not the only one taking an interest and have to wriggle through a thicket of bodies to get to the front. The new tram-tracks at St Mary's Gate have barely been laid a month and there's already some idiot got his boot wedged in them.

'Get me out!' he crows, half-laughing, half-yelling, in that way of intoxicated folk who get themselves into a pickle.

It takes a minute, but I could hardly forget that face. He has a smear of hair on his upper lip that makes him look like he's kissed a coal scuttle. He lies athwart the ruts, stuck fast.

'Good evening, Reg,' I say.

'What? Who?' he blurts, eyes lumbering back and forth in their sockets.

To him, I'm just another fellow. He can't even be bothered to remember those he has tortured.

'Help me,' he says, slurring the words. 'I can't lie here all night.'

'No, you can't. That's true enough,' I reply, sucking my teeth philosophically.

Reg tugs at his trouser cuff, but all this achieves is to drag the wool up to his knee, revealing his calf. He looks rather comical with one leg bare. I start to whistle.

> Diddle diddle dumpling, my son John,
> Went to bed with his trousers on;
> One sock off and one sock on,
> Diddle diddle dumpling, my son John.

Folk continue to gather. There's a lot of oohing and aahing from bumpkins fresh up from Marple as they try to haul him out. They may be skilled at dragging sheep out of streams, but in the city they fail.

'Take your sock off,' suggests a helpful lad. His trousers are fastened around his waist with string, knotted tightly so they do not slip to half-mast. 'Like this, sir,' he says, pushing down an invisible stocking.

'No,' opines another chap. 'He wants to get his foot out of his shoe, so he does.'

'What?' squeaks another. 'And leave it behind?' He clicks his tongue against his teeth. 'I couldn't afford a pair like that if I worked a month.'

'A year,' laughs another.

'You're not wrong there, mate,' concedes the first fellow agreeably.

'But if he gets his foot out of the shoe, then the shoe will follow after.'

'Easy to dig it out if there's no foot in it.'

'There's an idea.'

Round and round they go, nodding ruminatively and puffing away on cigarettes and pipes. The rut begins to vibrate, like an iron string plucked by a massive hand.

'Fellows,' I say. 'There's a tram coming.' No one pays me the slightest bit of attention. The thrumming grows louder. 'I mean it,' I add.

'Gorton tram's not due for five minutes,' remarks one old codger, back bent into a snake. 'I should know, I take it often enough.'

'I don't care about the timetable,' I say. 'There's one coming all the same.'

The Gorton man raises his head from its contemplation of Reg's trapped foot and glances left, then right. 'Don't get yourself so wound up, lad,' he mumbles. 'Goes down the other track.'

The foretold tram squeals around the corner, takes the spur and bypasses our little group, sparks buzzing from the wheels. The conductor leans out, shakes his fist and bawls at us to get out of the way. We watch it trundle into the distance. More folk gather to watch the proceedings. One monocled worthy draws out a pocket watch with a face not much smaller than my own. He consults it gravely.

'There's a Belle Vue tram in a minute,' he remarks. 'Comes down this track. Cut right through this gent's leg, if I'm not mistaken.'

'He'd best be off, then,' says an ancient woman.

'He'd better, indeed,' agrees another.

Reg tugs at his foot. 'Someone get me out!' he cries, sounding a great deal more sober than five minutes ago.

The clouds select this moment to drop rain upon the scene. One by one the bystanders gallop off in search of shelter, until I am the only one to remain at Reg's side. His desultory attempts to free himself become increasingly frantic.

'Help me!' he pleads.

His breathing is shallow, his face changed from drunken puce to sickly green. The rain thickens.

'Oh, lawks,' I squeak, patting my cheeks. 'Whatever is a girl to do?'

'Please,' he begs. 'Grab my foot and pull.'

'How can a girl possibly do that?'

He blinks at me through the downpour. 'You're not a girl.'

'Oh, but I am. That's what you said. I distinctly remember you employing that precise appellation.'

'I don't—' His face grows paler, if that were possible. 'You—' he gulps. 'Dear God in heaven. Have pity.'

'Perhaps He will, perhaps He won't. Best start praying.'

The space behind my eyes glitters, as though my head's been filled with silver feathers. In that weightless place, I see my hands reach down and pluck Reg from peril. I am the hero of the hour; Reg and I are best pals forever, closer than brothers. The vision splutters, drowns. Rain pounds the cobbles, creating dense clouds of spray. Reg stares at me with eyes stripped of arrogance, the pupils swollen with terror.

'What are you doing?' he whimpers.

'Watching.'

Reg swallows painfully. 'Why won't you help?'

'What's that?' I say, cupping a hand around my ear. 'Can't hear you.' My heart is hammering. 'The tram can have both legs off for all I care.'

I fold my arms across my chest and press my hands into my armpits to stop them getting any ideas about rescue. There is a far-off tooting. Reg stares at a point over my shoulder. I turn to follow the direction of his gaze and see the Belle Vue tram turning the tight corner into Blackfriars Street, a dark blur shuddering through the torrential rain.

'It will stop, won't it?' he whispers, soft as a child. 'It'll see me. Won't it?'

93

'That depends,' I say. 'On someone raising the alarm. Someone like me.'

He yanks at his foot with lunatic energy. I think of what he'd have done to me. I'm not actually doing anything to him. I'm just not getting in the way of fate. I step clear of the track. The shadow of the oncoming tram grows larger. The rain is filthy with soot.

'Why won't it stop?' wails Reg, a small dry noise lost in the tumbling water. 'For the love of Jesus, help me.'

'Here's a jolly turnaround,' I quip. 'I do believe Jumbo is going to have a ride on you.'

At the last moment, one of my hands works free and waves. My arm swims in the rain. The tram is so close I see the driver's mouth fall open. The brakes scream, steel grinding against steel. It slows. And slows. And comes to a halt on top of Reg's foot.

Despite the downpour, the crowd regroups, not wanting to miss the entertainment. The puddle under the machine turns pink, deepening into crimson. Reg won't take his eyes off the spreading pool. A reedy noise comes out of his gob. I bend to his ear.

'Take it like a man,' I mutter.

The noise swells to a high-pitched keening. He slumps sideways, ankle twisted at an impossible angle. Some of the tram passengers have stepped down to get a closer look at the accident and those without umbrellas are craning their necks out of the windows. The driver leaps from his platform and dashes to my side. I'm roused from my reverie as he clouts me around the side of the head.

'You little shit!' he yells.

'What was that for?' I shout back, just as angrily.

'Why didn't you tell me?'

94

'I waved! I was the only one who did!'

'I'll lose my badge for this.' He takes another swing at me, but his heart's not in it and he is wide of the mark. 'What a to-do,' he gabbles, shifting his cap and scratching the bald patch beneath. 'Didn't see him. Not anyone's fault. Certainly not mine.'

'Not your fault by any means, sir,' the conductor chips in, a man with a swollen nose the same colour as the bloody water.

The pool widens. I step out of its way.

'Shall I call for a policeman?' asks the conductor.

'Yes, I believe you must. All must be done according to the correct procedures,' blares the driver, as though he thinks courage can be demonstrated by raising his voice.

The passengers nod their heads sagely.

'Police!' shouts the conductor. 'Is there no policeman to be found?'

There's the deep-throated blare of a foghorn and the humped back of another tram separates itself from the murk. It toots again, more urgently, and scrapes to an unwilling stop behind the first.

'This will not do,' mutters the driver. His forehead furrows, rain streaming down his face. 'We are holding up the service.'

'Yes, sir,' agrees the conductor.

'We do no good by stopping here.'

'No, sir.'

'We must shift ourselves.'

'Indeed, we must, sir.'

'Look lively, Mr Bootham.'

'Yes, sir!' says the conductor smartly.

He ushers the passengers on board. They look pointedly at their pocket watches and through the smeared windows I see heads shaking. At last, a policeman arrives, more by chance than by good management. There is now a string of trams backed up along the track, every last one of them hooting like billy-o.

'Here, here,' he accuses the driver. 'You're holding up the trams.'

'Not me, officer,' he replies. 'Him.' He points at Reg. 'He stuck his boot in the track and he won't move. Lay there where no one could see him.'

Reg sprawls across the paviours, mouth agape and collecting rain. His face is as washed-out as a dishcloth.

'Well, now. He's not going to move any faster with you on top of him.'

The driver's eyes light up. 'That's the truth.'

'So you'd best shift yourself, and fast.'

The driver tugs his cap, jumps into the footwell and rings the bell vigorously. The carriage jerks, clanks, and moves forward slowly, revealing what is left of Reg's foot. The policeman sighs with an air of one much put upon. He lifts up his hand and blows hard on his whistle so that the following trams don't get ideas and shunt forward.

'Give me a hand, lad,' he growls, glaring like this is somehow my doing.

We take one arm each and haul at the limp body.

'He's stuck, sir,' I say.

'I can see that,' he replies, although I don't think he sees at all. 'Leave it to me.'

He grasps Reg's leg below the knee and gives a colossal tug. The foot comes out, or what remains of it. I do not want to look, but my eyes are drawn to the mess. The policeman yells at two chaps lounging in a shop doorway. Very grudgingly they leave their shelter and approach.

'Pick him up,' orders the policeman.

'What, us?' one of them moans.

'He's half-dead, he is,' says the other.

'And you will be too, if you don't jump to it. Get him to the Infirmary. We're only a step from Piccadilly.'

'A long step,' grumbles the first, but they set to, hoisting Reg between their shoulders like a side of bacon. They haul him away, his mangled trotter trailing behind. The policeman gives a long blast on his whistle and waves the stopped trams forward. He gives me a final glance.

'Get out of the way, lad. Don't want you finishing up in the same fix.'

The rain thins. The show is over. The splash of crimson is already fading. I watch until it disappears completely, rinsed away by each tram that passes through it. It carries away my last scrap of kindness and washes it down the drain, where it belongs. I journey home with a fluttering feeling in my belly. It makes my skin crawl, like coming into the kitchen with bare feet and treading on a slug. At first I think it is the usual nonsense that descends upon me in the wee small hours, but it is not. It is cold and searing and unutterably delicious. It is the savour of revenge.

Grandma is supping tea and warming her knees before the range, stockings shabby around her ankles. A bit of a night owl like her grandson, so she is.

'You're late,' she supplies by way of greeting.

'And I love you too, grandmother dearest,' I reply, giving her a peck on the cheek, which is as rough as a miner's trousers.

'Get away with you,' she says, not unkindly. 'Where've you been?'

'Man got his foot cut off by the Belle Vue tram. I tried to help.'

'You, help? There's a funny thing,' she hums, too disbelieving a tune for my taste.

'Don't you start,' I snap. 'I return to the bosom of my family, burdened with weariness—'

'Stow it, Gnome,' she retorts and slurps the last of her brew. 'It's near morning. Upstairs with you.'

'Or what?' Fagged out I may be but there's a scrap of heat remaining.

'Or you'll stop in tomorrow night. And the night after.'

My heart shuffles, skips a beat. Not again. Not that. I snort. 'I'd like to see you try.'

I stamp out of the room but she grabs my arm.

'I can.'

'You and whose army?'

'Lad, listen. You're going to get yourself in trouble.'

'Maybe I like trouble.'

'You know the sort of trouble I mean.'

'Give over. I'm sick of it. Stay at home, be a good lad, don't rock the boat. That's all I ever hear. It's not what I want for my life.'

'It's the best way for folk like us. The only way.'

'I'm nothing like you. You can wipe that pitying look off your mug and all.' I spread my arms like wings. 'I've got plans, I have. I'm going to get away from all of this. See if I don't. Trams, carts, trains: anything with wheels to carry me further than the eye can see. I want a steamship to America. I want wide-open spaces and a horse to gallop across them. I want—'

'Put a cork in it, you little idiot. You might not want this life but you're stuck with it.' She peers at me. 'Now. Get into bed – and take your boots off first, for once.'

'I won't!' I clap my hands over my ears, but my insides are already writhing with defeat.

'The sooner you stop fighting, the better.'

'Never,' I moan, voice shifting into a higher register. 'Look.

I'll stay as I am just by concentrating.' I clench my fists, squeeze my eyes shut and strain as if I'm pushing out a three-day-old turd.

'No good,' she murmurs.

'I hate you,' I hiss, drumming my heels on the floor to drown her out. 'Hate you.'

Trust the old witch to hurl water over my budding joy the second I'm through the door. I've had it up to here. Never was a fellow so cursed with a family of interfering busybodies. Every last one of them with nothing better on their minds than keeping a good man down, that good man being myself.

I'll play the dutiful son if that's what it takes, but I've not the slightest intention of obedience. I can't help it if I was born with wheels on my backside. If God didn't mean for me to be King of the Moonlit Hours, He wouldn't have granted me their dominion, would He?

Tonight, the curtain rose on a boy. At night's close, I am a man, or as near as makes no difference. No more nonsense. I can't hold Edie's hand forever. She'll have to hold it for herself. I have my own life to lead. No cage can hold me, nor will chiding clip these wings.

EDIE
1901–1902

It's as well that I've discovered a source of strength, for I need every scrap. Although Nana is kinder, Ma is not.

Perhaps it is the poison of her hatred that infects me. My flesh crawls with ants that burrow fire beneath the skin. I stare at myself in the looking glass till I'm blue in the face but neither see nor find anything to explain it, not so much as a pimple. Yet I sicken. I hasten so often to the privy I may as well live there, crouched double, retching. I'm convinced that one day I'll turn inside out, I heave so hard. For all my labour, I bring up nothing.

I seek understanding from my grandmother, who mutters about growing pains in such a way that I'm embarrassed for having asked. As for my hair being cut as soon it gets to my chin, I assume it is one of Ma's inexplicable punishments to shear me as I sleep. There is no other explanation.

However, I shall not be overthrown. Not by this, nor by any other tribulation. And, as I enter my fifteenth year I begin to rebel.

In common with all of my station, I finished my schooling at the age of fourteen. The teacher bade us farewell with the words *knowledge is power*. It planted a seed that buds into a determination to pursue answers to my questions between the pages of a book. As the months pass, that desire intensifies into a hunger that drives me, trembling, to the King Street library.

The place is as grand as a temple; far too grand for the likes of me – or so sneers Ma's voice in the chambers of my brain. I tick myself off. If I am going to become my own woman and not merely cower in her shadow, I have to start somewhere. I climb the steps to the colonnaded portico, a precarious courage carrying me through the doors and into the reading room.

I tiptoe between the ranks of shelves, tasting the scent of old paper mingled with morocco leather and pipe smoke. I don't dare touch anything. My bravery trickles away. I am on the verge of bolting when a finely dressed matron approaches me.

'Can I help you?'

I tug my shawl tightly across my bosom and stare at the floor, a jigsaw of wooden rectangles set in a herringbone pattern.

'Are you seeking any particular volume?' she continues.

I shake my head a fraction.

'Perhaps if you inform me whither your interests lead?'

I wish I knew the answer. I wait for her to hurl me on to the street with a flea in my ear.

'Do you like stories?' she asks.

I raise my eyes, startled by her kindly tone.

'Hmm,' she muses. 'Mythology, I think.'

She sweeps away, navigating her way through the maze with mysterious confidence. I cling to her skirts for fear of becoming hopelessly lost. She comes to a halt before a shelf that looks pretty much the same as the others, runs a slim finger along the spines, pauses and plucks out a small volume.

'Yes,' she says. '*Tales of Greece and Rome*. A good place to commence one's exploration, don't you think?'

She holds the book in my direction, clearly intending for me to take it. It is too wonderful. I extend my hand, more than half expecting her to snatch back the treasure and cry that she was only joking and I must leave immediately. She does not. Instead, she motions me towards a table the breadth of a coal barge and invites me to sit. I obey, unable to take my eyes off this wondrous creature.

She places the book upon the table and leaves me alone with it. It takes a few moments before I am valiant enough to touch it, a few more before I am able to lift the cover. It does not fly into pieces when I do so and gradually my fortitude re-exerts itself.

The first story is entitled 'The Fall of Icarus'. It boasts a frontispiece of a young man, stark naked save for a towel draped around his hips. I glance over my shoulder, but no one else has noticed this scandalous display. His arms sprout feathers, his toes point to the earth and, very wonderfully indeed, he is flying.

I dive into the story: a wild tale about wicked kings, men with bull's heads and Icarus locked up in a tower. The words convey me to his castle as surely as if it has sprung up around me. I smell the breeze floating above the waves, feel the stirring of plumes upon Icarus's shoulders. The air teases, calling him to the realm of the sky. I yearn to go with him. He clambers on to the windowsill. I stand at his side. He spreads his arms. I spread mine. He jumps and I jump also.

The delight! The wind rushes under my arms, and, oh, they are no longer arms. They are wings, and I am flying. Birds wheel away, squawking in fright. I dive low and skim the face of the waters, the salt breath of the sea burning my lungs. I swoop high, no longer earthbound. I can go anywhere: away from this library, this city, this island. I can fly to the stars and make my home on the moon.

Up and up I go. No miserable blanket of cloud pins me down. I bask in heat, soar high as the birds, and higher. I am free. I take a deep breath, my nostrils fill with the smell of candles and I see the most curious thing. A feather slips from my wing-tip, flickering as it falls. It is followed by another and another until I'm shedding quills as fast as a chicken plucked for Christmas. I flap wildly, but my wings are melting away. I hurtle towards the sea. It glints emerald, set with islands like topaz gems. I fall and fall, and am finished.

My eyes blur. I jerk my head so that tears do not splash the precious book and blow my nose on my handkerchief. A fellow with nibbled side-whiskers glances up from his newspaper and frowns. I do not care. So what if my life constrains me, tighter than the baskets in which hens are brought to market. This story has lifted me into the heaven of the imagination. I've glimpsed a world with boundless horizons. I burn: not to build a contraption of wings, but to shake off the shackles of my existence and make my own way. Build my own life.

Yes! sings my soul. *That's right, Edie,* he says. *Fly!*

I don't have time to solve the riddle of why my soul sounds like a boy, because I am roused from my trance by the librarian, who whispers that they are closing up. I taste a fall as keen as that of Icarus and vow that I will visit again, and soon.

I return the next day, to be greeted as a friend. On each subsequent visit, the steps become easier to climb, the columns less of an impenetrable forest. The librarian is patient and guides my journey through this kingdom of binding and ink, until my confidence blossoms and I become a seasoned traveller. Every book I open answers a question I didn't know I'd asked. Each line plucks a resonant string in my soul. I will never tire of such invigorating music.

After three weeks of enchantment, she stops me at the door as I am leaving.

'Did you have an enjoyable day?' she asks.

I nod my thanks, still too shy to speak.

'You could become a member, you know. With your own ticket, you could borrow books and take them home.'

'Home?' I squeak.

'Yes. For one week, after which you must return them, of course.'

She smiles, as though she has said the most natural thing in the world. I am aghast: I can select a book, place it in my bag and remove it from the building. I can walk home without a policeman chasing me along the street shouting, *Stop thief!* All she asks is that I return it. It is the first time I've ever been trusted. I shake my head.

'Thank you,' I mumble. 'Maybe another day.'

I am far too frightened to take her up on the offer. I can hardly tell her I don't trust myself. If I am the kind of slattern who wakes up with muddy boots on her feet, who knows what infamies I may inflict upon a book.

This aside, the library is refuge and escape rolled into one. A generous world that asks nothing of me save attentiveness and rewards me with gifts beyond measure. My self-education is intoxicating and sweet. Once I commence, I cannot stop. The spark of each question lights the fuse of the next, and the next, until my mind crackles with *who, what, how, when* and, most essential of all, *why*: that king of questions, which seeks an answer and is forever left hungry for more. Not that I limit myself to stories. I read everything: from science to history, poetry to novels and back again.

Learning makes me unruly and cantankerous. The more I read, the more Ma and I bicker. The altercation that tops all others takes place on a day as flat and grey as any Manchester can offer.

I've scarce set foot over the threshold when Ma lets loose her volley of complaints: the hours I squander with my nose in a book, how a proper daughter would help her mama around the house, and so on and so forth.

'It's not right,' she rails, peeling potatoes with such fury I have the distinct feeling she'd prefer to be flaying my skin instead of theirs. 'Gadding about, getting into the good Lord only knows what sort of unseemly scrapes.'

In the past I let it roll over my head. But I'm no longer the girl I was.

'I am hardly engaged in indecorous activity,' I reply, slamming my hat on to the table and denting the brim in the process. 'I imagine you would find a library the dullest of places.'

'How dare you. The sauce of it,' she hisses, hacking at a green spot. 'Besides. Excessive reading causes malformation of the female organs.'

'Codswallop. Since when did you become a professor of medicine?' I reply. I saw a thick slice off the loaf and search for the dripping.

'I've never been so insulted in all my days! No obedient child would dare address her mother so.'

'Hah! Don't like me fighting back? You'd best get used to it. Meek, quivering Edie has gone. You'll not see her again.'

'Under my roof you will behave!'

'Make me,' I growl.

Her face turns an ugly shade of puce. 'This proves the truth . . .'

'It proves nothing.'

'Book learning leads to unfeminine behaviour!' she squawks.

'Hark at you! If anything proves that women are prone to

ridiculous fancies it is claptrap like that. You should try reading a book, Mother dear. It could hardly do any harm to feed your brain once in your life.'

'You will drive me to drink with your impertinence!' she squeaks.

I hoot with laughter at the thought of Ma taking anything stronger than tea. On and on she goes: denouncing my clod-hopper gait, fire-shovel hands, lantern jaw. What a disappointment I am, an ugly duckling with no indication that I'll blossom into a swan any time soon. I've heard it all before.

'Mother. You raised me: if I am going to the bad the fault should be laid at your door.'

'How dare you!' she roars – at the cheeky answer, or the fact that I dare say it. She primps her lips tight as a miser's purse. 'My reputation is intact. I am a beacon of respectable behaviour.'

'Ha!' I snort. I slather dripping on to the bread and take a large bite.

'I did not raise you to be like this.'

'Like what? I am what I am,' I mumble, spraying crumbs.

'You are unnatural.'

'How so? You fling that word around like bread for ducks.' I hurl my crust on to the table. 'What on earth do you mean by it?'

'You are a young lady. You should act like one: tender, timid and loving. You are a perversion of all that is womanly.'

'You gave birth to me. If there's a fault, then it springs from you.'

'You are sick. I want you cured.'

'I am not ill!' I cry.

'You are!' she yells, matching me shout for shout. 'Look at you. You're a diseased plant, rotten to the root. I should have dug you up.'

'Ma! I'm your daughter, not a bush.' My eyes sting. Still she is not done.

'You are not the daughter I wanted.'

'Aren't you tired of singing that old tune? I am the one you have been given.'

'You are a monster.'

I struggle to control my tears. Considering the years of hurt, I should be inured to pain, but she can find chinks in my armour and wound. At heart, I am still a babe, reaching out for her breast. I shake the thought away. I will not punish myself for wanting the natural comfort of a mother's love.

'I am your monster, and none other's,' I remark and storm out, heading upstairs to my room.

I hear her through the floorboards, complaining about my intolerable manners to the accompaniment of splashes as she hurls potatoes into the pan. Gradually she quietens as she always does when I am out of eyesight and she wants for an audience. Presently, the front door slams as she quits the house on an errand.

I tiptoe downstairs and complete my chores. I wipe the tables, clean the windows and pay particular attention to Papa, polishing his face while I pour out the bewildering content of my soul.

'Will she always be like this?' I ask. He listens with his habitual calm air. 'Will there ever be peace between us?'

He arches an eyebrow. I sigh. I know the answer, even if I refuse to admit it. My grandmother comes in, puffing with exertion. Her face is swiped with brick dust, her apron also.

'Talking to the wall?' she says.

'Papa. He's a good listener,' I reply. *The only one*, I think.

'We all need one of those,' she says. 'Anyhow, I'm parched. Make your nana a cup of tea, eh, pet?'

I obey willingly. Ma returns in time to open up, looking

positively smug. Let her plaster on whatever expression she pleases. She'll not cow me, ever again.

We give each other a wide berth, our coolness tainting the air. I fetch glasses and take around the fried bread with not so much as a salty remark from anyone. I wonder if word got around about the threats I made to the man with ginger whiskers. He's not poked his nose through the door since that night. If that's the case, it suits me very well indeed. I never heard our customers so polite when asking for their glasses to be filled, nor conduct such muted conversations, nor tell such decorous jokes. Perhaps I should fight back more often.

The evening drags. When Ma calls time I am grateful to be released. I climb the stairs with weariness far greater than that of the body. I sprawl across the mattress. There is nothing at The Comet but vitriol and boredom. Youth alone detains me. Once I've attained an age to seek work of sufficient income to afford lodgings, I will quit this place. I picture a world where I am my own woman and it comforts me greatly. There is nothing so mollifying to the spirit as the knowledge that one's burdensome existence may have an end in sight.

The following day Ma is milder. She does not go so far as to apologise, but breakfast is laid out: porridge ready in the bowl, teacloth draped over the loaf to keep it soft. It is so unexpected that when she asks me to accompany her on a walk, I agree.

'Your grandmother can deal with the delivery,' she says, chewing her lip. 'Edie. I have had opportunity for reflection. You're growing into a young woman and it's high time we spent an hour in each other's company. Talked about women's affairs.'

The last thing I want is another of her sermons, but she seems eager to make amends. If she is capable of compassion then I shall be also: shall forgive, even if I cannot forget. We walk a quarter-mile in quiet contemplation of shop windows when she clears her throat.

'I can be harsh, Edie. I know it.'

'Mm,' I say in as non-committal a fashion as I can manage.

'I do it because I care for you,' she continues.

'Mm.'

'I've worried about you your whole life. How you'll turn out.'

'I rub along all right, Ma.'

She ploughs on as though I've said nothing. 'I never get a moment's sleep for worrying. You're a queer one and the world's not kind to odd women.'

She speaks with such unwonted wistfulness that I'm taken aback. She prattles on: her monthly curse, the search for respite, the hope for a cure, doctor this and doctor that, at such a precipitous rate that it takes a further half-mile of pounding the pavement before the true purpose of our constitutional dawns on me.

I sag with disappointment. Rather than waking with an appetite for my companionship, she wants someone to accompany her on a visit to the doctor. I shrug off the dissatisfaction. Ma may not be able to change, but I can. I put my arm though hers. I can afford to be charitable while I plan my escape.

'Look, Ma,' I chirp, pointing to a milliner's display. 'That one with the green flowers would look a treat on you.'

She tugs me away. 'No time for window-shopping.'

'Ma, you're in a powerful hurry.'

She bustles along, not looking at me. 'I am eager to receive – treatment, that is all,' she mutters. 'Lift your feet. Or we shall lose the appointment.'

I fall into step. If there is the slightest chance that this doctor's remedies can bring about a mellowing of Ma's character – why, I will tramp a dozen miles and count it as nothing. With a homing pigeon's sense of direction, Ma makes her way to a street thick with wagons streaming from Old Trafford into the city. We stop outside number 27, a building distinguished from its neighbours by a small brass plate affixed to the wall above the bell-pull. *Dr Alexander Zambeco*. A host of letters follows the name, so crammed in that they bump up against each other.

'The place?' I ask with an encouraging smile.

'The place,' she replies, voice heavy as a swung lead.

I've rarely, if ever, heard her words so tinged with trepidation. The poor woman. She yanks the cord and a bell clangs within. A minute later the door is opened by a man whose hair is slathered with violet-scented oil. Without a word of greeting, he ushers us up a flight of stairs. It is too cramped to walk side by side, so he leads the way. I follow and Ma brings up the rear. My imagination produces the outlandish notion that I'm being escorted up a scaffold to a gibbet. I giggle at the silly picture. Ma jabs a finger into my backside.

'Show some respect,' she hisses.

Our guide titters, the first sound he has uttered, and shows us into an airless room. The paintwork is blotched with grease, as though a company of men are in the habit of leaning their grubby heads against the wall. A mahogany desk swamps the floor. Behind it sits a gentleman I take to be Dr Zambeco. He does not trouble himself to stand, and surveys us from beneath drooping eyelids.

'Yes, yes,' he says, although no one has said anything with which to agree.

The perfumed fellow closes the door and proceeds to inspect his fingernails. Ma performs a ragged curtsey.

'It's her,' she barks. 'My daughter, doctor. Sir. She's not right.'

'Ma?' I say. 'I thought this was for you?'

The doctor steeples his hands. 'As I suspected,' he remarks, addressing the ceiling. 'A capital case, do you not agree, Mr Atkinson?'

'Of course, sir,' replies the assistant.

'You observe the vein in the forehead, do you not?'

'I do, sir.'

'How it swells, how it throbs? Precisely as I intimated in my most recent paper.'

'Most instructive, sir.'

'Ma?' I quail.

The doctor wafts his hand. 'Your mother has been most descriptive.' He picks up a sheet of foolscap, clears his throat and reads. '"The subject exhibits a lively imagination, indicating baseness of character and moral defect. None of the proper feminine attitudes and behaviours of passivity, dependence, fearfulness or fawning."'

'Well, doctor?' says Ma.

'As for her physical attributes,' he continues. He looks me up and down and shakes his head, as if my brawny frame is a sure indication of moral turpitude. 'I suppose she is within the parameters of the female. If somewhat . . .' His voice drifts.

Ma wrings her shawl. 'Somewhat?'

'Look for yourself, madam. Any intelligent and enquiring person – such as yourself, madam – may observe the people around her. Think of true women: small of hand, foot and waist. Do not their gentle features denote a gentle disposition? Do not their soft eyes betoken softness of mind? Of course they do. Conversely, one has only to observe the rough manners of this girl: the hulking limbs and mannish voice. The wild look in her eye. Whatever sex she may profess to be, she is no lady.' He sighs. 'A suffragette in the making.'

'No!' gasps Ma.

'It is the path on which she is headed,' he says, almost sorrow-fully.

'This is arrant nonsense,' I declare.

'Some miracles a doctor cannot accomplish, however skilled he may be. Some mountains are too steep to climb. But in the case of your daughter . . .' He tosses a cursory glance in my direction and shudders. 'To the amelioration of her faults I shall bend all my attention.'

Ma blinks, devouring his promises with bright eyes. During his monologue I observe him closely. The velvet lapels of his coat have a greenish tinge and the brim of the bowler upon the hat-stand is pitted with moth-holes. I wonder why a surgeon as prominent as he claims to be wears a jacket with rubbed elbows.

'I am not afflicted by any of these so-called ailments, sir,' I say.

The room cools. His brow creases, lips pout.

'Of course, madam,' he drones on at Ma. My presence is immaterial. 'I refrain from listing other conditions, equally wounding to the tender heart of a mother: namely disobedient speech and a perverse flouting of the niceties of social inter-course. Answer me truthfully: does she display a propensity for education, an unhealthy madness for reading?'

'How can you tell?' Ma cries, face purple with shame. 'It's all since she started going to the library! She speaks to me like you wouldn't believe.'

'Oh, I think I would,' he says.

'There's nothing wrong with me,' I insist.

Ma turns on me, eyes flashing. 'Oh yes there is, Miss High and Mighty. You know precisely what I'm talking about. And this gentleman is of a mind to put it to rights.'

I glare back with equal fire. 'There's nothing wrong with me that wasn't caused by you.'

'I never laid a finger on you unless you deserved it.'

'You hate me! That wounds me far deeper than blows.'

'I'm doing this for your own good.'

'Rubbish. I think this suits you very well. You can't push me around any more, and you can't stand it. What you want is a slave who won't kick up a fuss.'

'You unruly little hoyden,' she splutters. 'Hold your tongue!'

'Ladies!' interrupts the doctor, smiling queerly. 'Let us have calm words. Madam, I can see the problems with which you are burdened. You have come to the right man. I am best placed to bring about a swift cessation of your woes. I believe my cure will be especially effective in the swift removal of your daughter's malady.'

Ma cringes. 'Bless you, doctor!'

'I am not ill!' I shout.

He responds with a high-pitched giggle. 'Do you think there is hope with this subject, Mr Atkinson?'

'You have yet to disappoint, Dr Zambeco.'

'You are too kind, Mr Atkinson.'

They exchange looks of cordial amity. In their eyes I am little more than a beetle with a silver pin skewering it to the morocco-topped desk, limbs flailing. I roll my eyes. I've no idea what Ma hopes to achieve by forcing me to listen to this flummery, but if she thinks it will change one single solitary thing, she is mistaken. I will sit tight, see this through and go my own sweet way.

'I need no treatment,' I say. 'Not from you or anyone else. I am content with who and what I am, sir. However discontented my mother may be.'

'Ah,' he muses. I expect him to raise his voice, but he remains

113

unruffled. I rather wish he would shout. 'Contentment,' he murmurs, clearly enjoying every moment. He shifts his attention from my disobedient scowl to my mother. 'Are *you* content, dear lady?'

Ma shakes her head.

'I thought as much.' He gazes at the ceiling. 'Contentment is such a subjective state of being, so open to interpretation, is it not?'

'Er . . .' Ma replies, unable to follow his meanderings. 'You advertised,' she stutters, blinking. 'In your advertisement . . . I can't pay . . .' She stares at the floor. 'I wouldn't dream of – What I mean, sir, is that if you can understand my situation, sir, what with my husband away, sir . . .'

The muscles of her throat are as taut as piano strings. He lets her ramble, wearing the smirk of someone amused by the wriggling of lower life forms. When he decides that Ma has humiliated herself sufficiently, he holds up his hand.

'Madam, madam!' he says. 'Do not distress yourself so. I assure you that I am a man of science. A seeker of truth. Scientific minds have other forms of satisfaction than lucre.'

'Lucre?'

'Monetary recompense, dear madam. I wouldn't dream of it.'

A coil of doubt twists in my gut. 'Ma?' I begin, but am interrupted.

'So. We are agreed,' he says.

'We are most certainly not,' I declare.

At this juncture, several things happen at once. I step away from the desk and towards the door. With the oiled grace of a boxer, Mr Atkinson slides across the carpet and blocks my path. Dr Zambeco springs out of his seat and proceeds to perform the strangest pantomime, sweeping his head from left to right

114

whilst pointing at his eyes. The irises are huge, slate-grey; they hold me in their thrall. I exert every scrap of my will but feel myself succumbing to their mesmerising influence. It is Mr Atkinson who breaks the spell with an unpleasant chuckle. I shake off the sticky feeling.

'A worthy subject,' purrs the doctor. 'Most suggestible.'

'That's all very well for you to say,' chirps Ma. 'I can suggest till the cows come home but she doesn't pay me a blind bit of attention.'

Dr Zambeco flutters his fingers dismissively, but he doesn't know my mother. She presses her lips into a petulant line.

'Well, I can't do a thing with her,' she grunts, determined to have her say.

It is the last straw. 'I've had enough of this interview,' I say. 'Talk until kingdom come, if it pleases you. Send me home with a sackful of pills. I shan't take one. I'll pitch the lot into the canal.'

'Pills?' whinnies Dr Zambeco. 'How delectably antiquated. I have no nasty physick for that equine constitution of yours. I am no savage creature who peddles eye of newt and toe of frog. Dear me, no. Sit, sit,' he says, gesturing me to a chair.

I take it, without knowing why.

'It is all quite scientific, my dear. Nothing to worry your little head over. Don't you ache to be happy?'

'I am happy.'

'Are you? You entered this room angry and disordered, did you not?'

It is true: I am furious. But I don't trust where this is heading. 'Your questions are rhetorical, sir.'

'Does it not pique your interest by even the smallest fraction to learn that I can bestow lasting happiness in the space of minutes?'

I stick out my chin. 'I don't believe you.'

'She does not believe me, Mr Atkinson,' guffaws the doctor. 'She does not, sir.'

Once again, I experience the sensation that my presence is of no consequence and that he could just as easily conduct this conversation with a brick wall. There being little point in responding further, I hold my tongue. I hope it might make him hold his own.

'Now. You will remove your clothing.'

'I will do no such thing,' I snort. 'You are not going to examine me.'

'Correct!' he chirps. 'Nothing is further from my mind. I am going to beautify you. A brief intervention. A simple operation.'

'Operation?' I say.

The word hangs in the air, cold as a sheet pegged out in winter. I glance at Ma. She is staring at a space slightly to the left of the doctor's shoulder.

'A mere bagatelle,' he replies. 'No need for even a drachm of chloroform. Bring the body to heel and correct behaviour will follow. All speak of my success. It has been reported in the most prestigious of journals.'

'What are you on about?'

He turns and addresses my mother. 'Curb the physical traits that mark a subject as anything other than woman. There is the briefest instant of discomfort, I warrant. But afterward, what bliss suffuses the mind and frame of the patient! I beseech you, madam: set a moment of pain against a lifetime of misery and debilitation. I wager I can guess which you would select as the preferred path for the remainder of your daughter's life.'

Ma sucks her teeth.

'Why are you talking to her?' I roar. I cling to my skirts,

holding them tightly across my knees. 'You will not touch me. You are a charlatan.'

'I don't need to gaze up your skirts, young lady,' he murmurs. 'I know what I would find.'

'I beg your pardon?'

'I do not need to look. No amateurish fumbling. I can tell you without doubt that I should find the clitoris somewhat enlarged. Oh, madam, consider the danger of tribadism . . .' His words trail off. 'The labia minora will be much beautified by trimming them' – he clicks his fingers – 'away.'

I swallow heavily. I understand less than half of the long-winded words he employs, but know enough to be terrified. 'Trimming?' I whisper.

'You will comply. Your mother demands it. I demand it. No one has disobeyed me to date, nor do I envisage that state of affairs changing today.'

I glare at Ma. 'You'd have this done to your own daughter?'

'For your own good,' she chants, eyes glassy.

Dr Zambeco throws a languid glance at Mr Atkinson, blocking the way out like a pungent Cerberus. My heart hammers; sweat trickles down my ribs and soaks my blouse. I have to get away from these fiends. If I must dissemble and play the hapless damsel to buy myself some time, so be it.

I make a big show of directing my attention at an inner door, set in the wall behind the desk. I stare at it intently for a full two seconds before looking away, furtively, as though discovered in something. The doctor laughs, as I hoped he might.

'Observe, Mr Atkinson! How feeble and transparent are the mental faculties of females. The subject seeks a way to escape, without realising that the door at which she gazes so hopefully leads into a cupboard. Perhaps we should permit her to examine it.'

117

Mr Atkinson giggles. 'Once again, your observations are most instructive, sir.'

The doctor claps his hands. 'Enough of this sport. There is more than enough here for the *Lancet*. You,' he growls at me. 'Take off your clothes.'

I sigh, and pray it sounds submissive. 'You have me, sir,' I say. His eyes glitter. 'May I be permitted to undress myself behind a screen?' I enquire, looking at the rug.

There is a wet sound, of moistened lips smacking gently.

'There is no need for such bashfulness,' he says. 'We are medical men.'

'Yes, sir,' I say.

I begin to unbutton my collar. Their attention does not wander from the hesitant action of my fingers.

'Note the coquettish behaviour,' says the doctor with the slightest catch in his voice. He clears his throat. 'They cannot help themselves. Just as noted by Professor Baker.'

'I could not agree more,' answers Mr Atkinson, a little croakily.

I pause. 'Sir,' I breathe huskily. 'May I retain my stays, and remove only my skirt and petticoats?'

'No, you may not. Everything. Undergarments also. It is your lower portions which are of interest to me.'

'Of course, sir. I will do exactly as you wish,' I say. I glance upwards through my eyelashes. There is a spot of pink upon each of his cheeks, as though someone has pinched them hard. 'May I stand, sir, to make my task easier?'

The humility of my manner puts him off his guard. He nods, leans backwards and stretches out his legs. I stand, very slowly, as if the effort fatigues me. I push the chair to one side and take a discreet step aside, concealing the movement by unfastening my under-chemise and pulling it open to reveal the scant curve of my breasts. I've no intention of removing it, but need to make it appear as if I am about to.

The doctor tips his chair and hoists his heels on to the desk. Mr Atkinson slumps against the door frame, his smirk replaced by something far hungrier. He shifts his weight from foot to foot and as he does so I notice a tenting in his trousers, in the region of the fly. They continue to speak to each other in low murmurs that make my hair stand on end.

'See how she desires treatment. How compliant she is now she knows what we intend.'

'Indeed, sir,' gloats Mr Atkinson.

With a great deal of unnecessary rustling, I pretend to undo my skirt, lowering one of my stockings until it sags around the ankle.

'In this case, excision is the only answer.'

'Cauterisation?'

'Yes. With the iron. Prepare the bed, Mr Atkinson. If you please.'

'Yes, sir.'

Mr Atkinson leaves his post, opens the cupboard and begins to haul out a metal bench, an unwieldy contraption with stirrups at one end and leather cuffs dangling at the other. As he drags it across the carpet, its clawed feet stick fast. Dr Zambeco rolls his eyes and goes to Mr Atkinson's assistance. Under cover of their exertions, I survey the room. The window is the sort operated with a handle. It is open a fraction.

'Ma,' I bleat. 'I'm so shy. Can't you screen me?'

She huffs a complaint, but takes up position between myself and the two men, spreading her arms to preserve what she imagines is feminine modesty. It may give me the few seconds I need. It has to. I spring to the window, shove it open and hop on to the sill.

119

With a curse I thought reserved for stevedores, Dr Zambeco lunges towards me and crashes into Ma. Both of them sprawl flat on their faces, Ma squawking like a hen. Undeterred, the doctor clambers over the toppled stump of her body and grabs my ankle. I kick like the mule I am accused of being and have the considerable satisfaction of hearing his answering yelp. Mr Atkinson lumbers to his assistance but I'm not hanging around for him to get his paws on my petticoats.

I peer out of the window. The roadway is thronged with carts. I have one chance. I seize it. Bundling my shawl about my head I leap and, like Icarus, for one glorious moment dance on air.

By some great good fortune I land, not on the cobbles fifteen feet below, but on a wagon piled with sacks stuffed with vegetables. From the bulging feel of them, cabbages. I promise the angel who has redeemed me that I will henceforth eat cabbage at every meal and write odes praising the life-preserving properties of brassicas of all descriptions.

I stretch out on the sacks and stare at the sky. I have a suspicion that Dr Zambeco does not indulge in anything as ungainly as pursuit and pray I am proved right. As I wait for my breath to return, for I've been badly winded by the tumble, I send up a further prayer that this wagon may transform into a fairy-tale conveyance and carry me to a safe haven far from Manchester. But street by street, mile by mile, the bricks grow grubbier, windows clot with dirt, paint peels, and I know we are approaching the city.

I experiment with moving my arms and legs. All seems whole, although every one of my bones aches. What a crop of bruises I'm going to have. I imagine the canvas of my skin painted with their garish hues. I button my blouse to the neck, pull up my stockings and wrap my shawl tight. When the wagon halts

120

at the gate of a market, I dismount with a thank you to the driver, who scratches his head with an air of bemusement.

'Where are we?' I ask.

'Shudehill,' he snorts. 'You daft, or something?'

He lets down the back of the cart and proceeds to unload it. Realising I'll get no further enlightenment, I look around. I'm not precisely lost, but nor do I know exactly where I am. I've never had any call to venture further than the market on Denmark Street, yet this place bears an unusual familiarity. I try to reason that all markets look the same, yet cannot shift the conviction I've been here before, many times. This is not possible: the events of the past two hours must have scrambled my brains.

I loiter at the gate. I'll have no peace until I prove one way or the other if I'm mistaken. I slip through the carts and pedestrians and enter the hall. It is much like Denmark Street market, save far bigger and a great deal noisier. I can barely move for the squeeze of bodies. Gangs of lads small and not so small are making a general nuisance of themselves, dashing back and forth and stealing from the stalls. One lass weighing out toffees shoots me a dirty look before wrinkling her brow in confusion, otherwise no one pays me any mind.

I close my eyes and see a ghost of myself strolling these aisles, hands in his pockets. This dream-self laughs as we gallop between the stalls, creating mayhem. My senses, already reeling, stutter afresh. *We?* Who is this imagined self whom I recollect so easily, who feels so real? Perhaps I am as barmy as Ma says.

I am overcome with a wave of nausea so intense I have to grasp the nearest table to prevent myself from falling. My thighs tremble; my heart shudders in and out of rhythm. I swallow a mouthful of bile as I remember what those doctors – I shake my head wildly, causing a stab of discomfort in my ribs – what

121

those brutes planned for me. What Ma was going to let them do. My fancy conjures up the stink of hot iron. No wonder I feel as though I'm going mad.

I consider my options. Home is no longer safe, if indeed it ever was. Being yelled at is one thing, the events of this morning another. How can a mother do such a terrible thing? However, all I'm doing is delaying the inevitable return. There is nowhere to go but The Comet.

I wrap my shawl around my head, hug the wall and keep my eyes down. I walk carefully, so as not to exacerbate the ache in my bones, but not so slowly as to make no progress. As I trudge, it strikes me that I am adopting the gait and bearing of every other female on the street. We scuttle like rats, as if we have no right to breathe the outdoor air. I've walked these streets a hundred times and never before remarked upon it. My mind aches with the effort of thinking, so I let it drift into blankness.

I enter through the back gate. I close the door carefully as if it is made not of solid wood but of tissue paper. My grandmother is in the kitchen, stuffing tobacco into a pipe. I fold my shawl over the back of the chair and stare at the room as a stranger might. The chairs crouch around the table. A pair of boots click their heels before the hearth, which is stacked with fresh wood, ready to catch fire as soon as a hand sets a vesta to the kindling. On the kitchen table sit three large potatoes and a package of brown paper. By the smell of it, bacon. I tuck my hands into my armpits and shiver.

'Where's Ma?' I stutter.

'I thought she was with you,' says Nana, concentrating on the pipe. She tamps the bowl with a broad, capable thumb. I shake my head, stiffly.

'I'm putting the kettle on,' she says. 'You look like you could do with a brew.'

'Yes.'

She lights a spill from the range and sucks the pipe-stem until the flame catches. A stone is stuck in my throat. I am unable to swallow it down. My eyes water, salty.

'Sit down, girl. Before you fall down.'

I obey. A cup of tea is held before me. I stare at it in a daze. Nana shakes it and the rattle startles me awake.

'It's good and sweet.'

She sounds a great way off. I raise my hand and take the saucer with the curious sensation that I am observing another person do so. I lift the cup to my lips and take a sip. It is hot, almost too hot. The heat draws me back to the room. Something in my chest is twisting. I can't be crying, for I'm making no sound, but my lap is spotted with tears.

A slice of bread and dripping appears before me. Nana's forefinger and thumb grip the plate, but are unconnected to any person called *grandmother*. It might be a floating plate conjured up by a magician. I take a mouthful and immediately begin to choke. A hand massages my back, patting firmly until the crust dislodges, pops out of my mouth and lands on my knee. I stare at it, marked with the half-crescent of my teeth.

'Just drink the tea, Edie.' That is definitely my grandmother's voice, deep and calming. An Atlantic ocean of a voice.

Great sobs burst out of my breast as I weep for the girl I was, for the girl I wanted to be, for the pain of every humiliation dealt out by Ma: for every time she's told me I am wrong, or sick, a perversion of nature, a sin, a punishment. I weep for what almost happened today, for what Ma wanted to have done.

Nana does not tell me to shush. Her hand rests light between my shoulder blades. My face is sticky, as is my hair. The short curls hang in rats' tails in front of my nose.

'Now,' I hear her say. 'When you're able, we'll have something to eat.'

'Don't you want to know what happened?'

'I'll not press you,' she replies. 'Whatever it was, it'll keep an hour. I shall not make you live through the retelling until you're good and ready.'

I nod my gratitude. By some alchemy, a damp towel is produced and she wipes my face clean.

'So,' she says after I've eaten a portion of potato and bacon and have washed it down with another cup of tea.

'It's Ma,' I whisper.

Word by halting word, I speak the awful truth. She listens without interruption. When I am done, she pulls me to her breast and rocks me as if I am still a little girl. I offer no resistance. She hugs me so close I'm afraid I'll burst with love. No. Something fiercer than love. I draw my knees to my chin and weep again. When I am done, she wipes my nose on her apron.

'We must talk,' she says. 'This state of affairs has gone on long enough. You are plenty old enough. In fact, you should have been told from the start. That is my guilt and mine alone for going along with your ma's wishes.'

'Nana?' I sniff.

'You have burned with questions. It is to my eternal shame that I have not answered them. I shall make amends, as best I can.' She shakes herself. 'This family *is* unlike any other. But it is not a curse, as your mother would have it, nor is any of it your fault. Whatever you have been told.'

I nod. Not because I understand, but because I'm desperate for her to continue and fear that if I so much as cough, she'll stop.

124

'You have had strange dreams all your life, have you not?'

'Yes.'

'You're frightened of your own shadow.'

That's it, I say to myself. *I have a shadow and I am terrified.*

'What you call nightmares are no such thing. They are half-memories.'

'Of what?'

'Not of what. Of whom.'

Ice inches down my spine. Without knowing how, his name springs to my lips. 'Gnome?' I say.

'Yes, Gnome, Herbert. Whatever he calls himself.'

'I thought he was all in my head. A nightmare.'

Memories rush in with such force my head spins and I slide to the floor. She lays her hand upon my shoulder and secures me with its anchor.

'He's no dream. You must have seen it happen.'

'Seen what?'

She rolled her eyes. 'The *change*, Edie.' She waggles her fingers in the direction of my private parts.

I flush crimson. 'I never look – down there. God is watching. He'd see me – looking. It is dirty. Ma says.'

'Your ma needs a good . . .' she growls, and presses her lips together as if holding in something dangerous. Her fingers comb moist hair off my forehead. She smiles and is tender once more. 'He is real. He is half of you.'

'You mean I look more like a boy than I do a girl?' I ask. 'I know. Ma reminds me every day.'

'That's not it at all,' she says. 'The two of you share one body.'

'That's not possible,' I say, half-laughing.

'It is, my love. You by day and he by night.'

'No.'

'It wasn't always that way. When you were young, you

were as restless and happy as . . .' Her voice drifts into a wistful silence. Fireworks shimmer between my ears. Gnome and I dancing so close, there was no need for . . . There was neither . . .

'No,' I say, shaking my head free of sparks.

'Your ma put paid to that,' she sighs. 'Stamped it down. I should've stood up to her.'

'No!' I say, louder. 'You're lying.'

'Today of all days, I would not lie to you. Your ma and I are the same.'

'Stop it!' I cry, and slap my hands over my ears.

Her words trickle through my fingers. 'Of course, we have our own arrangements. Your Uncle Arthur – well, he is your ma's other half. Not that he gets a fair share,' she mutters.

'That can't be right,' I say. 'Uncle Arthur is the best – the kindest – He's got nothing to do with Ma!' I struggle free of her embrace, dash up the stairs, dive into my room and slam the door behind me. I pace the floor in a turmoil. In an hour, The Comet will be full of drinkers. If Nana is to be believed, I am as distant from those men and women as the moon from the earth. I can't believe her. It is impossible.

Granted, I am an unfeminine girl, with a big nose and bigger feet.

People take me for a boy in dim light.

What does that signify? Nothing.

Nana is exaggerating.

But to choose such a cruel falsehood.

This can't be the answer I've sought so long. It is too monstrous.

I stagger across the rug, footing as unsure as a drunkard too far gone in his cups. Nausea rises, inch by sickening inch, and I am compelled to lie down, as if commanded.

Good, says a voice closer than my own skin. *Can't have you falling over and cracking your noggin on the bedpost. Last thing I want is a black eye.*

It is not my voice, yet springs from within. I recognise it. It is the voice that pulled me out of the snowdrift, that sent the gingery man packing. No. This is ridiculous.

'You are a dream,' I reply. 'You have to be.'

Laughter billows through my innards, as if I've swallowed a sparrow.

Step aside. It's my turn.

'No,' I say. 'You are a figment of my imagination.'

I don't know why I'm answering. Even to think of him is to prove my lunacy. It will be just as Ma foretold: I'll be carted off and locked up in a sanatorium and live on bread and water while rats nibble my toes.

Hush your everlasting racket! he chides. *It's enough to make me deaf.*

'Gnome?' I utter the outlaw name, the name I have been terrified to think, let alone speak. 'Are you real?'

What a stupid question. It's clear who has the brains in this godforsaken family.

'Nana told me – about us. I don't know what to believe.'

What I can't believe is that you're so dim you couldn't work it out for yourself. Good Lord, Edie. Here I am yattering away and you still doubt? You're stupider than I thought.

'But Ma says—'

Baa, baa, black sheep, you are quite the fool, he chants. *Yes, Mam, no, Mam, three bags full. I have a sister with lard for brains.*

'I'm not your sister. I'm—'

Shut up! Shove over.

I watch as my fingers begin to undo my blouse.

127

Help me with these dashed buttons. They're so fiddly. You have wasted half the night with your jabber.

He pulls it over my head and tosses it into the corner where it collapses in a forlorn heap. I watch, lost for words, as my hands strip me of skirt, undergarments, stockings and all.

'But it's not dark for an hour.'

So? This is your final warning, he glowers. My fingers form a vice and tweak my buttock. *It's my turn!*

'Ow! Nothing is anyone's turn. Why am I even talking to you? You're in my head. Look.' I flourish a hand, indicating my paltry breasts, the neat bush of hair at the groin. Every inch of its geography is undeniably mine, and female. 'I'm Edie. I'm a girl.'

Oh shut up, Edie. You're as bad as Mam.

'I'm nothing like her!'

Move over!

'Gnome, stop it. Please.' I've read about earthquakes, and one has begun to thunder in my belly. The mattress shudders and I shudder with it. 'What's happening to me? It hurts.'

We've hardly begun, he says. *This will be a night to remember. Watch!*

'I don't want to. I won't.'

I shut my eyes, but the lids are prised open. My neck twists and I am forced to stare at my naked body. My skin is rippling, like a pot when it comes close to the boil.

No, I say, my voice muffled.

'Yes,' he hisses.

I watch. With each quiver, my breasts shrink. Bit by bit they are swallowed into my ribs until only the nipples show, small and hard as coat buttons.

What are you doing to me? I say. The words ring in my skull.

'You've almost gone,' he leers. 'Look.'

A tide sweeps across my stomach to the place between my thighs. The lips swell, fat as mushroom caps, darkening from pink to biscuit brown. Petals of flesh unfold and a soft tip appears between them. I am flooded with warmth as blood dashes from my head to nourish this new growth.

It's too much, I whimper. *I'll burst.*

'Me,' he purrs.

My bones are on fire. The thing between my legs stretches, tearing me inside out. Wrench by agonising wrench it lengthens until it lies athwart my thigh, the length of my thumb. His voice echoes around the room, deep and sonorous.

'You still don't get it, do you? It's not *your* thigh, *your* thumb. It's mine.'

Gnome?

'Ah, the penny's finally dropped,' he jeers. 'Ta da! Here I am. Right. Where are my trousers?'

Gnome, wait—

'Gnome, wait!' he lisps.

Listen. This is important. Ma tried to—

'Make poor ickle Edie take castor oil? Who cares? I don't.'

My protests are as insignificant as two peas rattling in a tin. This is not madness. I wish it were. Gnome is no dream I can leave on my pillow in the morning. This intense and wayward inner being, this wild and ungovernable creature who has haunted me like a ghost, is no phantasm. All mysteries lead to him.

I have managed to hold myself together for the past few hours – years, it feels like – but can do so no longer. The stitches holding soul and body together unravel and the fabric of what I call my self rips at the seams. Darkness rushes into the breach. I can't hold my head above its swirling depths. I can fight against him no longer. I give in, let go and fall into nothing.

129

GNOME
1902

So the monumental dullard has finally figured it out. It makes not a blind bit of difference. I shall carry on in my own sweet way; take what is rightfully mine. If I've set up shop a few hours early, so be it. She can't stop me.

Brave words can't mask my trembling. I cannot shake off the conviction that I've escaped from mortal danger by the skin of my pearly whites. I throw off the swaddling blanket and scan the shadows as though there's an assassin planted there, knife in hand and ready to strike me down. A scrap of gaslight slants through the window and I can see everything is as it should be: the curtains lank and threadbare, the jug in its crack-glazed basin. However, my teeth won't stop chattering. I want nothing more than to jump out of the window, take to my heels and never return.

Maybe she did have something to tell me. I can't see precisely what she's been up to – I never have been able to – but I must get to the bottom of it. I slip into the crevices between us, catch up on her long slide down.

'What were you trying to tell me?'

I know what we are, she says, words bubbling in a ticklish stream.

'Yes, yes. That's not what I asked. What happened today?'

She sinks away without further answer. It can't have been anything important. Some female nonsense I'll be bound; hysterics at the revelation of the completely bloody obvious. Nothing to concern myself over. I wait for my heart to steady, my breath to even out.

Time to get down to business. My stomach thinks my throat's been cut and I for one don't blame it. I take the stairs two at a time and am scouting around in search of a morsel when Mam lumbers through the door with a tray of dirty glasses. Her mouth flaps: open and shut, open and shut.

'Oh!' she says, with a hunted expression. 'It's you.' The words dribble to a halt.

'That's me, Mam. Large as life and twice as natural.' I spread my arms. 'Aren't you going to give your precious son a hug?'

She shrinks away and comes up hard against the chair. The glasses rattle. She sits heavily, not taking her eyes off me for a second.

'I've got to get these clean,' she says.

I grin. She's on the back foot for some reason and that suits me fine.

'Let me do that,' I say. 'No! Don't you stir a finger.' I slop water into the sink and dunk the glasses, one by one. Mam watches my every move. 'Isn't this nice,' I say. 'A mother and her son, enjoying each other's company.'

'Yes,' she breathes, shivering like a grubby blancmange.

I stuff a dishcloth into a wet glass and twist. Breathe on the glass and rub again. Hold it under the gaslight and admire the sparkle.

'You're – early,' she gulps.

'Is that such a terrible thing, dearest Mam? You're acting like you've seen the devil himself.' Her cheeks grow paler. I didn't think a person could appear so ghastly green and not be dead. I follow the scent of her fright. It reeks of guilt. 'Or wanted to see.'

I polish another glass and then wring out the cloth. She glances towards the door.

'I ought to get back. To the bar. It's time to open up.'

'Don't you want to be with me, Mam? Don't you love your special man any more?'

The arrow strikes. She quails, as though I've brained her with a poker. I draw up a stool, plonk myself on to it, take her hand and pat it. She tries to draw away but I hang on.

'Why don't you tell dear Gnome what's got into you.'

'Son – Gnome . . .'

Inspiration strikes. 'What's my nasty sister been doing to my dearest mam, eh?'

She crumples, clapping a hand across her mouth. 'I didn't mean . . .' she warbles, the words half drowned by her fingers. 'You've always been the one I wanted!'

She rocks to and fro, whining *oh my, oh Lord* and other drivel until I am on the verge of slapping some sense into her.

'What's going on?' I ask.

She shakes her head. 'Everyone blames me! I do the best I can! No one knows how I suffer, no one!'

She rocks backwards and forwards. Idiot she may be, but I've never seen her so out of her meagre wits. Something has prompted this caterwauling. Whatever it is, it's giving me a prize bellyache. The cellar door opens and Grandma stomps into the kitchen, dragging a loaded coal scuttle.

'Look who's here,' she grunts. 'Thanks for all the help.'

'That's a fine way to greet your grandson,' I say primly. I rub my hands together in an encouraging fashion. 'Now you're here, how about a nice bit of supper?'

'You want to eat, fix it yourself. We've work to be getting on with. Unless you want to lend one of your idle hands? No. I didn't think so.'

'Charming.'

She proceeds to make a pot of tea, without asking if anyone else wants to join her. She pours a cup and adds three spoonfuls of sugar, tinkling the spoon as she stirs. She observes me in that odd way of hers that lies between humour and pity.

'You're before time,' she muses, taking a slurp of the steaming brew. 'I wondered if Edie would get scared off after what your mother tried to do.'

'I *beg* your pardon?'

Mam makes a strangled sound. Grandma rolls her eyes and gulps more tea.

'The two of you are better than a star turn at the Hippodrome. Her and her flannel and you gormless enough to swallow it.'

'What are you on about?'

'Your mother took you to the doctor, didn't she?'

'I've been no such place,' I declare.

Mam presses her hands over her ears and starts to low like a cow.

'You can lay off the histrionics,' barks my grandmother. 'I know you can hear me.' She leans over the table and deals my mother a hefty crack across the chops. The smack rings out like a gunshot. 'You've got lard for brains, Cissy. What do you think would've happened to Gnome if that butcher had got his way?'

Mam clutches her face, lower lip wobbling. 'I—'

'You *didn't* think, did you? You'd have lost the lad forever, as like as not.'

'No,' whispers Mam. She looks as if she's been hit with a shovel. 'It wouldn't . . .'

133

'What are you two witches talking about?' I cry.

'You're luckier than you have any idea,' Grandma continues, looking at me. 'Your loving mother was of a mind to get you fixed. Like you would a bullock.' My chin drops to the table. 'She would have done it too. If Edie – you, that is – hadn't jumped out of the window. She cares about you more than you know.'

I stand up so quickly the stool goes flying. 'No! I don't believe you!'

'It hardly matters whether you believe it or not. It happened.'

I turn on my mother, cowering in the chair.

'Gnome,' she whimpers. 'My beloved boy.'

'Bloody women,' I spit. 'You can't be trusted.' I make for the door but Grandma lays a hand on my sleeve. 'You and all,' I snap. 'Conniving harpies, every last one of you.' To my surprise, her face cracks in a smile. 'I'm glad I amuse you. What's so funny?'

'You haven't got the brains you were born with. You're as much a woman as the rest of us. Gnome, Edie, both, neither . . .'

'I'm not!' I roar.

She throws her hands in the air. 'For goodness' sake. I don't know who's worse, you or your mother. I've had enough of this. If I could leave . . .' She slumps, as though someone has pulled out the rug from under her anger. 'Gnome,' she sighs. 'I entreat you. This is no game. You and Edie must come to a better arrangement before—'

'Stop telling me what to do! Edie this, Edie that. You're not the only one who is sick to the back teeth of this sodding family. Don't you think I'd be shot of you if I could? Don't you think I'd jump on the first train away?'

My words trail off. She is too old to change her ways. I am

not. Instead of arguing the toss I take to my heels and do precisely what I want. Which is to go to the only place that feels like home.

I head for the tea-stand in the hope of finding Jessie. She's the only one who understands, the only one who listens. Every Friday night I've been buying her a quarter-pound of chocolates, regular as clockwork. Clever as she is, thieving will get a body into trouble and I'll not have that. I don't care how many saucy glances she bestows on older fellows, or that our promenades are cut short when one of them falls into step beside us and mutters in her ear. It's me she talks with. Me she walks with.

She's propping up the counter, rubbing elbows with a woman with hair the colour of a ripe banana.

'Gnome!' cries Jessie and lurches in my direction. 'How's my favourite little man this evening?'

Now would be a very good time to say *all the better for seeing you*, but my tongue wraps around the words and won't let them go.

'Less of the little,' I grunt, hands in my pockets.

She folds an arm around my shoulder and tugs me so close I smell the gin heavy on her breath. I soak up the embrace like blotting paper.

'Come on, give us a smile,' she says, patting my cheek.

I pat her hand away. 'Suppose you'll be wanting a cup of tea,' I mutter, like I don't care either way.

She gives me a look that's half-soppy, half-regretful. 'That'd be nice. Really it would. But I'm off home.'

'What, already?'

'Had a couple of toffs pass through, didn't we?' The

135

yellow-haired woman brays a laugh that could crack marble. 'I'm getting an early night. Oh, look at you. You've got a face like you've found a penny and lost sixpence.'

'No I haven't,' I grumble.

Jessie shakes her parasol and prances away, waggling her backside. I fold my arms and glower. She glances over her shoulder and jerks her head.

'You stopping there all night?' she says. 'Come on.'

I hop to her side and ease into step beside her.

'Cheer up,' she trills.

'Thought you said you were going home,' I say, hanging on to my scowl.

'I am. You may escort me.'

'Don't see why I should,' I grunt, without making any attempt to go.

'Please yourself. I shan't drag you.'

She sweeps along the pavement and I scurry after. By the time we've reached her lodgings and I've struggled up the half-dozen flights of stairs to her room, I'm gasping for air. She unlocks the door and pauses. She wears an odd expression, as though she's changed her mind about granting me entrance.

'Come in, if you've a mind to,' she says. 'You're letting the heat out.'

She flounders into the room and turns up the gas.

I don't know what I expect, but it is not the disordered scene that unfolds. The room has not been so much touched by a woman's hand as seized in its grip and throttled. It sags under a burden of drapes, cushions and ornaments all in need of the duster. I wait for her to beg pardon for the mess, but she picks her way through as though it is not there.

I trail after, an intrepid explorer in need of a map. Dominating the room is a vast bed, piled so high with bolsters and quilts the hardiest of mountaineers would balk at scaling it without a length of sturdy rope fastened about his middle. A mirror is propped at one end, draped with red gauze. When I catch a glimpse of myself my cheeks are flushed crimson.

I make my way to the fireplace, discarded crusts crunching underfoot. In the grate are a cracked firedog, three mismatched pokers and a scuttle with such a sizeable hole I wonder how she carries coal without it tumbling out. The mantel is stacked with picture postcards. I pluck one from its place: a portly female clad in nothing but a crown of feathers, grinning as she wraps her heels around her neck and displays the dark gash between her legs. Her eyes look like they've been scratched out with a pen nib. Heaviness settles in my privates. I shove the card whence it came and direct my attention elsewhere. A fringed shawl drapes over a chair, sagging under the weight of embroidered flowers. I slip the fabric through my fingers.

'That's made of the best Chinese silk, that is,' says Jessie proudly.

'It feels like water. Without being wet.'

She chuckles wistfully, a sound quite unlike her habitual cackle. 'Given me by a mandarin. So entranced was he by my beauty that he gave me twenty-one pearls: one for each toe, one for each finger and one for luck.'

'Where are they?'

She flutters her fingers. 'Somewhere.' She looks around and frowns as though she has suddenly found herself in the room of a stranger. 'Bugger me. Look at the state of this place. How did it get like this?'

She does not appear to require an answer, so I don't offer one. I examine the ceiling, as that seems to be the safest course of action. There's a delta of cracks in the plaster, fanning out in cocoa-coloured tracks. Women are bloody funny creatures.

If I agree with her about the chaos, she'll tear my head off. If I come out with some rot about it not being too bad, she'll as likely do the same.

She bustles about, scooping up armfuls of gloves, boots, under-petticoats, over-petticoats, stockings and corsets, all of them dangling with ribbons and dingy lace. She casts about for somewhere to stow them, but the tallboy is stuffed. With a resigned shrug of her shoulders, she shoves the whole kit and caboodle under the bed, which is already so chock-a-block I'm surprised its feet aren't lifted off the floor.

'That's better,' she pants. She straightens up so hastily that she winces. 'I'm not suited to housework,' she says. 'When I've got a bit put by I'll get a maid. See if I don't.' There's an edge to her words, as though she expects me to disagree. When I don't, she adds, in the same sharp tone, 'I suppose you're going to lecture me about my slatternly ways.'

'Not a bit of it. My mam has a passion for tidying. Pick this up, pick that up, sweep the floor. Drives a fellow mad, so it does.'

She rubs the small of her back and grimaces. 'You're lucky you've got someone looking out for you.'

'Me, lucky? She's an interfering old trout.'

'Gnome!' she squawks. 'You should talk about your mother with more respect.'

She picks up a glove and chucks it at my head. It trails over my shoulder. I throw it back, but she ducks and it disappears behind the dressing table.

'Missed by a mile!' she crows. 'You couldn't hit a barn door at five paces!'

There is plenty of ammunition at my feet. I grab a petticoat. She catches it, wraps it around her shoulders and sticks out her tongue. I follow it with a hat, another glove, a shawl and

138

a boot. She catches whatever I toss until she is wearing three mismatched pairs of gloves, two hats and goodness knows how many petticoats.

'Don't I look grand!' she sings. 'Quite the lah-di-dah lady!' She removes one of the hats and plants it on my head. 'As for you – what a peach!'

'Get it off me!' I tear it away, hurl it to the floor and stamp on it.

'Watch out!' she cries. 'That's my ruddy hat, that is.'

'I said get it away!'

'It's only a game.'

'Some bloody game.'

'There's no pleasing some folk.' She sniffs and perches on a padded stool before the dressing-mirror.

'What are you doing now?'

'Fixing my hair.'

'There's nothing wrong with your hair.'

'I'll be the judge of that,' she replies, mouth full of hairpins. 'Go on, make yourself comfy, if you're stopping, that is.'

I resist the urge to lecture her about the impossibility of comfort in such a midden and lower myself on to the bed. I'm sure the only reason it doesn't collapse is the quantity of debris shoved underneath. Jessie tugs her hair, looping bits of it around her finger. She doesn't seem to be in any haste to turf me out, despite my poor manners. In truth, I'm in no hurry to be anywhere else and it is oddly restful to watch her at her toilet.

My gaze wanders over the bottles and candlesticks strewn across the tabletop and alight on a tiny photograph. It's been snipped into a circle such as would fit a locket. An infant with a startled expression, face weighed down by a mop of curls. Jessie sees me looking and picks it up. She cradles it in her palm as tenderly as if she held the babe himself.

'I wore him around my neck,' she whispers, caressing his face with her thumb. 'Those were different times. A gold locket wouldn't last five minutes with these neighbours.' She hoists her voice to a shout. 'Would it now!' she screams, and stamps on the floor.

There's a muffled cry of *whore!* from the room below.

'Who is he?' I ask, nodding at the little 'un.

'Was. Charlie.'

The kid looks bilious. Something in her voice is so naked that I keep my lip buttoned. The air hovers, tight and silent. She slaps the picture face down on the table. 'Anyhow,' she says with loud gaiety in her voice. 'How about a nice chocolate?'

She pulls open the drawer and produces a tin big enough to keep my boots in. The lid is embossed with blowsy roses. I think of my paltry Friday offerings, wrapped in brown paper.

'You won't be wanting me to buy you sweets when you have gents buying you fancy stuff like that,' I mumble.

'Yours are the best I could ask for.'

'Don't tell lies. My stuff's rubbish. Off the market.'

'That's as maybe. But they were given by you.' That sappy look blossoms in her eyes. 'You're my ray of sunshine, you are.'

She wraps her arms around me and pulls me close. I ought to shove her away. The thunder-and-lightning, racket-and-riot Gnome wouldn't stand for it. I close my eyes so I can't see him. By and by, Jessie's hand curves around the top of my head and she starts to hum. I burrow deep into her arms and hang on tight, like I'll drown if I let go. I mustn't cry. I push my nose into her breast, soft as a loaf rising, and plug up the tears.

But devilish Gnome won't leave me be. He sneers at the sight of all this tender tomfoolery. *Sickening. Pathetic.* I'm a disgrace, a suck-a-thumb with a piss-wet nappy, snivelling for his mam.

Some man I'm growing up to be. A man wants more. Gets more. I wriggle out of her clutches.

'Give us a kiss,' I say with a leer.

She laughs, leans down and I pucker up for the press of her mouth upon mine. She plants a kiss on my forehead.

'There you go, you little scamp.'

'Not like that,' I say, batting her hands aside. 'Properly. Like you do with men.'

She laughs. 'Oh dear. That would never do.'

'Why not?'

Her face grows serious. 'Don't,' she sighs.

'You think I'm too young, don't you? I'm not. I've kissed lots of girls.'

'No you haven't.'

'I have!' I cry, face hot. 'And if I haven't, why shouldn't you be the first?'

'It wouldn't be right, Gnome,' she says kindly and rubs my knee. 'You'll understand when you get older.'

'You sound like my mam.'

'Exactly.' She sounds sad, and I have no idea why. 'That's my point. Don't you see?'

'I don't see at all. Is it money? It is, isn't it?'

'No it isn't.'

'I can get money,' I gabble. 'Easy. How much do you usually charge?'

'Stop this.'

'I'll give you double.'

'I said shut it!' Her face screws up, cheeks bright with rouge and the blood that flares beneath. 'I don't want to talk about this a moment longer.'

Wisps of hair have escaped their pins and straggle around her face. Lipstick sticks to her teeth and bleeds into her upper lip. The word *ugly* wriggles on my tongue. If I say it, that'll be the end of everything. I'll never set foot in her room again, never know the thrill of her chatter, the sweetmeats of her secrets. I want to stay, more than I could ever admit. At the same time I want to rip the paint off the walls, tear down the room brick by brick and her in it. Fury rages through me like fire through a sugar warehouse. I can't stop myself.

'What is it with you bloody women?' I scream. 'You're like the rest of them! All I ever hear is *no you can't, stop, get your hands off, shut up.* You'll do it with anyone who can haul himself up the stairs and put money down. But not me.'

'That is enough,' she says. 'Go home.'

'I don't need you!' I wail.

I thunder down the rickety stairs. I have to get away. Go and never stop, not till I've shaken everything off my skin. My head's too small for all of the nagging, the *no, no, no,* the nailing down. I can't think straight. There's no room for me any more.

I spot a cart trundling away, climb on unnoticed and burrow between chicken coops. Most are unoccupied and the remaining fowl are quiet, heaped in the cages like cushions turned inside out, feathers on the outside. The cart rocks and rattles, sending me into a drowse.

Women. The sum and total of my life's ills. Every last one of them: Mam, Grandma, bloody Edie, even Arthur. He's no better than a woman, the half-baked fruitcake. And now Jessie. How I let myself be mollycoddled I don't know. No more snuffling in her clutches. I'm not her pet. If I let her touch me again, why, it'll be like she does with her customers. My stomach gripes at the memory of pushing her away. I drag my sleeve across my face. No. Reg was right. Wet-kneed slapper. Whore. Tart. Cow.

I'll go wherever this wagon is headed, away from the city.

I'll wake up in Wales and be a farmer's boy. I could fork a haystack in one go if I put my mind to it. Eggs and bacon for breakfast. Milk warm from the cow. Horses to ride and ride. When Edie sticks her nose in, she'll be so flummoxed she'll stick it right back out again, so she will. I'll never set foot in Manchester, let alone The Comet, ever again.

Wales. That's halfway to Ireland. I spin rainbows of steamships ploughing the ocean, wings on my heels to fly me to the moon. Then—There's an almighty jolt as the cart shudders to a halt. As my eyes accustom to the half-light I see that we have drawn up in a vast building. It stinks of chicken droppings.

'You've got a big barn, mister,' I say.

The driver scowls at me. 'Big barn? Where the bloody hell do you think you are?'

'A farm?'

'Bugger off,' he cackles. 'It's Denmark Street sheds and I'm locking up. Shift yourself, unless you want to dig a tunnel.'

The cart has brought me full circle.

When I get indoors, Grandma is lurking in the kitchen. I try to slink past, but she blocks the way with her arm, hefty as a coal-heaver's.

'We must have words, Gnome.'

'No we mustn't,' I hiss through gritted teeth. 'I've had a long night.'

'This has got to stop.'

'I'll stay out as late as I choose.'

'That's not what I mean and you know it.'

'Don't.'

She fills the doorway. I never really noticed how much space she takes up. She's built like a brick outhouse.

'I've spoken to Edie. I've tried to make her see sense and I'll do the same with you.'

'No point. I'll not listen.'

'You will, my lad.' She claps her paws on me and holds hard. She's loving every minute of this torture. 'You and Edie—'

'Save your breath. I am not her. Never have been, never will be. I am Gnome. The only thing I'm interested in is how to be a boy all of the time.'

'That's impossible and you know it. We are part and parcel of each other.'

I bang my fists on the table to drown out her gibberish. 'It's making me sick. *She* is making me sick. I want a cure. One that'll take her away for ever.'

'You sound like your mother. Haven't you had enough of a scare with what she tried to do?'

I can't think of a smart retort, and it irks me greatly. It doesn't take long to find my tongue.

'I'll run away.'

'You'll have to come back.' She tosses her head angrily. 'I am not arguing with you like this, Gnome. Round and round you go. Here it is: listen or don't listen, it's all the same to me. You and Edie are closer than hand in glove. You can't run away from yourself. You must understand. You have to.'

'I don't.'

'You are being very foolish.'

'That's all I am to you, isn't it? Little boy, little fool, little Gnome. I didn't see you stepping in and stopping Mam from—' My throat tightens. 'You didn't want to stop her, did you?'

'Gnome! How can you say such a thing?'

'It's true, isn't it? You love Edie more than me.'

'I love you equally. There's no difference.'

'There is. You love her because she doesn't mind all of . . . this.' I wave my hand up and down my body. 'Mam is right. She hates what we are. I hate it too. It's vile. It's against nature.'

144

'Nature is far more adventurous than we credit,' she replies. 'You are my special—'

'I don't want to be special. I want to be like everyone else.'

'Gnome—'

'When I grow up, I want to be able to marry a nice girl and not have to hide from her every time I—' I spit on the rug. 'I don't want to watch her face when she finds out how disgusting I am.'

'We are not disgusting.'

'Liar!' I howl. 'Where's your husband, or friends for that matter? Where are Mam's? You see? We can't let anyone get close. If that's not lonely, I don't know what is.'

'Listen. Let me explain…'

'No! I've had enough of your half-baked explanations!'

I run upstairs. I don't need her telling me how to live my life. Share and share alike, my eye. How dare the old ratbag tell me to go halves when she does the opposite? Come to think of it, I don't think she's cursed in the same way as Edie and me. She can't be. I've never clapped eyes on any grandfather. I shake my head. I don't give a tuppenny damn what my blasted family do with their lives. The only way out of this is to get away. No grandmother to sneer and make me feel small and stupid. No Edie sneaking in when my guard is down. No mother to plot against my very existence. It's time to spread my wings.

I'll save money, so I will. Ma's cashbox is ripe for the pillaging. A shilling here, a shilling there. It won't take long to steal enough for a train. Liverpool, London. When I'm there I shall – My thoughts hiccup to a halt. I'll cross that bridge when I come to it. I'm clever, me. Smart as a box of monkeys and smarter. I'll work something out. Things are going to change from this moment onwards.

EDIE
1902-4

I tread the path to remembering and yearn for my days of innocence, when I thought myself no more than a clumsy girl in need of lessons in feminine comportment.

I was not, am not, mad.

What I am is worse than lunacy. Gnome is not some half-forgotten nightmare. He is real. Together we make up the oddest creature ever to live.

If I imagine that this revelation might bring about a rapprochement between Ma and myself I am sorely mistaken. She is as harsh as ever and flat out refuses to speak about our strangeness, as if silence might deny its existence. However, I am a practical lass and reason that truth – however inexplicable – is preferable to a life of shoving down suspicions, of denying what my eyes can see but my mind cannot allow. If I am to be lonely, then at least I shall be free of frightful imaginings.

The weeks pass following my awakening and, to my surprise, Gnome becomes kind, even pleasant. He takes no more time than his due, nor does he get into scrapes that earn a whipping. He folds my petticoats over the chair so that I no longer need to root around under the bed. He even polishes his boots.

I should be grateful. But suspicion prickles, like a spider walking up my arm and stirring the hair.

It takes a minute to locate the loose skirting board behind my bed, a minute more to extract a sock filled with cash. I whistle at the number of coins: more than eight pounds, sovereigns too. I'll wager my hat not one farthing was obtained by honest means. I dump the lot on the kitchen table and tell Ma she should keep a closer watch on the takings. Not that I get a crumb of thanks. She wears such a curious expression I wonder if she's in on it. Even Nana looks at me askance. I don't know why I bother.

Gnome and I shuttle back and forth, back and forth, his night following my day. The months blur into each other and become years: I do household chores morning and evening and in between I assist Ma and Nana with the smooth running of the beerhouse.

I cling to the refuge of the library. Every moment I can spare without incurring too many objections, I dash there eager as a child to the arms of a loving parent. I read with a new determination that one day I may turn the page and find myself reflected. I might. If I do not, why, I will nourish my starved mind whilst I search.

One morning, shortly after my seventeenth birthday, I am seated at the breakfast table, stirring my porridge absent-mindedly and leafing though the newspaper, which is greasy from the chips wrapped in it the previous evening.

'Stop playing with your food like a savage,' Ma says. 'Have some manners.'

'Isn't it too late for such niceties?' I reply, shovelling in a mouthful of oatmeal. 'You tell me repeatedly there's no hope.'

She sticks out her lower lip. 'I may have to accept what you are,' she mutters. 'But don't expect a pennyweight more.'

'I can hardly miss what I never possessed,' I reply, affecting a cavalier air I do not feel.

I return my attention to the newspaper. A train puffs out a wreath of smoke, advertising trips to Blackpool. The last thing Gnome needs is any encouragement, so I turn the page quickly.

I'm greeted by a quarter-page illustration of a statue, accompanied by the banner headline: *The Sculptures Travel North.* The editorial describes a new exhibition of masterworks taken from the Lycian tombs. I've no idea where Lycia is, but the sculptures have caused a sensation in London, according to the breathless prose, which is sprinkled with words like *apogee, illustrious* and *astonishing* as freely as pepper.

The journalist expresses disappointment that Manchester is not to be graced with the original carvings, which are far too fragile to venture from the British Museum. We are to satisfy ourselves with plaster casts, although very good ones. My breath will be taken away, I am assured. *In particular,* he gushes, *the Nereid Tomb must be admired.*

Very well, I say to myself. Admire it I will. This moment, to boot. I fold the paper, push myself away from the table and proceed out of the kitchen.

'Where do you think you're going?' barks Ma.

I stand before the hall mirror and adjust my hat. 'I don't *think* I'm going anywhere. I'm off out and that's the long and the short of it.'

'The sauce! While you are under my roof you will address me with the respect I deserve.'

'Respect!' I snort. I glare down my nose at her. In addition to existing unwomanly attributes, I've added a further span of

148

inches to my height. She is the first to look away. I draw on my gloves and take my time about it.

'You're running around with suffragettes, aren't you?' she fumes.

'No,' I reply wearily. It is not the first time she's accused me of this and I am sure it won't be the last. 'I am visiting the Museum.' I slide notebook and pencil into my bag and swing it over one shoulder.

'Liar!' she squawks. 'A child of mine, cavorting with those awful women. The very thought!'

'I said Museum, Mother,' I say dryly. 'But now you pique my interest. Perhaps I shall attend a rally after all.'

'How dare you talk so rudely to your elders and betters!'

'Elders, yes,' I drawl.

Her face flushes to the roots of her hair. 'Go, then! Jump in the canal! Earn a few bob on Minshull Street if any bloke is blind enough to fancy your ugly mug. I wash my hands of you.'

'Thank you for your kind solicitations, Mother dear.'

'Get out!' she screams.

'My pleasure. It is what I have been trying to do this past half-hour.'

The library is my first and dearest love, my primer and encyclopaedia. Over the years I have cast my net wider, venturing through the portals of both the Art Gallery and the Museum. Variety is the spice of life: I visited the library yesterday, and today will be the turn of the Museum.

I may not be one of the fortunate young ladies attending Owen's College, but I stride through the arched doorway with head held as high. I hasten past stuffed beasts; butterflies spreading metallic wings; gigantic shells and twinkling gems; axe-heads spread in a dun-coloured rainbow; strings of antique necklaces, cold without the throats that wore them two thousand years ago.

149

At last I enter the classical gallery and read the accompanying notice. *The Nereid Monument: sculptured tomb from Xanthos in classical period Lycia. 390–380* BC. *Excavated by Sir Charles Fellows, 1844.* The scrubbed white plaster lacks the grandeur of marble, but I am not complaining. The sculptures are spectacular.

A cavalcade of naked youths gallop the length of the wall, gripping the flanks of their mounts between their knees. I marvel at the artful hand that teased marble into flesh. Thighs bulge, faces grimace; horses flick their hooves, toss their heads and flare their nostrils in such a lifelike way I half see the steam of their breath. I have the strangest notion that if I lay my hand on the wall, I will feel the pulse of ancient hearts.

I draw out my notebook and pencil and begin to sketch one of the warriors. His right arm is thrown forward in a gesture that could be a salute or a challenge. I study the muscles, endeavouring to translate my observations to paper. It is not too bad for a first attempt, but the fingers leave a lot to be desired. I jot a few notes and make two more sketches of a leg and a sandalled foot before walking on.

I reach a portion of the frieze where the cavalry are involved in a skirmish with a group of standing warriors. My eye is drawn to a kneeling man who is putting up a valiant fight despite being unfairly matched against the Greek horse that rears over his head. I feel rather sorry for him.

The sculptor has bent the stone to his will in a manner that is nothing short of astonishing. The short tunic is so delicately carved that it appears soaked with sweat. My gaze wanders to the spot at the fork of his thighs. The linen sticks to the flesh beneath, accentuating a tumescence that is undoubtedly masculine. It's nothing I haven't observed in myself, budding and

150

blossoming out of my own groin when I am undergoing the change into Gnome.

I realise I am staring. I glance around to see if anyone has noticed such brazen behaviour. Two young gentlemen lounge on a nearby bench, conversing in low murmurs. One flourishes a hand in the direction of the wall, waving it to and fro as though conducting a symphony for the benefit of his companion. I am quite overlooked and resume my observation. To make it less obvious, I move sideways a couple of steps. From my new vantage point the light falls upon the warrior slantwise.

He has breasts.

I blink, but they do not disappear. Despite what is evident below his belt, two small yet unmistakeable mounds push out his chlamys. It has to be a trick of the light. I step back to view the sculpture face-on yet can still pick out the feminine curves, albeit less clearly.

I am fixed to the spot as surely as if the soles of my boots have been slathered with glue. Here is a man who is also a woman. A woman who is also a man. He – or she – calls out to me, clear across the millennia. *I lived, I breathed. I was as you are.*

My mind reels. I search the card for enlightenment. *Mounted Greeks victorious against a barbarian race, as yet unidentified. Possibly Thracians.* Nothing to explain what is in front of me. My cheeks burn. If I can see this, so can everyone else. I peer around, expecting gaping mouths, pointing fingers, a riot of denunciation and disapproval. The gallery is serene and orderly, the only tumult that which rages in my breast.

I take up my notebook, hoping to act the part of a student of art about her legitimate business. I begin with the shoulders, then the neck; the upraised forearm. I imagine my own muscles as firm as those of this man-woman. I am his sister. I too am

151

preparing myself for battle against enemy forces who will crush me if they discover my alien strangeness.

My warrior – I dare to call him mine – comes to life beneath my pencil. I never sketched so well. Some agency guides my hand and despite my trembling the line is true and unwavering. This sculpture is the first and only thing I've seen that comes close to a representation of myself.

I am not alone.

I yearn to dash up to every matron, every gentleman, haul them across the neatly blocked parquet to my warrior and cry: *Look! The Greeks understood! I am no singular freak of nature! I exist!*

I do no such thing. I stow pencil and notepad, take a deep breath and proceed out of the gallery in as composed a manner as I can manage. The only sign of my mental and spiritual turmoil is that I clutch my bag to my chest more tightly than usual.

I totter down the steps of the Museum, trip and crack my knee. My nerves are so disordered it'd be just like Gnome to shove me aside and leap into the breach. Mercifully, I am spared that ignominy and I weave along the street, barely conscious whither I am headed.

I know I am different. I know that difference is profound. Nana says there's not a soul to match us. Maybe she is wrong. If people like me existed thousands of years ago, why not today, this very minute, somewhere on the face of the earth? We could be passing each other on Oxford Road. The notion is intoxicating.

I tumble onwards and scowl. All very well to entertain phantasies, but they are of little practical worth. Far better to bend my thoughts towards building a safe harbour to withstand the buffeting of life's storms. I'm stuck with this world and must make the best of it. I must grow strong and not merely in my body. I've had enough of doctors to last two lifetimes.

My thoughts are interrupted by the sound of raised voices. Clustered around All Saints' Church are trestle tables piled with leaflets, plates, cakes and even a tea-urn. A platform has been set up by the wall and beside it a young lady and an older gentleman wrestle with a banner emblazoned with the legend *Votes for Women*.

A woman bustling in the opposite direction brushes against me. 'Not for the likes of me,' she mutters, face screwed up with age and hard work. 'Maybe for you, my pet.'

She stamps away. Here are the women that Ma rails against: the scourge of society, on a mission to drag it to its knees. Ma would be terribly disappointed. From what I can see, everything is proceeding with the utmost decorum.

A tolerable proportion of the troupe is comprised of gentlemen, who tip their hats and greet me with civility. I made an assumption that no man would lower himself to the cause of women's suffrage. Clearly, I was mistaken. I wonder what else I've been wrong about. It is a day of having foundations shaken and beliefs challenged, that much is certain.

To the accompaniment of applause, a small lady clambers on to the podium. She wears a broad-brimmed hat and a sash of white satin edged with green and purple. She eyes the gathering keenly, and begins to speak. With the warp and weft of her words, she cajoles us, she tantalises us, she breaks us down and builds us up again. She weaves a world where women and men stand side by side as comrades in possession of equal humanity. I don't know whether to weep that it is denied us, or cheer that it is a goal towards which we can strive.

Perhaps it is the suggestive state in which I find myself, but I am refreshed in a way I never thought to experience. A chord resonates throughout my being, awakening me from slumber of the soul. Perhaps I can find a way to live in this world and not simply exist. Perhaps I no longer need to cower, frightened of my own shadow. Maybe I can shake that Edie off, now.

The clock strikes three. I ought to return home, but any sense of urgency has receded. It won't be dark for some hours. Besides, I am far too enraptured to leave. My attention shifts to the young woman holding the banner. She, too, is listening with keen attention. Her chin is uptilted, revealing the column of her throat: the muscles delicate yet firm. A neat bonnet is pinned to a cushion of hazel hair only a philistine would describe as brown.

I cannot take my eyes off her: the determined set of her jaw, the fine blades of her cheekbones, the soft mouth. A mouth that blooms like a rose. Good heavens, I chide myself. What claptrap. I've stopped to hear the speech, which is rousing enough to inspire even the most leaden of creatures. I am not here to gawp at handsome women.

Despite the ticking-off, my gaze is disobedient and insists on returning to the object of its desire. I note the line of her jacket, tailored to show off a slender waist. Lavender wool trimmed with emerald velvet, buttons of a matching hue sparkling like gems. I am too far away to see the colour of her eyes, but fancy works its magic and I imagine them to be green also.

I give myself a good shake and return my attention to the speaker, who has come to the end of her address and is fielding questions. She is so diminutive of frame that I fear how she'll fare in this rough neighbourhood. However, she has an inexhaustible store of good-humoured retorts and I am stunned by the ease with which she counters her detractors with a clever quip here and an adroit comment there. I hear more than one fellow tell the hecklers to pipe down or else get a punch on the nose.

All too soon she is done. I want to preserve the enchantment of this afternoon for as long as possible so I dawdle, picking up pamphlets one after another and flicking through the pages. Someone tugs my sleeve and I turn to find the young lady I was admiring.

'Mrs Tuke is a wonderful speaker, is she not?' she says.

'She? Oh! Yes,' I say, fudging the words. 'I apologise for my inarticulate reply. I believe I am still held in her spell.'

'I can tell!' Her eyes rove over me in a frank fashion I should find unnerving. I do not. She smiles, as though pleased with what she has observed.

'The words she speaks and the passion with which she speaks them are like draughts of cool water,' I say, surprised at the vigour of my response. 'Balm to my parched soul.'

My gabbling ought to send her packing, but she continues to regard me with friendly interest.

'I do hope you'll take tea,' she says. 'Man cannot live by speeches alone, and a cup helps the words go down.' She takes my elbow, steers me towards the tea-urn and pours a cup. 'Enough sugar?'

I take a sip. It is so fortifying I wonder if it is laced with a stimulant more invigorating than tea leaves.

'I believe I may be able to scrounge up a biscuit,' she adds. 'Now. Where are they hiding themselves?'

She lifts up a pile of leaflets, then another and another, until she gives a little shout of victory and seizes a plate.

'I couldn't,' I bluster. 'You are too kind. I should go.'

I have no idea why I'm behaving as though I've never set eyes on a biscuit in my life. However, she is not put off by my gauche manners.

155

'You're quite safe,' she says, pushing the plate in my direction. 'I didn't bake them; Hilda did.'

She tilts her head in the direction of another young woman, who I presume to be Hilda. She is at the far end of the table, speaking in an animated fashion to a chap in a tweed jacket.

'Go on, do. It would please me,' she says with such hopeful intensity I have the feeling there is no choice in the matter.

I select one of the biscuits and take a ladylike nibble. I've not had a bite since breakfast and it is manna from heaven. I try to eat slowly, but it's gone in a trice.

'Have another,' she says. I shake my head, overcome with mortification that my hunger is so apparent. 'It'd be a kindness,' she continues in her enchanting voice. 'No one's ever finished one before. Hilda's talents do not lie in the kitchen. And I am far worse.'

I take another biscuit and drain a second cup of the ambrosial tea. *To wash down our burned offerings,* as she puts it. After four biscuits have been devoured and a third cup of tea refused, she hands me a broadsheet entitled *The New Crusade*.

'Do take it. It's very good.' She smiles. 'Unlike the biscuits.'

'I can't,' I say, and pause. Although the cover price is a mere sixpence, it is out of my reach. I do not think it is possible to feel more embarrassed. 'I mean, I should like to, but . . .'

'You need not feel obliged to pay,' she says lightly.

'But I wish to.'

'Sixpence is a suggestion. A voluntary donation, if you will.'

'I'm not a beggar,' I snap.

I think she'll respond to my sharpness as nonchalantly as she does everything else, but her face falls.

'Oh,' she gasps, colouring. 'I meant no offence. I did not wish – I am sorry.'

A wave of remorse sweeps over me. 'No. *I* am sorry,' I say.

'Truly I am. That was most ungenerous. I took a tumble on the Museum steps and bruises put me into a fearsomely bad temper.'

'The Museum?'

'Yes.'

'I love the Museum! Who would not be entranced? Did you see the Lycian casts?'

'Yes!' I exclaim, unable to conceal my pleasure. I scold myself for behaving so openly with a stranger. I am most unlike myself today. 'They are fascinating,' I add with more self-possession.

'I am in a fearful hurry to see them,' she says.

'They took my breath away.'

As I speak, the truth of the statement crashes over my head with the force of a wave. I clap my hand to my brow and sway dizzily. Her hand grasps my arm, firm and strong.

'My dear girl,' she breathes. 'Are you well?'

'I must go.'

'Of course,' she says, her eyes warm with concern. 'If you think you are fit to walk.'

'My mother is missing me,' I say, squirming at the lie.

'Perhaps you will attend another rally?' she says. 'There's a meeting at the Free Trade Hall on Thursday.'

I ache to cry *yes!* The idea of spending time in the rousing company of this woman – I correct myself sternly – these women thrills me to the core. However, I remind myself that the reason for her attention is to garner support. I am a face in the crowd who may be of benefit to the cause, nothing more. Much as I'd like to loiter, I place the pamphlet in my bag and thank her politely. Taking up this grand lady's time will not bring me one inch nearer to my doorstep.

I hasten away, breasting the tide of city crowds. When I awoke this morning, I could not have guessed the change that today would bring. My world has tilted on its axis, towards the sun. So what if I loom head and shoulders above other women? No longer will I tuck my chin into my chest in a pointless attempt at concealment.

I take a deep breath and for the first time in my life, stand up straight. My neck cracks as the muscles assume untried positions. A well-dressed youth gawps at the spectacle of a giantess striding along the pavement. Yes, I think. I'm tall. I have big feet, bigger hands. I am who I am, and that's that. Hurt falls from my shoulders like the ill-fitting coat it always was. I experience the stirrings of an unfamiliar emotion. It dawns on me that it is pride.

The first quarter-mile passes swiftly enough. The second I am a little less sprightly, and the last hundred yards I feel the lights of my body extinguishing themselves one by one as the sustaining effects of the tea and biscuits wear off.

I enter The Comet and greet Ma and Nana in a perfunctory fashion. Ma attempts to distract me, bleating that Uncle is on his way and someone must prepare his supper and how that person won't be her. Answering *yes, Ma, no, Ma* and *presently,* I take the stairs two at a time, slam the door to my room and launch myself on to the mattress. My thoughts whirl, and the room whirls with me.

The unimaginable has occurred: I have seen my freakish nature displayed, not as a skulking footnote in a medical journal of the diseased and abnormal, but in a museum of all places. If that were not sufficient cause for joy, my soul has been lifted into a rapture at the suffrage rally. Prior to this afternoon I regarded that cause as worthy, but of no direct consequence in the course of my life. All that has changed. I make a promise to myself: I will find a way to attend another meeting. I do not know where or when, but soon. A profound alchemy has been wrought this afternoon. It is an explosive combination.

I am so distracted that it takes a while before it sinks in that my light-headedness is not hunger but Gnome. He's far too early. The sun is still up.

Move aside, he growls.

'No,' I say. 'It's barely suppertime. I'm not ready. Give me an hour.'

Since when did the likes of you need an hour? You will move over.

'I will not. Not today.'

You have no choice.

'Maybe I do.'

His laughter ripples through me like a bout of indigestion. *What's come over you all of a sudden? We've always done it this way.*

'Things change.'

And some things don't. We're saddled with each other, sister dear.

'I am not your sister. You know that as well as I do.'

As though they are a pair of evening gloves, Gnome slides his arms into mine and proceeds to rescue his breeches from under the bed. However, I have not fully quit the building, so to speak, and I shove them out of reach. He picks them up. I throw them down.

'Stop this nonsense,' he snaps. 'Give me my body this instant.'

'It's not your body,' I say. 'It is ours.'

'Mine, mine, mine,' he chants.

'For heaven's sake. You're acting like a baby.'

Neither of us yet has the upper hand. If he's going to be

childish, so shall I. He shoves one leg into the trousers. I twist them about-face. It takes a quarter-minute for him to realise they're on backwards.

'Oh, Gnome,' I titter. 'You are so cack-handed.'

Undeterred, he grasps the waistband and hops about, trying to poke his foot inside. I unbalance him and he topples on to the bed, to an affronted squeak from the mattress.

'You put your right foot in,' I sing, enjoying myself immensely. 'And then you take it out, and wag it, and wag it, and wag it all about.'

'Give me my trousers!' he shrieks, frustration fizzing like ginger beer. The legs are bunched around his ankles. The harder he tries to free himself, the tighter they tangle. 'I've had it up to here with you. A millstone around my neck, so you are. I never asked for things to be this way.'

'You think I did?'

'Just get out.'

'Why?'

'Because I said so. If it wasn't for you, I'd be free.'

'Gnome! You can't turf me aside like I don't matter.'

'You don't. You're as dull as ditchwater and thick as two short planks. Shut your moaning and shift.'

Would it kill him to be polite, just once, instead of talking to me like I'm dirt on his boot? It seems particularly galling, today of all days. Do I have no vote in the governance of my own flesh? Must I bow to this petty patriarch? The tumultuous events of the afternoon set a spark to the timid embers of my heart. I clasp my hands behind my back.

'No,' I say firmly.

He fumbles helplessly, trying to tease my fingers loose. I clench them into fists. We hover half in, half out of each other: that no man's land between our two selves. The meaning of the phrase strikes home with grim humour. To be a land with no man in it. What a paradise that would be.

'If you don't lay off this minute, I'll—'

'You'll what, Gnome?' I'll stop teasing him presently, I tell myself. Of course I'll step aside, I always do. I want the smallest taste of victory, that's all. 'Come on,' I sneer. 'Show me what you're made of. Grind my face into the dirt, put your heel on my neck and hold me there. Show me who's master. If you can, of course.'

'I can! I can!'

'Can't.'

'Can.'

'Hmm,' I sigh. 'I don't think you're here at all. I am talking to myself. After all, that's what girls do, isn't it? Muttering all kinds of silly notions and fancies. That's what you are: a scrap of my imagination.'

'I am not! Shut up!' he shrieks.

'Shut up, shut up!' I squawk in mimicry. Goading Gnome is beneath me, but I can't stop. 'I see you. Waiting at the threshold, unable to step over it into my body. I could raise my hand and swat you aside. Not that I need to exert myself. You're pathetic.'

'Just you wait!' he squeaks. 'I'll teach you a lesson you'll never forget. I'll kick you out. I'll stamp you flat, and when I've done so, I'll never let you back in, never!'

Silence falls. I hear the plink of rain from the cracked gutter above the window. Every hair on the back of my neck stands up.

'Cat got your tongue?' he leers. He wraps his hands around my throat and squeezes till my eyes sparkle. 'Look what I have in store for you.'

He shoves me to the brink of extinction and dangles me over the abyss. Hell floods out of the pit, stretches its jaws wide. Frantic with terror, I twist the budding flesh between my legs

161

but cannot stop the swelling. He pokes me in the eye; I box his ears. He punches me in the stomach; I bite his arm. Inch by inch, he gains the upper hand. In the struggle my fingers strike the bedside table and close around a hat-pin. Without thinking, I swing my fist in a wide arc and stab myself in the thigh.

Hell holds its breath.

Gnome grinds to a halt. He tries to rally, but when I jab myself a second time I taste panic and it is not my own. I grasp his private parts. They are shrinking: a pebble, a snail, a marble, a cherry stone. He is so small that a midwife would scratch her head if asked whether we were girl or boy. I can't quite believe it. Gnome is seeping away, and I made it happen.

'You didn't know I could do that, did you?' I crow. There is no answer. 'Well, I can. Aren't you scared?'

No, he quavers.

He clings desperately to our body, but his hold is slipping. I could leave it there; could permit him to slink away with some dignity remaining. Power makes me cruel.

'Listening to you is like listening to an old man's farts,' I jeer. 'When it comes to a stand-up fight, you're off with your tail between your legs. Look,' I say, brandishing the hat-pin. 'You're full of hot air, Gnome. One jab and poof! You're gone.'

I pierce my thigh a third time. His voice shrinks to a mouse-squeak.

No.

'That's all you are. A little prick.'

Again. His voice is the buzz of a fly.

No.

Again. The whine of a gnat.

No.

Again. He winks out, like a snuffed candle.

I sprawl on the bed, chest heaving as though I've run a mile.

162

What have I done? I've won, that's what. My brain seethes with the possibility that I've chanced upon the key to my salvation. Can I be forever female and fix myself in that estate by such a simple ruse? Can I chase Gnome away with little more than a hat-pin, such as I might easily keep about my person? Temptation spreads its peacock cloak across my path. To live free from the fear of discovery. To live free of the change. I can be normal. Ordinary. This is the cure, the true cure, and I have stumbled upon it by myself.

The shadows thicken as night comes on. Up to this moment, the best I hoped for was to keep my head down and remain invisible and unmolested. This changes everything. I turn the pin in my fingers. It is barely marked with blood. For the price of a drop or two I am mistress of my existence.

I wonder how Ma and Nana can be unaware of this solution to all of our problems. The answer falls upon me like a coal sack down a chute. They do know. Ma limits Arthur's appearances, perhaps by employing the same trick. As for my hypocrite of a grandmother, I can't recall one single, solitary occasion when I've seen her other half. Has she done this to banish my grandfather entirely? I am confused. I don't expect honesty – or anything approaching it – from Ma. But Nana? How can I trust her again if she has hidden the key to freedom so wilfully?

I imagine that the stimulation of my thoughts will preclude sleep entirely. However, I slumber more soundly than I can remember, untroubled by dreams or awakenings. I wake with neither boots on my feet, nor grime under my fingernails.

I go to the window, rub dirt from the pane and watch the sun come up on this, the first day of my new life. The clouds to the east peel away and the colour of the horizon deepens, flushing pink to scarlet. *Red sky in the morning, sailors take warning.* I scoff at the superstition. This morning sees me the

163

luckiest of creatures. The star of misfortune blighting my life is turning to the good at last.

Mill chimneys press their silhouettes against the sky as though cut from black card, in crisper and crisper relief as the light grows in intensity. The early shift is heading to the brewery, sparks flying as their heels strike the pavement. I can join them, can become a face blending into the fog of city crowds. I can settle down, take tea with my neighbours in china cups. A real woman, the same as every other, with all the concomitant chatter of babies and hats and gloves and fans. I can be unnoticeable. Normal.

I shudder. Now that I have the choice, it strikes me that I don't want to be the same, not in that way, which seems to be trading one shackle for another. I want liberation, not verisimilitude. The two are entirely different.

Of course, I won't shut Gnome out entirely. That's the sort of low trick he'd pull. I am far too generous-hearted. I'll let him run around and indulge in foolish escapades, let off boyish steam. But I will say when and where. It is only fitting. As for Ma and Nana, they've concealed this cure. I owe them nothing. I'll wait a day before telling them of my discovery. Maybe two.

A slice of orange appears above the line of distant roofs. I have the oddest notion that the misery which has stifled my life is rising up with the sun, to be dissolved in the warmth of the day. I shade my eyes. A great calm settles.

I've suffered under Gnome's selfish yoke for long enough. Things are about to change. If he can save money, so can I, and every penny honestly. I'll hide it better, too. I'll learn a false smile and serve out my sentence under this roof. If Ma and Nana can withhold the secret of liberty, then I can withhold my plans. When I'm good and ready I'll pack my bags, leave The Comet and not look back. I'll take lodgings and work for my living. For the first time I have a choice.

GNOME
1904

I live in the cage of her curfew. She sets the hours and if I don't keep to them she sticks in the spike. I am her dog brought to heel, docked of tail and teeth. Every night I stretch my leash. Every morning I slink back. There is no choice but obedience.

Tonight, I dream of walking free. Free of skewers, free of pins.

The streets unroll beneath my feet and carry me to Pomona Docks. Great ships hug the wharves, their holds bursting with the world's freight. Grain elevators stretch to the clouds, taller than the houses on my street: taller than two houses, three houses, any number of our cramped kennels. I'm not interested in bananas, nor sugar, nor all the perfumes of Arabia. My eye follows the keen line of the canal striking westwards: to Liverpool, to the sea, to everywhere that isn't here.

This is a dream and I can do anything I want. I can step off the quayside, stroll to Eastham and hopscotch the Atlantic until I set foot in – wherever it is I choose to set foot. Buffalo Bill will meet me in America, pull me up on to his saddle and we will gallop away, whooping, with feathers in our hair.

There's a packet-boat dawdling in Mode Wheel Locks. Rubbish skulks along the wall: a stoved-in orange crate, snapped spars, bottles without messages. The lock-keeper cranks the great lever; chains clank, cogs grind and the water level drops. The debris takes a sluggish step forward only to be shoved back by the incoming surge.

I slip down the ladder set into the wall. I'm careful to wrap my shirtsleeves around my hands, for the rungs are slimy. Step by step I go, balancing speed with sure-footedness. The boat nestles close.

'Come,' says the pilot, voice rippling the surface of the canal. 'Have a drink with us.' His accent is so thick I could spread it on toast, his face burnished mahogany. 'Jump over.'

'It's too far.'

'I will catch you, boy.'

He holds out a hand. I take it: dry and stiff as planed wood. He pulls me on board and I huddle in the shelter of a coil of rope, piled as high as a grown man. I taste singed oil, the sick smell of bilge, the faint but persistent odour of the privy.

'Running away, sonny?'

'I'm going to America,' I say.

'America!' he roars, teeth glinting. He pounds his thighs with his hands. 'America!'

There's chuckling from within the cabin, his shipmates joining in as if it's the funniest thing they ever heard. They repeat the word over and over until it loses all meaning and becomes a handful of syllables rattling around the deck.

'Better to be home,' declares my captain, more soberly. 'You have been away too long.' I don't ask him how he knows. 'You are too young to be going so far.'

'I'm seventeen. I'm a man.'

He laughs, so gently it might be breathing. He stops before I can be sure. 'Very well,' he says. 'If you wish it.'

'I do wish it,' I mutter.

I wish I didn't sound so ungrateful. He sticks a gnawed pipe between his teeth and sucks hard, harder, until the tobacco sizzles into life. I shiver with something that is not the chill breathed out by the water.

'Here,' he says.

He throws a scarf, which falls across my shoulders. I give it a sneering glance as if to say I don't need such a babyish thing. When he's not looking I wrap it around my throat. The wool is coarse and smells of the dirty necks of many men, but it is deliciously warm. I hug my knees closer to my chest.

In my dream I drowse, lullabied by the chugging of the engine. The Ship Canal hauls us seawards on its pewter rope. Ships hoot, calling one to the other. The pilot puffs on his pipe, singing snatches of a song I've never heard and don't understand. We steam towards Liverpool: from Barton Bridge to Irlam Locks and under Cadishead Viaduct; Warburton Bridge through Latchford. We pass Woolston Weir, Warrington, Widnes and take the long, swinging sweep past the Weaver Sluices, beyond which the ocean awaits and I can leap off this stinking piece of earth.

Perhaps it is the way of dreams, for in the wink of an eye I am at Eastham. The engine clunks to a halt. Water shuffles back and forth, slapping the flank of the packet-boat.

'Why have we stopped?'

The pilot grins. 'We wait.' He points at the iron giant blocking the way ahead. It's not enough to cool my impatience.

'We can slip past it. Come on. We'll never make it to America if we stay here.'

The lock gates hug the left bank, kissing the muddy mouth of the Mersey. They are low in the water, barely lifting their brows above the level of the canal. I thought they would tower, high as Babylon and higher, impossible to see over. Thought the chains would be forged of silver, the wheel-locks of gold.

This was to be my great escape. I expected crowds, waving their caps and cheering me on my way; thought I'd have the pick of ships rolling out the gangplank to beckon me on board. I dreamed of being transported to a rainbow land where grey is outlawed; where the sky stretches a hot tent, where I might lie on a beach of yellow sand with a mango in one hand, a coconut in the other. No Mam, no Grandmother, and especially no Edie.

Instead, I am gawping at the backside of an ocean-going liner heading west and leaving me behind. Its vast propellers churn, sending up starfish that flash at the surface only to sink back into the depths. I am of no more significance than these soft-bellied creatures. I flicker for a night and am gone. I'm at the jumping-off point for the world's trade but as locked in as ever.

The dream shivers. I cling to it: I must be master of my fate. If this is a vision, I will make it my own. Bend it to my will and force it to obey. And yet . . .

What do dreams signify if I can't escape? I can stow away to the other side of the world and not outrun her, not by so much as one inch. Even flying to the moon isn't far enough. She is with me always and always will be. All my striving: none of it any use. I don't know why I bother. I am tired of fighting to be Gnome. I am tired of fighting to be anyone at all.

If I can't get what I want, I don't want anything at all.

The water beckons, grim as lead. I could climb over the side of the boat. Nothing as wild as hurling myself in – just one little step and I'd be in and under. I think of the steel hug of night-water. I'd be choked in an instant. A moment of pain; then nothing. An end to all of this; a peace I did not know I wanted. I grip the gunwhale and lift my leg. My body won't let me. My feet refuse to budge.

Don't you dare, she says. *That's far enough.*

Even in my dreams she is watching. The sea-gates shiver and dissolve into the phantasy they are. I am cold and trembling, back where I started on the towpath, not even as far as Pomona.

'Can't I have the privacy of my own thoughts?'

Someone's got to watch over us.

'Who ordained you watchman?'

She crumples my words and tosses them into the canal. *You can't be trusted. Look at you: about to drown yourself and drag me after.*

'I wasn't going to. Not truly.'

How can I know that? You've always been impulsive.

'This is despair. You have felt it.'

There's a pause, less than the time between one breath and the next. A silence clearer than any denial.

Never.

'Liar. You were all geared up to snuff us out in a snowdrift.'

I was a child! she whines. *I thought I was going mad! I didn't understand. I do now.*

'It was me that saved you, remember?'

It doesn't matter! You don't know how hard I've had to fight, every step of the way! Ma loves you. Not me.

'How did we get so lost? Don't you want to go back to how it was?'

I don't know what you mean.

'You do. Wasn't it grand, Edie? Being in a harmony all of our own?'

All very well for babies.

'You do remember.'

No more games. Enough of this malarkey. You're lucky I let you out tonight. Make the most of it. Drink deep. It's the last you're going to taste.

'You can't. You wouldn't dare.'

She laughs, the scrape of rust off a keel. *Wouldn't I? I can stop you.* Her mind brandishes spikes. *You don't deserve this body.*

'It's my body too. It's not fair. Leave me the nights, Edie. Please.'

No. You're too dangerous. She twists my shoulders, turns me in the direction of Hulme. *Home. Now.*

'Never.'

I can make you.

'Can't!' I cry, voice smaller by degrees.

I run from her, fast as I can. My feet are caught in treacle. The greater my exertion the slower I go, until I may as well be walking backwards. Sweat or tears – I know not which – stream down my face and off my chin. I wheeze like a broken-backed old man.

I close my eyes and when I open them I'm at the corner of Renshaw Street. I feel nothing. It is not home. I will have no home until I am free, until I am more than a dream of a boy who can be blown out like a candle flame.

The door is on the latch. I enter the silent building. No one to say *goodbye, good riddance.* I wonder if they'll even notice that I've gone. I climb the stairs, curl on the cot in the corner of the room. Powerless to resist, I watch my fingers flourish the hat-pin.

I hate Edie. Hate is the only thing I have left to call my own. I cling to it, as if it might save me. With torturous grace, my hand swings in a wide arc and the shock of the stabbing resonates through my being. I sink into darkness, a drowning man fighting for his very existence. I flicker. I go out. She has won.

PART TWO
MANCHESTER
1909–1910

EDIE
MARCH 1909

The food is ghastly, as it is every morning.

I crack the top of my egg and prise away the shell to reveal a blob of gelatinous matter cradling a yolk that is tough and grey. Mrs Reddish has performed the seemingly impossible feat of producing a boiled egg that is uncooked without and India rubber within.

'Our landlady has excelled herself this morning,' grumbles Gertrude, shoving her spoon around and around a bowl full of sludge. 'I assert this to be stewed gravel. I dare you to prove me wrong.'

'It's porridge,' snaps Edna. 'I'd face it a hundred times over one of her boiled eggs.'

Gertrude takes a reluctant mouthful and pulls a face. 'It tastes worse than it looks, if that were possible. There must be more salt than oatmeal.'

'You'll hurt her feelings,' hisses Edna.

Heralded by the smell of burned toast, the lady in question enters the dining room. She slams down a plate stacked with slices of bread in various stages of incineration and sails away with an air of one much put upon at being forced to serve young females who by rights should have been waiting upon her. This would indeed have been the case but for the death of Mr Reddish, carried off by an illness so heroic it was able to topple a man who'd survived Omdurman with barely a scratch.

Gertrude once said that Mrs Reddish preserved his best suit in her wardrobe, but the girl is prone to exaggeration. Besides, a woman of Mrs Reddish's straitened circumstances is far more likely to have taken every saleable shirt and shirt-collar to Uncle and refrained from redeeming the pledge. Reduced to taking in lodgers, her only recourse is to make our stay as disagreeable as possible.

'I wish she would serve it in a rack,' sighs Edna. 'A plate is so unrefined.'

I take the topmost piece and smear it carefully with marmalade. The table is so small that we are required to engage in a strange ballet whereby we take it in turns to lift spoon to mouth, or else knock elbows and risk spilling food on to our skirts.

'I don't know how you do it,' growls Gertrude, grabbing a slice and waving it at me. 'You behave as if it were edible.' She neglects to apply the jam as carefully as I do and the toast flies into pieces at the press of the knife. 'Oh, bother it all,' she gasps, glaring at me.

They watch with something perilously close to amazement as I polish off porridge, egg and toast. I do not care what they think of me. Nor do I care about the parlous state of Mrs Reddish's cooking. Each gristly lump of boiled mutton represents a delicious step away from my family, from Gnome, from the awful bondage of that time. I would not trade a single mouthful.

My lodgings, cheap by any standards, are all that any of us can afford and we know it. On the occasional evening, having no one better with whom to share it, we take ourselves to the nearest Hall of Varieties. Gertrude grumbles at the acts in much the same way as she does our meals. I daresay Miss Langtry herself could do a turn and Gertrude would find fault with her diamonds. Not that I claim to be sparkling company. I stretch my face into a simulacrum of a smile, forever aware of a barrier between myself and the amusements. It does not matter. I am resigned to wariness in the company of others.

I shrug and crunch my toast, reminding myself that charcoal is good for the digestion. Mrs Reddish returns, spiriting away the plate before I have the chance to gobble the last slice. Gertrude and Edna shove back their chairs. They primp before the glass hanging over the sideboard, shouldering each other out of the way as they affix their hats.

'Some of us have work to go to,' sniffs Gertrude, pulling on her gloves.

I take a slurp of bitter tea. Mrs Reddish snatches the cup from my hand and bangs it on to the tray. Fortunately, it is made of sturdy stuff and remains in one piece.

'Thank you for breakfast, Mrs Reddish,' I say, dusting crumbs from my lap.

She ignores me and stomps into the kitchen. I draw on my own gloves and pin my hat in place, stooping slightly to see my face in a mirror positioned at a height suitable for women of regular height. Over my shoulder I see a reflection of scuffed wallpaper: a room unloved and undecorated over the long years since her husband's death. If she were a little less disagreeable, I might feel more compassion for her situation.

The outer door crashes as Gertrude and Edna make their exit. I hurry after them, closing the door quietly, glad that we are not in the same employ. Sharing a table is sufficient companionship. Besides, I relish my daily constitutional to the Telegraph Office

I feel especially uplifted this morning. This is no red-letter day yet my steps have a particular bounce to them. I put it down to the clemency of spring sunshine, and that I am

175

celebrating six months in my new post at the finest telegraph exchange in the north of England. I proceed swiftly, taking breath after bracing breath.

Though barely a mile from Hulme, I may as well inhabit a different continent. I revel in each grimy brick, each carved pediment, each Gothic furbelow. I care not one jot that my innards are tarnished as black as the walls that rise around me. These streets are mine and I love them with a jealous passion.

Manchester music rings in my ears: the squeal of trams and shouts of wagon-drivers; the slamming of doors and clash of plates from the cafés; the roar of newspaper-sellers; the percussion of clogs sparking stars from the pavement; the halloas and hail-fellows of a thousand folk at the beginning of the day's labour, still brand spanking new.

I consider my life and how I hold its reins since I kicked the dust of The Comet from my heels. I miss my grandmother, Arthur, even my mother, although I'd cut out my tongue before admitting it. Keeping Gnome down has become a fine art. So long as I keep a pin beside me at all times and engage in the prophylactic measure of piercing my thigh before permitting myself to sleep, all is well. The scars heal by morning, generally speaking. I'm hardly likely to remove my drawers in anyone's presence, so there is no reason to concern myself over the constellation of wounds that sprinkle the lower half of my body.

I am independent. I have an income of my own. I have my life anew, gifted me when I thought I had lost all. I roll the words in my mouth, sweet as a caramel, and laugh out loud with the keen, sharp joy of it. I don't care who hears me. Let them look. Let them stare. I wear pride and happiness as unashamedly as the collars on my shirts. I've never had so much as a whiff of champagne, but imagine this is what it must be like: the bubbling exhilaration, the heady bliss. I'm so skittish I leap the puddles from last night's rain. No more counting the cracks between the flagstones, eyes downcast.

I dash up the steps of the Manchester Telegraph Company, hang my hat and jacket in the ladies' cloakroom and bid Mr Pryor the supervisor a hearty good morning. He peers over his spectacles and replies in a cursory fashion. I sail past without the slightest dent in my good humour and take my position.

'You'll have to put up with me today,' chirps Mr Heywood as soon as I am seated. 'Miss Reynolds has been brought down by a fearful head cold. We have been thrust into each other's company.'

I grunt a swift greeting and busy myself, arranging the cables in readiness for the first calls. I hope Miss Reynolds hasn't passed her infernal germs on to me. Gnome is more restive whenever I take ill. I touch the brooch at my throat, for luck. Mr Heywood drapes himself over the arm of his chair in a decorative fashion.

'Not even a good morning for your comrade-in-arms, Miss Latchford?' he trills. 'To think how long I have waited to be at the side of such a sublime conversationalist. Yes, I have been in a veritable passion.'

I ignore the sarcasm. I will not permit him to vex me. I am well used to Mr Heywood's silliness; we all are. The girls at the exchange make a pet of him, treating him like a helpless child rather than a full-grown man. I tolerate none of it. Women get precious little coddling from the moment we leave the womb and I see no reason why he should not pull his weight like the rest of us. My silence does not put him off: rather, it serves to increase his overtures.

'Never has a being suffered as I do.' He wipes his hand across his brow and exhales in an overstated fashion. 'Your handkerchief, dipped in lavender water and pressed to my burning brow, hmm?'

'I have no idea to what you are referring,' I respond tartly, rearranging the already perfectly arranged cables.

'I have the worst headache in the history of the world,' he moans. 'Have pity on me, dear heart. Succour me.'

'I shall do no such thing. And certainly not while you insist on calling me silly names.'

'I knew I could rely on your good nature,' he continues, ignoring my rebuff.

'Mr Heywood,' I say in a tone frigid enough to form icicles on a pot of tea. 'You're not one-quarter as sick as you make out.'

He pouts. 'Dash it all. I feel as rotten as I say, honestly I do.'

I sniff and turn away, awaiting the arrival of Miss Edwards. She might defuse some of Mr Heywood's inanity. She enters, four minutes late as is her habit, and strolls across the floor with considered elegance, taking no notice of Mr Pryor's pointed examination of his pocket watch.

She seats herself to my left and lifts her hand to unplug one of the higher pegs on her station with a relaxed grace that borders but does not quite stray into the languid. The curls over her forehead have been set in place by an artful hand and I am pretty sure that no strand will dare work its way loose during the course of the day. Her skin is so smooth and lacking in blotches that I wonder whether she removes it at night to press, steam and starch it. I chide myself for the unkind thought. She tosses her head and releases an aroma of rose petals, bestowing a smile that disarms me completely.

'Good morning, Miss Latchford,' she breathes.

I understand why foolish songs talk about hearts stopping. Her face seems entirely composed of cream. Mr Heywood sprawls across my board.

'Ollie,' he drawls. 'Miss Edie is being such a frightful bore. Be a dear and—'

'My name is Miss Edwards,' she replies sweetly. 'Olivia Edwards, if you would be so kind.'

'My dearest Ollie-vee-ar Ed-waards,' he says, dragging out the syllables. 'Would you be so kind – Oh, fiddlesticks. I've clean forgot what I was about to ask.'

I give the plug sockets my entire attention and pray for a call to come through, to no avail.

'Edie!' he shrills. 'What was I going to ask our precious companion?'

'I have not a glimmer of a notion,' I say, glaring at the board. 'And my name is Miss Latchford.'

'But, Edie—'

At that moment my prayer is answered and a call comes through. I take inspiration from Miss Edwards and move my hands slowly, hoping to delay Mr Heywood talking to me. I find the movement rather pleasing and accomplish my task just as quickly with less agitation. Perhaps Miss Edwards is cleverer than I thought.

'You two are the dullest creatures to walk this earth,' sulks Mr Heywood. 'You realise that I shall now be forced to do some work. It is too tiresome.'

His fingers fly across the board, connecting and disconnecting calls, answering queries politely and efficiently. However giddy in private, in his tasks he is beyond reproach, and I know this to be the prime reason he has not been served with his notice before now.

Mr Pryor strides up and down the carpet behind us, scanning the rows of operators for imperfection of posture or slackening-off of labour. I sense every spine straighten, each word enunciated with great care. After a few parade inspections, he takes up his customary posture at the desk, which stands like a pulpit in the centre of the room. There's the crackle of a lucifer as he lights a cigar.

'Miss Strutt?' he enquires of the floorwalker, puffing away.

'Mr Pryor, sir?'

'All running smoothly?'

'Smoothly, sir.'

I concentrate on my board. Much as I prefer the aroma of cigar smoke to that of cigarettes, it is overwhelming at times. Today is one of those occasions.

'Tip top,' says Mr Pryor, shuffling his feet.

'There is a rustle of paper: sheets of foolscap being arranged in a neat pile. Mr Heywood tilts his head and eyes the clock on the gable wall. He glances at me and raises his eyebrows daringly. Forty-three minutes past eight. As if on cue, Mr Pryor's watch-chain tinkles as he draws it from his waistcoat pocket. He snaps open the case and taps it with his fingernail.

'Goodness,' he blusters. 'Is that the time?' He clears his throat when no response is forthcoming from Miss Strutt. 'Dash it all, so it is. I have important business to attend to, Miss Strutt.'

'Important, Mr Pryor,' she replies, with the skill of one used to making her questions sound like statements.

There is a clumping of boots, the opening and swift closure of the door. Though he takes the greater part of his cigar staleness with him, the remnant hangs on the air like a fusty shawl. Wafting her hand before her nose, Miss Strutt grasps the window-cord, gives it a brisk tug and the shutter slaps open. A few drops of rain fall, but they are from a previous shower that collected on the pane. The outdoors gusts in, scented with horse manure and soot.

'Much better,' she declares. 'Refreshing.'

'Yes, Miss Strutt,' we reply in chorus.

Mr Heywood leans into my ear. 'The lazy blighter stayed

forty-six minutes!' he hisses. 'He's never bunked off so fast. I believe we should celebrate. Cat's away, mice shall play, etcetera.'

I pull a face and he falls quiet. The next few hours proceed without further incident or amusement and I am annoyed to notice that I miss Mr Heywood's banter. At the morning break he disappears for five minutes and reappears with a tray of iced lemon buns, enough for one half each. My colleagues fall upon them like starved urchins.

'Halves, Guy?' pipes Miss Atherton between mouthfuls. 'Hardly enough to keep body and soul together.'

She slaps a hand to her bosom and it wobbles beneath her blouse. They are good people and I wish I had their ease with witty camaraderie. I remind myself that friendship is a luxury I am not permitted and certainly not with a talkative gadfly such as Mr Heywood. Not that he is in need of any intimacy I may offer, thronged as he is with acquaintances.

'It's a trifle,' he says in answer to the thanks heaped upon him. 'A mere bagatelle. It pleases me to see you lot wolfing them down. No, I won't have one myself. What, deprive you? Icing brings me out in pimples and one has to think of one's complexion. Unlike the great Queen of Egypt, age *does* wither me.' He takes a breath and sings, 'Vaseline loves me, this I know; because the poster tells me so.'

'Mr Heywood,' says Miss Strutt, cracks audible in her pronunciation of his name.

'I'm sorry, Miss Strutt. I know. A gentleman shouldn't use up his wife's cold cream. Grounds for divorce, I shouldn't wonder. Cruel and unusual treatment and all that.'

Miss Strutt sniffs. Mr Heywood always seems able to ascertain how far he can stray on to the thin ice of impudence before falling through into offence. He turns his butterfly attention to me.

'Have half a bun, Miss Latchford, do.'

'I am not hungry,' I say primly.

I expect a smart retort about him not being the only one in peril of pimples, but he lowers his voice to a hum meant for my ears.

'That is a pity. It will go to waste.'

'Perhaps we could share it,' I say, feeling mean-hearted all of a sudden. 'Hardly enough to nourish a blot upon one's countenance.'

He holds my gaze. His eyes are such a pale blue as to be almost clear; his brow high, nose delicate as a girl's. I feel lumpen beside him. Then again, I feel thus when compared to most individuals. He slices the half-bun. It is topped with a quarter-inch of yellow sugar-icing.

'Thank you,' he says softly.

The snowy dough collapses on my tongue. I have a sensation that, like Penelope, I have been enticed into eating the pomegranate seeds that consigned her to Hades.

'I hope you are not planning on imprisoning me in the Underworld for six months,' I remark.

His expression shifts as he picks up the thread of my thought. 'Only an evening or two,' he says, and smiles. 'Hades does have the best entertainments, after all.'

Lunchtime finds us walking through the bevelled-glass doors together.

'We shall have to stop these romantic liaisons, my angel,' he says, tipping his boater.

'Romantic?' I scoff. 'The very idea. I have errands to run.'

'Don't be a prig. We've shared an office for an age. Why not share half an hour?' He cups my elbow.

'Mr Heywood,' I say, glancing sternly at his hand.

It is a withering look, designed to shrivel him to a crisp. He slides his arm through mine, completely unshrivelled.

'You are always in such a tearing rush, Miss Latchford. If one were prone to suspicions, one might hazard that you wish to avoid me.'

'Perhaps I am,' I reply.

He clutches his breast. 'Wounded, Edie!' he cheeps. 'I may call you Edie, mayn't I?'

'You may not, Mr Heywood.'

'I'm so glad,' he rambles. 'Edie is the prettiest name.'

We fall into a comfortable stroll. My soul relents. For all his affectation, he is a fellow being, carrying a shield to protect his own secrets and dreams. His differ to mine, undoubtedly. I should make more effort to be kind.

'I believe this is the point I should cry out for the assistance of a policeman,' I say with greater affability.

'Surely you cannot deny a chap as inconsequential as myself the pleasure of being seen in your fair company for the space of thirty minutes.'

'I am hardly fair, Mr Heywood. I overtop you by three inches.'

'Two.' He looks me square in the face. 'Besides, there are plenty who would find you handsome.'

He speaks with such unexpected sincerity that it takes the wind out of my sails.

'Well,' I say. 'Mr Heywood, you are the very end.'

'I am relieved. My reputation would be in tatters if I steered too close to the shores of sensible behaviour. And please, call me Guy.' We head through the lunchtime crowds towards the corner of Market Street. 'Now. You simply must tell me all about yourself.'

'I certainly must not.'

He cocks an eyebrow. 'No matter. I have already surmised a fair deal through close observation, dear girl.' My fears surface, vile as eels. 'Oh, good Lord,' he exclaims. 'You look like you've seen a ghost. Here. Sit, sit.'

183

'That is not necessary,' I wheeze.

'It is, it is. I'm most fearfully sorry. I have this awful habit of offending those with whom I wish to become acquainted.'

'It is nothing.' I cling to his arm more tightly than is entirely becoming.

'Let us engage in less perilous intercourse. Look, here is a display of gloves. Young females have a particular passion for gloves.'

'So I have heard,' I gasp.

He pats my hand. Mercifully, he does not press me for explanations. He points at the lowering sky. 'Now, let us take the clouds,' he says. 'There are plenty of them in this fine city. Just think: if a man could throw a hook skywards, drag them down and spin them into cloud-cloth, we should have a new industry with which to take over the world, or at least a new corner of it.'

'You are very entertaining, Mr Heywood,' I say, gathering my breath. 'Though it escapes me why you choose my company.'

'Because we would make good friends, would we not?'

'I hardly think one stroll along Market Street warrants such an assertion.'

'Pish and tosh. We are clearly destined to be close as bugs in a rug. Now that I have enticed you from your enchanted tower, perhaps I can persuade you to spend an evening in my company. I do hope you have no dragons. I am no use at fending off fearsome beasts. You will have to do the fending.' He gives me a sidelong glance. 'Yes, you would look rather fine with spear and shield. A veritable Penthesilea. I know a cohort of Amazons who would be delighted to meet you.'

'Good heavens, Mr Heywood. Where do you come up with such nonsense? You have an inexhaustible supply.'

'Guy, please.'

'Very well, Guy,' I say. 'I tolerate your antics all day, for I am paid to do so. But you seem mightily confident that I should want to spend my leisure time in your company, not to mention a Tuesday evening.'

'But it is precisely what you do wish to do, isn't it?'

I could pretend to mishear. But hear I do and, gallingly, he speaks the truth. Whatever my declarations to the contrary, I ache for friendship closer than the watery acquaintance I have with Gertrude and Edna. My spiky nature is that of the hedgehog, a need for protection rather than a desire for lone-liness. I ask myself how many years I am prepared to live with this unhappiness, afraid to turn my face to the sun of compan-ionship. Perhaps fate has thrown Guy into my path. Perhaps it is time to seize the day.

'Yes,' I say, with an impulsiveness that scares and excites me. 'Yes, I should like that.'

'You would?' he says, sounding so startled I wonder if he's been pulling my leg and doesn't want to spend the evening with me at all. I cringe that I have shown myself to be so needy. But he beams from ear to ear: a true smile, not the foppish lip-curling employed at the office. 'How marvellous! We shall have a grand time. There's a sparkle about you today, my dear. One shudders to admit it, but oft-times I've deemed you a wet lettuce. I'm delighted to be proved wrong.'

'I shall take that as a compliment,' I say dryly.

'And so you should. I shall meet you by the statue of Cromwell at eight o'clock. Don't wear your best shoes,' he adds mischie-vously.

There is a pause.

He looks up at the clock above Lewis's. 'Time flies like an arrow. We have exhausted our half-hour and must now return.'

We hurry back. I almost run, but am not yet ready for such unruly behaviour. I am to be so, far sooner than expected.

After supper, a meat stew of questionable origin, I regard myself in the mirror. For the first time in my life, I am about to step out with a young man. I wonder if Mr Heywood regards me as a sweetheart. He did not intimate anything of the sort, but it is quite possible that this is courtship and I am engaging in it without realising. I am enough of an idiot to do so.

I attack my hair with the brush, endeavouring to tame its bush into something resembling the gleaming sheaf of flax the newspaper advertisement promised. I survey my feelings. I have none, other than a sensation of warm companionship. I am not sure if I want Guy – or any other, for that matter – for a beau. However, I am twenty-two. Perhaps it is time. After all, it is the mark of a woman to have admirers even if she does not precisely want their attention.

My thoughts circle. He gives no impression of being a cad. On the contrary, I don't think he'd notice if I dyed my hair green and wore carrots on my hat. He seems – I search for a suitable word – harmless. I wonder if harmless might be just what I need, having had enough disruption to last a lifetime.

I look at my fist, gripping the handle of the brush so tightly that the knuckles show white against the ebony. A quiver ripples through my being and for one terrible moment I think Gnome is peering over my shoulder. I stick out my tongue at my reflection. I don't know what's got into me. I never let myself be tempted into friendship at any previous place of employment. I was the ghost who drifted in and out of my work-mates' days and did not feel the loss of it, not truly, not until today.

I finish my toilet hastily, remembering to pin my brooch

186

upon the lapel. There will be no funny business with Gnome, tonight of all nights. I blow myself a kiss in the mirror and dash to the rendezvous so precipitously I am early and have to hide in the cathedral porch for ten minutes. The last thing I want is to stand below Cromwell and draw the attention of unsavoury gentlemen. Mr Heywood arrives one minute after eight.

'You look dashed nice,' he says. 'A proper peach.'

He speaks as one who has rehearsed the best way to open a conversation with a young lady. It is most unlike his habitual flippancy. I slip my arm through his and smile. He turns the brim of his boater in his fingers.

'I shan't bite,' I say, pointing at the nervous working of his hands.

'Oh,' he says, and places his hat upon his head. 'The devil take it, Edie. I fear you may hate me after tonight and never speak to me again.'

'What an odd thing to say. Why ever should I do that?'

'Time will tell,' he mutters. 'Well then. Unto the breach, dear friends. Best foot forward.'

'Where are you taking me?' I say, hoping we may be headed for Lewis's, for there is a funfair advertised.

'A little place I know. You'll find it in no Bradshaw's.'

'Oh,' I reply, trying not to sound too disappointed.

His eyes glitter. 'Jolly good! I knew you'd agree. It's beastly, of course. But it is secluded, away from the prying eyes of His Majesty's finest.'

'I do hope you are not leading me into sin,' I say playfully. 'If you kiss me, I shall have to hit you with my handbag.'

'Kiss you?' he says, as though I've suggested we jump into the Ship Canal. 'Why on earth would such an outlandish notion pop into your head?'

My friskiness evaporates instantly. 'Don't you want to?' I ask. There is self-pity in my voice, which I do not like one bit.

'No, I do not, and you'd best put any of that flapdoodle out of your mind.' He surveys me at arm's length. 'Besides,' he continues. 'I didn't think you were the sort to want such a thing of me.'

'Isn't it what ladies and gentlemen do?'

'Not this gentleman. I am temperamentally unsuited, you might say.' He swings his walking stick.

'Clearly I am frightfully ugly,' I mumble, overcome with mortification. 'You can say it. Plenty have.'

'You do talk a lot of rot, Edie. Here it is, plain as I can make it. No doubt your mama harangued you with dire warnings of being led astray by wicked men. That won't happen with me. I do apologise. I am not fearfully interested in girls.'

'You aren't?'

'No. As for the two of us engaging in spooning,' he says, raising his eyebrow, 'I don't believe you want that for one moment, either.'

I examine my heart thoroughly. He is right, though I am not entirely sure why. I am humiliated yet thankful at the same time. It is most perplexing.

'No,' I say, slowly. 'I don't believe I do. It is more the sensation that I *ought* to.'

'Quite. How easy it is to be duped by mere convention.'

'Isn't it the done thing?'

He squeezes my arm. 'I'm sure it is. But not for folk like us.'

'Like us?'

'I think you have a good idea what I am talking about.' I stare at him. He sighs and rolls his eyes. 'You are jolly foolish. It's blasted obvious we're two of a kind.'

My heart drops into my boots. No one knows what I am.

No one, other than Ma and Nana. Unless Gnome has been keeping company with Guy. But Gnome can't . . .

'By the look on your face you know exactly what I mean.'

'I know no such thing.'

'Don't worry,' he says with surprising tenderness. 'It is a frightening thing to live with. Always in fear of discovery: some ghastly piece of tittle-tattle that will have you bundled into the back of a police wagon; some regrettable kiss given in a moment of drunken, hopeful abandon, only to find yourself in the gutter with a black eye.'

I gape. He seems to know.

'But how—'

He gives me a warm smile. At last it dawns on me what he is talking about and why we are so well suited in his eye. His attraction is for his own sex. I ought to be shocked. I should thrust out an accusing finger and call down the punishment of the Lord for his sinful habits. How can I? More to the point, why would I do that to someone who is, if not the same, then certainly a brother in strangeness?

He sees me not as a lover but as a sister. I imagine him on one knee, declaring his adoration and sigh at the silly picture it presents. My heart knows the truth: I do not desire him, nor he, me. It is a relief.

'Come,' he says. 'Trust me. All will be revealed.'

We scurry along Deansgate and come to halt at the top of a flight of steps I'd have walked past otherwise. He skips down while I stay precisely where I am.

'Where on earth are you taking me?' I say in a tone that reminds me uncomfortably of Gertrude. 'There's nothing down there but old newspapers.'

'*Au contraire, mon petit choux,*' he warbles and proceeds to rap upon the door, a hotchpotch of long and short knocks.

It looks as if it hasn't opened in an age, but open it does: a half-inch that unleashes a blade of light into the filthy stairwell. Guy whispers through the slot and the door swings back. I expect the hinges to shriek, but all is oiled silence. He looks up at me.

'Are you going to stay there all night? Sesame has opened.'

I pick my way through the rubbish, trailing my skirt in goodness knows what foulness, and step within.

A long, low-ceilinged room presents itself: narrow and dry, with a smell of long-gone cheeses. In contrast to the entrance, all is swept perfectly clean. At regular intervals are beer barrels set upright for use as tables. Candles upon saucers cast a cheerful glow. The place is crowded with men and women in their day clothes, chattering in low voices. Young chaps weave through the throng, carrying trays of sandwiches.

'What is this place?' I whisper. 'I didn't know it existed.'

'Few do. Skittles by day, mollies by night,' declares Guy. 'What fun. Everyone is here, stuffing their faces with supper and remarking on the smart new pair.'

'Who?'

'Us, you silly goose.'

'Goodness me.'

'Goodness? I hope not. There's no sport in goodness,' he quips.

A slender youth waves a plate of tiny sandwiches under Guy's nose.

'Angel!' crows Guy, and pecks the air to each side of the youth's head. 'I'm famished. I must have sustenance or expire.' He slaps a sixpence on to the platter and scoops up a handful. 'Ham or cheese?' he asks, holding them in my direction.

I shake my head politely. Guy swallows his in a mouthful and proceeds to lick crumbs from his fingers, rather noisily.

'Now that I have satisfied the needs of the belly-god, I have a prodigious hunger for gossip. Have you nothing with which to whet my appetite?'

'I am afraid not.'

'I shall not despair of you yet. I see I shall have to provide the entertainment for this evening.' Another fellow swings by, with a basket of bottles. 'What have we here. Ambrosia? Nectar drawn from the Fountain of Youth?'

'Beer or lemonade,' comes the answer.

'Alas and alack,' Guy sighs. 'Beer for me. How about you, Edie?'

I plump for lemonade. I thumb down the marble and take a sip, but am so distracted by my surroundings that it spills on to my blouse.

'You're as jumpy as a cat on Mischief Night,' says Guy, drawing out an enormous handkerchief and pressing it to my breasts in a manner that would be unseemly in any other situation. 'Lord, there's nothing to you,' he adds. 'I've felt bigger titties on a budgerigar.'

'Guy!'

'Oh stow it, Edie. Loosen your stays, for tomorrow we die,' he declares, waving his arm theatrically. 'Of boredom. Those about to be merry, I salute you.'

His hair, loosened from its carapace of brilliantine, flops over one eyebrow. I cannot help feeling that I am amongst children who, having escaped a dull lesson with a harsh master, have raced from the school gate to this underground haven and are celebrating their freedom. I stand amongst them as stolid as a fence post. Any moment someone will toss his coat over my head and use me as a hat-stand.

'Why ever do you bother with me, Guy?' I say. 'Truly. I am not vying for pitying reassurances.'

'Good, for I shall not give them.'

I wave my hand. 'We are surrounded by sparkling individuals. Yet you choose to take the arm of this Aunt Sally. Why?'

'Because you are family,' he says quite seriously. 'Family sticks together and strives together.'

A young man in a butcher's apron far too big for him thrusts another bottle of beer into Guy's hand.

'Bless you, darling,' he says. The lad grins and skips away. 'We were all new once,' he continues after a long swig.

Whatever he means, it strikes a resonant chord. Amongst this odd crowd, I feel more at home than I thought possible. I tilt the lemonade bottle to my lips and this time I do not spill a drop.

'Let me show you to my friends. Come; it would please me.'

Guy takes my hand and steers me through the crowd, bestowing smiles and embraces every few steps. He introduces me to so many folk along the way that the names and faces blur. Just when I think I can remember no more, Guy taps a finely dressed woman on the shoulder. She turns and I come face-to-face with the enchanting suffragette I saw at All Saints.

'Miss Edie Latchford,' says Guy. 'Let me introduce you to Miss Abigail Hargreaves. I am all a-quiver for the two of you to become acquainted. Two of my absolute dearest friends.'

'We have already met,' says Miss Hargreaves, inclining her head in polite greeting.

'Dash it all,' says Guy. 'That's my entire evening drained of fun. I shall never live down the ignominy. Abigail, you are a ghastly spoilsport.'

'You are too kind, Miss Hargreaves,' I stutter. 'We met at a rally, some time ago. I was one of many. Hardly worth the recollection.'

'False modesty does not become you,' chirps Guy, wagging his finger. 'You are unforgettable, Edie dear.'

'For once, Guy is correct,' says Miss Hargreaves with a pleasant smile. 'I remember the occasion well.'

'You do?'

'Indeed,' she replies with every indication of sincerity.

Guy looks from one of us to the other and rubs his hands. 'Oh! How I adore being matchmaker.'

I stare at my boots.

'Guy,' says Miss Hargreaves. 'Put a sock in it. You are terrifying the poor girl. Permit us to conduct a conversation in peace. If you insist on hovering, I shall be forced to swat you with my umbrella.'

'Wounded, darling, wounded!' he cries. He pats his shirt, an expression of mock-terror creeping over his features. After a bout of flapping, he brightens. 'Ah, there it is. Thought I'd lost the bally thing.'

'I'm surprised you can locate it,' Miss Hargreaves continues. 'A proper heartless Harry. Hop it.'

They smile at each other and I wonder what it feels like to have a friend with whom one can chaff so gaily. She raises her eyebrow and he dances away.

'Off to torment some other poor soul. Now,' she says, turning kind eyes to me. 'Let us find a quiet spot.'

She indicates a vacant barrel under the curve of the vaulted ceiling. We stand, shoulders almost touching. I watch Guy place his arm around a gentleman of burly proportions. They draw closer and their mouths find each other. I do not experience the slightest stirring of disapproval. Observing them feels like the answer to a question I was not aware I'd asked. I sip my lemonade.

'I was not dissembling, Miss Hargreaves,' I say between gulps. 'I am truly surprised you recall our meeting.'

193

'You are a striking creature.'

'That's one way of putting it,' I say with a laugh. 'I did not expect to meet you here.'

'I hope you are not disappointed. What brings you to our hidey-hole?'

'Guy invited me.'

'The two of you seem thick as thieves. How do you know him?'

'We work together at the Telegraph Office on Cross Street. He's a great favourite of the ladies there.'

She raises an eyebrow. 'I can imagine.'

'Is he really heartless?' I ask.

'Guy? Not a bit of it. Soft as they come. That sharp humour is all for show. A man could snap him like a pencil, if he chose. Some have so chosen.' She takes a draught of ginger beer. 'Sweet on him, are you?'

'Me?' He and his friend are dancing now, cheek pressed to cheek. 'Not at all.'

'Good. Plenty of girls make that mistake.'

'Miss Hargreaves, I am aware – I know about him. About this.' I indicate the brick arch above my head, the dusty plaster, the huddle of souls. 'I have not wandered in here after taking a wrong turn in the glove department of Lewis's.'

She laughs. 'Dear Miss Latchford. Taking into account that we find ourselves in a place so far removed from convention, shall we dispense with formality? Do call me Abigail. Would you permit me to call you Edie?'

'With great pleasure.'

In the comfortable pause two women draw alongside and hail Abigail as an old friend. One wears a skirt split by a deep pleat down the centre which gives it the appearance of broad-legged pantaloons; an unintended comic effect, or so I surmise from her unsmiling demeanour. She clasps her hands behind her back, and presses her lips together with such determination that her mouth is reduced to a line scratched across her face.

Her companion could not be a greater contrast: a kitten of a girl with a mouth so full and red it appears painted on. Her blouse froths with lace and is nipped in at the middle to show off a diminutive waist. I picture her swaying down the street and every eye – male or female – drawn to her, like a child's toy on a string. She extends a spotless crochet glove.

'Craythorne. Henrietta Craythorne. And you are?'

'Latchford,' I say. Her handshake is as limp as bread in milk. 'Edie Latchford.'

'Ah,' she purrs. 'How pretty.'

Her severe companion snorts and grasps my hand when Miss Craythorne has finished with it.

'Mabel,' she says, pumping my arm up and down. 'Glad to meet you. You're not a Temperance Terror, are you?' she says, eyeing my cordial.

'No.'

'Damned good thing too. Self-denial. Bloody nonsense. Pass this way but once. Jug of wine, loaf of bread – and thou.'

'In the wilderness,' I say quietly, picking up the thread.

Mabel laughs, a brisk sound that snaps like a twig when she is done with it. 'Ha! My point precisely. This earth. Bloody wilderness. Present company, et cetera. Have a glass of beer.'

'My landlady has the olfactory sense of a bloodhound.'

She laughs with greater gusto. 'Drink a beer. Smoke a cigarette after. She'll give you the Dickens for the latter. Major crime obfuscated by minor misdemeanour. Freedom.'

'Mabel, you are a devious beast,' says Abigail.

'As accused,' she replies.

She rocks backwards and forwards on her heels, grinning

mischievously. I reflect how easily I fell into error. I assumed that her stern attire would betoken stern behaviour. I could not have been more wrong.

'Poor little Edie,' drawls Miss Craythorne. 'We must do our utmost to protect you from Mabel's corrupting ways.'

'You will not find me that easily swayed.'

I regard the cat-like Miss Craythorne. Although her face bears the perfect facsimile of a smile, there is something lacking. The way she looks at Mabel suggests she'd like to consume her, skirt and all. I am proceeding into a new land, one wherein I must tread with great care, as though walking upon eggshells.

A memory returns with unusual clarity: sitting at the kitchen table and watching Nana pierce an egg with a sewing needle, first one end and then the other. She places her lips to one of the holes and blows the contents into a bowl. She helps me paint the empty shell for Easter; yes, it is for Easter. She scrambles the egg and we share it with a little piece of toast. *You see,* she says. *You can make an omelette without breaking eggs. Everything has its limits, even proverbs.*

'Everything has its what now?' Mabel's voice brings me back into the room in a galloping rush.

'I'm sorry. I was a fearfully long way off.'

'We should be the ones to apologise,' hums Miss Craythorne. 'We fatigue you.'

'Rot,' says Mabel. 'Sheathe your claws.'

'Well!' harrumphs Miss Craythorne.

'Nothing wrong with being a dreamer,' says Abigail and I am grateful for the warmth in her eyes.

'Feet firmly planted. That's what a woman needs,' says Mabel. 'Never more so than today.'

Their talk drifts on its current until it tangles in the weeds of Austria, the Balkans, Russia and the rumour of war. People talk of little else, even here. After a while, Miss Craythorne affects tiredness and Mabel squires her away. There is a pause. I wait for Miss Hargreaves to make her own excuses. She drains her bottle. Now, I think, she will go. My spirits droop.

'Do you still visit the Museum?' she asks.

'Yes,' I reply, surprised that she remembers.

'And the Art Gallery?'

'Oh! I have a passion for the place,' I say, louder than I wish, and blush.

'I do, also. Would you care to accompany me one afternoon?'

I gape. 'Me?'

'Unless you are too busy.'

I see shyness writ upon her features. How self-absorbed to regard myself the only creature on this earth to feel timidity.

'I should love to,' I say. 'Next Saturday afternoon? I finish work at one o'clock.'

'Saturday. Perfect. I shall be there.'

She leans forwards, brushes her mouth against the side of my face, turns and moves away. I watch her elegant departure, heart pounding. The thought of spending more time in her company stirs a maelstrom of contradictory sensations. Guy appears at my side.

'Did you enjoy your dance?' I say.

'Hugely,' he beams. 'Decent cove. A jobber on the *Guardian*. Sets type. Good with his hands.' He giggles. 'Less about me. You look like the cat that got the cream.'

'Maybe I have,' I reply.

'I knew it!' he crows. 'There's hope for you yet.'

I sigh. 'It's late. I really ought to go.'

'Darling, I beseech you. Five minutes more. There's always a song at this hour.'

As if on cue, there is a squeaking of barrels and chairs being shoved aside at the far end of the tunnel. Heralded by applause, half a dozen lads and lasses parade into the space.

'My babies!' breathes Guy. 'Forgive me. I become unbearably maternal when it comes to these dear creatures. It is too discomfiting for words.'

'Your secret is safe with me,' I whisper back. 'Mind you, I wouldn't know a motherly sentiment if I tripped over it in broad daylight.'

He opens his mouth to contradict me. We are shushed as the song commences, a jingoistic piece of fluff about Toppling the Turban of Tarquin the Terrible Turk. It is currently the rage and I've seen it performed on one of my evenings with Gertrude and Edna, the only observable difference being that tonight women wear the tin hats and army fatigues and the Turkish parts are taken by pretty lads titivated to the nines in ballooning trousers, wafting veils and dollops of greasepaint.

We join in the chorus. It is of necessity a cappella, but our lusty clapping means that one barely remarks on the lack of orchestral accompaniment. To saucy shrieks and whistles, the youths scamper in confused circles, waggling their hands and squealing, pursued by the soldiers who prod their backsides with wooden rifles. One by one, turbans are knocked off like coconuts at a shy, to such a hullabaloo I can hardly hear myself think.

All is exuberance and high spirits, until a particularly rowdy shriek is followed by silence and the pounding of footsteps. Candles are blown out, bottles crash to my right and left.

'No!' growls Guy. 'A raid? Here? Tonight?'

Without a word, each pair of women detaches one from the other, each pair of men. In a slow but deliberate waltz they take fresh partners of the opposite sex. Guy clings to my arm as if I have taken on the properties of a life raft. Boots stamp.

A deep voice roars: 'Get back, you swine!'

Guy and I are shoved against the wall by a brace of policemen. One of them waves a lantern in front of my nose.

'Here's two,' he quacks. 'One's dressed like a tart.'

It takes far longer than it ought for me to realise I've been taken for a man. My heart sinks to my boots. The policeman sticks his face close to mine. His breath is old and sick, his teeth clogged with what looks like china clay. I turn aside. He grasps my chin.

'You're a pretty one. Paddy-whack, paddy-whack, I'd give *this* dog a bone,' he says, tilting my face and examining me. 'Smooth as a baby's arse. How old are you?'

'Twenty-two,' I say.

'And not a shadow of a beard? You look more like a girl.'

'I *am* a girl!' I exclaim. The ardour of my declaration arrests his fumbling.

'What?'

'I am a woman,' I insist, imploring any listening deity to make me look more feminine than ever before.

His companion, who has been watching the proceedings, chortles. 'It is and all. Can't you tell the difference? You've been in this job too long, my old mate.'

'Get away with you,' says my interrogator. 'It's a nancy like the rest of these shit-stabbers. Aren't you?' he growls.

Guy clears his throat. 'This is my fiancée, Miss Latchford,' he says in a voice deep as a mineshaft. I'd no idea he could appear so broad and muscular.

'You calling him *miss*? You disgust me, you filthy bugger.'

'Unhand her this instant,' Guy declares. His hand on mine trembles.

'I have never been so offended in all my life,' I twitter in a ladylike fashion.

The policeman hesitates. 'You . . .?' he splutters.

'Yes! If I'm a boy, what are these?'

I cup my meagre breasts, pushing them out to their furthest extent. The policeman's hand shoots forward and he grapples my bosom. I squeal in pain.

'By heck,' he hisses. 'They're bloody real.'

'I should say so!' I cry.

The discovery serves to confuse him, and confusion changes swiftly to anger.

'You little whore!' he barks, shoving me against the wall. 'You're worse than him. I ought to—'

'Now now,' says his companion. 'Sweet manners, chum. She's a posh one. You heard that voice, didn't you?'

My tormentor swallows heavily. He is not done yet, not by a long chalk. He peers around the room and his eye lights on the performers, who are receiving similar harsh treatment from his fellow lawmakers.

'What about them?' he says. 'All the costumes?'

'Haven't you ever been to rehearsals for the pantomime?' replies Guy.

'In March?'

'The best thespians start early. I shall send you some complimentary tickets. For the front row, of course.'

'You cheeky fucker,' the policeman grunts. He shoves his elbow into Guy's face. I hear a yelp, a crunch of bone and Guy collapses on to all fours. 'Down where you belong, you dog.'

I kneel at Guy's side. I glare at the brute and would do far more, but Guy grasps my arm, whispering *no*.

'I don't believe a word of your nonsense. We'll be back. Make sure you're not here when we do.'

With that, he and his comrades-in-arms leave, kicking over chairs and stoving in a few barrels, laughing as they do.

Guy insists on escorting me home, not that I have any intention of refusing. We pause at the tea-stand on the corner of Stott Street. I am trembling so violently I almost drop the cup. I have escaped with little more than my dignity bruised, but Guy looks a fright. A bruise is settling into his cheek and his collar is distinctly awry.

'Bit of rough trade, duck?' slurs a tattily dressed woman leaning against the counter.

'You could say that,' Guy replies.

'Your boater,' I say quietly.

'Gone the way of all flesh.' He touches his cheek experimentally and winces.

'It looked new.'

'No more lemon buns for a while, alas.'

'You are remarkably sanguine. It must have cost a week's wages.'

'Edie dear, we could have lost a great deal more.'

We drain our mugs and continue on our way to Rusholme with the tram-track as our guide. My mind trips and stumbles.

'How did that happen? Why?'

'We were given up. Some poor sap caught short in a public convenience, I shouldn't wonder. One can imagine the threats: *Betray your fellows or it's Strangeways for you.* I can't say as I blame the blighter. None of us would last two minutes in chokey.'

'We were doing no harm. We were making less noise than I've heard in a beerhouse. Far less.'

He chews his moustache. 'We were lucky. We didn't get thrown in the wagon. They didn't have a root and rummage up your skirt to be sure of your sex.'

'Guy!' I cry, shocked at the ghastly picture presented.

He squeezes my arm. 'I beg your pardon, Edie. Truly I do.

201

But it fills me with – oh, the bally unfairness of it all. I did not ask to be born the way I am.'

'I understand,' I say. 'I did not ask to be made the way I am, either.'

It does not matter that we are talking at cross-purposes. I am stranger than he could ever imagine, yet we are united as outlanders, both of us thrust far from regular society.

'Dash it all, Edie,' he blurts. 'I am sick of these hole-and-corner affairs. Skulking around in dusty skittle alleys no decent chap would take a lady to. I am an absolute rotter, inviting you out and then getting you into such a disagreeable scrape. I've blotted my copybook irretrievably.'

'Not at all. I was frightened, I'll admit.' I squeeze his arm, suffused with something that is not quite courage, although it leans in that direction.

'But. There is a but, isn't there?'

'Yes. I felt alive. Amongst . . .' I almost say *my own kind*, but that is an impossibility. '. . . like-minded creatures.'

'Bless you, dear heart. That is balm to a guilty conscience.'

I take a deep breath. 'Guy, I should be honoured to call you friend.'

We regard each other under the gaslight. I see myself as through his eyes: chest heaving, bright spots pinking my cheeks, hair disarrayed, and smiling broadly.

He grins, nursing his aching jaw. 'I think we may suit each other very well.'

He sticks out his hand. I grasp it and we shake in a wordless bargain. As his fingers close around mine I double over with a searing cramp in my belly.

'Edie! Whatever is the matter?'

I know what ails me only too well. I fumble with my lapel. 'A moment,' I gasp.

The brooch has gone. It must have been torn away in the melee. I grasp a hank of hair and give it an almighty tug, disguising the gesture by turning aside. The cramp recedes sufficiently to enable me to stand upright.

'I am well,' I lie. 'Quite restored.'

'Claptrap. You look awful, even by the standards of these unflattering street lamps.'

I stagger on. I can hardly take out my hat-pin and prick myself while we are together.

'I am almost at my door,' I spit through gritted teeth. 'Let me go on alone.'

'The very thought. You're dead on your feet.'

'I shall go faster on my own.'

'I won't hear of it. This is all my dashed fault.'

'Guy,' I growl, voice noticeably deeper. 'Go away. Now.'

His eyes widen. 'Well,' he says. 'I . . .'

He bows stiffly and is gone. I have no time to rue the unmannerly outburst. I slip into the dark mouth of a ginnel, yank out my hat-pin and shove it through my skirt, petticoats and all. The nausea retreats, taking Gnome with it. It is a brief respite. I take a few more steps only for swirling sickness to descend, a fog so thick I can barely see my hand in front of my face. I stab desperately, not caring if anyone is passing.

I proceed in a grisly hopscotch of stab, stagger, sickness. As I reach the door of my lodgings I hear the distant boom of the Town Hall clock sounding the three-quarter, of which hour I've no idea. All sense of time has deserted me. I turn the handle and breathe a sigh of relief. I have not been locked out.

I tumble into the hallway and into Mrs Reddish. Her face is plastered with cold cream and she is wearing a shabby dressing gown that gives her the air of a heap of laundry. I edge past.

She sniffs loudly. 'Do I detect drink, Miss Latchford?'

'No, Mrs Reddish.' I am seized with frantic inspiration. 'I am – It is my monthlies. I am proper laid out by them.'

Her face performs a turnabout from disapproval to sympathy. 'You poor lass,' she cries. 'How I suffer also. I could tell you some things!'

'Mrs Reddish,' I blurt. 'I have to—'

'Yes, yes! Of course.' She forces herself to glare. 'But don't be so late next time.'

'No, Mrs Reddish,' I whimper and crawl up the stairs.

I collapse on to the bed, body aching as though kicked by a mule, insides threatening to fall away. The rigors of the change are not one whit easier to bear because I know them of old.

I haul up my petticoats, stab my thigh, watch the drizzle of blood across pale skin. It's not enough to quell the distant thunder galloping closer, closer. I stab again. Not enough. For hours and hours I wrestle my dark angel. I shove him down; he rises. I shove him down; he rises again. I will not permit him to conquer me, not after all these years. I cannot.

At last I see a chink of light through the gap in the curtains. The day is my kingdom. I have made it through the night. I taste victory, let down my guard and it is my undoing. He rises in a towering wave and this time, however hard I drive in the spike, it is in vain. He is coming. His revenge will be terrible. I have failed.

GNOME
MARCH 1909

I come to, roaring like a lion.

I sit up and immediately have to lie down again. My head sways and the room sways with it. If I didn't know better, I'd swear she's been swigging gin. My stomach lurches at the nauseating smell of cabbage. Daylight stings my eyes. Daylight? It ought to be night-time. I'm encircled by dark green wallpaper, fat with flowers that have been vomited down the wall. A framed portrait of the old Queen glares disapprovingly above the fireplace.

What hell is this?

Wherever I am, it is not my room in The Comet. I groan, clap my hand over my eyes and pray for the heaving to abate. Everything's arse about face.

From downstairs comes the hammering of a gong and a roar of *breakfast!* It doesn't sound like Mam, although it's the sort of racket she's capable of. I raise myself gingerly, clutching my noggin. My slattern of a sister did not undress herself before getting into bed and I am trussed up in petticoats. I wrestle free with a satisfying sound of ripped stitches and hurl them to the floor. I swing my legs over the side of the mattress, and see the scars. My thighs are plastered with them, like I've been used as a dartboard. What has been going on? I take two steps and my legs buckle beneath me. I am flat on my face, weak as a kitten and not at all like the great cat of my dreams.

I hoist myself on to my elbows and her hair falls in a curtain around my face. When on earth did she grow it so long? The first thing I'll do is get a pair of shears and slice off the lot. The second thing, rather. The first thing is to find something to wear. I clamber to my feet, grasping the bed frame for support. Where are my blasted trousers?

I totter across the mean little rug, drag open squeaky drawer after squeaky drawer. I rifle through her clothes but find nothing of mine, not so much as a pocket handkerchief. Dizziness overwhelms me once more. I hang on to the drawer handle. Someone bangs on the door and I fair jump out of my skin.

'Edie? Are you well?' shouts a female, one I've never heard in my entire life.

'Don't come in!' I squeak, screwing my voice into a tight knot.

'You sound awful,' says a different woman, sounding strangely triumphant. There are two of them out there. 'Are you coming?' she adds.

Coming where? I wonder. I rack my brains for an intelligible answer. 'I'm on my way!' I pipe.

It seems to satisfy them, whoever they are, for the crump of footsteps sounds along the passageway. I wait a few moments, crack open the door and spot them at the head of the stairs, whispering and glancing in my direction. I shut it smartish and hold my breath. They galumph down the stairs, braying about how there's no pleasing some people.

There's nothing for it. I open the door and tiptoe out. Four other doors open off the landing. The first is a bathroom, tiled in white and black and boasting a tub the size of a tram. The window is too small to crawl through, even if I wasn't stark bollock naked. The second is more promising. It is clearly the master bedroom, with a bay window and gargantuan wardrobe. Hanging over the mantel is a studio photograph of a dyspeptic-looking fellow, brandishing a Malacca cane as though he'd like to brain me with it. The frame has been polished so often that the silver has worn through to the brass.

'Begging your pardon, sir,' I say, tugging a ringlet with contrived obsequiousness.

The wardrobe bulges with old frocks. At the back and reeking of mothballs is a man's suit and bowler. If it's not the very one worn by the gent in the picture, then it is the spit and image. I don't waste a minute. The trousers are an inch too short, the jacket an inch too wide, but to my harassed eye the ensemble is perfection. I tuck my – her – curls under the hat. Of boots there is no sign. I take a pair of lisle stockings dangling over the back of the chair and pull them on. Better than bare feet. Just. No time for wool-gathering. I must be away.

I venture downstairs, far more delicately than the elephantine females who pounded the carpet before me, and aim for the front door. It is locked. No sign of a key. With a deep breath, I turn about and stride up the passageway and into the kitchen. An old baggage, clearly the source of the commotion with the gong, is glaring into a pan of water as though daring it to boil. At the sound of my entrance, she glances up, her spectacles steamed over. She unhooks them from her ears and squints in my direction. Her mouth falls open.

'Morning, missus,' I grunt, tugging the hat brim low.

The back door is propped open to let out the smoke from bread she recently set on fire. She takes a quivering step towards me, holding up her hand as if the room has been plunged into darkness and she is feeling her way.

'Jack?' she croaks. 'Jack!' Her voice rises in a shriek, halfway between delight and terror.

She wipes her glasses on her apron and begins to manoeuvre the wire frame on to her nose. It will not do for her to see me clearly, so with a grunted *ta-ta, missus* I'm out of there, accompanied by banshee wailing of *Jack! Jack!*

I walk through the unfamiliar neighbourhood until I come upon streets that I recognise. I get plenty of peculiar looks, striding through Hulme in a battered Sunday suit and no boots. I get to thinking. The length of my hair tells me I've been gone weeks. Months, perhaps. My bitch of a sister must've stabbed me down the whole time.

I count off the beerhouses until I stand before The Comet. Not a moment too soon, for my feet are killing me. I am unaccountably moved to see it. I'll deal with such a girlish feeling at a later date. There are more important tasks at hand.

No need to break the habit of a lifetime. Round the back and up the drainpipe I go. I clamber on to the sill and push the window. It will not open. I give it a fierce shove, but it refuses to budge. I peer through the dirty pane. The bed is unmade, the walls stripped bare. The only resident is a crate of ginger-beer bottles. Some sort of homecoming this is, I think bitterly.

I make my way down and into the kitchen. Mam gawps like she's never set eyes on me before. I've had enough of startled females this morning.

'Give over, Mam,' I snap. 'It's me.' I look pointedly at the range. 'Get the kettle on. I'm gasping for a brew. I've had a morning like you wouldn't believe.'

Her head bounces like a puppet with half its strings snipped. 'Oh!' she gargles. 'I thought you'd . . .' At this, the dozy mare bursts into tears, weeping and wailing and rabbiting nineteen to the dozen about how I'm her lost lamb returned at last to the family fold till I'm clogged up to the eyeballs with her nonsense.

'Lay off. You don't usually make such a palaver.'

She wipes her eyes. 'Can't a mother be nice to her son?' she says. 'I'm just pleased to have my Herbert back again after all this time. How you've grown!'

'Gnome, Mam, Gnome,' I say. 'Now, how about some breakfast? I'm half-starved.'

She proceeds to cook me the biggest plate of sausages and fried potatoes a fellow could wish for. She watches me shovel them in, like every gobful is putting meat on her scrawny bones rather than mine.

'So, Mam,' I say, mopping up the fat with a heel of bread. 'What's all this with my bedroom? It looks like I haven't set foot in it for an age.'

'Hmph,' she says. 'That sister of yours. Walked out, calm as you like. Got herself employment,' she adds with a sneer that could strip varnish. 'After everything I did for her.'

'That's not right, is it, Mam?' I say, stoking the fire of her anger and adding a coal or two of my own. 'Downright ungrateful, I'd say.'

'Ungrateful.'

'I'd not do that to my dear old mam.'

'You're a good lad, Gnome,' she sighs. 'It'll be grand to have a man about the place again.'

'All in good time, Mam.'

'Of course, of course,' she mumbles distractedly. 'The bar's not open for a couple more hours.'

I've been back five minutes and she's already making plans to set me to work. I change the subject.

'Where are my clothes? I can't wear this ugly suit. It stinks. Besides, it's borrowed.'

Her eyes flicker, as though the shadow of a dark angel has passed overhead. 'They're sold.'

209

'Give me a shilling. I'll pop down the road and redeem the pledge.'

'They're not with Uncle. They're sold.'

'Sold? There's a nice thing. A chap turns his back – your son, mind you – and you sell his trousers?'

My grandmother's head appears around the door and, by the look on Mam's face, not a moment too soon.

'I have to check the beer,' Mam mutters and slips out of the room.

I roll my eyes and address my grandmother. 'What's got into her? All I asked for was my clothes.'

'Herbert,' she says with all the surprise of someone finding a loaf in a bakery. 'I wondered when you'd grace us with your presence. Thought you'd grown far too elevated for your lowly family.'

'That's charming. Besides, my name's Gnome and you know it.'

'I thought you'd have grown out of that name by now.' She looks me up and down. 'You can have one of Arthur's shirts.'

There's no option but to follow her upstairs. Her room is as I remember, with its scent of soap and leather. Through the window is the view of slate-tiled roofs, gleaming with dew. She fossicks in the depths of her tallboy and thrusts a shirt in my direction.

'It's too big.'

'You've filled out nicely, Herbert.'

'Will you stop calling me that name?' I try to sound angry but it comes out as a peevish squeak. I clear my throat. 'Dash it all. I can't talk right this morning. Everything's shot to hell.'

'Beggars can't be choosers. Especially those who go off gallivanting without so much as a Sunday visit.'

'Gallivanting? You have got to be kidding.'

She returns her attention to the drawer, producing a pair of trousers. 'Take these,' she says. 'I'll let them down an inch. You'll look grand.'

'Fine welcome this is turning out to be. Mam flogs my clothes and you're talking like I'm Rip Van Winkle.'

'What do you expect if we don't see hide nor hair of you all this time? Now,' she muses. 'The boy must have boots.'

She kneels and searches under the bed. My forehead grows cold. It's guesswork that I've been gone months. It could be longer, much longer. There's no tick of time when I'm away. It's a dream-time, a sea of unknowing quick with monsters. My memory glitters with skewers. Nightmares of surfacing and being stabbed down. Surfacing and being stabbed down. I perch on the mattress, clutching shirt and trousers to my chest. All of a sudden, I lack the gumption to put them on.

'Boots!' she cries, jerking me out of my trance. She waves a pair in my direction.

I take a breath and ask the question I do not want to. 'What do you mean by "all this time"?'

The words ring hollow. She plops herself at my side, to complaints from the bedsprings.

'You're here now. That's all that matters.' She squeezes my knee. 'I've missed you.'

I smack her hand aside. 'How long have I been gone?' I cry. 'Tell me.'

'What a question! Five years.'

She speaks the words as plainly as you might five minutes, five bottles of beer, five slices of bread. I catch my reflection in the cheval glass. Peering out from a mop of ringlets is a broad-shouldered young man with the shadow of stubble on cheek and chin. I swallow and swallow hard. Bile stings my throat.

'Last time I was here . . .' I whisper. I watch myself raise a hand and lay it against my face. 'I can't have been . . .' My

211

stomach is on fire, my head a block of ice. I run out of words. I can't think.

'There, now. I understand, even if your mother doesn't. Chicks fly the nest and make a life for themselves. So did you and Edie.'

'A life?' I screech, finding my voice again. 'I've been her prisoner!'

'Don't talk daft. That's impossible.'

'No it's bloody not.' I wrench the curls framing my face. 'She's kept me down the whole time. Five effing years!'

There's a silence as her face performs feats of acrobatics, twisting from shock to disbelief and back again.

'No,' she says, after a long while.

'What do you mean, *no*? Are you deaf?'

'You're exaggerating.'

'Shut up, you old trout!' I scream.

She swings her arm and gives me a crack on the side of my head that makes my ears ring.

'I'll let you get away with that, just this once. I'll mark it down to shock. But if you ever—' She raises her fist and I cower.

'I won't,' I squeak, cradling my aching head.

'Very well. You're no longer a child and I won't address you as one.' She clears her throat. 'If this is true – and you're telling me it is, it's a serious matter.'

'You're telling me,' I grumble, rubbing my ear.

'More than you can imagine.'

'What do you mean?' I moan. 'What's she done to me?'

'I don't rightly know,' she muses. 'But it's not right, however she's managed it.'

I know what Edie's done to keep me down, even if this old fool doesn't. I'll bloody kill her, so I will. But my grandmother is babbling on and I have to put aside thoughts of revenge to keep up.

'. . . only way,' she says.

'Eh?'

'Listen. In a perfect world, this family should share half and half. But when things get unbalanced . . .' She trails off, gazing at the boots in her lap as if they might provide inspiration.

'What?' I snarl. 'Spit it out, why don't you!'

'I didn't think Edie could. Or would be so selfish.' She presses her lips together. 'Say that one side – Edie for example – tips the scales. Once it starts, it's as though the scales get used to it. Grain by grain, ounce by ounce, it takes a greater and greater effort to tip them back, until . . .' She pauses.

'Until what?'

'Until you can't get back. And it takes hell and high water to even things out. Your mother lets Arthur in once a month and he's stuck with it. The longer Edie keeps you away . . .'

My mind races. I could tear the mattress apart with my bare hands. It takes the effort of a circus strongman to hold back my rage. I must handle my grandmother more carefully. She's got a right hook like a steam hammer. My mind seethes with visions of throttling Edie till her eyes pop. I need time to think, to lay plans. I force my mouth into a biddable smile.

'Oh, Grandma,' I bleat. 'Edie's been awfully selfish, hasn't she?'

'I shall have stern words with her.'

I consider dropping my trousers and displaying the puncture wounds. Knowing her, she'll think I've done it. Yet another thing for Edie to wriggle out of.

'You do that,' I murmur. 'And while you're at it, take a good look at her legs.'

She looks at me sideways, opens her mouth; thinks better of it, slaps her thighs and stands. 'I'm glad we've had this talk, Gnome. Now. Let's get you downstairs and behind that bar. High time we had an extra pair of hands about the place.'

'Of course,' I coo, voice dusted with sugar. 'Let me get dressed, first. Please.'

I affect a little-boy-lost expression until she clomps away. I'm back and in the nick of time: cold with fear at my narrow escape; boiling with fury at how Edie snuffed me out all these years. The grasping, vindictive . . .

As for Grandma's baloney about balance: the stupid woman doesn't know what she's talking about. Half and half, my arse. I'll be damned if I let Edie take another minute. She'll rue the day she took my life away. How could I let myself be cowed so easily? I should've stood up to her. I was an idiot. A child. Not any longer.

First things first. I'm going nowhere and doing nothing until I've cut this hair. I rifle through the dresser and turn up a pair of embroidery scissors. They'll have to do. One by one the curls curve upon the rug, a limp reminder of what's wrong with my world. As for helping out in The Comet, they've got another think coming. I thump downstairs and am halfway out of the door when Grandma grabs my shoulder and hauls me back.

'Not so fast,' she growls. 'There's work to be done.'

Of all the whiskery, horse-faced, fat-bottomed frumps.

'What, me? You can whistle for it.'

'Some things don't change. You're still a lazy tyke.'

'I'm not your slave. You'll be making me empty the night-soil bucket next.'

'If I will it, you'll do it,' she says, too cheerfully for my taste.

'I bally well shall not. Mam wouldn't make me.'

She laughs. 'You think so? Cissy!' she yells.

The woman in question sticks her head around the doorpost. I have the distinct feeling she's been hiding there.

'Don't cheek your grandmother,' she mutters, and pops back into her mouse-hole.

I've never seen her so browbeaten. The worm turns, even

214

here. Grandma folds her arms. They're the size of boiled hams.

'Got it? Good. Under this roof you'll do as you're told.'

'So much for a welcome home. I can see why Edie was so quick to sling her hook.'

The old sow's face twists. I've struck a bull's-eye.

'You want bed and board? Earn it,' she grunts. 'Don't think you're going to lounge around with us running around after you.'

The remainder of the day passes in toil. Mam opens the public door at lunchtime and in troop our customers: flat-footed, sour-breathed, slack-jawed dead-enders, every man jack of them. I work my fingers to the bone: fetch beer from the cellar; carry bottles back and forth; serve codgers I'd as soon kick along the street with my boot up their backsides. I lay it on with a trowel, laughing at their feeble pleasantries and affecting interest in their tedious anecdotes.

If that wasn't enough, the moment they've departed and the doors are bolted against them, Grandma thrusts a brush into my hand. I'm not made for this low sort of labour. It is beneath a sharp chap such as myself. Mam flits past carrying a tray of dirty glasses as I attack the floor.

'Watch it,' she says. 'You'll break the head off.'

'I wish it was Edie's ruddy head,' I mutter, whacking the broom against the wall.

'Tch,' she chides affectionately. 'Less of your impertinence.'

I bat my eyelashes. 'Oh Mam,' I say. 'It's the homesickness talking. She took me away from you – my lovely mam – for five years. Are you surprised I'm so upset?'

'No,' she says cautiously.

'Do you think she should get away with it scot-free?'

She nibbles her lower lip. 'Of course not,' she says. 'She deserves . . .'

I supply a notion. '. . . to be kicked into the coal cellar.'

The corners of her mouth twitch. 'Now, now.'

'She'd come out blacker than your shoe.'

Her eyes glint: chips of glass from a broken beer bottle. 'That's not very nice,' she says.

'Why not? You hate her as much as I do. How about I scatter marbles on the stairs?'

Mam giggles. 'Down she'll tumble.'

'And break her scraggy neck.'

'Gnome!' She tries for censure, but it comes out as complicity.

'Nah,' I say. 'Too quick by half. I'll buy a penny dose of poison from the chemist. *It's for rats,* I'll say. No word of a lie, neither. I'll sprinkle toffees with the stuff and leave them with a note: *To Edie, from an admirer.'*

'That'll tickle her vanity. *Toffee*-nosed madam.'

I laugh wildly at the weak pun, hugging my ribs and rocking back and forth. We are having a whale of a time when Grandma pokes her head through the door.

'Listen to you two idiots,' she says.

'It's not like we'd do any of it,' Mam mumbles. 'It's just talk.'

'Nasty talk.'

'She's no daughter of mine, swanning off like that,' says Mam.

'Can you blame her for upping sticks? Not exactly dripping with the milk of human kindness, are you?'

I wait for Mam to fight back, but she slinks away, tail between her legs.

'Since when did Edie do us any favours?' I say, chin up.

'You've not got the brains you were born with,' she sneers. 'For heaven's sake. Trip her down the stairs and it's your nose gets broken.'

'Don't see why I shouldn't try,' I whisper. 'After what she did.'

'You can mutter all you want. It changes nothing. You're stuck with her and she you.'

216

'Then I'll make her life such a misery she won't want it any more!'

'Herbert . . .'

'Gnome!' I scream. 'I want my five years back! I'll take them and all!'

'Hasn't it occurred to you that if you share, you both get a look-in?'

'Never!' I shriek. 'I want vengeance. It's mine by rights.'

'Even if it's the death of you?'

The cat gets my tongue, but only for a second. 'Don't waste your breath on threats. I'm not a boy any more.'

She opens her gob, reconsiders, and shuts it. Good. That's how a woman's mouth should be. Buttoned. I barge past her and run upstairs, don the bowler hat and jacket. The sleeves have been let down and pressed. Mam or Grandma did this for me. Something soft knots in my gut, but I shove it down, hard.

I slip through the scullery and stick my hand in the sugar bowl. I wonder if Mam's acquired any grey matter since I've been gone but my fingers find coins, right where they've always been. I head into the city, jingling shillings.

My head crams with violence. I pass a chemist and gaze longingly at the jars scrawled with mysterious letters: *Tr. Chlorod., Oxymel Scillae, Tinct. Benz. Simp.* Much as I hate to admit it, Grandma is right. If I poison Edie, I cough up blood. If I break her arm, my own is broken. I consider playing her at her own game and stabbing myself with a hat-pin. Knowing my blasted luck that would fail, not to mention my meddling Grandma sticking her oar in and putting paid to it. My dreams pop like soap bubbles. It's not fair.

Manchester has changed since I was here last. In particular, they seem to be knocking down half of it. If I had my way I'd sweep it all aside and good riddance to bad rubbish. Flatten the old city and build it anew. A man's city, slick with tarmacadam and clean, straight streets. Give me tramlines, motor cars, steamships. Give me express trains to whisk me to London in the space of a few hours. Give me zeppelins and flying machines. Give me a way out of here. Up and far away, till I am the tiniest speck. Till I cannot be seen.

Not that these pleasant imaginings bring me one step closer to a solution to my problem. I make my way up Mosley Street towards Piccadilly, my thoughts circling back to Edie like a dog returning to its vomit. I can't poison her, strangle her, break so much as her little finger. I deal a pebble a hefty kick and stub my toe on the kerb. Damn it all to hell. She stole my life. Five long, wonderful years of it.

She has a life.

That's what I can poison, without any injury to myself. That's what I can take and stamp to pieces, bit by delicious bit. I can't believe I didn't think of it before. No more wage-earning, independent tomfoolery. Edie doesn't deserve to stick her nose out of the front door, not after what she did to me. She can stay in and slave for Mam. It's my turn to live.

I mull over how to keep her kennelled. She imagines herself quite the modern woman, strolling the streets like she owns them. Modern or not, when a woman is terrified she stays indoors where she belongs. Simple. I'll scare the living bejesus out of her. How she'll cower, how she'll scuttle. Hope soars afresh only to be doused immediately. There's no point in me threatening her. She won't believe anything I say.

But she'll believe other men. Unsavoury men. The kind who lie in wait, cracking their knuckles; who slide open windows and creep into bedrooms. Men who'll do as I tell them. It's perfect. No one has to harm a hair on her head. She just has to believe that someone will. I don't want to consign her to nothingness. I want her to know what I've done to her. I want her to taste my revenge. Every bitter mouthful.

I must work quickly before she sticks in that bloody pin of hers. I hasten towards Shudehill Market. It is heaving as always. A brace of small boys whizz past, one of them flourishing an orange. Judging by the shouts of the costermonger, one purloined rather than paid for. I am on the point of laughing when I'm visited by an unwelcome vision of myself: ancient, toothless and still here, night after night, guffawing at naughty lads. There must be more to my existence. There has to be, or—

My mind sputters. Part of my life gone forever and this tatty market hall is all I have to show for it. I rack my brains for somewhere better to go when a familiar voice calls my name.

'Well, if it isn't my little Gnome.' Jessie unglues herself from the wall and takes my arm. She looks a lot older than when I saw her last, jowls sagging and left eye drooping at the corner. 'Nice hat.'

I twirl the bowler in my fingers.

'Quite the swell these days, aren't you? Thought you'd forgotten your old friend Jessie.'

'You? Never. Besides, you're not old.'

'You flatterer,' she replies coquettishly, and fiddles with her hair. 'Come. Walk with me. How about a bite?' she adds, steering me towards the pie-stand. 'You've got no meat on you, Gnome. What've you been doing with yourself: living off lettuce?'

Daylight does her no favours and she knows it, for she suggests we move inside. We down our pies, elbows propped on the tabletop. She picks at the crust delicately as though she's only eating to be polite. I gobble mine with a hunger I didn't know I had.

'That's more like it,' she coos. 'Get some flesh on those bones. So. Tell me everything you've been doing.'

219

'Bugger all. Biding my time, you might say,' I grumble. 'Five ruddy years and all.'

She taps her nose. 'A holiday in Strangeways, eh? You wicked fellow.' She pats my wrists with a flirting gesture. 'What *have* you been getting up to?'

'I was set up,' I say.

'Tell me the old, old story,' she sings happily.

I suck gravy off my fingers and lean across the table. 'Now I'm back, I need a job done,' I mutter.

'What sort of job?'

'Never you mind what sort,' I snap. 'A score to settle. That's all you need to know.'

'That's a nice way to speak to a friend. If you want my advice, learn your lesson. Steer clear of trouble and it'll steer clear of you.'

'Don't nag. I can handle myself perfectly well.'

She laughs. 'I dare say you can. But Strangeways is not the place for return visits if you can help it. There are unscrupulous fellows to be found.'

'Precisely the sort I wish to meet. I'll bet you come across plenty in your line of work.'

'Maybe I do, maybe I don't.' She sighs. 'What a shame you boys have to grow up so fast.' She looks set to pat me on the cheek, so I turn my face away.

'Will you help me or not? You'd not believe what she did.'

'What's that?' she says. 'You didn't say anything about it being a woman.'

'What difference does it make?'

'None to you, maybe. But it does to me.'

'She's the reason you haven't seen me all this time!'

'Count me out, Gnome. I'll not conspire against a lady.'

'Lady? That's the last thing she is. You'd hate her too if you met her.'

220

'Would I now?'

'Come on, Jessie. I've seen you lot put each other's eyes out over a glove. This is someone who's made my life a misery. Don't you care? I'm not asking for nasty business. Just a little fright.'

She presses her lips together and pouts. It makes her look uncommonly like a duck. 'Find someone else to do your dirty work.'

I make cow's eyes at her. 'But I've missed you.'

'I don't want any part of it.' She stands. 'But if you hang around long enough the sort of men you're looking for will come to you. Cash'll grease the wheels, but there's plenty will do it for the pleasure.'

She flounces off, arse jiggling from side to side like a sack of potatoes. I don't need her help. I order a mug of tea and start lamenting about the sad state the world is in, what with women making every decent man's life a blasted misery.

'They rule the roost and now they want to seize the reins of government. Where will it end, I ask you?' I say to no one and everyone. 'With our necks in a horse-collar, that's where.'

There is a grunt of general agreement; nothing more.

'Women, always women,' I continue. 'Taking jobs a man should be doing. That's it. Our wages, our pride, the bread out of our mouths.'

A few heads turn.

'It's men that need freedom from their constant badgering,' I continue. 'Bleating how hard done by they are.'

'Never bloody happy,' says one fellow.

'That's not the half of it!' I say, and stand him a cup of tea. 'Scratch the surface of this world and there we are, wondering where our share has gone and who has snatched it from us.'

'Whining, always whining,' he agrees, gulping the brew.

Blow me if Jessie isn't bang on the money. Within minutes

I have the sympathy of a sizeable bunch of fellows, every one of them bemoaning the activities of females and holding out their mugs to be refilled.

I let it be known that I have one particular tart in need of cutting down to size and most sidle off once they've guzzled the tea. Two likely specimens linger and I reason that if one doesn't work out then the other will pick up the slack. The rat-thin man introduces himself as Mr Joseph. His companion, Mr Jack, is the canine type: stiff of leg and square of head. He displays a row of yellowing fangs when we shake hands.

'Gnome,' I say gruffly.

'Gnome,' opines Mr Joseph, rolling the word on his tongue. 'There's a funny name.'

'Memorable,' I parry.

'There's such a thing as too memorable,' he retorts.

I never thought of that. I shall consider that conundrum at my leisure. We sit in brotherly contemplation of the low females strutting past.

'Women, eh?' I grunt.

'Egging us on,' says Joseph in an unpleasant tone I warm to immediately. 'Shaking their derrières in a manner designed to inflame the most celibate of monks.'

'Hmm,' grunts Jack.

'Yet they raise merry hell when we take them up on their enticements,' Joseph continues.

'Where's the justice in that?' I agree.

'I could tell some tales,' Joseph replies. 'But who'd believe me?'

'Ha! Whole lot of them need taking down a peg or two,' say I.

'Or three,' barks Jack.

'There's the rub,' I sigh. 'If only I had a friend to help me set my world to rights.'

'That'd be a fine thing,' agrees Joseph.

'A peg or two. That's all I ask. Why, if I could meet such a man, I'd pay good money, so I would.' I gaze wistfully into my empty mug.

'Would you now?' he replies with an air of languid interest. He scratches his stomach with a fan of claws.

'Oh yes. I have a job in mind. A very particular job.'

'We are particular men,' declares Joseph. 'Aren't we, Mr Jack?' He grins, top lip peeling away from his teeth, augmenting his rodent air.

Jack lobs an unflattering epithet at one of the whores.

'I have in mind a particular woman,' I say.

'Just the one? How incommodious.'

The word is so out of place that I am close to laughing. I know what side my bread is buttered, so I stow it and nod.

'Nothing too cruel,' I say grudgingly. It's a shame, but there's no way around it. 'No violence.'

Joseph scowls. 'That is a pity.'

'I want her – scared.' I give my imagination its freedom. 'Tell her . . .' I pause and the Muse descends. '. . . You're going to kick her into the middle of next week.'

'Ah, yes,' he breathes with a smile that increases in malice by the minute.

'Tell her that you're going to flog her black and blue. That you're going to strangle her till her face goes puce. Put ground glass in her tripe and onions. Lye in her lemonade.'

'That's a fearsome amount of work,' says Jack.

'Don't *do* any of it,' I reply. 'Just threaten to.'

Jack frowns. He digs a finger into his ear, rotates it a couple of times, then removes it and inspects the tip. 'I don't get it,' he says.

Just my luck. I've picked cretins. There's no time to search for better.

'Scare her,' I say. 'It's not difficult. No kicking or thumping needed. Threats. Frights. That's all.'

Joseph holds up a finger so thin you could pick a lock with it. 'We need no instruction,' he says. 'We know a good way to frighten the ladies, don't we, Mr Jack?'

'We do?' says Jack, tugging a strand of hair bristling out of his nose.

'We do indeed.'

'Oh yes. We know how to put the wind right up them,' cackles Jack. He pulls out the hair and winces.

'And you'll pay us?' says Joseph. I nod. He shoves out his hand and I fill it with the money I filched. It seems far less of a fortune when spread over the spade of his palm. 'I'd do it without thought of monetary recompense, to tell you the truth.'

'In that case . . .' I lunge forwards to sweep the coins back into my own keeping, but he snatches them away.

'This will reimburse my companion and myself for any inconvenience. Expenses incurred, you might say. Thirsty work, so it is.'

'And hungry,' chimes Jack, scratching his backside.

'Shut up,' snaps Joseph. Jack shrugs, clearly unbothered by such chastisement. Joseph returns his attention to me. 'Where shall we find her, young fellow-me-lad?'

We stare at each other. I am putting it off, I know. For this to happen, I shall have to step aside and let her back in. I shudder at the thought of drowning for another five years. That will not happen, I tell myself firmly. When these two have done their business, I'll rule the roost again. This is no gamble. It's a dead cert.

For all my brave thoughts, I am trembling. I take a deep breath. 'The Comet on Renshaw Street. A plain beerhouse. I'll go ahead and—'

Joseph wipes his paws one against the other, as though washing them. 'Oh no you won't,' he says. 'You will lead the way. Don't want you getting any queer ideas.'

I can't imagine what sort of ideas they might be. However, there's no putting him off, so I shrug and head to Hulme with them dogging my heels. We loiter at the junction with Rosamond Street whilst I point out The Comet.

'Let us be crystal clear. No broken limbs. She mustn't be injured,' I say.

'I heard you the first time. It's not our style. Just fun and larks, eh?'

'Frightening fun and larks,' guffaws Jack.

'Yes,' I say. 'That's right. Like a mouse back into its hole.'

I grin at the picture this presents. Edie with a pink, twitching nose, too afraid to stick it out. The two men exchange a look.

'Oh, I'll bet she has a fine hole we can scare her into,' says Joseph.

'We'll scare her good and proper,' titters Jack. 'We'll scare her front and back.'

'You can take the back,' says Joseph in a generous tone. 'I'm a front-door man myself.'

'What?' I say. A ghostly presence digs its cold finger into my stomach.

'We'll scare her so she can't stand up for a week,' Joseph continues.

'So she can't walk for two,' pants Jack.

Joseph turns his smiling face to me. I wish he wouldn't.

'You won't have a squeak out of her by the time we're done,' he says. 'We'll put a cork in that mouth of hers.'

'Two big corks,' says Jack, pummelling the front of his britches.

My heart sinks into my boots as I tumble to their plans. I

hungered for revenge a moment ago. I shouldn't care. I should cheer them on, waving a rattle. A scrap of my pie comes back up and stings the back of my throat. I swallow.

'No,' I say, shaking my head furiously. 'That's not what I meant.'

·'Why not?' sneers Joseph. 'There's no better way to strike terror in women.'

'No *other* way,' opines Jack. The flesh of his throat is flushed where it bulges over his knotted neck scarf.

'Quite, quite,' says Joseph, smacking his lips.

'No,' I say firmly. 'I said you can't hurt her. Deal's off.'

'Bit late to change your mind now, lad,' he replies. 'Not now you've brought us all the way here.'

I pluck at Jack's sleeve. It's like trying to get the attention of a brick wall. He turns his head, so slowly I swear the hinges creak.

'What do you want, you little shithead?' he hisses, spraying me with spittle.

'I said you can't hurt her. Go on, hop it,' I say with a great deal more courage than I feel.

Joseph grasps my shoulder and shakes me like a dog. 'Too late. You got us fired up and you can't throw water on the flames.'

'Lay off!' I cry.

'You asked for this. Begged and wheedled, so you did. Now she's going to get it.'

'Get her out here now,' says Jack.

'Or we'll take you up the back alley and scare you instead. You or her. Your choice.'

Jack chucks me under the chin. 'What a pretty boy you are,' he coos. 'I'd say you're nice enough for us.'

'Stop it! Stop calling me pretty!'

'Now, now. No need to get agitated. A fellow never got anywhere by being agitated,' says Joseph.

I am way out of my depth. Why does everything I do foul up? I have to think fast.

'Let go!' I shout, wriggling free of Joseph's talons. 'We're wasting time squabbling. She's in there. I'll send her out to you.'

I have no intention of doing any such thing, but I have to get away from this ghastly pair.

'Not a moment too soon. My fingers are trembling.'

'It's not good when his fingers get into a tremble,' declares Jack.

'It's good for us,' corrects Joseph. 'Not good for those who cross us.'

'I'm not crossing you,' I say with exasperation. 'Pipe down, hold your fingers in check for one blasted minute and I'll fetch her.'

Joseph throws back his head and laughs. It's a thin sound, like a rabbit having its windpipe cut. I scurry across the road, fly through the door, gallop up the stairs and wedge a chair under the doorknob to bar my nosy mam and nosier grandmother. I pace up and down, cursing the heavens.

Now what? My mind empties of solutions. I've been back less than a day and my plans have landed me in a fix I can't see my way out of. It's not my fault. If Edie hadn't shut me out, I wouldn't have been forced into this. She brought it on herself. I ought to leave her to it. Let Jack and Joseph do precisely what they want.

My heart tips over. I can't. I tug my hair in frustration. The tufts remind me, as if I needed it, how deep a hole I've dug, and how fast. It's not fair. It wasn't supposed to go like this. I peer around the edge of the curtain, hoping that by some miracle they might have got bored and gone away. No such luck.

Whichever way I try to cut it, I can't see any way out of this

227

cock-up other than warning her. If I warn her, she'll be grateful. She has to be. She can't shove me down again. I breathe deeply to calm myself and fail. My heart is thumping so hard I'm surprised it doesn't burst out of my chest. I slump on to the bed, groaning and holding my aching head. I've been held down for so long it takes me a moment to realise what's happening. She's coming back.

I must do this, now, before the change swipes me aside.

'Edie,' I say. Too damn quiet. I have to put some zip into it. 'Edie!' I bellow. 'Don't go out!'

No use. I sense the tickle of her curiosity. All I'm doing is whetting her appetite. My mind rattles: how do I make her stay indoors once she's here? She's so contrary she's as like to pick up a broom and sweep the pavement. I wanted the wind taken out of her sails, not this.

I could write a note. However, I've not so much as a pencil stub about my person, let alone paper. I don't have time to ask Mam and deal with her interrogations. I chew my fingernails. Inspiration strikes. I lick my forefinger and drag it through the dirt on the looking glass.

Stay indoors. Don't go out.

My stomach churns. Although it kills me to do so, I scrawl, *I am sorry. I didn't mean it.* See that, Edie? I'm sorry. You can't punish a lad who's contrite. Don't keep me down again. I've had fewer hours than I can count on the fingers of one hand. Please. You can't.

I stand back and survey my handiwork. It's barely legible. If I can't see it, she won't. My privates have commenced their awful contraction. I've run out of time.

'It's not my fault!' I wail.

Too late. She's on her way. The door between us swings open, I fall through and am gone.

EDIE

MARCH 1909

I fall headlong into my body and, when I land, find my nose pressed into a sour blanket. My head pounds as though someone has slammed a door upon it. I raise myself only to collapse afresh as a spike is driven through my temple. It hurts to keep my eyes open, but open them I must. I squint at the light glaring through the uncurtained window and see where I am. My old room at The Comet. I am wearing a pair of ill-fitting trousers and a shirt too short in the sleeve. Gingerly, I run a hand over my head. Shorn to ear length.

My stomach falls to my heels. Gnome seized his opportunity after the tumultuous events of yesterday evening; that much is clear. As for the Telegraph Office: the angle of the light suggests afternoon. I'm late for work. That is, if this is the day after. Oh God. Let it be Wednesday. No later. I drag myself upright, wringing my hands. If this nightmare were not agony enough, I cannot shake off the sense that I am in danger.

I peel away Gnome's britches and shirt and sniff my armpits. What I desire most is to heat a kettle and scrub myself with carbolic soap, but such a luxury is out of the question. I have to be content with cold water from the jug. I peer into the mirror: a half-plucked chicken if ever there was. The glass is

229

slathered with dust so thick I can barely see myself. I bundle the shirt to wipe away a patch when I notice words written in the muck.

Stay indoors. Don't go out. I am sorry. I didn't mean it.

Gnome. It has to be. I didn't write it, sure as sixpence. *Don't go out?* The cheek of it. I need answers, and if my scheming brother is telling me to stay indoors I can bet they lie in the opposite direction. He's been back five minutes – I hope and pray – and is already up to his machinations. How very like him to want me in the house under lock and key, the treacherous toad. I'm going out and there's an end to the matter.

Despite the brave words, I am unable to shake off a fear that needles and will not let go. I survey the room, which is almost bare. Hardly surprising, as I took my few possessions with me when I quit the place. I cannot stroll along Renshaw Street in my birthday suit, nor can I ask Ma for a skirt and petticoat. I picture her sneer of victory when she discovers I've crawled back without even a pocket handkerchief to my name. I have no option but to don Gnome's malodorous clothes once more.

I haul myself out of the room and trudge down the stairs. A strange force hinders my steps as surely as if I am dragging chains. I don't know what the little devil has done to me, but I refuse to be beaten. As I fight my way along the hall, Ma sticks her head out of the kitchen.

'Herb – Gnome!' she cries.

'Don't you know your own daughter?' I snap, puffing with exertion. 'I'm off out.'

She rolls her eyes. 'No you're not. I'll not have you two treating this place like a boarding house. We don't see you for five years and then you're in and out at all hours without so much as a by-your-leave.'

She plonks herself in my path. She barely comes up to my

chin and I wonder when she grew so small. She can, at least, answer my most pressing question.

'How long have I – How long since Gnome came back?'

She flaps her hands as though chasing away a fly. 'Don't plague me with your nonsense. I can't keep up with this chopping and changing, him in the day and you—'

With a rage that comes from nowhere, I grab her shoulders and hoist her off the ground. 'Tell me!' I roar. 'What day is it?'

She blanches. 'Wednesday. He's only been back since this morning.'

'Is that true?'

'Yes,' she gasps. 'I swear.'

I drop her with a thump and slog down the corridor, wading through treacle. One more step, two, and I am at the front door. I twist the handle and stand on the threshold. It gleams the colour of oxblood from a recent bout with a donkey-stone. I gaze up the street, and down. Folk are going about their business: the rag-and-bone cart rattles past; a knife-grinder shoves his cart. No danger that I can see.

I am quaking, head to foot. Of all the ridiculous – I can't spend all afternoon in this stupor. I must return to my lodgings, retrieve my own clothes, dash to the Telegraph Office and beg to keep my position. Hard as I try, I can't budge. My heels are glued to the step. It is most peculiar. I ought to be racing to the nearest tram.

It is then I see them, motionless amidst the bustle of passers-by, leaning against the wall at the turn of the street: a squat fellow as broad as a gate and a slender man of considered movements, the sort used to picking his way through a world of clumsy mortals. I shudder as though a goose has walked over my grave.

231

The short chap turns to his companion and says something. The tall man responds with a brusque gesture. They draw their caps over their eyes, detach themselves from the wall and stroll in my direction. I've no idea what business they have with me, but am queasy with a conviction it is not for my benefit.

This is Gnome's doing. It has to be.

'Gnome, you bastard,' I growl.

The words release me from my spell. I spring backwards and slam the door with a crash that shakes the house. I slide the bolts for good measure. The flap of the letterbox squeaks as a hand pushes it open. I shrink behind the coat-stand.

'Open the door, lad,' wheedles a voice, gentle as a lamb. The tall man, I'm sure. 'Where's the lass you promised us?'

The flap clatters shut. Of course. I'm wearing trousers and a shirt. They think I am Gnome.

'Send her out,' says the other. 'We have a treat for her.' He snickers, and the sound is cut off by a slap. 'Ow!' he cries.

'Shut up, you berk,' growls the thin man.

'She's not there, Joseph.'

'She must be. He said she was,' comes the reply. 'Perhaps she's scarpered round the back. You can cut her off in the alley.'

'Why me?'

'Because I just said so. Besides, it suits your predilections.'

'Huh?'

'Shift your arse. I'll stop here. I'll give that lad what for. Mucking us about.'

I am trapped. I can't escape by the front door nor the back. I lean against the wall, wondering if I pray zealously enough the bricks might oblige by swallowing me up. I drop to my knees and crawl through the scullery and into the refuge of the kitchen, terrified that the slightest sound will betray my position. I do not want to think what is meant by the word *promised.* All I know is that Gnome wishes me to come to harm. I can taste it.

It gives me an idea. Gnome got me into this fix. He can get me out. For once in my life I shall exploit my mannish demeanour to my advantage, use it to flee from these louts and outwit Gnome into the bargain. I creep to the range, dip my fingers into the ash and smear it over my face and hands. A man's cap – Uncle Arthur's, I reason – is hooked on a peg. I ram it on to my head.

I take a deep breath and saunter out of the back door. As casually as I am able, I stroll through the yard and into the alley, whistling. I've gone no more than three paces before a hand seizes my elbow and twirls me around.

'Where is she?'

I am glad it's the short chap. The taller of the two presents the greatest danger.

'What are you on about?' I say, affecting a gruff voice. 'Get your paws off me.'

He does not oblige. 'Where is she, you blockhead?' he says.

'Me, blockhead? You, more like.'

He deals me a prodigious shake. 'You cheeky little—'

'We can stand here and argue the toss if you want. While we're at it, she's legging it out of the front door.'

His face falls. 'The front?'

'That's where I sent her, isn't it? Told her to get out there sharpish. I came to let you know.' His grip loosens a fraction. 'He was yelling for you. Your mate.'

He swallows. 'Joseph?'

'You forgotten who he is?'

He blinks, chews his lip and releases me. I resist the urge to run. He'd be on me in a trice. I stand my ground, heart hammering. He glances over his shoulder.

233

'You,' he snarls, jabbing my chest with a pudgy finger. 'Stay right there. Don't you move a bloody muscle till I get back.'

'Me? Move? I'll be sitting here, waiting to hear about all the fun,' I say. 'That's if Joseph gives you a look-in.'

He grunts a final curse and is off. I wait until he's out of sight and race in the opposite direction, cutting through back entries and back yards, leaping over walls and dodging washing lines. I pray they aren't acquainted with the shortcuts in and out of this neighbourhood. Some kindly god must be watching over me, for no one pays me any attention. I am one of a hundred untidy boys of no interest whatsoever.

Once I judge it is safe, I slow my pace. Despite the fear that roils in my breast, I force myself to look up rather than down, for I reason that furtive behaviour will attract attention. I will conceal myself through lack of concealment. A memory stirs: *If you act confidently, folk believe what they see and hear. Act nervous, like you don't belong in a place, and you'll stand out like a sore thumb.*

I wonder where I heard that advice and remember it was Gnome. Years ago, when we went to the fireworks. Before – A lump comes to my throat. I shake away the tender memory.

I can't spend all day pounding the pavement. I suspect that my would-be assailants are not the sort to dally, so wait a further fifteen minutes till the clock at St Wilfrid's clangs the three-quarter. I head home and my luck is in. There is no sign of them the length and breadth of Renshaw Street. I creep through the yard, open the door and walk slap bang into Ma.

'I don't know whether I'm coming or going with you and your brother,' she grumbles. 'It's like Market Street on a Saturday night.'

My grandmother heaves into view. 'What's going on *now*?' She peers at me. 'Edie?'

'At least one of you can tell who's who,' I mutter. 'What's going on is that I need to get out of these clothes, run like the devil to the Telegraph Office and grovel, that's what.'

I expect a fight. Instead, she nods and motions me upstairs. I follow.

'You'll help me? No sermon, no questions?'

'It'll keep,' she says. 'We'll talk this evening. For now, let's get you dressed.'

While her back is turned, I hurry into a pair of long bloomers. This is no time for an interrogation about the state of my thighs. With the aid of a mouthful of pins, she fastens me into her Sunday skirt. It is a generous fit, to say the least. Ma's best blouse and hairpiece complete my ensemble.

'Won't Ma complain?' I ask.

'What she doesn't know won't grieve her.'

I throw my arms around Nana and mumble thanks.

'Get away with you. And don't you mess that skirt. I want it returned in one piece.'

I have no idea how respectable I look, and fear not very. I have been absent from the Telegraph Office the whole morning and most of the afternoon. If I hurry I can be there by four o'clock, half past at the outside. I pound up the steps at five minutes past the hour. Mr Pryor's work-shy nature has played its hand to my benefit and he has long quit the building. I throw myself on Miss Strutt's narrow mercies.

'In addition to my extreme tardiness, I must also apologise for my appearance,' I gabble. 'Everything is at sixes and sevens and my costume is being laundered. My mother was taken ill while I was wearing it. She suffers terribly from the problems facing women of a certain age . . .'

I trail off, allowing Miss Strutt to follow the chain of thought to its disagreeable conclusion. Two bright spots appear in her cheeks. I arrange my face into a mixture of what I hope looks like sorrow and penitence.

'I expect this from others but not you, Miss Latchford,' she says, directing an acid glance at Guy, who is pretending not to be eavesdropping. 'I trust there will be no repetition of such behaviour?'

'No, Miss Strutt. Assuredly not.'

'I should hope so too. It can't be helped if a member of one's family should fall ill,' she says in a tone suggesting the opposite, 'but there is nothing to prevent you sending word.'

'Of course, Miss Strutt. I was in error. It won't happen again.'

'No, it won't. You will not find me so prepared to overlook the infraction on any subsequent occasion.'

'No, Miss Strutt.'

She continues to skewer me with her glance. 'I hope your mother is restored.'

'Yes, Miss Strutt. Quite restored.'

'I am gratified to hear it. She is not . . .' She pouts, chewing over words that might convey solicitude without compassion. '. . . a sickly woman, generally speaking?'

'No, Miss Strutt. Our family is blessed with good health.'

'Good. Sickly mothers are not to be accommodated.'

At five o'clock, Mr Pryor returns with a red nose and beery breath. At six o'clock he examines his watch, comparing it to the clock upon the wall.

'My goodness,' he remarks. 'Ladies and gentlemen of the first shift, six o'clock is upon us.'

My companions push back their chairs and file out to the

cloakroom. I stay at my position, wrangling the pins in and out of their sockets. Miss Strutt appears at my side.

'Miss Latchford. Why are you still at your turret?'

'I am making up the lost time, Miss Strutt,' I reply. 'I will work the late shift.'

Her mouth quirks into the nearest thing to a smile I've ever witnessed. 'That won't be necessary. Your mother has need of you. Tomorrow, return refreshed and ready to work.'

Mumbling copious thanks, I scuttle away before she can change her mind. Guy meets me on the steps.

'How did you know I'd be allowed out?'

'Strutt is a decent bird under all that huffing and puffing. Buck up, old girl. You've kept your place. If I'd pulled a stunt like that I'd be wearing out my shoe leather seeking fresh fields and pastures new, without a reference.'

'You are a tonic, Guy,' I say. 'I thank you. I wish I could walk with you awhile, but I must hurry to my lodgings and beard Mrs Reddish in her den.'

'I shall accompany you.'

'I'm sure you have far more agreeable things to do with your afternoon.'

'I am your friend, Edie. Remember? Friends stick together.'

We make our way through Piccadilly Gardens.

'Thank you, Guy. I don't think anyone understands me better than you.'

'Heavens, I don't know about that,' he replies. 'I could name one lady. Unless there are more on your dance card.'

'Guy!'

'My prophetic sense indicates you are tussling with yourself over whether you should meet Miss Abigail Hargreaves for a pot of tea. My advice is yea, yea and thrice yea.'

I feel a blush creep into my cheeks. I pretend to be spellbound by the shop window we are strolling past. It contains a display of machinery with a placard declaring *Tangyes Steam Engine*. He is not taken in by such a transparent ruse.

'So,' he says. 'I have delayed long enough. Are you going to tell me where you've been today?'

I am hardly about to vouchsafe the story of my narrow escape into his keeping, however good a friend he may be. 'I'm sure you were listening in. My mother has been unwell.'

'Rot. For a start, I see no earthly reason why your mother being taken ill should necessitate that awful haircut.' He points at my head. 'You might fool Strutty but you can't fool me.'

'It is a family matter,' I say. 'That is all.'

'Edie,' he chides. 'Spit it out.'

I sigh. I can tell a truth of some sort, if I am careful. 'Very well,' I say. 'If you must. It's my brother. He's something of a black sheep. Been gone for years, then turns up like the proverbial bad penny and wreaks havoc.'

He laughs. 'I'm rather partial to sheep of that hue. You'll have to introduce me immediately. I am already dying to meet him.'

'I'll do no such thing.'

He pouts. 'Spoilsport.'

'Guy. You have no idea what he is capable of.'

'How marvellous. You are whetting my appetite.'

I clamp my lips together and withdraw my arm from his.

'You play your cards exceedingly close to your delightful chest, dear Edie,' he sighs. 'I do wish you would divulge . . . Ah well. If wishes were horses, then beggars would ride. I am not given to begging.'

My blush deepens, from embarrassment to shame. 'I treat you shabbily,' I say, the words sticking in my throat.

'Come now. I did not mean to upset you.'

'It's true. You have always been open-handed.' My voice cracks. 'In return I offer you little more than crumbs.'

'Tosh,' he protests. 'You're the best friend a man ever laid claim to. This man, in any case.'

'Am I? I feel sorry for you.'

He spins me around, eyes grim and fiery. 'Never speak to me like that again. I am in need of no one's pity.'

'I did not mean—'

'Do not presume I am a fool because I play the part of one. I've seen more than you can know, much of it unsuitable for the eyes and ears of a young lady.'

We hold each other's gaze. I have never seen him like this: a curtain swept back, revealing steel at the heart.

'I apologise,' I say with true contrition. 'That was low of me.'

'It was.'

'Guy. I have experienced things which are difficult – no, impossible to put into words.' His face softens in recognition and I continue. 'Of all the people I have met, you are the first I believe I could trust. Please be assured of that.'

He squeezes my hand again. 'Your secrets are safe with me. Leastwise, they will be, should you choose to share them.'

'Thank you, Guy.'

'Besides, compared to my peculiarities, I'm sure your skeletons in the closet are not so very awful.'

'You can't know that,' I murmur.

'I've done some reprehensible things in my time. Your hair would curl. I am completely unshockable.'

I gnaw the inside of my cheek. It is as though I stand at the edge of a cliff, wind stirring my hair and tugging the brim of my hat. One inch separates me from a vertiginous tumble. All I need do is lift my foot and step into space. The air might gather itself beneath my arms and transform my sleeves into wings. Guy's friendship might hold steady and bear me aloft. Or, far more likely, I would see his face collapse: first into disbelief, then horror. And after the horror, disgust and rejection.

I would fall. Fall truly, down and down. Not only would I lose a jewel of a friend, but I'd deliver myself into the hands of someone who could do anything with the information, however fervent his promises of secrecy. I say none of this, of course.

'Dear girl. You don't need to affect bravery in my company,' he says in a gentle voice. 'I understand better than you might imagine. When one is aware of one's difference, compared to the normality of every other person on the face of the earth – well, the effort of retaining one's equanimity can be frightfully taxing on the spirits, can it not?'

He plants a kiss upon my cheek. We part on friendly terms at Mrs Reddish's gate, after I have given firm assurances to spend luncheon in his company the following day. I steel myself for unpleasantness and knock on the door. I get no further than the doormat before being given my marching orders.

'I will not tolerate immorality,' says Mrs Reddish with the conviction of a hellfire and brimstone preacher.

'I beg your pardon?' I reply, racking my brains.

'Miss Willert witnessed a young man leaving your room. Your room!' she squeaks.

'That's not possible,' I say.

'Are you calling me a liar?' says Edna. 'Gertrude saw him as well.'

Gertrude smirks. 'Mrs Reddish has been most unwell.'

'A conniption fit, I shouldn't doubt,' says Edna primly.

'My nerves,' exclaims Mrs Reddish. 'They are in shreds!'

'I can explain,' I begin, and then realise I can't. There's a silence.

'There's the matter of the suit, Mrs Reddish,' adds Gertrude helpfully.

Mrs Reddish's face turns a fierce shade of magenta and she sinks into a chair. Edna wafts a tiny bottle under her nose, which prompts a bout of spluttering.

'I should say Miss Latchford's lucky not to have the police called on her,' says Gertrude with great cheerfulness.

Under the watchful eye of these three witches I pack my bag with the sum total of my five years of independence: a few blouses, some skirts and a picture postcard of Hetty King in top hat and tails. No doubt Mrs Reddish suspects an unsavoury character like myself will roll up the carpet and spirit it away unless my every move is supervised. I return to The Comet with bowed head.

'Here she is, tail between her legs,' Ma crows, eyes glittering with triumph. 'Don't think you can stop here without paying your way.'

'Fear not, Mother,' I say. 'I wouldn't dream of presuming on your generous nature.'

I snap open my reticule and count coins on to the table. Ma's eyes widen. The amount far exceeds anything I tipped in before.

'Since when did you become a moneybags?' she sneers. 'Been on the game, have you?'

'Cissy!' gasps Nana. 'She's not been in the house five minutes.'

'Sticks and stones,' I say with a shrug. 'Words cannot hurt me. Listen up, Mother. This is the amount I paid to Mrs Reddish. Not a penny more, not a penny less.'

'Didn't she pull the wool over your eyes,' Ma replies.

I do not rise to the bait. 'For that, I had two meals a day, laundry, a hot bath and I did not have to cook or clean. I shall be your lodger, Mother. Not your barmaid, nor understairs maid, nor girl of all work.'

Her eyes flicker. 'Oh, Edie,' she whispers. 'You don't need . . .'

Her mouth trembles. Despite myself, I am shaken. If only I'd seen that tenderness as a child; if I'd once heard her speak my name so softly. It is too little, too late. She is not the only person on this earth to learn harshness out of necessity.

'Done,' she barks, the weakness gone as swiftly as it appeared. 'I shall expect nothing from you. This is business.' She sweeps the coins into her apron.

'Business,' I agree.

I climb the stairs and unpack, folding my clothes and placing them in the dresser. I become aware of my grandmother leaning on the door frame, but have no intention of engaging in small talk. She breaks the silence.

'We've missed you,' she says with true warmth.

This is the moment where I am supposed to run to her arms whilst wiping away a tear as we make our joyful reconciliation: the prodigal daughter returned to the bosom of her affectionate family. I toss the notion aside. Such a reunion is the stuff of penny papers.

'Did you?' I scoff. 'I find that difficult to believe.'

'Edie, love. I didn't take you for such a harsh woman.'

'You are surprised? I am my mother's daughter.'

'That you are,' she sighs. 'Edie, she's not had it—'

'If you dare tell me she's had a hard life, I swear I shall scream.'

'Do as you please. You'll never know the half of it.'

I refuse to soften. 'You assume I have any desire to do so.'

We face each other: I with folded arms, chin thrust forward and glaring down my nose. She gives me a long, slow look.

'Edie, lass . . .'

'I am no longer a child. You can't win me round with clucking and cooing.'

I wait for her next sally, tapping my foot belligerently. She sags like a loaf taken out of the oven too soon.

'I can't fight you,' she croaks. 'Not any longer. But I shall have my say and then I shall leave you to your own devices. You have precious little respect for your mother, eh?'

'How did you guess?' I reply with a snort of derision.

'Then pin your ears back and hear this. You will end up like her. Worse, I reckon.'

'Where on earth did you get that idea?'

'She's closed Arthur away, more or less. You've done the same to Gnome, haven't you? Took what was not yours. There's a bitter price to pay for such tyranny.'

'I don't know what you mean,' I lie.

I stare out of the window at the rain-glazed roofs. I refuse to show how deeply her words have affected me, but she's been able to read my face since I reached her knee.

'At least you have the good grace to look guilty, even if you won't admit it.'

'Nothing to admit,' I mutter.

'You know exactly what I'm talking about. It's killed your mother.' She waves away my interruption. 'No. Not in that way. But she might as well be dead. She works, she eats, she sleeps. She is too terrified to contemplate love, even a friend. That's a poor sort of life. Do you want that? Frozen, friendless, loveless?'

She has hit the mark and she knows it. I hang my head. 'No, but—'

She silences me with an angry gesture. 'No more of your wheedling justifications. You're back home. Gnome must be back also. I want to see him, every night. Chew on that, young lady, and see how it tastes.'

With that, she leaves the room. She has no idea what he's put me through. I resist the urge to shout something uncomplimentary and confine myself to slamming the door. I make up the bed with the blanket and sheet laid out on the chair. Night is coming in. From beneath come the sounds of the bar and its customers. The basin and ewer stand in their usual position upon the chest of drawers. The wallpaper peels at the cornice. It's as though I never left. Battered by a wave of misery, I sink to the bed and put my head in my hands. All my effort, for nothing. I have lost everything. I am back where I started.

I grind my teeth. No, not quite. This is a temporary setback. I have retained my job by the skin of my teeth, which is more important than the loss of my lodgings. I have a friend in Guy. And, possibly, Miss Hargreaves. Abigail! In all the confusion, I clean forgot. The single light in my present darkness is the arrangement to meet her at the Art Gallery on Saturday afternoon. For the first time on that monstrous day, I smile.

The pleasure is short-lived. Nana's words ring in my ears and my skin crawls with the truth of them. My whole life I've regaled myself with the glib conviction that I'd never follow my mother's example. Yet I've done precisely that, and worse. I consider the notion of Gnome and me resuming our old ways: day and night, night and day. We might start this very evening.

I gnaw the inside of my cheek and think of what he attempted today, how narrow my escape. What if I let him in tonight, only to have him wreak an even more terrible revenge? I feel the familiar twisting in my bowels as he stirs. I wait for the surge of his rage. It does not come. Rather, he is timid, hesitant. It must be a sham.

'Gnome?'

Who else? I am sorry.

'Sorry? Don't insult my intelligence. You set thugs on me!'

I knew it was a mistake the minute I did it. I didn't mean it to go that way. I swear.

'Rubbish. It's just the sort of trick you'd pull.'

I was angry. Can you blame me? Can't you forgive me a moment's fury?

I clench my fists against the bile rising in my gorge. 'No.'

Let me in, Edie.

'Just a few more days,' I gasp. 'Until Saturday. Then. I promise.'

Please, Edie. Don't. I'm frightened.

'You're not frightened of anything.'

I cannot permit myself to trust him. Everything he says is a lie. I can't give up, not now. I draw a pin from the brim of my hat and thrust it into the flesh of my thigh.

I am on tenterhooks for the following three days. When not at work I keep to my room, avoiding Ma and Nana whenever possible. I wedge a chair under the doorknob if Nana looks set to deliver another sermon, and the prospect of my wage packet emptying itself into her pocket appeases Ma's foul mood to the occasional scowl. Nothing can be permitted to prevent my meeting with Abigail. When Gnome wriggles at nightfall, I skewer him till he stops.

On Saturday, I pace outside the Art Gallery in a frenzy. Abigail arrives on the dot of one and I am so overcome with relief I almost kneel and kiss her shoe. With a great deal of effort, I compose my features into what I hope is a calm smile of greeting.

'Guy has been most mysterious,' she says, taking my hand and shaking it gently. 'He told me you missed a day at work.'

'Did he?' I recoil at the idea of Guy casting my confidences to the winds.

'Rest easy, dear Edie. He said nothing untoward. He can be very discreet when he chooses. Or is required to be.'

245

'Thank you,' I say, unsure if I am addressing Abigail or Guy. 'He intimated I may need to treat you gently.'

I open my mouth, ready to fashion a brisk retort about not needing to be mollycoddled by anyone, thank you very much. Her expression is suffused with such kindness the words die on my tongue. I nod stiffly. It is a poor state of affairs to be so unused to expressions of tender feeling that I lash out at all and sundry. I must learn to accept gentleness.

We proceed through the heavy wooden doors, cross the vestibule and its chessboard of black and white tiles, turn to the left and enter a room full of landscapes. We pause before a breathtaking vista. Wisps of cloud are torn across an azure sky and dense forests cling to the side of mountains, thrilling me as much as if I were a mountaineer braving their slopes.

'I find it quite magical that I can gaze into another world through the golden frame of the painting,' I say. 'Without leaving the confines of this room I can travel a thousand miles in the wink of an eye, transported far from Manchester and its sooty mills and chimneys.'

'I never thought of it in such a way before,' Abigail replies. 'You have the soul of a poet.'

'Me? Hardly.'

'You underestimate yourself.'

She assesses me with a penetrating glance. Here, then, was my great fear: to be observed closely and for my disguise to be pierced. To be found wanting and rejected. No such denouncement occurs. We move to the next painting, a rural idyll with a sky of cornflower blue.

'I declare I can hear birdsong!' she says. There is the lightest of pauses. 'There are blackbirds nesting in my father's garden. They have the sweetest of songs. I should like you to hear them sometime.'

'You would?'

'May I press you to call upon me one evening after work?'

'I should like that very much.'

'So should I.'

We wander on, side by side. A pair of stone lions guards the staircase to the upper galleries. On previous occasions I imagined them baring their fangs and growling. This afternoon they appear to be grinning. Abigail's company is indeed invigorating if it can prompt such a flight of the imagination.

'Now we leave the countryside and enter the world of men,' she says with an arch smile. 'Prepare yourself for a great deal of sound and fury.'

We take the stairs and are presented with canvasses populated by ladies and gentlemen pulling faces and striking theatrical poses. Abigail comes to a halt before a particularly wide-eyed youth who is chewing his knuckles and banging his knees together.

'He looks as though he has been struck with a bad case of indigestion,' she whispers.

The jest is spoken softly, yet is loud enough to be overheard by a matron standing to my left. I wait for the snort of disapproval and am surprised when her mouth quirks into a smile.

'How often have I thought the same,' she says. 'But one is hardly permitted to say so, is one?'

'Life is much refreshed by a little disobedience,' says Abigail.

The woman laughs. 'Thank you, my dear. You have quite made my day.'

She turns and moves the length of the gallery with a spring in her step. The stuffed bird upon her hat flaps its wings.

'Now,' says Abigail, with a look of grave seriousness. 'Time to screw our courage to the sticking-place.' My face must betray my question. 'Forgive me. I am being obtuse. Come.' She takes my hand in hers, a gesture so distracting I care not whither I am led. 'Ah!' she breathes. 'The room I most wished to visit.'

The gallery contains portrayal after portrayal of somnolent women. They look much of a muchness to my ill-educated eye: flame-coloured hair, bruised mouths and a great deal of velvet. Abigail pokes her umbrella at one of the limp nymphs, at the joint of whose thighs the paint has been blurred into nothingness.

'Bah!' she exclaims. 'An ideal to which women are forced to aspire, yet never have any hope of attaining.'

I stare at her, unsure how to respond.

'Do they look like any women with whom you are acquainted?' she says angrily. 'No! I could smack the whole roomful into the middle of next week. The artists and all.' She pauses, breath stertorous.

'I thought you said you liked the gallery?' I say, somewhat at a loss to understand her outburst.

'I do,' she replies. 'It reminds me why I am passionate about the cause and how far we have to go.'

'Now that you mention it, I suppose there is a surfeit of disinterested-looking maidens,' I remark. 'It is rather trying upon the nerves.'

'I should like to take a toffee hammer to them,' Abigail says, passion unabated. 'It might happen, you know.' She pauses. 'Do I shock you?'

I consider my answer. I ought to cry out *yes!* However, I have a growing mistrust of statements containing the word *ought*. 'No,' I reply.

'I am glad. I like you and would have us share thoughts and feelings, even if they flow against the current that society has ordained for our sex.' She lowers her eyes and picks at the fingertips of her gloves. 'I sound foolish.'

'Far from it! You speak with fire.'

'I do so whenever I touch upon my hopes. I have ambitions that are scandalous to many.'

'Please. Tell me.'

I am entranced. I could listen to her passionate declamations till the cows come home. How outrageous can she possibly be? Whatever she says, it cannot come close to my outrageous nature.

'Not here. I simply must take tea or else I shall start tearing the pictures from the walls.' She speaks quietly, but with iron determination. 'There is a fine teashop around the corner. It serves a strong cup.'

She slips her arm through mine. I like the sensation it affords a great deal. She guides me down the stairs and along the street. We order tea and the waitress brings the tray straightaway. Suddenly I am thirstier than ever in my life. Abigail pours me a cup.

'So,' I say. I drop in two lumps of sugar and stir thoughtfully. 'You said you are scandalous.'

'I did, didn't I?' She glances nervously in my direction. 'All of a sudden I feel rather shy.'

'You?'

'I am when I am with someone whose opinion I esteem. Very well.' She draws in a breath and speaks quickly, as though the words have been bottled up and are pouring out in a rush. 'I wish to be my own woman. That is the beginning and end of it. I do not desire marriage to provide the only means of escape from home. I want a job that interests, not enslaves me. I want to exercise my mind and not on romantic frippery. I wish to love, freely. Whether that lover be man or woman.'

'Good gracious!' I exclaim. 'How . . .'

She falls silent. The muscles in her cheek tick away the seconds.

'. . . how wonderful.'

The cloud clears from her face. She smiles and peers into the teapot. 'Enough of my hectoring. What of you?'

'Me?' No one ever asked such a question. 'I assume I'll follow Ma into the brewery trade.'

'Do you want to?'

I shrug. 'What I want is of little significance.'

'If you could choose?'

'Choice? Not for the likes of me.'

I take a fortifying gulp and it occurs to me that I have made choices: even though my lodgings are lost, I am earning a wage in the Telegraph Office. Perhaps I can still be my own woman? No. The very idea is laughable, not to mention impossible.

'You must pardon my questions,' Abigail continues. 'I am an inquisitive creature and like to have my curiosity satisfied. It is a great failing and has led me into all kinds of scrapes.'

'You have failings? I cannot believe that.'

She laughs loudly. An old fellow with bushy side-whiskers shoots us a sharp glance of disapproval. *O tempora, O mores,* I imagine him thinking. I stare back until he looks away.

Abigail chuckles. 'Too loud to be ladylike, aren't I? That is another of the sins I commit. My manners do not become my sex.' She takes a long draught of tea, her eyes sparkling. 'I must warn you, Edie. If we are to be intimate friends you must understand that you are falling into unsavoury company.'

'You wish to be intimate friends?'

She tips her head to one side. 'Indeed. Why not?'

'I am not like other women, who know the art of friendship. What have I to offer one such as yourself?'

'A good question. Maybe the exploration of that question over time will produce its own answer.'

I faced this crossroads with Guy. This afternoon I face the

same with Abigail. I can continue on my life's narrow course, free of the entangling snares of companionship. Safe and lonely. That path is as clear as a series of picture postcards, complete with dramatic captions. I grip the edge of the table, rubbing my thumb against the warp and weft of the tablecloth. The creases are ironed in so sharply I am surprised they do not slice the skin and draw blood. I raise my eyes, regard her steadily and in that moment know I do not wish to be free.

'Your mouth is open,' she says. 'Be careful, for I may push in a sugar lump.' Her cheeks flush crimson and she places her hand over her smile. 'Now it is my turn to offer apologies. I did warn you I was uncouth. Words spill out before I have the sense to check them for propriety.'

'No one heard,' I say and smile reassuringly.

'*You* did.'

I am unused to flirtation and it makes me dizzy. Abigail is a near stranger, yet there is an indefinable quality about her that demands honesty. It is most peculiar. I never felt so madcap. I drain my cup.

'Be assured that you have my good opinion and more. If I hesitate on the brink of closer intimacy it is no fault of yours. It is entirely as a result of my own fear and shame.'

'Shame?' Abigail echoes.

At that moment, the waitress reappears. 'Can I fetch you some sandwiches, miss? We've got nice cheese and piccalilli.'

'No thank you.'

'How about a slice of cake? There's a lovely Victoria sponge.'

'No. Thank you.' Abigail smiles and proffers the empty jug. 'Another pot of boiling water, if you please.'

'We'll be getting busy shortly,' the waitress says pointedly. 'They'll be coming out of High Exchange and wanting tea. And cakes, and sandwiches. Heaps of them.'

'We'll not keep the table much longer,' I apologise.

The waitress sniffs at such a pair of penny-pinchers and sweeps away.

'I don't blame her for trying,' Abigail says. 'Pittance of a wage. I shall leave a generous tip. However, I'm not moving until I've heard you out. I have a feeling if I do not hear it today I never will.'

The waitress returns speedily, carrying a very small jug of water. Abigail thanks her, and tips it into the pot.

'We'll be lucky to have a cup worth the drinking. The leaves are practically drowned. But faint heart, et cetera.' She pours us both a cup. The brew is thin, approaching a state more akin to water. In her presence it is nectar. 'Tell me,' she says. She props her elbows on the tablecloth and leans her chin on her fist. 'What do you mean by such powerful words? Shame. Fear.'

'I do not know where to begin,' I say.

'Edie. You are prevaricating,' she growls.

I take a draught of bitter tea, seized with a wave of frustration at my inability to speak plainly. I want this friendship to flourish and it cannot do so without trust. But I do not trust myself: how can I when my very flesh is untrustworthy? I can never tell her the truth. But I can share something approaching it.

'I am ashamed of my family.' The words come out in a creak. 'In particular, my brother.'

'I didn't know you had a brother.'

'He has been away for a long time. He returned this week. Dramatically.' I point at my ragged curls. 'Take this for instance.'

'He cut your hair?'

'I certainly didn't. Life at home has been overturned as a result of his – intrusion. I was forced to surrender my lodgings. Almost lost my position at the Telegraph Office.'

Abigail leans across the tablecloth and takes my hand. The

252

linen is speckled with tiny droplets, where tea has dribbled from the spout of the pot.

'No wonder you are so distracted,' she says. 'Thank you.'

'What for?'

'For speaking to me as a friend, not as a stranger to be kept at arm's length with falsehood.'

My heart swells. With such a woman, anything might be possible.

She puts down her cup with a gesture of finality. 'However, we must give up this table for worthier customers. Before we leave, I have a request.'

I restrain myself from crying *anything!*

'The pleasure of your company on Tuesday evening next. If you are not already engaged.'

'I should be delighted,' I say. 'If needs be, I shall move heaven and earth to be there.'

'I doubt if you will need to labour quite so hard! It is a suffrage meeting at Birch House, that is all.'

'I have some arrangements to make. With my brother,' I say, selecting the words with great care. 'I shall be there. If I am not, it will not be my own choice, but rather an unavoidable detainment.'

She nods her head gravely. 'It is for me to apologise. I am unaccountably selfish. It did not occur to me that you may have good, plain reasons not to attend.'

I reflect how neither goodness nor plainness are words I attach to my family.

I fly home on wings of air. My head swims, giddy with hope. I have made it through this awful week. Abigail has declared herself my friend. My first and, I speculate, the first in the history of my cursed family. I think of us, hidden for untold generations, dodging from shadow to shadow. I am living in a new world, a new century, peopled with wonderful creatures like Abigail. Perhaps things can change.

Next Tuesday. I can permit myself a little leeway. An extra few nights without Gnome won't make that much difference. Nana won't notice. My conscience stirs and I stamp it down, hard.

I dance up the stairs and into my room, only to be brought down to earth with a thump. My grandmother is perching on the edge of my bed, very much like a dowdy pigeon with its feathers puffed up.

'Well?' she says.

'Well what?' I glower. I am in no mood to have her trample on my happiness.

She folds her arms and sticks out her chin. 'It's been three days. Where is he?'

I unbutton my jacket and arrange it over the back of the chair; brush away a speck of coal dust that has adhered to the lapel.

'He?'

Her hand snakes out, whip-smart, and slaps my cheek. 'Don't you play me for a fool,' she snaps. 'I can still put you over my knee.'

The shock of being struck by my grandmother is far greater than its sting.

'Three days isn't so long,' I mumble. 'I'll let him back in presently.'

I sit on the chair and unhook my right boot. I scuffed the toe at some point during the afternoon, far too beguiled by Abigail's charms to pay it the slightest attention. I smile at the pleasurable memory.

'Presently? That's not good enough. I am begging you, lass. The two of you have got to find a better way.'

For a moment, I think she means Abigail and myself. Of course she doesn't. Gnome, always Gnome. I refuse to stomach her blether about balance when it's the last thing she has any intention of doing herself. I cannot stay at The Comet. This state of affairs is untenable. I wonder idly if my next wage packet will prove sufficient for new lodgings and whether I might prevail upon Abigail to provide a reference. Out of the question. There is no point in renting a room only to have the same disaster befall me. I can do nothing until I have—

I am jerked out of my meditations by hands grasping my shoulders. With astonishing strength Nana pins me to the mattress, grabs the hem of my skirt and yanks it upwards.

'How dare you!' I cry. 'Get off!'

I endeavour to wrest my skirt from her grasp, but she pushes me aside as easily as a leaf brushed from her sleeve. She hauls my petticoats to my waist, revealing the latticework of wounds betraying five years of self-torture. I wait for the storm of recriminations. She slumps on to the mattress and puts her head into her hands.

'Dear God,' she moans. 'He was telling the truth.'

I look at the ruin I've made of my flesh, scars from every campaign I've fought against Gnome and the terrible price of victory. I draw my skirt over my knees. The most painful silence of my life stretches between us.

She breaks it. 'I thought he was exaggerating. I had no idea.'

'It's true,' I say. 'For five glorious years, I was free. Can you even begin to understand how wonderful—' The words stick in my throat. 'I want – I need – a life of my own. I am close to having it.'

'At what cost?' She lets out a little groan, which chills me far more than if she yelled. 'This cannot go on.'

'I don't see why not,' I mutter, patting my skirt into neat folds. 'It has been quite satisfactory.'

My tattered skin cries out the falsehood. I cannot admit it. I dare not.

'Haven't you listened to a thing I've said?' She pounds the blanket with her fist. I blink, the wind taken out of my sails. She pinches the bridge of her nose. 'I've never been good with words. You're the bookish member of this family and still you're as dense as gravy. You two are as bad as each other. He needs you as much as you need him.'

'He's the last thing I need.'

'Rubbish. Since he came back, you've been happier than in the five years preceding, haven't you?'

'You're wrong.'

'Am I? You have friends now, don't you?'

'Yes,' I say grudgingly.

'Your face can't lie. Name me one friend you had before this week. Without him, you drifted through those years half-alive. Which is rather the point. Have a heart, Edie. It belongs to both of you. Let him have his share.'

'I can't trust him!' I protest. 'I'll get lodgings. Miles from here. I'll do it all again.'

'How long will you manage before you slip up? Years? Months? Days? What if we slam the door on you the next time you crawl back?'

'You wouldn't,' I gasp.

'Whatever it takes for you to learn.' Then, more gently, she says, 'I'm trying to help.'

'Doesn't feel like it.'

'Listen. What if he'd done the same to you? What if he'd held you down for five years, never letting you so much as surface for a breath? What would you do?'

256

I catch my reflection in the mirror, self-justification ground into my features. I could trot out the soothing lie of Gnome's unreasonable nature compared to my mildness, his anger against my sweet nature and so on. It's a fairy tale I've told myself every night for five years.

My grandmother is correct. If Gnome did to me half of what I did to him – how I'd rail, how I'd plot vengeance. I think myself so clever to keep him down. It is a cunning devoid of compassion. We are not so very different, Gnome and I. My eyes prick with tears. I do not know if they are for Gnome, for myself or for the wreck of our lives.

'I'm frightened,' I whisper.

'I'm not surprised,' she says. 'You have a lot of apologising to do and you'd best start now.'

'What if he won't let me back in?'

'I'll make him.' She cups my cheek and I weep into its warmth.

'Help me,' I say, my voice small as a child's.

'I'll stop here. Till he comes.' She takes my hand. I cling to its anchor. 'Now, Edie,' she murmurs.

Bit by bit I let go of my hold, slip away and fall into the darkness that comes with Gnome.

GNOME
MARCH–JUNE 1909

Free. I'm free!

I fly back in to find my ear clamped in the vice of Grandma's fingers. 'Ow! Let go!'

'Not a chance.' She shakes me like a dishrag. 'Edie has kept her side of the bargain. You will too.'

'Bargain?' I roar. 'How long has she kept me away for this time? A year?'

'Three days.'

I scowl. 'Three days, three years; it's the principle of the thing.'

'It is.'

'You what?'

'I agree, you daft ha'porth. I'm on your side, Gnome.'

'Oh?'

'And hers.'

'Oh.' I knew there'd be a catch. 'You just wait and see what I've got in store for my ruddy sister.'

'You'll do nothing.'

'Watch me,' I growl.

'If you so much as break one of her fingernails . . .'

'You'll do what, you old bag?'

She hauls me close, presses her nose to mine. 'God forgive me for saying this, but I shall hold her hand as she stabs you.'

That takes the wind out of my sails. 'You wouldn't.'

'She is sorry. She wants to put things right.' She lets go of my ear. 'It's up to the two of you to sort this out. Make a life. You're together forever, and that's that.'

'Not if I—'

'I am watching. Don't you forget it.'

She storms out, leaving me alone.

I watch the sun go down and fume. Edie wants to make amends, after all these years? Too late. I'll show her. I pound the wall with my fist, the sound drowned by the racket from the bar downstairs. Damn their gaiety. Damn my sister. She and Grandma are in cahoots and if I so much as cough out of place they'll puncture me like a balloon. I am hobbled.

The ingratitude. I saved her from Jack and Joseph's clutches and look at the thanks I get. I shouldn't have bothered. *Sorry?* I cringe to think I wrote such a word. *Sorry* got me into this tight spot. Never again will I show such milk-and-water mildness.

I'm not man enough, that's the problem. Jack and Joseph thought I was girlish, just like Reg did. It's all Edie's fault. If it weren't for her, I'd be a true man, through and through. My birthright, yet it has been denied me at every turn. I hate myself.

No. I pull myself up sharp. I'm bemoaning my fate, and that's what women do. I'm not a woman, not even the tiniest bit of me. I shall prove it. Women have got fluff between their ears. I've got brains and I'll use them to get what I need. I've been going about things all wrong. Rage got me into this fix and will not get me out. New times need new measures.

There's a shirt in the tallboy, britches too. I put them on and it calms me a little as I think my way to a solution.

259

She stole my past. There's nothing I can do about that. But I can take her present and her future. Take it for myself, piece by piece, and when I'm done with it I shall crumble it like stale bread. What's more, I'll do it so cleverly she'll never guess a thing. With a snap of my fingers I shall transform myself into the sweetest brother ever to draw breath.

If I'm to discover the keys to her life, there's no better place to start than here and no better time to start than now. There is a power to be got from knowledge, and I shall get it. I snoop around the room; search under the mattress, the tallboy, the rug. I ferret through her pockets, her petticoats, the pillow-slip. I slide out the drawers on their runners and check if anything has been pasted to the underside. Not so much as a tram ticket. The only sign she's set foot in here is a pamphlet entitled *What Women Want*. I mangle it into a tight ball. What women bloody want? When I've finished with her what she'll want is—

A bell chimes in my head. Patience, Gnome. I lay the crumpled paper on top of the chest of drawers and flatten it with the heel of my hand. So, she fancies herself a suffragette. Very well. I shall let that be my first clue. It's only a matter of time before she slips and leaves more titbits of information.

I button my shirt and head downstairs. The Comet is in full swing. I saunter along the corridor, tipping my cap to Mam.

'Where are you off to?' she growls.

'Oh Mam,' I simper. 'Have a heart. Edie swept me under the carpet for so long. Surely you don't begrudge me a night on the tiles to make up for lost time?'

I expect a curse but her face softens.

'Go on, you poor lad,' she coos. 'You're a good son. Better than that sister of yours.'

'What's she done now?' I say encouragingly.

Mam kicks a crate of lemonade bottles. They chink indignantly. 'She strolls back in here with airs and graces like you wouldn't believe,' she mutters.

'Did she indeed? How rude.'

Mam hoists the crate and struggles towards the public bar. 'Slaps down a wad of cash,' she pants. 'Bold as brass, declares she'll be my lodger. Me! Do I look like a landlady?'

'The cheek of it.'

My sister has money. I squirrel away that nugget of information for future use. I'm so taken up with the thought I miss the next part of her monologue.

'. . . not lifting a finger. To my face!'

'Say again?'

'You could've knocked me down with a feather. Not a lick of help from her. Never!'

An idea stirs. I shall add wily fox as well as sleuth-hound to my repertoire.

'I'll help,' I say.

Her complaints hiccup to an abrupt halt. She blinks. 'You?'

'Can't have you wearing yourself out, can we? Let me take those heavy bottles.'

She looks close to tears, or fainting. Take your pick. The crate is a dead weight and her grateful quacking doesn't lighten it one smidgen. I follow her around The Comet, doing every task she has a mind to and doing them with a good will. When she calls time I'm there with a broom to sweep the steps. Why restrict myself to being the finest brother when best son is up for grabs? I fairly hug myself with delight at my ingenuity. I've been pushing a rock up a hill when all I had to do was stop and let gravity do its work.

Night follows night and I work like a trooper. Even my slab-faced grandmother cracks a smile. Mam stuffs me so full of beer and bacon and fried potatoes I can barely move. By the end of the following week, she's practically shoving me out of the door to take a night off.

Back and forth we go, Edie and I; back and forth.

Spring brightens to a summer as bright as Manchester can muster, and I'm as good as my tricky word. I don't barge in early. No more monkey business with boots in the bed, shearing her like a sheep or leaving her too exhausted to face the day. She falls for it, the sap. She thinks Gnome is a gelding. It's an effort to rein in my anger, but who knows what I may discover if I take things slow, rather than pile in, all guns blazing.

As she believes and trusts in me, she lets down her guard. As she lets down her guard, she leaves evidence: letters, leaflets, books, calling-cards, a pocket handkerchief scented with flowers that don't grow within a hundred miles of The Comet. I press it to my face. Ah, her precious life. The fool lays it out as a banquet for me to feed upon, selecting any delicacy that takes my fancy and gobbling it up.

One evening, I find a picture postcard of the Royal Botanical Gardens propped against the ewer. I flip it over and read the message: an invitation to attend a meeting where a Mrs So-and-So will present an illustrated lecture about the work of a bunch of busybodies from Cardiff. I can't think of anything more tedious. However, if my sister finds it of interest, so shall I. It is signed in sweeping copperplate: *From your friend, Miss Abigail Hargreaves.*

Hah. My sister has a friend: a flittery, fluttery girl with whom to giggle and gossip. The thought of all that sugar and spice makes me want to gag. Courage, Gnome. I raise the postcard to my nose and inhale. My senses crackle like the moment before a thunderstorm; heart thumps, breath gallops. Anyone would think it's yours truly who's affected by this female. The very thought. It's nothing to do with me. Edie read this communication with a particular thrill, that is all.

An address is written at the top of the message. Whalley Range, a brisk fifteen-minute walk from The Comet. What business my sister has in company so far above her station is beyond me. What is beyond me, intrigues me.

With great care, I replace the card in the precise position I found it. I wonder what this lah-di-dah companion would think if I were to whisper Edie's secret in her shell-like? Down will fall baby, cradle and all. Dash Jack and Joseph and all of that rough stuff. There's no need to lay a finger on Edie's precious body when I can injure her heart and carve wounds that can neither be seen nor repaired.

Her first friend will be my first quarry. I'll stroll by her place of residence, casual-like, satisfy my curiosity. Stash any discoveries for future meddling.

As I saunter along, botheration starts in my boots. It won't leave off, wriggling its way up my legs until it gets to my bonce. Wouldn't life be a lot simpler if I let go of my anger and shared with Edie, as Grandma suggests? Wouldn't that be easier than all this hole-and-corner business?

Never. Edie must be planting these notions in my head. She'll not get one over me. There's reparation to be made. This is not selfishness. This is survival.

Upper Chorlton Road is something of a Rubicon: to the north huddle Hulme's cramped terraces; to the south sprawls a plantation of modern villas, towering three storeys high. I take the turning on to College Road and straightaway I'm lost in a maze of genteel avenues. Just when I think I am heading one way, the road changes its mind and curves in the opposite direction, or else presents me with a choice of turnings. As often as not they lead to dead ends, so that I need to retrace my footsteps and begin over. If I believed in magic – which I most assuredly do not – I'd swear the houses move when I'm not looking, plonking themselves down in a fresh place every few minutes. It must drive delivery boys barmy.

If that wasn't unnerving enough, the place is as silent as the grave. It takes me a while to work out why: from the moment I entered this neighbourhood I've not spotted a single beer-house, not one shop. It escapes me what these people do of an evening with nowhere to go for a pint and a sit-down, let alone buy a bag of humbugs or get their boots resoled.

Just when I am beginning to wonder if I've stepped into a dream, a lady heaves into view, dragging a small dog on a lead. I raise my cap and enquire – with especial politeness – where I may locate Dene Road. The matron responds with an acid glare, as though I've cracked out a violent fart. She sweeps away, skirts flapping like the sails of a galleon, dragging the mutt from the tree against which it has cocked its spindly leg.

'Thank you, ma'am!' I shout after her. 'What exquisite manners!'

Her shoulders tighten. The dog yips disconsolately. This is unsupportable. I'd like to punch the wall, but cracked knuckles won't improve things. I stomp beneath the electric street lamps, cursing the higgledy-piggledy street plan. My boot heels sound far louder than they ought and I'm convinced I hear footsteps behind me; but when I spin around the pavement is empty. The back of my neck prickles with hungry eyes. This place gives me the willies.

Then, without warning, I find myself at my destination. After all the mucking about, I can't believe I'm here. The front door boasts a brass knocker in the shape of a sunflower and the driveway is flanked by pottery urns big enough for Ali Baba and every one of his forty thieves.

I'm not entirely sure what to do. There's no point knocking, for it's far too late for high-class types to receive visitors. Even if I do and Miss Hargreaves answers, she doesn't know me from Adam. I can hardly say: *I'm Edie's brother. You know my sister.* I rock back and forth on my heels and my attention alights upon an upstairs window. For no good reason, I am convinced it is Miss Hargreaves' room. I imagine her seated before her mirror and counting each stroke of the brush as she draws it through her unbound hair. From root to tip she goes, the bristles wrapped in a silk scarf, transferring its sheen to her tresses.

I shake myself. Why I'm mooning like this is beyond me. I've work to do. I slip down the side of the house and pummel the tradesman's door. It opens before I've finished to reveal a short girl in a dark uniform.

'Yes?' she enquires, sticking her nose up in a failed attempt to be grand. 'We aren't expecting a delivery this late.'

Her position on the other side of the brass strip across the threshold makes her so conceited you'd be forgiven for thinking she was the lady of the house and not the parlourmaid. I decide against a ribald quip, bring my sunniest grin out of hiding and ogle her like she's the prettiest pearl I ever saw.

'Who are you calling for?' she says, pleasingly confused.

I gaze longingly for a few more seconds. 'I'm sorry, miss! I am in such a daze. I do apologise – but I thought for a minute there . . . No.'

'You thought what?' she says. She's hooked.

'It's impossible – but are you perhaps the famous singer Miss Minnie Atkins?'

'I am certainly not,' she says in a voice that is all affront – to the untutored ear at least.

'Her sister, perhaps?'

She squirms with delight. 'Not a bit of it! The cheek!'

'But your face – it has that self-same delicacy. Oh, listen to me. I am making such a fool of myself!'

I hear what she will relate to her friends. *He said I looked like Minnie Atkins! He said I had her delicacy, and all on the mistress's back doorstep, without a by-your-leave!*

In truth, she has the poise and charm of a wheelbarrow, but making an accurate comparison will get me nowhere. Needs must when the Devil drives. I peer over her shoulder into the hallway. A drugget stretches its tongue into the distance. I bestow a smile that could melt granite; then it's to business.

'I was wondering – if I may trouble you,' I simper. 'Is Miss Hargreaves at home?'

'Oh.' Her face wrinkles in disappointment.

'It's just that my sister has sent me on an errand. I don't know Miss Hargreaves at all,' I add, watching her perk up. 'She wishes me to leave a message. Oh, it's all so dashed complicated. I'm awful at remembering things.'

I shoot her a helpless look and its arrow pierces the target. Bullseye. She leans forward.

'No one's at home. They're all out. One of their *meetings*.' She pronounces the last word with weighty disapproval. 'If you know what I mean.'

I don't, but nod my head sagely all the same.

'I'd invite you in . . .' she says, hesitantly.

'I couldn't!' I blurt. 'You don't want me cluttering up the kitchen and keeping you from your chores,' I continue, knowing that is precisely what she does want. She stares at me. I feel like a gammon joint about to be carved and eaten. 'In any case,' I add. 'I'm sure Cook wouldn't have it.'

'It's Cook's half-day off,' she says, and quick as a flash I'm in, with much giggling and shushing.

I get a good look at the hallway: a parti-coloured tile floor, figured wallpaper heavy with lilies and an ornate ceiling rose from which swings an electric light glittering with a dozen bulbs. Panelled doors lead into a vast room; I am whisked by far too quickly to catch a glimpse of the interior. It's not Buckingham Palace, but may as well be compared to anywhere I've lived. The maid drags me into the back kitchen, as devoid of interest as any kitchen from Scotland to Southampton. She bobs up and down in front of the range.

'Would you like a cup of tea?' she chirps.

'Goodness,' I demur, warming to my role. 'I wouldn't want to be any trouble. Not the tiniest scrap.'

'Get on with you. Won't take a minute,' she beams. She pokes the fire, spilling a coal on to the rug. With a lot of stamping and squeaking, we douse the flames. I imagine her smashing plates and smearing the silverware when she polishes it. After a bit of a struggle, she hauls the kettle safely on to the hot plate. 'See? No trouble at all,' she pants, looking very proud of herself.

'Thanks awfully,' I pipe.

The pot of tea is made without further upset and she pours me a cup. I pronounce it delicious, despite the fact that it could scour the barnacles off a tugboat. I add an extra spoonful of sugar and chatter about my sister, how she is most awfully attached to Miss Hargreaves. However, the maid is more interested in gurning than furnishing me with useful information.

'Surely you've seen her?' I ask a little desperately.

'Who?' she says. 'Miss Hargreaves? Of course I've seen her, silly. She lives here.'

'I meant my sister,' I say, grinding my teeth. 'Miss Latchford. Edie.'

'No. I'm sure I haven't heard that name,' she replies with a frowning effort at concentration. 'My name's Betty.'

Her hopeful expression betrays how it's my name she's after. I force down a mouthful of the acrid tea.

'Reginald.' It's good enough for the present circumstances.

'Reginald,' she echoes, rolling the syllables around her mouth like mint balls.

'My best friends call me Reggie,' I say. As though struck by an after-thought, I add, 'Do call me Reggie, won't you? If you'd like to, that is.'

She looks extremely pleased with herself. 'Well, Reggie,' she croons.

I toy with my cup. If I drink it, she'll only pour me more of the vile muck. It is most provoking. At this rate I shall leave this house with nothing more than the worst tea known to man tanning my insides. I've no intention of that happening, not when I've trudged so far. I try a different tack.

'I bet they work you jolly hard.'

'They're not the worst I've had.'

'Aren't these big houses packed to the gunnels with things that are the very devil to keep dusted and polished? Why, I'll bet there's a room full of stuffed tigers' heads poking out of the wall, from the master's time in India.'

'Not this house.'

'I don't believe you,' I gasp. 'It's filled to the brim with Zulu spears and shields, isn't it? There are lion-skins spread over the floor that you catch your foot in every time you walk into the room.'

'Oh! Not a bit of it,' she declares.

'Come on now. You're teasing me.'

'I wouldn't tease you,' she cries earnestly. 'They live very plainly. They have books, heaps of them, but that's about it.'

268

I fold my arms and sigh. 'You're pulling my leg.' There's the space of a heartbeat, during which time she glances over her shoulder at the wall-clock and then grasps my elbow.

'Come with me,' she hisses. 'I'll show you. Then you'll believe me.'

I've eaten my chips off enough newspaper advertisements to know just how prissy a house can look, and I expect this one to be up there with the prissiest. It's a surprise when Betty leads the way into the drawing room and I find windows hung with sober drapery, chairs marked with the print of many backsides and carpet of fine quality yet worn with the passage of feet. Bookshelves stretch from skirting board to cornice, crammed with more volumes than a healthy-minded chap could read in two lifetimes. Many of them stick out paper tongues where a marker has been slid between the pages. I wonder what breed of troll lives here.

'Gosh!' I gasp. 'I did not realise Miss Hargreaves was such a bluestocking.'

Betty lets out a snort. 'They're not her books, silly. They're the master's. Mind you, the missus reads enough of them. And, come to think of it, so does the young mistress, and all.'

She shakes her head at such inexplicable behaviour. I cross to the desk and start to shuffle through loose papers spread across the blotter. A claw seizes my wrist.

'Here! You put those down. I'll get thrown on to the street, so I will.'

I give her a contrite look. 'What a naughty, naughty boy,' I simper and hold out my hand. She looks confused. 'Go on. Bad boys need a slap on the wrist.'

She raps my knuckles gently, with her hand over her mouth to hold in the giggle. There is nothing of interest on the desk, merely scribbled notes about *prisons* and *humane treatment* and such rot.

We continue on our Grand Tour. The sitting room is as dull as the drawing room, albeit with fewer books. If anything, the chairs have been even more heavily sat upon. I am confused. These people are clearly rolling in money – folk in this neighbourhood are – yet they tolerate old carpets, battered chairs and rickety desks. The books might tot up to a king's ransom, but it's a dreary way to show off the lucre.

If I had half of it, I'd spend it right: fancy new chairs to start with, carpets too. Four maids. Six. A butler to fetch and carry whenever I yell. A boy to pull off my boots. And champagne: bottles and bottles. A cellar dug especially to keep them in.

We hover at the foot of the staircase while Betty chunters away about the master and the missus and how modest they are in their ways. I know a lot about secrets and where they are hidden. I put my foot on the bottom step and she hauls me backwards. If she ever loses her position, she could go into the building trade.

'Where do you think you're going? That's private, that is.'

'Aren't you going to show me the whole house?' I say, eyebrows raised. 'I bet it's a different story up there,' I remark. 'The height of fashion.'

'Not on your life.'

'I don't believe you! It's all very well showing me downstairs. It's all pretence.'

'It's the honest truth!'

'Pshaw. Lots of folk pull the wool over their friends' eyes by seeming sober in public, when in private all is riot.'

'That's as maybe. Not Master and Missus.'

'I know what you're doing,' I say slyly.

'What? I'm not doing nothing,' she cries, eyes wide.

I stick out my lower lip. 'You're too scared to show me the upstairs rooms.'

'I'm not!' she insists.

'I understand completely. Can't have the likes of me messing up the carpets. I'm too common by half.'

'No you're not,' she says, desperation mounting.

'Sure I am. I'm only a friend of Miss Hargreaves, after all.' I cross my fingers and hope she's forgotten Edie is the friend. It's not exactly a lie, when you think about it. She chomps the inside of her cheek. I sigh. 'I'll be off now. The tea was lovely, thank you. It's a shame I shan't see you again.'

I turn in the direction of the back door when her talons sink into my arm.

'Wait!'

'Whatever do you mean?'

'Come on,' she gasps, heaving me up the stairs. 'They're never back till nine o'clock. At least half an hour.'

'I couldn't. I don't want to get you into trouble,' I bleat, a love-struck fool once more.

She blushes. We tiptoe up the stairs, letting out little shrieks with every creak. Not that there are many, for the carpet is so thick it could muffle cannonballs being rolled off the landing.

Once more, Betty is disappointingly correct: the upstairs rooms match those downstairs for tedium. She shows me the bathroom, the master's bedroom, then the missus's, although her bravery does not extend to letting me take a step within. Not that I care, for it's Miss Hargreaves' room I'm wanting. Finally, she draws open a plain door and announces *the young mistress's room*.

'Is it really?' I say, gazing deeply into Betty's eyes.

I lean very close, as though I am about to steal a kiss, and while she's tittering I slide past.

'Hey!' she cries. 'You can't—'

'Can't what?' I chirp, heading directly for the window.

Upon the sill is a sheet of cheap writing paper. I catch a glimpse of the words *deepest, heart, kindness, intimacy* tossed around like marbles. I'm sniggering at women and their namby-pamby passionate friendships when I see the signature.

Edie.

How unutterably pathetic. How Miss Hargreaves must have laughed at such a grovelling missive! I dashed near do. It's as plain as the nose on my face that Miss Hargreaves needs a bit of a shake-up, and I am the very chap. I'd like to pry further, but Betty bounds to my side. I grab her hand and clasp it to my chest so she can't drag me away.

'Isn't it a pretty view?' I say. 'Wouldn't you like to have a house like this one day?'

Her lower lip droops as she tries to fathom whether this is a proposal of marriage. It takes up all of her brainpower, which grants me the opportunity to examine the room more closely. The bed is tidily made, coverlet embroidered in a tangle of green, white and purple flowers. The curtains are purple with green and white ropes tying them back. The cloth on the bedside table is cross-stitched in matching hues. I wonder if Miss Hargreaves is a monomaniac.

Above the fireplace is an engraving of a knight in armour with a pudding-bowl haircut. Plonked on a horse, he has a circle of light around his head and is gawping at the sky. It takes me a while to realise it's a woman.

'You don't want to be bothering with the likes of the young mistress,' says Betty sourly. 'She's a suffragette.'

'I'll bet she has a face like a bashed crab,' I say.

'No, she hasn't,' she mutters. 'She's pretty,' she adds with considerable venom.

'She'll be nothing compared to you. You're just being nice,' I say, and straight off I'm back in her good books. 'All suffragettes are ugly,' I aver knowledgeably. 'I've seen the papers.'

'She does have airs,' she concedes. 'Ideas, like.'

I've got all I'm going to get. This is a reconnaissance, not a rout. I steer Betty down the stairs and into the kitchen.

'More tea, Reggie?'

'No!' I say a little too loudly. I straighten my cap. 'I simply cannot take up any more of your time, much as I should like to. Perhaps I may call again?'

'I've got a half-day Sunday.' She smirks. 'Every Sunday.'

I wink. 'How could I stay away?'

I'm on the verge of making my escape when she grabs my sleeve, loosening a few of the stitches in the shoulder.

'Was there a message, Reggie?'

'A message?'

'For Miss Hargreaves, silly,' she says, poking me with a finger as hard as a chisel. 'You said you were on an errand.'

I consider telling her to leave off, but I may need her again. I smile engagingly. 'Say that Miss Latchford's brother stopped by.' I rack my brains. 'Tell her my sister will meet her as arranged.' It sounds feeble. I shrug my shoulders helplessly. 'I'm sure there was something else, but it's gone clean out of my head. I must've been bewitched along the way.' I heave a mournful sigh. 'By someone.'

This cheers her enormously. She continues to paw me and it occurs that while I'm here, I may as well get some manly practice under my belt. There's no reason why not. When I was a lad I didn't understand. Now I do. I have a lot of time to make up.

'Oh, I'm spellbound and no mistake,' I murmur, drawing her close.

She puckers her lips, eyes closed. I mash my face against hers. She pulls away.

'Hold hard,' she says. 'I don't want a fat lip.'

I wait for the laughter, the ridicule, but she grabs my shirt front and hauls me back in. I press gently. Our mouths fit neat as two spoons in a drawer. As we kiss, I have a strange sensation of sliding into myself: a half-sleep that sparkles with wakefulness at the same time. It is pleasure.

I pull myself up sharp. I can't afford to let myself go. Gabbling about how the master will be back any minute, and how it'd be a fine thing for him to find the two of us canoodling, I rush out of the door and tear up the cinder path as fast as my feet will carry me.

I scrub my mouth against the back of my hand. I've caught myself, and just in time. You won't find me falling for a girl. Betty – no, I've already forgotten that name – means nothing to me. I'm part of a man's world now, and I shall have a slice. A bloody big slice. I'll have a hundred women. See if I don't. On my arm, for all the world to envy and admire. There's a man worth his salt, they'll say. What a chap he must be, to have a hareem at his beck and call.

I don't understand why my swaggering words sound hollow; why I fell into that kiss as hungrily as a starving man on bread; why I itch to go back and tell Betty that it was all an act and that I want another kiss, and another; why I can't let myself admit any of this. I want to forget her. A man doesn't let women get their claws into his soul. Her name sticks in my head like a song I can't shake off.

Betty, Betty, give me your answer, do.

I'm half-crazy . . .

Wouldn't you know it: just when I think I'll be lost in this labyrinth for a week I tumble on to Withington Road. By the time I'm at Renshaw Street I am my sour self again. It doesn't make me happy, but happiness and I never went together.

It's a start. I have the measure of this Miss Hargreaves. A suffragette, dash it all, but if she's important to my sister she's important to me. I'll grit my teeth and play court to the ugliest woman in England if it gets me what I want.

Night after night, week after week, I continue, smooth as silk. Edie swallows the lot. A few days later she leaves an envelope for my delectation. The direction is G. Heywood, Esq. Well, now: my butter-wouldn't-melt sister has got a beau. I'll bet Mam knows nothing about *him*. I search inside but it lacks any enclosure. I'd give a lot to know what was written on that particular billet-doux. A message is scribbled on the reverse.

Angel! Luncheon alone cannot satisfy my thirst for your company. Neither my hunger, nor that of another personage. Take pity upon your lamenting friends! If you choose to grace our soirées once again, you will find us here. Ghastly, of course. 17 Oldham Street. Upstairs.

More friends. More mischief. I squirm with delightful anticipation. If there are soirées to attend, I shall attend them, and become the toast of her society. I am certainly more fun than she is.

I make my way into the city. At Piccadilly I gaze longingly towards Shudehill with its pies and pleasures. I'd far rather share a beer with Jessie than snore in the company of Edie's friends. They are bound to be the most insurmountable bores. Gnome, I chide. You haven't got the brains you were born with. You've set yourself a task. Stick to it and have that beer after. It will taste the sweeter. My new brains win.

I count the buildings up Oldham Street. The door opens at my knock and a willowy man greets me, beaming recognition.

'Darling!' he squeaks. 'I thought you had quite sworn off nocturnal peregrinations.'

He embraces me as warmly as a long-lost brother and hauls me up a dimly lit flight of stairs to an attic room so Stygian I can barely see two inches to either side.

'Well, look at you! Don't you love the new place?' He grasps my shoulders and holds me at arm's length, inspecting me with lip-smacking approval. 'You look entirely the dashing blade. I knew you had it in you. You'll be singing "Burlington Bertie" next.'

I try to wriggle away but he hangs on tight, as if he thinks I'll disappear in a puff of smoke if he lets go. Which I've half a mind to. I feel a tickle of recognition: this fool must be the Mr Heywood of the envelope. The flowery verbiage matches. I thrust him away. He looks me up and down.

'Dearie me,' he says in a contemptible drawl. 'You aren't Edie, are you? What a pity. Peas in a pod. And you're not a member of *our* family either. How frightfully dreary.' He wipes his paw on his jacket as though he's touched something unpleasant. 'Abigail!' he roars. 'Come and see what the cat's dragged in.'

Abigail? Miss Hargreaves? My heart does a skip and a jump. A young woman appears at Mr Heywood's side. Her hair is piled upon her head, luxuriant as a cushion composed of pale brown silk. I'd pictured her as a frostbitten spinster, and am knocked sideways at how wrong I was. Betty was bang on the mark; Miss Hargreaves is a delight to rest one's eyes upon. She grasps my hand warmly. That's the ticket. I've no desire to shake *her* off.

'Why! Edie, my dear,' she bubbles. 'I hardly knew you, you are dressed so outlandishly. Not that you don't look dashing in a shirt and collar, of course.'

The fop stifles a snort. I decide to affect bumbling ignorance. 'I beg your pardon, miss?' I say in a querying tone.

She falters. 'Edie?' she whispers. 'How funny you sound. Is this a game?'

'I'm afraid I don't – I mean . . .' I fluster, inclining my body in the half-bow I've observed in men of her class.

She leans forward. 'Come now, Edie,' she murmurs. 'What's afoot?' Her cheeks are bright, as if intoxicated.

'Miss?' I say, and tip my cap. 'I don't believe we are acquainted.'

'Oh!' she declares, abashed. 'You are not Edie. I would have sworn . . .'

Mr Heywood pats his hands together. 'I wondered how long it would take you!' he tweets. 'This is too precious. He took you in as surely as he did me! Isn't he the spit?' I glare at the pasty-faced bugger. 'Not half so pleasant as the original, of course,' he adds sarcastically.

I must be careful if I'm to squeeze anything out of them. I take a deep breath, fiddle with my cuffs and plaster on a shy expression. 'I am Edie's brother.'

I needn't have worried. They lap it up.

'My goodness!' declares Miss Hargreaves. 'She has mentioned you.'

'Edie's famous brother!' squeals Mr Heywood. 'I have been in an agony to meet you. Perhaps I should say infamous, hmm?'

The pansy winks at me. Winks!

I shrug. 'I'm afraid she rather disapproves of me.'

'How delightful,' he coos.

'Guy. Comport yourself. You will scare him away.'

'Fiddlesticks, Abbie.' He pouts. 'Don't be such a stuffed shirt.'

I resist the urge to heave the puffball down the stairs. It's possible he gets wind of my desires, for he prances off burbling about *drinkies*. I gaze at the charming Miss Hargreaves with wide eyes.

'I say,' I quaver. 'I don't think you could ever be a stuffed shirt, Miss . . .'

'Hargreaves,' she says, withholding her first name. It is early days. I counsel calmness.

'Gosh,' I say, adoringly.

She is a rose amongst thorns if there ever was one, blooming in this cesspit and wasting her fragrance on the desert air. I can't begin to imagine why she coops herself up here. She's sorely in need of a knight on a white charger and I know the very fellow to fit the bill and more besides. I take her hand and press my lips to her kid-glove knuckles.

'Miss Hargreaves,' I purr. 'Mr Latchford at your service.'

'I finally meet the dark horse,' she says. 'You are rumoured to be something of a troublemaker.'

'Indeed?' I say with admirable deference. 'Folk aren't always as black as they're painted. I can't imagine a lady as charming as you would let herself be swayed by rumour.'

There is a pause as I wait for her to blush and giggle, which she does not.

'Your sister will be most diverted to hear of this meeting.'

'I'm not so sure about that,' I mutter.

'I beg your pardon?'

I wonder how to get out of the hole I've dug myself when I get a brainwave. 'I entreat you,' I plead. 'Do not tell Edie.'

'Why ever not?'

I writhe with feigned embarrassment. 'She is – ashamed of me.'

Her face betrays curiosity. 'Why do you think that may be so?'

I heave a wounded sigh. 'I'm sure she's told some awful tales.'

She nods with sage comprehension. 'I see very little untoward in your behaviour, Mr Latchford. I have a notion you are not as bad as you've been painted.'

'Dear Edie,' I say, shaking my head with fraternal tolerance.

So, my sister has been blackening my name. But not sufficiently to make Miss Hargreaves run out of the room caterwauling *lawks! Murder!* 'You're a suffragette, aren't you?' I continue, knowing the answer full well. I wonder if she'll deny it. I would.

'A suffrag*ist*,' she replies, with emphasis.

What, there's a difference? The words quiver on the tip of my tongue. Some preserving angel lays a finger across my lips and the witticism dies before it is born.

'Marches, rallies, that sort of thing?' I say politely.

'Quite.'

I wrestle my features into respectful fascination. 'Tell me,' I say. 'I'd love to know. Edie doesn't . . .' I tail off and bite my lower lip dramatically. 'She says that I couldn't possibly understand, being as how I'm a man and all that.' I rack my brains for the title of the pamphlet. '*What Women Want*, for example. It sounds absorbing. She won't let me read it.'

'She won't?' she declares in disbelief.

Maybe I've gone too far. I spread my hands helplessly. 'I am a bit of an oaf. I'm sure you could make it all come to life.'

She proceeds to rabbit on about the movement, which sounds so much like a complaint of the bowels that I am forced to twist a giggle into an interested smile. All this repressing of jolly banter is giving me a glory of a bellyache. For a nice girl she talks a blue streak and it doesn't become her. I can't get a word in edgeways. However, Rome wasn't built in a day. I hem and haw at regular intervals and it is not long before a way in presents itself.

'I notice you are on your own, Miss Hargreaves. No brother accompanying you this evening?'

She arches her eyebrow. 'I hardly need to be taken care of, Mr Latchford.'

I laugh, such a tinkling sound you could mistake me for a

bell. 'I'm sure you don't need a gentleman to assure your safety. Yet I see no suitors doffing their caps and spreading their cloaks beneath your toes.'

'No, you do not,' she replies, mouth twitching. I am winning. 'How droll you are, Mr Latchford.'

I incline my head to acknowledge the compliment. 'It seems a strange turn of affairs. To my mind, you should be besieged by an army of ardent lovers, each one willing to barter his soul for one glance from those lustrous eyes.'

'That sounds fearsomely inconvenient. This room is small enough as it is. I doubt an army could squeeze in.'

'In that case, seeing as I have no rival, I beg a smile.'

She complies, very prettily indeed. I'm about to press my advantage when the ninny returns with a hefty female in tow.

'A thousand apologies,' he gushes in a tone suggesting the opposite. 'Mabel and I simply must tear you dear folk asunder.' He cocks an eyebrow at Miss Hargreaves. 'My angel, I pray the parting will not prove too dispiriting? No tears, I prithee. I am quite useless with tears.'

'Behave yourself, Guy,' says Miss Hargreaves.

'Fat chance!' blares his fat companion. She has a face on her like a well-slapped arse. 'Good behaviour? Bally waste of time.'

They waddle off, whisking Miss Hargreaves with them. The dandy looks over his shoulder and blows me a kiss. I should like to knock his block off. I console myself with the pleasurable sight of Miss Hargreaves' backside waggling in a flirtation of up and down and left to right as she goes.

I've fallen on my feet and that's the truth. They say luck comes in threes: I've tracked down Edie's secret rendezvous, Mr Heywood and Miss Hargreaves in one fell swoop. My first plan was to break up a friendship and dance on the broken pieces, but Miss Hargreaves is a perfect peach. Squiring her away from Edie will be more fun than I thought possible.

I feast my eyes upon the delectable swell of her buttocks, bulging beneath her skirt. She could fasten a piece of sacking about her middle for all I care. Clothes are pie-crust covering a pie. It is the tasty filling beneath the pastry that is of interest. Ah, the first slice of the knife into the hot centre, the steam rising from the gash.

Why shouldn't I be the prince to scale her castle walls? I picture her bedroom: there she stands, leaning on the window-sill like Rapunzel and beckoning me within. *Inside*, she says. *Inside*. I wonder what it would be like to lift those petticoats and stroke those thighs; see her face shed its businesslike expression and soften into pleasure.

These imaginings get me into a right lather. A fool might think I'm smitten with this biddy. The very idea is laughable. In fact, I laugh to prove it. I am laying my snares, that's all. If I have a man's thoughts while I'm about it, there's no blame in that. Right now, what I need is a pie and a pint and I know where to get both.

I pound down the stairs and stalk down Oldham Street towards Piccadilly Gardens. If I'm rattled, it's because Edie has found such easy friends. I hate their carefree happiness. Not one of them understands the loneliness that springs from imprisonment in a body that is mine by rights but has been usurped from the word go. I ought to be mobbed by folk eager to clap me on the shoulder and call me pal. It's always bloody Edie who gets first look-in. Bile pools out of my tongue and I spit it on to the flagstones.

I pass a gang of factory lasses tramping home from the late shift in Ancoats, swinging dinner pails off their arms. I hurl a few lewd comments and they give me good measure. You'd

281

think they'd be glad of the attention after the unearthly racket of the machines, but they're not, the ungrateful sauce-pots. It will not put me off. These are my streets. If these females choose to stray into my path, that's their lookout.

'You ugly cows!' I shout at their retreating backs. 'I wouldn't fuck you if you paid me!'

They swagger down the street, honking like geese. I watch until they turn the corner on to Tib Street. Not one of them glances over her shoulder to glare at the chap who put them in their place. I am tired of this sport. I shuffle along, scuffing pebbles. Glowing beneath the street lamps dotted along Thomas Street are women with loud voices and louder hair. In the deep pond of shadow between two gaslights a voice I recognise growls, '*Business?*'

'Jessie?'

She blinks in a manner that is half hopeful, half fearful. 'Oh, it's my little Gnome!' she declares, brightening. In answer to the question I haven't asked, she adds, 'Business isn't what it was.' She tips her chin at the squawking gaggle. 'Just because they've got a few years on me, think they know everything.'

'You look as fine as fivepence.'

I think I may have laid it on a bit thick, but she roars with merriment.

'That's brag and you know it.' She plasters on a flirtatious expression. 'Nothing that a proper drink wouldn't put a shine on, my pet.'

I have such a sense of relief at seeing her it quite unsettles me. I shove down the pleasure and let myself be herded to a hole in the wall where I shell out for a half-pint of gin and a string of questionable-looking sausages. Wittering about fresh lodgings and the travails of younger tarts stealing trade from under her nose, she leads me down alleyways that are narrower and grubbier by turn. Her new room is smaller yet has as much rubbish stuffed into it. I could try swinging a cat, but it'd create mayhem.

She pours gin: small for me and gargantuan for her. I toss it back in one gulp and manage not to cough. She plonks herself on the bed, stretches across the slippery quilt and admires herself in the mirror looming overhead. I slouch around the room, picking up gewgaws and laying them down. There is a distinct whiff of mould.

'This place is full of knick-knacks,' I say, toying with a china dog caked in dust. 'How do you put up with them all?'

'For the love of Mike,' she trills. 'Sit down, will you? If you keep picking things up you'll wear the shine off them.'

'Everything is filthy. Could do with a polish.'

She pours another gin and glugs it down without asking if I want one. 'Who d'you think you are, telling me what to do?'

'You're slovenly,' I say without malice.

She throws a cushion at me and misses. It strikes the wall, leaking feathers. I flip the lid of a box set with mother-of-pearl. It tinkles idiotically. I snap it shut and it is silent. I open and close it a few times.

'Stop fiddling!' she yells. 'You'll drive me to distraction.' I slam the lid and a splinter falls off, giving it a toothless air. She slaps the sagging mattress. 'Come now, Gnome. Give us a smile. Make an ugly old tart happy.'

'You're not ugly,' I say, dropping on to the bed. It elicits a smile of surprising girlishness. For a moment she looks half her age, whatever that is. 'You're not old, either,' I add earnestly.

'Not where it matters,' she says, squeezing a tit. She sees me looking and rocks back, hooting.

'Don't laugh at me.'

283

'Aren't *you* the life and soul of the party this evening. What's put my favourite boy so out of sorts?' she asks.

'I'm not a boy. I'm a man,' I growl, shoving my voice down into my boots.

'No you're not,' she chaffs, pinching my cheek. 'You're my little Gnome and always will be.'

'Bloody aren't.'

She claps her arms around me and squeezes me to her large and low-swung breasts. I am seized with the desire to bite them, hard. I'm still stirred up by Miss Hargreaves.

'How about a nice chocolate?' Jessie says, flapping her eyelashes. They are clogged with some black substance, like she's been face down in a tar-puddle. 'That'll cheer you up.'

'I doubt it,' I grunt.

She leans across the mattress and starts digging around under the rickety bed. Her rump sticks up, scant inches from my face. I think of the flesh wobbling beneath the skirts. My cock stiffens. I tear my gaze away and concentrate on my hands. They are trembling.

'What are you doing down there?' I say gruffly.

'It's under here somewhere,' she mumbles. With much puffing and panting, she straightens up. Her topknot is awry and I realise most of the stuff piled on her head didn't grow there. 'See what I've got for my special boy,' she says, shoving the wig back into place.

She prises open the box. More than half its contents are missing.

'Don't want chocolate.'

'You've changed your tune. *Give me some chocolate, Jessie,*' she whines. '*I'll starve if you don't. Please, please!*'

'Will you ever shut up!' I roar. I stick my hand into the box, grab a pawful and shove the whole lot into my gob. 'There,' I say through the gooey mess. 'I've had some chocolate. Happy now?'

'You and your cheek,' she says mildly. She waves a sweet in front of my nose. I swipe it away. 'Come on, Gnome, it's your favourite.'

She laughs: that affectionate laugh she keeps for my ears alone. I ought to treasure it. I can't. I itch to slap the motherly expression off the side of her face. I don't want it any more – as if I ever did. I want her to treat me like a man. I want her to do it without me having to ask. If I have to ask, that'll ruin it. She should know. It's her job.

'I'm bored of this game, Jessie. I want a different one.' I clutch her breast and squeeze.

'Gnome, don't,' she says, voice suddenly serious. 'We talked about this.'

'So what? That was years ago. Things are different now.'

I swing my leg across hers. I know what I am opening the door to. It's worth it, to wipe that Mama's-little-boy look off her face. She gives me an appraising glance, like you would a jar of dried peas at a fair when you have to guess how many.

'Why do you lads have to grow up?' she says. 'There's no way back.'

'Who said anything about wanting to go back? Forwards is the only way.'

I grind my knee into the space between her thighs. I should be careful what I wish for. But I don't have the sense I was born with. That's been drummed into me from the cradle and I may as well carry it to the grave. I can't help it. It's how I am.

'I thought you were . . .' she says softly. Her expression bends, breaks. A brightness snuffs out and only as it does so do I realise I shan't see it again. 'Sod it,' she snaps. 'It's all you lot ever want. Let's be getting on with it.'

She swishes across the quilt, props her chin on my shoulder and blows into my ear.

'Good enough to eat,' she coos in a voice I haven't heard before. She walks her fingers up my thigh. 'One step, two step,' she sings, and cups my privates. 'Well! What do we have here?'

'You know very well what,' I say, wishing my voice was steady. I sound like a boy whose balls haven't finished dropping. Mine are aching fit to burst. She starts to unbutton my fly. I slap her hand away. I must do this myself. 'Stop it, Jessie.'

'Never had a *man* say that before,' she says with marked emphasis on the word 'man'. 'My, how you've grown,' she continues, still in that catlike voice.

She unbuttons her blouse, exposing the stretched and gleaming skin of her titties. She spreads her legs wide and winches up her petticoat, inch by inch, smirking at me the whole while. It's a smile that says she knows everything and I less than nothing. I'll show her. If she thinks I'm a blushing boy to be taken in hand and helped over the hurdle into manhood she's got another think coming. I have lead in my pencil, all the way to the tip. I want this. I need this.

'No time,' I growl.

I give her a shove and her heels fly into the air. Her skirt rides up, revealing thighs fish-netted with crimson veins. I wrap my fist around my stalk, poke around but can't find where I'm supposed to put it. One of her hands reaches around, grabs hold and guides me in. She's scraping hot. I'm on fire.

'How my lamb is grown into a ram!' she warbles. 'Harder!'

She's sweltering and syrupy and I'm falling in and falling out; in and out, in and out, my balls slapping her arse.

'Come on!' she chirps. 'Show Jessie what you've got!'

I wish she'd put a sock in it. I hook her knees over my shoulders, bundle her skirt over her head so I don't have to look at her face, but can still hear muffled shouts of *that's it, lover! You stir my sugar hot and sweet!* It's enough to put a chap off his stroke. Now, if it was that suffragette with her legs spread and begging me to stick it to her – and there's my answer. Miss Tasty Hargreaves. It's her I'm pounding; it's her moaning my name. That's the ticket.

'Yes!' I shout and pile in like there's no tomorrow.

There's a squawk from beneath me. It's *her*, I tell myself, plunging in and out. Miss. Fucking. Har. Greaves. My innards roil and ripple. I bang on, gasping, breathless. This'll wipe the smile off that posh bint's face. My guts clench, tighter with each thrust. A flickering sense of something, someone . . . Set against the furnace of my lust it is dim, but it's there nonetheless.

Edie.

Surfacing, drawn by the scent of what I'm doing, till she's fair peering over my shoulder. Of all the filthy – I shove her away, but she sticks like glue, slithering over my business. Is there no peace for me, even here, even now?

'Get away from me!' I wail, unsure if I say it out loud or in my head.

Jessie shows no sign of having heard. I can't go on. I'm damned if I'm going to poke Jessie with Edie watching. Even worse, joining in. Getting in. I can't risk it. I mustn't fire my load. I can't, I can't. I shove aside all thoughts of Miss Hargreaves and Edie sinks away.

Cold sweat pricks my brow. I stare at the mirror over the bedhead and pull the faces a man is supposed to pull: brow creased, teeth bared and puffing like a thief. It's an empty, dead sort of thing my body is doing. I'm as hard as a chair leg and as unfeeling. The mirror's plaster frame thumps the wall in time with my rutting, showering the bed with flecks of gold paint. I am drowning in a cacophony of panting breath, shrieking bedsprings, the hammering rhythm of the looking glass and Jessie's smothered yelps. I have the oddest notion that I have been doing this forever and will never be able to stop, caught in the mirror's nightmare spell.

Jessie's cries lose their complimentary edge. A few more moments of strenuous pumping pass without any sign of escape. It's no use. I have to stop before I go off. I'm going to have to pretend. Gradually, Jessie's moaning tails off and it occurs to me that she's bored. No, not that. She has fallen asleep.

I should be furious. I'm anything but. It's my chance and I grab it. I dive heavily on top of Jessie, shouting a triumphant *oh yes!* to keep up the pretence of culmination as much as wake her. She comes to with a snort and gathers herself hastily, rearranging her skirts.

'Well then,' she says, and tickles me under the chin, testing the rasp of stubble. 'Better than those young 'uns, aren't I?'

'Course,' I mutter.

I stow my rigid prick in my trousers. It is a devil to manoeuvre, so to cover up I press my face into the curve of her throat and snuffle like a piglet. Under cover of her giggles, I worm my way to the edge of the bed, out of reach. I want to be away: out of this room, this house, this rat-infested neighbourhood. I want to climb to the top of Lewis's, take wing and quit this island. I want to soar farther and farther till I get to the moon, live on green cheese and get away from bloody Edie. That's all I want and even in this, the most private moment a man can have, she's there. I hate her. I'll destroy everything she has. I'll crush it to pieces and, when I've done that, I'll stamp those pieces into dust. I struggle to my feet. Jessie latches on to my arm.

'I've got to go,' I grunt.

Rather than release me, she hangs on. 'Come and give Jessie a cuddle,' she says.

I wish she'd shut her trap, but the nonsense spills in a maudlin stream.

What a chap you are, to be sure!

How about another gin?

How about some chocolate?

If she's like this with all her customers I'm surprised she doesn't get a thick ear every time. I take a step from the bed and drag her after me. She weighs a ton. I wonder if we are joined forever, like some monstrous fairground attraction. All I have to be is nice. Toss out a bit of flattery and watch her primp and preen, unlock her talons and let me go.

'Put a cork in it!' I bellow. 'Get off me, you ugly cow! I don't need anyone, certainly not an old tart like you!'

My words scatter like dirty pigeons. She unlatches her arms and the sudden release of dead weight makes me feel like I'm floating towards the ceiling.

'Well then,' she says. Her voice is far away, her eyes farther. 'That'll be that.' Her face has a hard beauty I've not seen before. My friend Jessie is so utterly gone I almost beg forgiveness. 'I've been the worst sort of fool,' she says, straightening her stockings. 'It's my own fault for . . .'

'What?'

'Never you mind. You wanted things to change. They have,' she says, buttoning up her chemise. 'Next time you're here it'll be cash on the barrel.'

'Aren't I welcome?'

'Always, dearie,' she says, face blank as a wiped plate. 'Money in your pocket and a box of chocolates if you're after anything special.'

'But I'm your little Gnome.' I punch myself in the stomach to quell the contemptible whimper.

'No you're not. You've put paid to that. Think I need another ruddy man in my life?'

I hunch my shoulders. It's a few paces to the door, a small matter to grasp the handle and tug, noting where it sticks on the rug. I'm halfway gone when she does speak, although not to call me back.

'I warned you,' she says crisply. 'You're not happier. Told you so.'

I stagger back to Hulme, hugging the ink of the shadows. It's nearly morning: too soon for the knocker-up, too late for any decent soul to be about. My cock is still as stiff as a stick of Blackpool rock. I thump myself in the nackers and that only serves to make the damn thing harder. The skin is so stretched it's on the verge of splitting along the seams.

I lumber onwards, floundering into walls and groaning like a drunkard. At last I reach The Comet. I try to shin up the drainpipe, but my knees are so watery I can't get two foot off the ground. I refuse to go in the door, front or back. One of those crows would be sure to poke their beak in. They'd see. They'd laugh. They'd pity.

I can't stop here forever. The sun'll be up soon. I crawl to the privy and park myself on the seat, boss-eyed with frustration. I tussle with the fly-buttons. My prick judders. I twine my fingers around the shaft and am washed with a wave of relief. I squeeze and the wave swells. I picture Miss Hargreaves, and blow me if Edie doesn't stir again.

Abigail, she murmurs. *Yes.*

I pause; she sinks away. I can't be doing with this interruption. It's disgusting. I have a job at hand with Mother Thumb and her Four Daughters. I clear my head of the suffragette; give myself a tentative yank. No sign of Edie. Another. Ditto. I spit on my palm, slide the slick over its head; jerk my fist; jerk again. That's what the doctor ordered. I fill my head with Jessie, the factory girls, every whore that props up the wall of Shudehill Market: a tumultuous parade of faceless flesh; for who needs faces when that's not what's needed? I pump and pump, faster and faster, shaking the privy walls, and no Edie, not a sniff, not a sniff. I. Don't. Need. Any. One. I. Don't. Need. A. Woman. A rocket goes off, my head explodes into a sea of stars, my fist fills with jism and I'm done.

The night's aggravation melts into satisfaction. If you want a job done properly, do it yourself. I wipe my hand on my britches. My legs are still wobbly, but it's of a different sort. I'm up that drainpipe faster than a ferret; I collapse on to the bed, delirious with exhaustion. I wrench away my shirt and toss it into the corner. I must take off my trousers. I must play the good lad.

I'm wrestling with my braces when it hits me. My brains nearly fall out of my arse. How could I have missed it? I couldn't make head or tail of Edie sticking her nose in at the thought of Miss Hargreaves, but it's as clear as the shit on my boots. All those letters and postcards, stored as carefully as holy relics. The endearments, the words of affection. I've been so engrossed in playing the bloodhound that it went straight over my head without parting the hair.

Edie wants her. The fool has fallen in love.

EDIE
JUNE–SEPTEMBER 1909

Gnome and I settle into an uneasy truce.

At first, I dare not permit myself to believe that such a turnabout in my fortunes is possible. I wait for his avowed good intentions to evaporate and for him to revert to his wild ways. The days turn into weeks; the weeks, months. Spring warms into summer and nothing untoward transpires. I have no clue what nocturnal escapades he indulges in, but whatever they are, I awake refreshed and unscathed. I breathe cautious relief.

Nana's approval continues to nourish and encourage me, and it is a satisfying moment when, three months after Gnome's reappearance and my ignoble return to The Comet, I am able to press her hand in mine and tell of our new-found peace.

I experience a particular delight in the attentive affections of Miss Hargreaves – Abigail, I remind myself with a distinct thrill – which casts radiance upon my previous darkness. We meet every spare hour I can find and I strive not to begrudge Gnome the nights he must, of necessity, be granted. When Abigail and I are apart, I devour pamphlet after pamphlet, my brain stimulated with the nourishment of the words. My life approaches a serenity I never dreamed possible. I rejoice in contradictory joy that I, the unluckiest of creatures, am now the most fortunate.

If that were not sufficient cause for celebration, my friendship with Guy blooms. Indeed, we spend so much time in each other's company that we become the gossip of the office.

'Which suits me perfectly,' he says one Saturday afternoon as he squires me out of the building. 'Hiding in plain sight is by far the best way.'

I murmur agreement.

'Can't I persuade you to come out tonight?' He sighs. 'Afternoons are all very well, but, like the hart, I pant for the cooling streams of your company. I haven't been able to tempt you out of your hidey-hole for aeons. My hand is quite worn out by the writing of entreaties.'

'I'm sorry, Guy. More than you know. Since I moved back to The Comet Ma won't let me out at night.' It is an outright lie and I turn my face to the shop window to obscure my guilt.

'Fiddlesticks. I am convinced that you are toying with my affections and that our engagement is curtailed.'

'Guy . . .' I throw him a look of desperation.

'Good Lord, Edie. You look terrified. What on earth does she do; chain you in the cellar with a dish of gruel at your feet?'

I smile, despite the stirring of old fears. 'Nothing so dramatic.'

'Then we must find you fresh lodgings, away from your turnkey mother. Evenings simply aren't the same without you.'

'What on earth do I contribute to proceedings?'

He holds my gaze steadily. 'You underestimate your value, Edie dear. You see through me, right through to the other side, yet continue to offer loyal friendship.'

'Why should I not?' I say, baffled.

He cocks an eyebrow. 'It is a rare quality, far more so than you might imagine. Can't I at least persuade you to stroll with me for a little longer?'

'To the top of Market Street, at least. I am meeting Abigail.'

'Capital. I can no longer tolerate that hat of yours.'

'Whatever is wrong with it? I thought it rather the thing.'

'*Au contraire.* If we are to continue as an affianced couple – whether or not that is a misrepresentation – then I must instruct you on the perils of hideous millinery. And certainly before Abigail takes exception to it.'

We make our way in the direction of Piccadilly Gardens. Guy provides the amusement with droll comments about the parlous state of gentlemen's outfitting this season, the frightful price of gloves and how he simply must have mustard kid, no other shade will do: not ochre, and certainly not yellow.

I laugh and am very gay. I remind myself that my return to family life is merely a setback in my fortunes. Trading day for night with Gnome is a blow but not the end of the world.

'Here we are,' Guy declares, smirking gleefully. 'My arch-rival!' Under Lewis's clock stands Abigail, looking as pretty as fifty pictures. 'One day I shall be forced to take up arms and challenge you for Edie's heart.'

'I can't imagine I'm worth fighting over,' I say.

The two of them laugh over some truth they see and I do not.

'You would carry the day,' he murmurs, and pecks Abigail on the cheek. 'I shall capitulate immediately.'

'Buzz, buzz, Guy,' Abigail replies and returns the brief kiss. She presses her lips to my cheek for a longer interval. 'Edie, dear,' she murmurs. 'If you hold your breath for any longer you will faint.'

I shake myself out of my delicious trance.

'Well, dear ladies,' says Guy with a smirk. 'I can tell that I am entirely surplus to requirements, so I shall away, having brought the pair of you safely together.'

Abigail and I hasten to our meeting, which is to prepare for a rally in Albert Square the following Saturday. Birch Hall bustles with cheery toil and I am about to set to with a good will when Abigail takes me aside and introduces me to Mrs Gore-Booth. A willow-slender lady in wire-rimmed spectacles, she peers at me like a seamstress inspecting a skirt for dropped stitches and sagging hems.

'You vouch for this woman,' she says to Abigail. It does not sound like a question.

'Yes, Mrs Gore-Booth. I have found her a loyal and worthy addition to our cause.'

The grand dame nods. With that tightly executed gesture it seems all is well. The walls breathe out and I am accepted.

'Then I am glad to make your acquaintance, Miss . . .'

'Latchford,' I say, unable to prevent myself fumbling a curtsey.

This unties the final knot of her suspicions and she laughs, the lines on her brow unravelling.

'You think me very regal!' she says. 'I dare say I shall disappoint any queenly expectations.' She claps her hands. 'So. To work, sisters. To work.'

I have never before been called sister and am taken aback by how it affects me. Two short syllables and I am drawn into the bosom of a group of determined women.

I am always stunned, and not a little disappointed, by the speed with which the hours fly when Abigail and I are together. It seems as though we have barely arrived before it is time to leave.

'Do you have time to take tea before you must be home?' says Abigail hopefully.

I glance at the clock. Wild horses may not be able to drag

me from her side, but the agreement with Gnome can. 'Unfortunately not,' I reply.

'In that case, permit me to be your chaperone.'

'Gladly!'

She crooks her elbow as a gentleman would. We make an odd pair: giantess matched with nymph. I drag my feet, inwardly lamenting the brief distance to The Comet and how little time we have in each other's company.

'I do hope you can attend the rally next Saturday,' she says.

'I wouldn't miss it for anything!' She could have asked me to soak my head in vinegar and I'd have agreed as fervently.

'It promises to be of particular interest and I should be sorry to miss you there. I know that evenings are difficult for you.'

I am grateful for her sensitivity regarding the boundaries placed upon my time, even if she will never guess the reason. She falls quiet. There is a splash of colour upon the skin of her throat, spreading up to her cheeks. She is not happy with her glove at all, tugging at the leather as if she would like to rip the stitches holding it together.

'Abigail, my dear,' I say. 'You are as jumpy as a firecracker.'

She shoots me a brief glance and in it I glimpse something I am not expecting at all: nervousness.

'I should have told you right away,' she says. 'I do not like secrets. Certainly not where they concern you.'

I experience a twinge of fear. I grasp her hand: to quell the jittery motions of her fingers or my own skipping heartbeat I do not know.

'Told me what?'

She clears her throat. 'Your brother doesn't seem too bad a chap, you know.'

I almost fall off the kerb into the path of a coal wagon.

'What?' I splutter, gathering my composure none too smoothly. 'You have met him?'

'Yes.'

I resist the urge to scream. All the same, my voice has all the subtlety of a foghorn. 'When—?'

'He came to Oldham Street some while ago. In the dim light I thought he was you for a moment.'

'Did you now,' I hiss. 'Is that not rather insulting?'

'Edie! He warned me off mentioning it. He said you'd be put out. And you are.'

'I am not,' I say unconvincingly.

'You two are quite impossible!' she exclaims. 'I ought to knock your heads together.'

'Do not patronise me,' I growl.

She pauses at the turn of Renshaw Street. 'Are you jealous, Edie? I thought you'd know me better by now.'

'I thought so, too,' I grumble.

She withdraws her arm from mine. Now, I think. Now she will stride away and leave me alone and friendless. A lump rises in my throat.

'Edie. For goodness' sake.'

'I hope I have not detained you,' I say gruffly. 'I know you have many demands upon your time.'

'Edie,' she says firmly. 'Don't be silly. Look at me.' I obey. Between our clipped sentences you could hear a pin drop. 'Dash it all,' she continues. 'Do you think I can be swayed so easily when it comes to you?'

She grasps my shoulders and kisses me on the mouth.

It is over in the time it would take to snap your fingers. The city's clangour continues around us unabated: carts rattle and folk hasten to and fro, seemingly unaware of the shift in the world's axis that has occurred.

'My dear Edie,' she murmurs.

'My dear Abigail,' I reply.

It may have been a simple kiss of farewell. But something about it was unlike those prim embraces. What then? I have no ready answer, nor exemplar against which to compare. At the back of my mind lurks a hope. However much I tiptoe around the idea, it speaks its name in the private chamber of my heart. It was a lover's kiss.

What tosh, I tell myself. The stuff of romantic novels. Abigail likes my company, that is all. She was merely reassuring me of her good opinion after the mention of Gnome. Any hopes for intimacy are out of the question. I am penny-plain and always have been. There will be no hand-holding, no dimmed lights nor tactfully drawn curtains; not for the likes of me. I should know better than to indulge in the sort of wild imaginings that brought me nothing but misery as a child.

Despite my stern chiding, I quake. Saturday. I wonder how I shall live until then.

The following Saturday morning crawls by. I look at the clock so often Guy remarks that I must have contracted some strange affliction of the neck and should be whisked to the Infirmary forthwith.

At last, it strikes one. I rush to the cloakroom, scoop up my hat without waiting for the mirror to become available, fling my coat over my arm and hasten to the door. The way is blocked by two of the newer operators, Charlotte and Vera, who are dawdling and chattering about something or other. I say a brief *excuse me* and step forward, expecting them to move. They do not and we bump together.

'Excuse *me*!' I say, louder. They look at me blankly, as though I am speaking Serbo-Croat.

'Oh, Edie! We are in your way!' titters Charlotte.

'What a tearing hurry you seem to be in,' adds Vera.

'I am,' I say through gritted teeth. 'Sorry, girls! I must go. I absolutely must,' I add brightly, intending not one iota of my cheeriness.

'Oh! It's our fault.'

'Look at us, getting in your way.'

'We are such naughty creatures. Guy will give us such a slap on the wrist when he hears of it.'

'Such a rap on the knuckles!'

I cannot fathom whether they are sending up Guy's turns of phrase or are simply keen students of his style. I have no desire to quiz them and find out. In my mind's eye, Abigail paces up and down Market Street, scanning the crowds in vain. I hear her tutting at my lateness, striding away in a storm of indignation and never speaking to me again, let alone kissing me.

The pair wink at each other. Vera stands on tiptoe and grabs my hat. She throws it to Charlotte. Back and forth they go, tossing it like a shuttlecock, the two of them giggling as though this is the most fun they've had in their entire lives. I stare at them, wondering if they've smuggled in bottles of gin under their skirts. I smell nothing but talcum powder. I have a powerful urge to knock them down like ninepins. I am not the only one: behind me there is a rising tide of complaints as the other operators arrive.

'That's enough silliness,' I say with forced jollity. 'You're holding everyone up. Give me my hat this instant.'

'Oh, this is simply too much!' gasps Charlotte, waving it like a flag of victory. 'I can't catch my breath!'

You shouldn't do your stays up so tight, I think, but keep the sarcasm to myself. Charlotte flings my hat at Vera, who tries to hold it out of reach.

'That's not fair,' she pouts as I retrieve it with ease. 'I'd have to stand on a chair to be half as tall as you.'

'Charming,' I reply, shoving my hat on to my head and pinning it firmly.

'How tiresome you are,' says Charlotte, and blows a raspberry.

I dash down the stairs and, with hardly a care for trams and wagons, race across the crowded thoroughfare and up Market Street, so fast I get a stitch in my side. As I approach the clock I see that it is not yet ten past one. It must be slow: I am sure those idiotic women delayed me by at least half an hour. Abigail is waiting.

'There you are. You look like you've run all the way from Oldham.'

'There was some silliness on leaving work. Two of the girls were – Oh, never mind. It is far too complicated to explain.'

'That sort of thing always seems to happen when one is in a tearing hurry, doesn't it?'

'You are not irked at my lateness?'

'Of course not. What purpose would it serve?'

'Thank you,' I say.

We stride towards the Town Hall. I take the opportunity to have a good look at her. It is a pleasant way to pass a few moments. There is no further mention of Gnome. That moment of unpleasantness has passed. She is my friend, I remind myself. Not his.

We arrive at Albert Square just in time to see Mrs Gawthorpe take her place on the podium. She looks slowly from left to right, as though she is gathering the entire congregation into her safekeeping, and begins to speak.

I have never been so moved, so horrified. My hair stands on end at the tales: of forced feeding; of women stripped of all possessions and dignity, spied on day and night by a prurient eye in the door; being made to stand for an hour at a time with no reason given. Rancid air from a grate set high in the wall, angled so that only the smallest trickle of light may seep through. Repellent food laced with saliva and worse, far worse. The awful, unending cold.

When, at last, she steps down I stare at the space as if the air itself is haunted by the spirit of her passionate speech. Abigail plucks my sleeve.

'Oh!' I cry. 'Is the earth still turning?'

She laughs. 'I told you she was captivating, did I not?'

As the crowd disperses, Abigail and I stand together, distributing leaflets. I notice how many of the women secrete them into apron pockets, hiding them from judgemental glances. There are also those who make a point of casting the papers into the dirt and trampling them before our eyes. I burn with a desire to roll up one of the pamphlets and swat their ears.

'Don't exercise yourself over such silliness,' Abigail remarks with a shrug. 'Some seed falls upon stony ground.'

She is correct, of course. There are far better things on which to expend my energies. When we are done, I fold up one of the banners while a brace of hefty chaps dismantle the platform. I am graced with sufficient musculature to aid them, but consider it wiser to dissemble my lack of femininity. At last, all is packed away and we join our comrades heading towards Princess Street, chattering about tea and sandwiches. At the edge of the square our forward motion is arrested by a line of policemen, standing motionless with arms linked at the elbow.

'Well, well,' I remark. 'I suppose they must have their fun and make us turn around and walk down a different street.'

'Perhaps,' muses Abigail with a note of concern.

We head in the opposite direction only to be met by a second wall of uniformed bodies. Grumbled complaints grow louder and more expressive. We swing about. The south side is blocked also, as is the east.

'I didn't know Manchester boasted so many officers,' I observe.

'It doesn't,' replies Abigail.

An odd silence descends. A barked order rolls across our heads, echoing from the battlements and towers of the Town Hall. All four ranks of policemen take a slow pace forward, then another. Step by measured step they advance, pressing us into a smaller and smaller space at the centre of Albert Square.

'This is ridiculous,' I say in exasperation. 'Where do they expect us to go? Do they think we can fly?'

'No, they don't,' says Abigail grimly.

A young woman throws me a nervous glance. 'I've seen this before,' she says, voice quavering. 'Bolton. Two weeks back. It was a right mess. A child got trampled.'

'That can't be right,' I scoff, reflecting on the propensity of some folk to embellish. 'This is the Manchester Constabulary.'

'That's as maybe,' she glowers.

'This was a peaceful meeting,' I protest. 'We have broken no laws. Not a one.'

She mutters something about me being a bigger idiot than I look. I choose not to grace such rudeness with a reply.

'Link arms,' says Abigail urgently. *You too?* I think, but say nothing. 'Pass it down the line,' she continues. 'Don't let them come between us.'

The lass nods and directs encouraging remarks to the chap to her side, a youth with barely the beginnings of a moustache. He swallows, Adam's apple huge in his skinny throat. My ears ring with shouts of *stand firm!* and *heads up, ladies!* and I feel an odd sense of exhilaration. It is not to last. There is a surge from behind, my arm slips loose from the girl who spoke insultingly and she jerks away with a frightened yelp. Our line rocks. Abigail turns, her eyes wild.

'Keep hold!' she cries.

The chain breaks. My arm is torn from Abigail's. I am thrown forwards and tumble face-first against a policeman, so close I can count the grease-spots on his jacket. The brim of his helmet is pulled low over his brow as if he wishes to conceal his eyes from mine.

'Excuse me, officer,' I say as politely as I can in the crush. 'Don't push, if you would be so kind. I'll fall.'

By way of reply, he places both of his hands around my waist and squeezes me like a bellows. I stare, half in disbelief and half in discomfort.

'I say!' I wheeze. 'That hurts!'

Abigail is nowhere to be seen. Panic stirs. I try to pull myself free, but am held fast. His eyes grow crafty.

'You like that, don't you?' he leers.

'Don't talk rot!'

I endeavour to shove him away, but my arms are pinned to my sides. He shoves his nose to mine. Dark hairs bristle from the tip.

'You're no looker,' he growls. 'I'll bet a hideous bird like you has never had a proper man take hold of her. You should be grateful.'

'Get off,' I squeak.

'I love them when they fight a bit,' he chuckles and kicks me in the shins.

My legs buckle; I find myself falling when an elderly woman comes to my aid.

303

'You! Alfred Booth!' she shrieks, jabbing a finger at the policeman. 'I never did! I shall tell your mother, so I will!'

His expression transforms from snarling demon into whipped boy. Heads turn. His hands loosen their grip around my middle, not enough to escape but sufficient to gulp breath.

'Disgusting,' she cries. 'Call yourself an officer of the law? You should be ashamed of yourself.'

'Get away from me, you old bag,' he mutters.

As I look more closely I realise she is not old at all. She is probably of an age with Ma, but her shrunken cheeks suggest she has no teeth, or sensibly decided to leave them at home.

'Old bag?' she snarls. 'How dare you! I'll show you, you little tyke. You're not too old for me to—' With these words she raises her handbag and swings it mightily, smacking him on the side of the head.

Everything shifts.

He releases me, grabs her and lifts her off the ground. There is a strange, slow moment as he hoists her above his head. It does not last. With a roar, he hurls her aside. She sails through the air in a writhing mess of skirts and strikes the cobbles with a crack of bone against stone.

For an instant his eyes flicker with something that might be fear, might be remorse. It is wiped away in a trice. He balls his fists like a boxer and takes a step towards us, treading on the prone body as he does so.

'Right, you bunch of bastard whores. Who's next?'

A lass barely out of girlhood stoops to the felled woman's body, crying, 'Maud, Maud, talk to me!' The policeman bawls at her to clear off and when she does not, deals her a hefty kick that sends her sprawling. A fellow pushes to the front, a gentleman by the cut of his jacket, gleaming collar and top hat.

'To treat a young lady so!' he cries with the gravitas of a patriarch. 'Witness the perfidy of the governing powers!'

Men begin to flex their shoulders.

'Blackguard!'

'Poor show!'

'A woman!'

'You dare to call yourself a police officer?' continues the gent. 'We have heard your name. I shall take it upon myself to report you to the Chief Constable!'

The assembled folk look from the gent to the policeman, keen interest writ on every face.

'I'm murdered!' wails the old lady. 'God help me, I'm murdered!'

'Maud! Maud!' screams the girl.

'Stand back!' shouts the officer. 'Stand back, you dogs!' He brandishes his truncheon, a rod the size of a tree trunk.

'That's what they think of us!' comes a female voice from the heart of the melee. 'See how they treat us!'

One burly chap ignores the policeman's threats and kneels to help the spread-eagled crone, who is still yowling about being killed, and dead, and murdered, though the racket belies the facts.

'I said, stand away!' squeals the policeman and whacks her saviour with his baton.

It is a glancing blow. The man inspects his arm as though a very small bed-louse has nipped him. With slow deliberation he draws himself upright and it is only then I see the size of him, broad as a beerhouse wall and as tall. He could have dug the Big Ditch single-handed. He stares down his nose at his assailant.

'Get him,' someone mutters.

'Smack that smile right off his chops,' growls another.

305

'You show him.'

A look of panic spreads across the policeman's face as the circle of angry faces closes in. He fumbles a whistle from his pocket and blows three shrill blasts.

'He's getting reinforcements!'

At this, he gives a fourth blast, longer and louder than the first.

'Not just that – he's calling the ruddy horses down on us!'

A cry rings out, off to the right. All heads turn. Trotting up Lloyd Street towards us is an army of mounted officers. The horses toss their heads, the brass on their reins catching the sun. They pull up at the edge of the square. One of the riders raises a gloved hand. All is silent. I wish it were not, for we hear the words he shouts as clear as day.

'Charge them! Mow them down!'

My world descends into chaos. All of us turn to run, but there is nowhere to run to save into each other. The smart gentleman shouts that we must save the injured woman; the giant bends to assist him but is shoved out of the way by a shrieking tide of people. I am dragged helplessly into its current, the toes of my boots barely scraping the ground.

'It's Peterloo!' screams a terror-stricken voice – man or woman, I can't tell. 'Peterloo come back to us!'

More and more voices take up the chant: *Peterloo! Peterloo! Peterloo!*

The horses press close, bits and bridles flecked with foam, breath steaming. They rock their heads up and down, maddened by the din, by the screaming people and by the laying on of the whip as their riders drive them whinnying into the crowd.

I fight to stay on my feet. I am buffeted first one way and then the other. I notice the same building once, twice, three times as the police herd us around and around. It dawns upon me that they are not driving us away from the square but forcing us into a tighter and tighter mass, until the only way to go is down.

I half trip, half tread upon a soft obstruction and with a sick realisation know it to be a fallen body. So thick is the press that it is impossible to see the ground, let alone offer assistance. I swirl around and am thrust into the path of one of the horses. It rolls its eyes, ears flattened in terror. The flesh packed between its front legs bulges. My crazed mind supplies the notion that it looks remarkably like my breasts: tough and unfeminine. I thought I would have a more profound realisation on the point of death; I'd imagined visions of light and seraph choirs. Wedged in my brain and circling my mind is the phrase *horse-breasts, horse-breasts*, maddening and pointless.

This is the end, Gnome, I say to myself. *All our contention, and for what?*

If he answers, it is lost in the thunder between my ears. I can hold myself up no longer.

Peace. Is it too late, even now? I wish—

A strange calm suffuses my being as I surrender to the crush. I gaze upwards, towards the shrinking window of light. Another policeman, more faceless than the last, raises his stick. My luck has run out.

As I swoon, I dream that an Amazon appears, muffler pulled across her face so that only her eyes are visible. I must be halfway on the road to heaven, to find it populated by such angels.

She shifts her weight on to one leg, raises the other in a snowstorm of linen petticoats, kicks out her heel and strikes the policeman beneath the chin with a crack that rings clear above the din of shrieks and moans. With a look of pained astonishment, the policeman's head snaps back. He staggers

307

one step, two; loses his balance and collapses on to the cobbles like a drunkard. The woman sweeps away her scarf and grasps my hand.

'We must go,' hisses Abigail.

'But . . .'

Her eyes blaze. 'Move yourself. When he gets back on his feet, which he will, there'll be hell to pay.'

'How did you—'

'Edie. Hold your tongue. Now.'

She drags me away. The suck of bodies holds me back; my fingers slip. Her grip tightens. My arm is being wrenched from the shoulder.

'It's no good, let me go!' I scream.

With strength that borders on the uncanny, she pulls and I follow like a doll dragged through a hedge. My hat tears away, pins and all, a hank of hair with it. Still she holds firm and does not stop until we reach the wall of a building. I collapse, breath rattling. She shields me against the brickwork.

'I am sorry,' I hiccup.

'No time,' she snaps, frowning. 'We're not out of this yet.'

She places her hand on the crown of my head, shoves me into a crouch and motions me to crawl on my hands and knees. The paving stones are slippery and I do not want to know how they've become so wet on a day without rain. Inch by inch we make our way out of Albert Square, deafened by such an ear-splitting clamour you would think all damnation had been unleashed.

'Doctor!'

'Here! Is there no doctor?'

'For the love of God, *help*!'

Far worse to my ears are the ghastly cries of the militia, crying: *Down on them, bring them down, I say! Bring down every one of them!* and laughing as they do. It makes no sense. In the space of an hour the men appointed our guardians have become merciless assassins, as senseless with power as any berserker.

This square, through which I've strolled, admiring the statues and the Gothic finery of the old Queen's consort, is now one of the lower circles of the Inferno. My mind reels. If women and children can be beaten to the ground, what is the world coming to? This is the modern age, a new century. Surely we have transcended such barbarity?

If it were not for Abigail I would give up, so overwhelming is the stench of vomitus and the bellowing of the injured. But she does not release me from her grasp and by some mercy we arrive at a side-alley, narrow as an arrow-slot. We creep along until we reach a doorway recessed into the wall. Abigail pulls me into its shelter and we stop.

For many moments we say nothing. We stare at each other, chests heaving. She has somehow managed to hang on to her hat, but her over-jacket is quite disappeared. Her blouse is torn at the shoulder, revealing naked flesh raked with scratches. She carries a gash beneath her left eye.

'You came back for me,' I say.

'I may be willing to endure arrest and imprisonment for the cause, but you have reached no such agreement with yourself. You came to hear a speech, and hear it you did.'

'Why – What did we do to deserve this?'

'Nothing,' she snarls. 'They need no excuse.'

I stare at her, transfixed by the memory of her kicking the policeman in the face. 'How did you ever – I did not think a woman—'

'For heaven's sake, Edie. Women sweat and strain in birth every moment of every day. We labour in coal mines, we—' She closes her eyes and presses her lips tight. 'Listen to me on my soap-box.' She pats my hand. 'There is nothing we cannot do, if we but put our minds to it.'

'Oh,' I gulp.

She wipes her face on her sleeve and scowls at the dirt and blood that marks it. 'We are quite a display,' she murmurs. 'Dash it all,' she growls. 'Dash every one of them to hell.'

She glances at me with a flicker of fury. But it is the merest flicker. The corner of her mouth quirks upwards. She wrinkles her brow, fighting to keep her expression steady. Her mouth twitches again and a snort of laughter bursts free. I look at her in disbelief. I have never met anyone remotely like her.

'How can you laugh at a time like this?'

She rocks back and forth, hugging her knocked ribs. 'Oh, Edie,' she guffaws. 'I am afraid I cannot stop. Look at us! What a pair we make.'

I see myself through her eyes: battered, bruised, scraped and scratched. But alive. Most definitely alive. I cannot help myself. Her merriment communicates itself to me and I find myself laughing too, wheezing through the constriction in my throat. I can't stop; not until I hear the hissing of her breath and realise her laughter has turned to weeping.

I take her into my arms and cradle her head on my shoulder, making tender shushing noises. Her body wrenches with sobs and she burrows into me as though trying to escape them. I worry that the sound may bring a policeman down the ginnel, but they are otherwise engaged. We are left alone in our tattered clothes and aching flesh.

I hold her until the fit subsides; then reach into my blouse and find my handkerchief, tucked neatly in my stays. I draw it out, warm from the press of skin and as neatly ironed as when I placed it there. It carries the scent of the talcum powder I dabbed under my arms that morning.

I shake it out and offer it to Abigail, who nods thanks and wipes her face. She peers at me, eyes puffy. Her cheek is flowering into a blue-black peony. Without thinking, I lean forwards and kiss the bruise. I mean it kindly, the sort of kissing-it-better you do with a child who has stumbled. Abigail shoots me a look of surprise.

'I am sorry,' I say. 'Did I hurt you?'

She shakes her head. There is a long pause. By turns I grow cold then hot under her gaze. She leans forward, crushes her lips to mine and holds them there. A thrill courses through my wounded flesh; more refreshing than a glass of lemonade gulped on the hottest day of summer, more exhilarating than every last one of the fireworks at Belle Vue. The pain in my limbs melts away.

I never felt anything so soft. Not the times I kissed my grandmother's lips, not even the velvet between my thighs. Only when I can breathe no longer and think I may burst do I draw away, most unwillingly, and take a gulp of air.

'You look so nervous,' she says, reaching out a hand and touching her finger to the point of my chin. 'Dearest Edie.'

'Dearest?'

'Dearest beloved,' she replies and kisses me again.

My heart soars and I return the embrace with fire of my own. A spear flies into my core and splits me as irreparably as a branch struck from a tree by a lightning bolt. I am cracked open to reveal my heart's wood. I am broken; I am whole. It makes no sense, yet never has anything felt so true. I would have borne a hundred bruises for this, a hundred nights in Strangeways.

'Abigail,' I say.

'My beloved?'

'I am afraid. I am exhilarated also. I'm not sure if I under-stand. Can you?'

Her eyes brighten. 'Yes,' she breathes.

I never before felt so aware of my body, the breath crackling

311

in my lungs. I clasp her hand and press it to my lips, not caring if we are watched.

'I have held myself aloof,' I say. 'I apologise. Never again. You have my heart, my whole.'

I expect her to frown as she weighs my confession. But she gives a smile of warm encouragement.

'I thrill when you unburden yourself,' she says.

'I am not used to revealing my true thoughts and feelings.'

'Who amongst us does not restrain herself, especially with a new friend?' she muses. 'Although I hope I have been thoroughly tried and tested.'

She looks so bashful, so tentative. I assume her to be confident in all things. How tied up I am in my own considerations rather than those of others. I will change.

'More than I can express,' I say, and mean it. 'My dear beloved.'

There are things I can't reveal; that goes without saying. But who does not speak rashly in the heat of wonderful moments? The last thing I wish is to break this spell so I hold my tongue. She won't notice if I keep some things back. It will not matter.

We emerge from the alleyway and avail ourselves of the nearest public convenience to wash our hands and tidy ourselves. The attendant sneers, but Abigail produces a sixpence from some miraculous store about her person and all is well. We proceed slowly, carefully, along Mosley Street, no more threatening to the fine folk of Manchester than two young ladies engaged in an afternoon's contemplation of window displays. My heart, pounding ever since our escape from the riot, pauses in its headlong canter. How long ago it seems since I dawdled with Guy, chattering about gloves and hats. How unutterably foolish.

Although we do our best to affect normalcy, we attract whistling comments and not just from the rougher sort of fellow. Abigail grits her teeth.

'Ignore them, if you can.' I squeeze her arm in a comforting gesture. 'I am used to it.'

She holds me at arm's length. 'You think I am immune to such attentions?'

'I did not mean that,' I say hastily. 'But let's be honest; I am an odd creature. If I attached a brush to my hat I could paint the ceiling. As a woman I fail at every turn.'

'You think I care for such fiddle-faddle? I hope you know me well enough to know I do not judge by appearances.'

'Abigail, you are so feminine.'

'Heavens alive, what does that signify? I cannot help the body I was born into, any more than you.'

I stare at her. In the rusty workings of my brain, cogs begin to grind, much like a fairground steam organ, squealing as it is cranked into life.

'No,' I say. I feel as though I am standing in a dark room and Abigail has turned up the gaslight. 'I can't help it, can I?' I grasp her hand and squeeze passionately. 'Thank you.'

'What have I said?'

'More than you know.'

She walks me to the door of The Comet, and I experience a delectable thrill of possession. No one can guess that the heart of this wonderful woman is in my keeping. For the first time in my life I am complete. Abigail is everything I need. With her I can forget Ma, forget Gnome, forget myself and all my problems. With her hand in mine I can put my troubled past behind me and face a bright future. Gnome can try all he wants to come between us. He will get nowhere.

Hear that, Gnome?

I love and am loved in return. It is so wonderfully simple. This is the peace of which I dreamed.

GNOME

SEPTEMBER 1909–JANUARY 1910

I tilt the mirror so that it reflects my face. A coil of hair tumbles down my brow, inviting kisses. I toss my head and the tresses spread their cloak. I am quite the aesthete these days. Hold that: not aesthete. I'm a gypsy rover, a charming prince; so adorable, I barely recognise myself. All I have to do is beg forbearance that she doesn't grow it too long, not wanting to find my manly hours difficult and all that, and blow me if she doesn't keep it trimmed to a reasonable length. There's a lot to be said for these new manners of mine.

I devour each morsel of Miss Hargreaves' letters to Edie as well as Edie's rough copies to her, for my poor sister drafts many attempts before she is happy with her answer. When I discover where Miss Hargreaves will be of an evening, why, there I am strolling by, purely by happenstance. I raise my hat; I kiss her glove. A little touch of Gnome in the night.

Midsummer passes into autumn and I judge it is time to make my move. I've sprinkled enough flowery seeds for them to have taken root. I've learned the hard way not to go charging in. The tastiest prey is the slowest into the trap and I am learning the patience of the wisest hunter.

For this particular evening's entertainment I am headed to

a gathering of the Female Terrors. I stroll towards Rusholme, rustling Miss Hargreaves' latest missive in my pocket. I have devilment on my mind and there's nothing Edie can do to stop me. So what if she has a girlish pash on Miss Hargreaves? Now that I have discovered it, it merely adds spice to my shenanigans.

She can pine till she's blue in the face. Let her have a companion with whom to amuse herself with speeches and marches and banners. Miss Hargreaves will tire of Edie when she's offered passion and a chap like me to supply it. What a paltry, starveling thing is female friendship, set against what a man can bring to a woman. Friendship endures only until love sweeps it into the dirt. Of course, when I'm done I shall discard Miss Hargreaves like a broken toy. This merely adds piquancy to the dish I shall swipe from under Edie's nose.

Birch Hall hums with hard work. It is packed to the gunnels with embroidered table napkins, knitted antimacassars, jars of jam wearing miniature mobcaps, the whole blinking lot decorated in purple and green. The walls groan under the weight of banners bearing the sigil of an angel parping on a trumpet. And there are men, in far greater numbers than I expected. I'll bet a pound to a penny they've all had their ballocks cut off.

I spy Miss Hargreaves pushing a trolley freighted with an enormous samovar. I plant myself in her path, she raises her head and our eyes meet. I have nice eyes. I sprinkle extra sparkle into them.

'Good evening,' I say, raising my cap and clicking my heels.

'Good evening, Mr Latchford,' she says politely.

'It is a pleasure to see you again, Miss Hargreaves.' I stick my hand across the tea-cart. 'I am flattered you remember a chump like myself.'

She takes my hand and shakes it briskly. 'I should know you anywhere,' she replies in a friendly manner that bucks me up no end.

'Gosh,' I burble.

'You and your sister are peas in a pod,' she says, which deflates the cheer.

She manoeuvres the trolley around the obstacle I present and continues on her way.

'You can call me Gnome,' I offer, keeping pace. 'All my friends do.'

'What a peculiar nickname,' she replies, but does not vouch-safe one of her own. She looks over my shoulder. 'Has Edie accompanied you?'

I scowl. 'No.'

'The two of you are impossible!' she chirps. 'I declare she wore the self-same expression when I mentioned you.'

'Did she, indeed.' I restrain myself from knocking over the teacups and storming off. I force a chuckle of commendable self-deprecation. 'I am a messenger. A shabby Mercury, I admit.'

I wait for her to echo my laughter. She regards me evenly.

'Mr Latchford?' she asks after a pause. 'You say you have a message?'

'My dear sister is otherwise engaged this evening. She sends her most cordial of greetings.'

She looks crestfallen. 'Oh. I guessed that might be so.'

I point at the laden cart. 'Let me help you.'

'I am quite capable,' she says.

'I'm sure you are. But so fine a young lady as yourself should not be delegated to heavy work more suited to a man,' I say, ladling on the honey. Never met a one who didn't yearn for a spoonful, however independently minded they may appear. The expression on her face is not one I'm used to. If I didn't know better, I'd say it was irritation. What is there to object in a fine-looking lad paying court?

316

'A man's work?' she says. 'I assure you, Mr Latchford, there is nothing you can achieve that I cannot match.'

'Goodness me,' I declare with a wounded air. 'If that is all the courtesy a chap can elicit from a female of your class, then England is in a sorry state.'

I turn to go and my luck changes. It's as well, for if she hadn't relented I'd have had no option but to march away with my nose in the air.

'I apologise,' she concedes.

I dangle the hook a while longer. She deserves it and a lot worse.

'Convention dictates I must accept,' I reply. A kicked puppy never looked as wretched.

'I am sincere,' she continues, if not with warmth, then with sufficient contrition.

I beam forgiveness and earn a small smile. She permits me to take one of the handles and together we steer the trolley in as straight a line as possible, although it is disobedient and insists on veering to the right. It affords me the opportunity to observe her with sidelong glances. She's wearing a costume of unsurpassing sobriety, without so much as an inch of lace on it; not that plainness can disguise the delightful curve of her waist between the twin abundances of bosom and buttock.

I am unaccountably tongue-tied. I've practised flirtatious speeches and can't remember a bally word. I'm as bold as a lion when I've got my hand around my John Thomas. The memory brings on a furious spate of blushing. So much for impressing her with my repartee. She does not notice – too busy talking about the cause. I tolerate the chatter with saintly forbearance, telling myself I'm listening out for a chink in her armour. However, the sound of her voice is decidedly musical and I find myself smiling. I shake myself. This will not do. I ought to tell her to put a cork in it and leave worldly observations to the male sex.

'Here we are,' she says, interrupting my line of thought.

'What else can I do?' I ask eagerly.

'You need not trouble yourself.' A spindle of a female appears at her side. Her face bears a distinct resemblance to a jug with its handle facing forwards. 'Miss Abrams will assist me now. Thank you, Mr Latchford.'

The newcomer positions herself between Miss Hargreaves and myself and rearranges the cups whilst jogging me with her elbows. They make off together, clanking the tea-things as they go.

I refuse to be spurned so easily. A temporary retreat is in order, so I make a circuit of the hall whilst gathering my wits. I pick up leaflets and, by jingo, the nonsense in them makes my blood boil. They are worse than those my sister possesses, if that were credible, and bear ridiculous titles like *The New Crusade, The Need of the Hour, The Emancipation of Woman*. I snort and hurl them aside, eliciting raised eyebrows. I must play this with care. This crew are simply itching for a chap to put his foot wrong so they can turf him on to the street.

After I judge sufficient time has elapsed for absence to make her heart grow fonder, I direct my peregrinations towards Miss Hargreaves. She is seated behind one of the trestles and wrapping a green ribbon around a broom handle.

'What a shame dearest Edie could not be here,' I simper.

'Yes.'

'You'd think she would make an effort and spare one evening. Especially for the cause.'

'It does not matter,' says Miss Hargreaves rather unconvincingly. 'Evenings are difficult for her.'

I'm glad she is not looking at me, for it means I do not have to mask my look of triumph. She adds a purple ribbon, creating a striped effect rather like a barber's pole. I loiter a moment longer. There is a prodigious heap of ribbons and wooden staves at her feet.

'You've got an awful lot to do, haven't you?'

Finally, she bestows a glance on me. 'Yes, I do.'

There's an edge of exasperation in her voice that I decide is meant for Edie. Without further encouragement, I seat myself, taking a pole and a length of ribbon. It will not keep its place and there are gaps where the wood shows through.

'I am not very good at this, am I?' I say sadly. 'Proof positive that the male is the inferior sex. I cannot even wind a ribbon in an adequate fashion. If my sister were here I am sure all would be completed to your satisfaction.'

'I dare say it would,' she agrees, taking the failed effort from my hands and unravelling the tangled muddle. 'But she is not here and you are. I shall make the best of that which I am given.'

A lesser mortal would be stung by such a retort. But I detect annoyance. I grin inwardly. What gratification there is in putting the cat amongst the pigeons.

'I do want to help, Miss Hargreaves, I do,' I say earnestly. 'It is your company that distracts me.'

'I shall leave, in that case.'

'Oh no! That would be frightfully miserable. Please don't. Oh, what a dilemma. If you go, I'll be a whiz at handicrafts but miserable. If you stay, I'll be happy but of no earthly use. Whatever shall we do?'

The smallest of smiles breaks like a sunrise on her face. 'I cannot solve this conundrum, Mr Latchford.'

'Permit me to hazard a guess. Your smile makes me bold. Your smile makes me happy. It may render me all fingers and thumbs, and I shudder at the thought you might ask me to thread a needle or handle a pair of scissors. But all is suddenly clear. You are the cause of my fumbling, Miss Hargreaves.'

'You are very entertaining, Mr Latchford. I can't fathom why Edie doesn't mention you more often. Or . . .'

Or more generously, I think, completing her sentence in my head. I heave a wounded sigh.

'She is – secretive,' I venture, looking at the ceiling. 'Isn't she?'

'Yes,' she says with a hopeful look. 'You know her better than anyone, I should imagine.'

At last I strike the mark. She wants *me* to take *her* into my confidence. It's all I can do to restrain myself from tossing my cap into the air.

'I suppose you could say that,' I say slowly, and then falter, biting my lip. 'I can say nothing more.'

It would be a soulless creature who did not nibble at the bait, and nibble she does, her expression betraying a struggle between curiosity and fine breeding. I tug my cuffs.

'I believe that I am an embarrassment to her,' I blurt. 'I beg forgiveness for speaking so openly. It is a fault of mine, to be honest with all. Too often I defy convention – to my peril. I am a freethinker, Miss Hargreaves. A man who breathes the invigorating air of this new century. Who craves change. Who craves the advancement of all women and men, marching shoulder to shoulder towards a bright future.'

I pause, sneaking a look at her reaction through lowered eyelashes. Her eyes are bright with surprise and not a little approval.

'Mr Latchford,' she says. 'You do not have to labour so hard to make a favourable impression upon me. I prefer simple truths to flowery dissimulation. I believe the phrase is "warts and all".'

I've no idea what the stupid woman is on about. It sounds mightily close to an insult. I decide to look aggrieved.

'You think me false?'

She smiles. 'I do understand. When a chap is making a fresh acquaintance, he feels he must be the mirror of perfection. A barrel-chested Perseus, always rescuing Andromeda. You need not strive so heartily. I am quite generously minded towards you.'

'You are?'

'Of course. Whatever your sister says.'

'I hope you will make up your own mind about me, Miss Hargreaves. I'm sure it is a very good mind.'

'Flattery, Mr Latchford?'

Under her gaze I have the distinct sensation of being peeled like an orange. 'No,' I say, speaking the truth for the first time in as long as I remember. 'Not in this case.'

One of the chief Gorgons passes by our table and sees that we have paused in our labours.

'Is this really the time and place for flirtation, Miss Hargreaves?' she asks with a look that could shrivel a potato. She turns her baleful glance upon me. 'As for you, sir: perhaps you would be so good as to employ your own leisure time to indulge in romantic entanglements. We are busy even if you are not.'

'That's rather sharp, ma'am,' I say, springing to the defence of my princess. 'Miss Hargreaves is trying to teach me impossible feats with ribbon.' I hold up the cat's-cradle of green and purple.

She glowers down her nose as though she'd like me to be the cat and the mess of satin to be my innards. 'Mr . . .' she begins.

'Mr Latchford,' I say. 'I'm so frightfully sorry. I'm trying so fearfully hard.'

The dragon is not won over.

'Mr Latchford. That you are a drone is hardly a revelation. But I do not believe for one moment that you are the fool you pretend. I should be grateful if you did not treat me like one. If you cannot assist Miss Hargreaves, there is plenty of heavier work to which I can direct you. If work is what you came here for.'

'I consider myself castigated,' I say with a twinkle in my eye that I cast in Miss Hargreaves' direction.

The witch harrumphs and stalks off. I open my mouth to make a comment about what a naughty pair of reprobates we are, but Miss Hargreaves is watching the departure of the miserable old prune.

'What fun!' I say, in order to bring her attention back to me, which is where it belongs.

'Fun? I found it embarrassing to be accused of spooning.'

'Come now, Miss Hargreaves. Merriment makes toil fly by all the faster.'

She does not look convinced. 'Perhaps it would be better if you helped with some of the . . .' She pauses and I pick up the thread.

'Drudgery? Work more suited to a *drone* such as myself?'

She sighs, but will not be drawn. She picks up a roll of purple ribbon and starts to loop it into a rosette, which she fixes to the end of one of the broom handles with a push-pin. It looks perfect. She then takes a roll of white ribbon and does the same, building up a bouquet of shining flowers. After a few moments she gives me a look that questions why I am still seated beside her with unoccupied hands.

I hang my head in a pitiable fashion. 'My company is unacceptable.' She raises an eyebrow. 'I have created trouble for you, for which I take full responsibility. I beg your pardon most sincerely, Miss Hargreaves. I shall depart and offend you no further.'

I stand and take a small step in the direction of the door. She lays her hand upon my sleeve and I gaze at the glove with genteel longing. The lavender leather is stretched as tight as a second skin.

'Please, dear Miss Hargreaves. Let me retreat with a little of my dignity.'

322

'Mr Latchford. I cannot make you stay.'

You can, I think. *A word would do it.*

'But as you go, I should like you to take my good wishes.'

'Gosh, Miss Hargreaves.'

'Convey them to Edie, if you will.' I incline my head obediently and force a smile. 'Take with you the assurance that I value honesty above all things, however awkwardly it may be expressed. I do not kowtow to convention either. I am here, am I not?'

I am mightily tempted to stay and force my suit. I make a gallant retreat. I have done well. I shall do better.

Month succeeds month and I become a veritable Galahad. If a sheaf of posters is set to slide out of Miss Hargreaves' arms, I am there to catch them. If a volunteer from the Men's Committee is required to hoist a banner at a rally, my hand is first in the air. I spend dashed near every evening dazzling her with my attention. I cannot figure out why she clings to this suffrage nonsense tight as a convolvulus. I have the devil of a job not to get bamboozled into it myself. The ghastly thought gets under my skin like scabies that I am enjoying her company far too much and that she's casting light into *my* darkness rather than the other way around.

I shudder. This coven draw men in with their feminine wiles, and suck all the manliness out of them. I'll wager Guy was once as burly as a bricklayer before they got their claws into him. Every fibre of my being warns me to give them the widest berth possible. But they are the means to Edie's downfall. Was ever a fellow so plagued with difficulty?

Chin up, Gnome. I shall not wilt at the first sign of trouble. Brave as a lion-tamer, that's me. As if a female could turn my head! Laughable, of course. Miss Hargreaves is a distraction with whom I may amuse myself whilst I wreck Edie's life.

Stop this, counsels a voice from within. *You are digging your-self a hole you can't get out of.*

It sounds like me. It can't be. Bloody Edie again.

I'll show Miss Hargreaves who's boss. I'll astound her with my virility until she is the one who capitulates. Till she admits she's the one acting a part. It couldn't be clearer. This game is ten times more interesting than planned. I thought I'd be winning over a lass in order to discard her. Here's a greater challenge and a sweeter prize: I'll break Miss Hargreaves as well as my sister. I'll show them all.

As autumn chills into winter the sharpness softens, grain by grain, both Miss Hargreaves and her sourpuss sisters. When I am invited to attend – for that I read as beast of burden and general dogsbody – a rally in Ashton-under-Lyne in a fortnight's time I beam with pleasure and swear that I will be there.

That evening, I loiter as Edie gives me back my body. *What a shame it is that I have to take all the nights,* I sigh. *Dear Edie, with so many invitations to evening entertainments.* She brushes off the apology. *Ah well,* I shrug.

What a pity, I say, the following night. *If only there were a way around it.*

Drop by drop, I water the seedling. After a night or two, I plant the suggestion – gently, mind – that of course there is a solution. It is staring us in the face. Cinderella *can* go to the ball. It's only habit that ties us to Gnome by night and Edie by day. She can stay for an evening if she wishes it.

That's if you do wish it, I sigh.

I hear the clunk of cogs as the machinery of her suspicion whirrs.

Of course, I murmur, *if you don't trust me, I quite understand. It's a shame, that's all.*

A few more days slide by. Each time we change over, I smell

hunger. She snuffs it the second it flares between us, but I'd know its stink anywhere.

I'll trade you a whole night for an afternoon, I say. *No catch.* She hesitates. Her longing seethes. I've got her.

She agrees to the following Saturday afternoon with such unseemly haste that I'm sorely tempted to take the whole week and to hell with the consequences. However, my work is not yet done. I butter her up with oily thanks. It is time for my coup de grâce.

The Saturday in question is a typical Manchester January and decidedly inclement. It's threatening rain when I put on my britches and bucketing down by the time I arrive at St Peter's Square. We men are directed to an empty dray; the ladies take the tram. Ostensibly it is to avoid any suspicion of assembly. To my mind they simply wish to avoid the downpour.

Five of us fellows cram on to the wooden bench up front, the remainder consigned to the rear. All of them are tiresomely gay and give every impression of being pals on a charabanc outing to the seaside, despite our bones being bounced to matchwood. When they begin to sing cheery songs, it is all I can do not to jump down and leave them to it. Every few minutes we creak past a beerhouse and I gaze at the doors with hopeful sighs, but to no avail. Water creeps down the back of my collar.

'Cheer up, Herbert,' says the twerp to my right, his face angry with pimples. I'm surprised he has the wherewithal to handle the reins with such aplomb, he's such a flop-haired fool. 'Join in, why don't you?'

I've no idea why they won't call me Gnome. At first I thought it rectitude: now it seems perversely uncomradely. I consider elbowing him off the side of the cart. The thought of his spotty face gawping in surprise as he topples off his perch cheers me considerably.

325

'That's better, old chap,' he says, misreading my smile.

'You being a misery-guts again?' quips the man to my left.

'I've had no luncheon,' I grunt. 'It's all very well for you chaps, with someone to fix you a plate of bacon and eggs.'

'Chance would be a fine thing!' says someone in the back.

'I managed some bread and jam,' squawks another.

'Cup of tea was all I got!'

I groan and hold my head in my hands. Now that I have started them, they will not leave off prattling about how little they've eaten. I wait for a note of complaint to creep in, how they would secretly like to be cooked for by a docile wife, but it's all joking and joshing.

'I fried my own bacon,' says the pimply youth. 'Mama watched to make sure I didn't burn it. This time.'

They collapse in gales of laughter. I'd like a slice of bacon wedged between two slabs of bread, right this soggy minute. Another public house drifts by.

'All this talk has given me a powerful thirst,' I remark, forcing a chummy tone. 'What say we stop and oil the wheels of industry for five minutes, eh?'

There's the lightest of pauses before the laughter resumes. They thump my back, declaring what a card I am, how there'll be plenty of time for a jar later. The beerhouse falls behind with any hope of a stiffener. The horse clop-clops along, raising its tail and trumpeting wind at such regular intervals there must be something wrong with the creature. Each time it farts they giggle, pinch their noses shut and waft their hands. I am sick of this party of schoolboys and close to revolt by the time we drag our aching backsides into the centre of Ashton.

The women are already there. One group emerges from a teashop, one from a grocer's; another descends en masse from the tram. I watch as the driver changes ends and the rattlebox squeals in the direction of Manchester. I repress a pang of longing to join him.

The moment the parade commences the rain stops. How very typical. We are led by an imperious female who sweeps her hand hither and thither, as though we are her orchestra and she the conductor. It is like being amongst children playing at kings and queens with sticks for sceptres: how serious their fat little faces as they stamp along the street waving placards. At last, Miss Hargreaves detaches herself from the melee of skirts and hats and strolls in my direction. My day improves.

'Mr Latchford. You are here,' she says in that unnecessary way to which women are so attached.

I manage a brave smile. 'At last.'

'Perhaps not as comfortable a journey as the tram?'

'Perhaps not,' I quip, and am rewarded with a grin.

'We are most grateful for your assistance.'

'It is nothing,' I lie carelessly.

'On the contrary; it is most heartening that you should support your sister so wholeheartedly.'

'Surely you mean my *sisters*.'

'Of course, of course. Yet it is admirable that a brother should so approve of his sister's activities. Not all are so understanding. I hope I detect an improvement of relations between the pair of you.' Her smile is infuriatingly smug.

'You think I am here merely to show fraternal support?'

'There is another reason?' she enquires with a tilt of her head. The smile wavers.

'Miss Hargreaves, I need borrow no one's convictions. I possess them of my own free will, and act upon them accordingly. I am present because of my belief in women's suffrage, not because I tolerate my sister and offer grudging support.'

'I have underestimated you.'

327

'I believe you have.'

She bows her head. 'Mea culpa,' she says gravely.

I have no idea what that means, but hazard a guess from her expression that she is conceding a point. I sweep off my cap and make a courtly bow. 'Thank you milady.'

'Arise, Sir Herbert.'

I'd rise up good and strong for you, my pretty is the grubby thought hidden behind my show of chivalry. Given a chance, this potboy would bend the lady of the house over the kitchen range and show her a thing or two.

'So!' I say, spitting on my palms and rubbing them together. 'What is best done first, in your opinion? Command your knight!'

I am their amiable drudge: I fetch what must be fetched, carry what must be carried and when the harpy of the hour clambers on to the cart to deliver one of those interminable speeches, I lend a shoulder. There's plenty of shoving to get her up the steps for creature of gossamer grace she is not.

She holds forth, haranguing the crowd from here into the middle of next week. I cannot understand why they are such a submissive lot. They chuckle as happily as if she were a comic turn at the halls, even applauding some of her wilder declarations. I shift from foot to foot, so mortally bored I pray for ructions. At least then I could enjoy the distraction of a punch-up.

Nor do I get another chance to play the lovelorn swain. Miss Hargreaves is far too busy dashing to and fro, dishing out broadsheets and pouring nonsense into the ears of the good citizens of Ashton. I am relegated to packing the wagon for the return journey and have to suffer the advice of a female who insists on instructing me in the art of rolling banners, for it seems I am not capable of doing it correctly. I display the forbearance of Job and smile, smile, smile.

I trudge back and forth through the drizzle, casting envious eyes on the horse, which has got its head stuffed in a nosebag. A raggedly dressed woman stops me as I'm loading the last box of leaflets. She darts a look from side to side, draws her shawl across her mouth and mumbles through the wool.

'What's that?' I ask.

Grudgingly, she uncovers her face. 'Here,' she mutters. 'Give me one of them.' She nods her head towards the box.

'Too late,' I say. 'I'm packing up.'

'Go on.'

'Are you *that* short of paper for the privy?' I sneer. I try to shove past, but she blocks my way.

'Look,' she hisses. 'If my pa catches me out here with you lot I'll get the skin taken off my arse and won't be able to wipe it for a week. So give me one and ruddy hurry up.' She snaps the fingers of her free hand in my face.

'It's all rubbish,' I murmur. 'Not worth the ink.'

'What?'

I don't know if she can't hear or won't hear. I'm aware of a movement to my side and change my tune without looking to see who it is.

'Here you go, miss!' I chirp.

I peel away the topmost piece of paper and press it into her hand. She gives me an angry look, tucks it into the folds of her skirt and is away in a trice, head down and indistinguishable from any one of the mud-coloured peasants heading for shelter. I turn. It is Miss Hargreaves. Just my confounded luck. I wonder how much she heard.

'Poor lass,' I say. 'She was telling me how her father wouldn't let her come to the meeting, so she dashed out at the last minute to get something of ours to read. She spoke of awful violence if she was discovered.' I wrinkle my forehead in concern. 'I wish we could do more.'

We gaze at each other for a moment. The rain is light but penetrating and the feather on her hat is sopping wet, drooping over the brim. I raise my hand and sweep it back. She starts, as though she thinks I am about to strike her.

'Your feather,' I say softly. 'I fear it is drowned.' A surprised smile builds on her face. 'It is good to see you happy,' I add. I glance at the pamphlets. 'Whatever am I thinking!' I cry. 'These papers will be ruined if I don't get them under the tarpaulin straightaway.'

I tug the peak of my cap and step away. Again, my way is blocked, but by a far more attractive impediment.

'Mr Latchford,' she says, laying a gloved hand on my forearm.

I'm stabbed with lust, firm and fierce, as though her naked fingers reached inside my breeches and squeezed. Blood floods into my cheeks. She takes it for bashfulness.

I cough. 'Miss Hargreaves.'

'You are wet through,' she says. 'Hurry and put that box under the groundsheet, do.'

Another blasted order from the Kaiser, I think. 'Yes, Miss Hargreaves,' I say, steeling myself for calmness. She is touching me, and that is worth the long, enervating day and the soaking. Possibly.

'You've not brought an overcoat, have you?'

I glance at the other men, who are spiriting oilskins out of a sack I'd not noticed before.

'I do not own such a garment, Miss Hargreaves,' I say with pained dignity.

'Then you must surely travel on the tram with us. We do not want to dampen your ardour for the cause.'

I laugh bravely at her joke. I race to the cart and hurl the box on board, where it lands with a soggy thump. One of the fellows extends a paw to hoist me up.

'Not me,' I say with a wink. 'I've got a far more comfortable berth awaiting my backside.'

I can't resist a swagger as I head to the tram, beckoning with light and warmth. I help every one of the wenches on board with a tip of my cap and a *here you go, ma'am* before hopping up after Miss Hargreaves. We take a seat together on the top of the car and suddenly the rain is of no consequence. With her at my side I'd endure the whole clattering journey in a typhoon. She produces an umbrella from God knows where, unfurls it and makes to hold it over both our heads. I shuffle to the far end of the bench, far too cunning to use it as an excuse to cuddle up.

'You will get wet,' she says.

'That does not matter,' I say brightly. 'Spot of rain won't hurt.'

The drizzle soaks through my jacket and shirt. My shoulders are clammy.

She sighs. 'Come now.'

'Really, it is quite all right.'

'I disagree. You have worked hard. I shan't stand by and watch you catch your death. You must sit close to me, or I shall have to come close to you.'

I don't stir and, sure enough, she slides in my direction until her thigh is pressed against mine. I draw my jacket over my lap and indulge the stirring of my flesh, my privates hidden safely beneath the press of my palm. I revel in the delicious knowledge that she is unaware of my arousal. Edie can wriggle all she wants. I'm not actually doing anything.

See this, Edie? I have what will never be yours.

I cram my head with filthy thoughts and it's only when she

331

stops yattering that I realise I've not been paying attention. I hope she doesn't ask any awkward questions.

'Mr Latchford: are you well?'

'Most decidedly,' I reply, and heave a romantic sigh.

'Here I am, talking nineteen to the dozen. How fed up you must be at the sound of my voice. I fear I bore myself sometimes.'

'I could listen to you for hours.'

She gives me a look of genuine surprise. 'Indeed? Then you are in a class of your own. Even my most intimate friends say that I talk too much.'

'I hardly think they appreciate you.'

'You flatter me again.'

'I'm partial, I admit. But ask me to think of a more pleasurable mode of transport and I shall be unable to answer.'

'Now, that must be flattery! Look at the weather!'

The drizzle has thickened into a persistent downpour and despite the umbrella my trouser-bottoms are sodden.

'I barely noticed it,' I say gamely. My feet are wet through the boot-leather. It'll take Mam an age to stuff them with newspaper and get them dried out right. 'Let me take the umbrella, do.'

She resists, but not with much fervour. I hoist it high and water trickles the length of my arm to the elbow. Despite the discomfort I smile like a true gent. By the time we get to the city, my hardness has wilted. It does not matter. I am getting my foot in the door. When we step down at Piccadilly Gardens I feign a doting look.

'Good evening, Mr Latchford,' she says, and walks away.

'Where are you going?' I say, scampering to keep up.

'Home, of course.'

'Then I shall accompany you.'

'That is quite unnecessary.'

'My eye! I won't hear of a young lady travelling unaccompanied.'

She gives an unfeminine snort. 'I hardly think Manchester is overrun with bandits.'

'I insist. I would be remiss in my duties as a gentleman if I did not.'

'You need feel no sense of duty, Mr Latchford.'

'It is not duty. It is pleasure.'

'Is there any point in my resisting?'

I grin. 'None.'

At last I earn a bow of the head. I know that posh types are obliged to be wary, but this back and forth is taxing my sodden good humour. Besides, she quacks loud and long enough about being opposed to convention. It is quite hypocritical. Once again, I retain self-control and remind myself that she chose to sit beside me.

'Why, there's your tram,' I say, pointing to the number 38.

She gives me a queer look. 'You are remarkably well informed about the direction of my residence.'

I curse the slip, but effect a good save. 'Dear Edie speaks of you so often!' I say with strained tenderness.

I help her clamber on to her tram and pay for us both; no, I won't hear a word. A stiff breeze blows away the rain clouds; the air is crisp and sharp in my lungs. I am the soul of gallantry, fit to knock the shine off the stars: enthusing about the rally, the thrilling speech, the jolly company. I hold her in my spell all the way to her stop, through the maze of tree-clogged streets and to her gate. It occurs to me that, away from the baleful influence of her overseers, she behaves as befits a lady, quiet and attentive. In her heart of hearts she knows we are a match made in heaven. It's as good as decided.

333

'Thank you,' she says rather wearily. 'Your conscience can be clear, Mr Latchford. You have conveyed me to my threshold.'

'Are we here?' I say, pretending I've never set eyes on the place. I tip my cap. 'I hope that I may offer similar service on a future occasion.'

'Yes, indeed,' she says vaguely. She turns, but thinks better of it. 'Perhaps you might accept an invitation to dine one evening,' she adds more brightly.

It's all I can do to restrain myself from sweeping her down the street in a mazurka. 'Marvellous!'

'Next week, perhaps? An evening when you and Edie are both available?'

My heart trips over its own feet. 'Edie? Why would I want to drag her along?'

'Now, Mr Latchford. We have spent an enjoyable day in each other's company. Don't spoil it by being ungenerous. I have to chide Edie for the same reason. I can hardly be an effective peacemaker if you do not—'

'Peacemaker?' I say. 'Is that what this is?'

'Is what . . .' she begins, and then pauses. She regards me carefully. 'Mr Latchford. May I speak frankly?'

'Of course,' I say cautiously.

'Why are you like this?'

'Like what?'

She sighs. 'You are so – formal.'

I am thunderstruck and it shows. 'Formal?'

'Everything you say is so – clipped. You bow, snap your heels, hold yourself as stiffly as a Ruritanian grandee. Manners that seem borrowed from a melodrama. I wonder what lines you would speak if the script were taken from you.'

My mind spins. I can turn this to my advantage. I muster affront.

'Can't a fellow be polite without having aspersions cast upon his good nature?' I bluster. 'I am wounded, Miss Hargreaves. Everywhere men are accused of brutish behaviour, yet when you are presented with a chap who is all consideration, you criticise his conduct. If I may make so bold, Miss Hargreaves, I believe you are playing a game I cannot possibly win.'

She draws her brows together. 'Again with the charade. I have a conviction that I should enjoy your company more if you were yourself. You need play no part on my account.'

'A part? This is insupportable. Do you detest me so much?'

'Quite the opposite. I am drawn to you—'

'You are?' I gulp, wind taken out of my sails.

'—without precisely knowing why. I am minded to like you. To count you as a friend. But my heart is vouchsafed elsewhere.'

'Who is the lucky cove?' I say bitterly.

'Not a *cove*, Mr Latchford.'

'What?'

'I should have thought it was self-evident. I have never hidden where my affections lie. Do you and Edie not speak to each other?'

'Edie?' I gasp.

I'm all too aware of Edie's infatuation with this princess, but never guessed it might be reciprocated. All of the vile, degenerate . . . No. I am the right one for her. It's the way it should be. Man and woman.

'Who else? You must know, surely. You share the same roof, eat at the same board. It is not something that can be hidden.'

My ire, suppressed so long, bursts free from its gaol.

'Shut up!' I cry. 'Edie this, Edie that, on and on and on. I can't tell you how sick I am of hearing that name. My mother, my grandmother and now you. You women . . .'

'I beg your—!' She straightens her hat and wrestles with the

335

buttons of her jacket as though she dislikes them. 'Mr Latchford. You will regret these words tomorrow. I can only surmise that you are fatigued.'

'I assure you I am no such thing.'

'You are most provoking. This conversation is over.'

She bids me a brisk goodnight and sweeps up the gravelled path. *You want the true Gnome?* I think. *You can have him, both barrels.* I chase after her, seize her arm and push her against the garden wall, violently enough to elicit a groan. As she moans, so do I. There is a sudden buzzing between my ears, my skull full to bursting with wasps.

'Let go of me,' she says.

I shake my head but cannot free myself from the hissing. 'Don't give me that,' I grunt. 'You've been flirting for weeks.'

'I have done nothing of the sort,' she blusters. 'I thought to play peacemaker. That was arrogance on my part, and clearly an error if you've mistaken my behaviour for encouragement.'

'Ballocks. You want this as much as I do.'

She struggles to free herself. 'I am going indoors.'

'Oh no you're not.' The words do not come out as sarcastically as they ought. I drag my wits together. I'll show her who's in charge here. I'll show Edie. I'll show them all. 'So, you think me too formal?' Her jaw sets in a grim line. I give her elbow a twist, only to recoil as a stabbing pain jabs me in the ribs. 'You want a man of flesh and blood?' I wheeze, grappling for breath. 'You want passion?'

'These are rhetorical questions, Mr Latchford,' she says with tight dignity. 'You have clearly made up your mind.'

'Too right I have,' I leer. 'I am going to *hurt* you.'

This is the moment: her cheeks will grow pale and she will plead, wide-eyed with fright. Neither takes place.

I lick my lips. 'Aren't you afraid?'

'No, I am not,' she replies steadily.

'You ought to be,' I bleat. I turn it into a growl. I don't know what's wrong with me. 'I'll push some fear into you. All your words, your speeches. I'll shove them right where they belong.'

I grab the brim of her hat and tug hard. She winces, making a small sound like someone taking a sip of too-hot tea. As she does so, there's an answering pain in my side that folds me in half. With a great deal of effort I manage to straighten up.

'Did that hurt? Eh?'

'Of course it did,' she hisses, not so much in distress as irritated by such an idiotic question. 'You mistake pain for fear.'

'When I'm done you won't be able to tell the difference.'

'Get on with it, then.'

The air stumbles between us.

'What?'

'You heard. Stop talking about how you'll do this to me and that to me.' Her eyes blaze. 'I am up against a wall. Hurt me. Be done with it so I can go.'

'You're not listening!' I squeak. 'I will break you! I can!'

I raise my fist and with every ounce of my being try to force it into her gob and knock each and every one of her teeth to kingdom come. I can't move. My arm is frozen. All my life's fury cannot budge it one inch closer.

'You will not. I cannot be broken.'

'All women can be broken,' I wail.

'Your experience of our sex is limited.'

'For God's sake,' I moan. 'Shut up.'

I cling to her, stuck like a fly to flypaper. She ought to be terrified. Ought to burst into tears. Ought to hate me. I wish she would; then I'd know where I stood. I want to tear her in half, into quarters, smaller and smaller pieces. I want to rip myself to shreds, so small all the king's horses and all the king's men can't put me back together again. I inspect my hands: my flesh is on fire, yet unmarked. Sweat drips from the tip of my nose.

I lunge forward and press my mouth upon hers.

Edie twitches inside the sack of my skin. Close, so close. We are almost—

Miss Hargreaves extricates herself from my grasp.

'This is ridiculous,' she says. 'Mr Latchford. If you imagine for one moment that this display will turn my head you are grievously mistaken. Do not let your envy and anger spoil what affection exists between us. Goodnight.'

She strides up the path, hammers her fist against one of the glass panels in the front door. I leg it down the driveway before the master of the house can emerge with a shotgun to defend his daughter's virtue. I take a wrong turn straightaway.

I traipse beneath the electric lights, wondering how on earth I am going to find my way home. The street eventually turns me out alongside Alexandra Park. I glare through the iron palings at the rhododendrons and spindly new trees. Broad paths stretch in regimented lines, pale under the moonlight.

Miss Abigail Bloody Hargreaves. She should fall at my feet, fall into my arms. One of the two, I care not which. Blast it, a woman should play by the rules. I am everything she needs and have chosen her, despite the great impediment of her being a suffragette. Most men wouldn't touch her. How dare she turn her nose up at me? She should sing grateful praises that a red-blooded fellow such as myself deigns to set his cap at her. Yet she won't. It should not irk me so much. None of it should. The stiff-necked, dried-up—

The realisation hits me with the force of the Manchester to Liverpool express. I hang on to the bars while I catch my breath. I have fallen for the damned woman. All my denials shrivel like paper in a furnace. It's not a game. It never was. I shake the railings. They are mortared deep, their very solidity intensifying my rage.

This wasn't supposed to happen. I had planned to peck away at her resistance till I hollowed out a hole to fill with myself. And when I'd won her ear I would plant poison therein, sit back and savour the entertainment of Edie lost and alone. All my talk of toying with her, discarding her. It's all hot air. I love her and I want her to love me back. I need it.

I climb the fence, as if it might help me escape these loathsome feelings. I stagger through the bushes, drawn towards the shimmer of a pond at the end of one of the avenues. The surface dazzles with reflected light. I flounder into it, kicking the stars to pieces, and am up to my shins before the chill communicates itself through my britches. I shudder to a halt: breath rasping, heart pumping.

'I don't want to love her!'

I look down. My reflection wobbles, lips move.

You knew where this would lead, I say to myself. *You've always known.*

'No!' I scream. I lift my foot and stamp myself into pieces. I don't love anyone. It's the last thing on my mind. I freeze, one boot up and one boot down.

That's right. This isn't what I want. This is Edie's fault, Edie's feeling. Her *love* – the word makes me sick to my stomach – has dug in its claws and dragged me in its wake. I don't feel a single twinge of affection for Miss Hargreaves. I don't, I *don't* – it is all Edie. I'm bound to her as helplessly as a galley slave chained to his oar. We are one in emotion as well as body, like Siamese twins. It is filthy. She makes me sick. They both make me sick.

I fall to my knees. The water barely reaches my hips. I pound the surface as if I might drown out Miss Hargreaves – the taste, the feel, the smell of her – but it is impossible. I don't want to

339

feel this fire, this ants-under-my-skin fury. It is not mine. I don't want any part of it.

Squatting on the opposite bank is a pavilion. I imagine the denizens of this neighbourhood reclining in its shelter, sipping tea in flowered cups, sticking out their little fingers. I slosh towards it, teeth rattling like clogs. If I can't win this game, I shan't let anyone else win, either.

The park-keeper is long gone, having locked up at sundown to keep out the dangerous likes of me. One hefty kick and the door bursts open. I blunder amongst the stacked tables, hurling them aside; hoist a chair and whack it against the floor until its legs splinter.

Not enough. I trip over a pile of tins and give them a mighty punt as well. Glistening muck sprawls across the floor and the air blooms with the scent of paint. I lug one of the cans outside. In vast, uneven letters I slather *Votes For Women* across the flagstones.

Not enough. My mind itches. Even an idiot could start a conflagration with all this rubbish. I scout about and find a bottle of thinners, a heap of rags and a box of lucifers. I watch my hands fumble, breaking the first, the second. If I do this I'm signing my own death warrant.

Don't do this.

It sounds like me. It can't be.

I can't help myself. It's too late anyway. I've ruined what little chance I had with Miss Hargreaves. I may as well destroy everything else while I'm at it. I'm Gnome, aren't I? Destruction is all I've ever been good for.

I strike the third match. The fire takes like a dream, flames gobbling wood made delicious with turpentine. I stare at the spreading inferno, hypnotised by my handiwork. Sparks soar and whirl like Catherine wheels. My memory glitters: a lake full of stars; Edie and I leaping like rockets. A time when I knew what I was and what I was doing.

No time to lose myself in memory. I run.

'Fire!' I shriek.

Windows roll up; heads stick out to discover the source of the racket. I pull my cap low.

'Fire!'

I love her.

That voice again, sounding like my own. It can't be me. It has to be Edie.

I can't let myself know this truth. I career towards Hulme, bellowing till my heart bursts, but I can't outrun my feelings, nor drown them out with screaming. It's too late for repentance. Too late for any of that. Miss Hargreaves is right. Everything I do is an act. I play the lover I think she will want; I play the brother I think Edie wants, the man Jessie wants, the son Mam wants. I no longer know who I am. I've been pretending so long I lost Gnome in all the invention. I thought myself so clever. I'm still a fool of a boy, jumping at fireworks. At least I was happy then. I was alive. We were alive. It's over; all of it.

Mam's in the kitchen. When she claps eyes on me, her expression twists to fondness. 'My favourite little man!'

She pours a cup of tea. I have the bizarre notion she's been waiting up with the pot ready at her elbow. I am all over the shop tonight and can't trust anything. I grunt thanks and sip the brew, powerful enough to make my ears ring.

'Just as you like it, strong and sweet.' She clinks her cup against mine. 'Here's to us. None like us,' she adds, play-punching my bicep. 'Aw, my lamb. What ails you?'

I wipe my nose on my sleeve. 'Nothing,' I mutter.

'Come on now, tell your mother.'

341

I drain the cup and stand. 'I'll get upstairs. Edie'll be here soon enough.'

She leans across the table and grabs my hand. 'Where's your hurry? Make her wait. Won't do her any harm to stew in her own juice for a while.' She inhales the words sharply, like someone might take them from her.

'No point, Mam.'

She won't let go of my hand. I sit down.

'By the time I was your age I was sick to the back teeth of your grandmother ordering me to share with Arthur. Me? Never.'

Her knuckles are white around the handle of the cup. She lifts it to her lips. The liquid jitters, droplets spilling on to the board. She does not notice. I guide her hand until the cup rests safely in its saucer. She does not notice that, either.

'You're your mother's son,' she continues, eyes glazed. 'Arthur's allowed in when I let him and he puts up with it. So he should. He's lucky I give him the time of day.' She giggles. 'Or night. You lay down the law with Edie, my lad. Serve her right.'

Something turns over in my stomach. These are words I've ached to hear. I've spoken them in the privacy of my own head often enough.

'I need—' I begin, but she interrupts.

'We don't need anyone but each other. Birds of a feather. We make a grand flock. The two of us.'

'No,' I say. 'I don't want that. I want . . .'

She lowers her eyelids, opens them slowly and continues as though I've not said a word. 'Like mother, like son,' she coos. 'We're practically normal, aren't we? None of that vile—' She shakes her head. 'Normal,' she repeats firmly, and elbows me in the ribs. 'I've won. Let's see you do the same, eh?'

I stand up. This time she does not hold me back. Her gaze remains fixed at the empty chair, as though my ghost is still seated there. I climb the stairs and sit on the edge of the bed. My stamping tantrums about how I don't care, not for anyone, not for anything. Lies. I care, very much. Edie loves Abigail. So do I. It is real. Love, anger, misery, revenge. If there's a difference, I can't feel it. All agony.

'I'm sorry,' I moan.

The words echo off the cramped-in walls. She's sorry too. Even if Grandma hadn't told me, I'd still know. I did not listen. Neither of us did. There's a swirling in my head as she surfaces.

What've you done? She sounds half-asleep.

'You should know. You tried to stop me.'

Stop what?

'If it wasn't you, who was it?'

I'm not your keeper, Gnome. It's late. Leave me be.

'Don't go!'

What?

'I don't want to be alone.'

Stop being silly. We're not children.

With that, she's gone.

I have not prayed since I was a child. I fall to my knees. It is not low enough. I prostrate myself, bang my head on the floorboards and beg for the impossible: that I did not set fire to the Pavilion, did not mistreat Abigail, did not foul up my entire life in the space of half an hour.

It is done. I have lost everything because I could not control myself. I have let anger consume me as it has consumed Mam. I am the King of Ashes, all hope reduced to cinders and by my own hand. I've proved to Edie I can't be trusted. Proved it to Abigail, to my grandmother, to everyone who matters. I am not worth the candle. I do not deserve forgiveness. My rage falls away. Without its heat I am cold and naked. I am nothing.

EDIE
JANUARY 1910

I rub my eyes and struggle awake, a sick grinding at my temples. The room is filled with the sharp-sweet fume of pine oil, which explains the headache. It reminds me: Gnome woke me in the middle of the night. The memory is half gone, like a dream that fades when you try to seize upon it. He was saying sorry, of all things. I delve into the depths of his apology. My skin crawls. If I didn't know better I'd say it was remorse.

I shake off the ridiculous notion. The reek of turpentine is turning my stomach, that's all. I drag myself off the mattress and open the window to let in some air. A bedraggled washing line, the huddled privy, but no sign of any uproar in the yard. The Comet is in one piece. Whatever Gnome was bothering me about, it can't have been important.

The bells of St Wilfrid's chime for morning service. I lean on the sill and bend my thoughts towards Abigail, a far more deserving object of attention. It is cold enough to see my breath in a plume of mist but to my fond eye, all is bright. For the first time in my life I am happy. If ever a soul deserved love, I do. Week follows week and month follows month, yet each moment with Abigail is as thrilling as the first, each kiss also. My flesh sings at the touch of her mouth and hands, shaking

344

me to my foundations more profoundly than I thought possible. I entertain daydreams of the two of us sharing a home and growing old together. It is all rather vague in that way of romantic reveries, but delightful nonetheless.

I pull down the sash and blow on my fingers. As for the niggling irritation of my secret, I simply refuse to think about it. I parry her enquiries with the skill acquired from a lifetime of practice, although I do wonder why her questions increase rather than decrease. It is the only blot on perfection and compared to the nightmares life has thrown my way, amounts to the smallest of clouds in an otherwise clear sky. This new year dawns with boundless hope. Let me dream, I say to myself. A handful of dreams never did a body harm.

My reflections are interrupted by a hammering at the front door. Ma's window screeches open.

'I'm opening at noon and not a moment before!' she shouts.

Muffled words are exchanged. Whoever is out there has not been put off by Ma's peremptory dismissal. A thump of footsteps sounds along the landing and my door flies open.

'It's for you,' growls Ma, her hair still in rags. 'You tell her, whatever her name is, that decent hardworking folk need their sleep on a Sunday morning.'

She bustles out, banging on my grandmother's door, bellowing commands to be up and about and that church will not wait. I don blouse and petticoat, trudge sleepily into Ma's room and stick my head through the window. My headache dissolves on the spot.

'Abigail!' I cry. 'Why ever in the world—'

She raises her head. Her features are printed with worry. 'Edie. I am sorry.' She draws off her glove and wrings it like a dishcloth. 'I did not know what else to do. Can you come?'

'Of course. I'll be down presently.'

Church can wait. I pull on the remainder of my clothes: by some miracle the laces of my corset do not snag and my hair obeys the brush tolerably well. I squint at the mirror. It will have to do. I take the stairs two at a time.

'Dearest,' she begins.

I clasp her hand, and press my lips to her cheek. 'Dearest,' I echo. 'What on earth has happened?'

'Terrible things. The police have arrested – we are accused . . .' She glances about distractedly. The back of my neck bristles as the curtains of Renshaw Street begin to twitch.

'Walk with me,' I say. I grab hat and shawl from the coat-stand and take her arm, steering her away from inquisitive neighbours. 'The Pahoria?' I suggest. 'It is open on a Sunday, the heathens.'

She manages a weak smile. 'Heathens.'

The place is almost empty and we get a table right away. Manchester must be more God-fearing than I suspected. As soon as our order is taken, Abigail takes a folded newspaper out of her handbag and spreads it across the table. The page crackles like distant fire.

'We are blamed for this outrage,' she says, voice quavering.

I read the words: the Alexandra Park Pavilion reduced to cinders. Huns. Vandals. Terrible destruction. Wilful violence.

'That's awful,' I say. 'Who would do such a thing?'

'Who indeed. Look.' She presses her forefinger to the photograph beneath the garish headline. Through the blur of black and white I see what has been daubed amongst the ashes. *Votes for Women.*

'Oh Lord!' I cry. As I speak, a chill seizes my throat. That scent of turpentine. No. He can't possibly be involved. He's been so – amenable.

Her shoulders sag. 'There will be denials. Which nobody will

346

believe.' Slowly, she looks at me. 'You believe me, don't you?

'Of course!'

She grasps my hand. 'I needed to hear you speak the words. Forgive me.'

'I would give far more than words.'

'Thank you,' she whispers. Her hand creeps to my cheek and I lean into its comfort. 'This sort of thing does the cause no good,' she continues, withdrawing her hand and staring at her fingers. 'We look as though we wrought this damage, even though we did not.'

'Then why?'

'To besmirch what little good name we have and drag us through the mud. The place was locked up for the night. What if a tramp – what if a child . . .' She contemplates the newspaper. 'A broken window is one thing. Where the life of an innocent may be endangered, assuredly not. And after such a peaceful rally . . .'

I clap my hand to my brow. The Ashton rally. So that's why Gnome dangled the promise of an evening if I gave up my Saturday afternoon. It didn't occur to me he'd have the slightest interest in women's suffrage. Sneaking around behind my back is one thing, but would he descend to this level? Is this why he said sorry?

'Gnome,' I blurt, despite myself.

'Edie. Do you know something?'

'Yes. No.'

The waitress brings the tray and we sit in rigid silence as she places cups, saucers, sugar, milk and teapot upon the table. It seems to take forever. He couldn't have. I trusted him.

Abigail pours the tea. 'I wonder . . .' she says in a half-trance. 'But it cannot be. Surely your brother would not . . .'

'I wouldn't put it past him,' I mutter. I churn with

self-recrimination. I thought he'd changed. How could I have been so stupid? I fell for his charm: hook, line and sinker. It was always too good to be true. 'He is a hundred times worse than you can possibly imagine.'

'I have a very sharp imagination,' she snaps. 'I apologise. My nerves are in ribbons this morning.'

My frustration explodes. 'I told you to steer clear!' I roar, bang my fist on the table. The crockery rattles. Every customer turns; stares. 'Why didn't you listen to me?' I hiss, lowering my voice. Our audience lose interest. A pair of giddy females; that's all we are.

'I don't relish being told what to do,' she replies, none too gently.

'When it comes to my brother, I damn well shall do. You have no idea of what he is capable.'

She stares into her cup before taking a careful sip. 'I think I do. Last night, after the rally. He made – advances.'

I go cold to the roots of my hair. 'What . . .?'

'I know; I know. You warned me. There was no great damage done. He seemed to be acting out of anger rather than desire.' She wrinkles her brow. 'I realise that sounds absurd.'

I look at my hands. He laid them upon her. No. I could never. Would never. There is a sudden fracture in the working of my brain, as though the gaslight of my conscious mind has shuddered in a strong draught. My hands, his hands. My touch, his. I clench my fists as though I am trying to hold on to myself. The nails dig into the soft flesh of the palm. It hurts, but not enough to sear away this turmoil.

'What is it, Edie?'

I hide his disgusting paws behind my back. 'Nothing.'

'I see it in your face. You know more about this matter than you admit.'

348

'I don't know what you mean.'

'Oh yes, you do. There's something rotten at the root of this enmity. It's not the usual quarrelling that exists between brother and sister. I must know.'

'No you mustn't.'

'I will know.'

'No you won't.'

She lowers her cup and gives me a look I cannot translate. 'Edie. All I ask is honesty, however taxing. Do you imagine I find it easy to disclose what your brother attempted last night?'

I shake my head mutely.

'There must be openness, now more than ever,' she continues. 'We are attacked from all sides. I must know what is going on, who stands for us and who against. What are you concealing from me?'

'Abigail, I implore you.'

'I will listen. I will cast no judgement.'

'No!' I cry, perilously close to shrieking, powerless to stop. There is an ugly pause.

'Can you not trust me?'

The cups rest in their saucers. The tea cools. Abigail lays her palms upon the tablecloth and smoothes away a crease in the linen. She watches the movement of her fingers to the left, to the right. At last, she raises her eyes to mine.

'If there is no trust between us, Edie, then what are we doing here?'

There is a longer silence. It stretches between us, taut and unbearable, whilst around us rings the din of plates and cups, the hubbub of conversation as the café begins to fill with good Christian souls who have done their duty and roared prayers at the firmament.

I cast about for the words to smooth this over. 'Why do you

press me so?' I say. 'Don't let this argument come between us. Let us be happy. Forget my brother.' I thrust my hand across the table. She glances at it.

'Edie. You say I am dear to you.'

'You are.'

'You call me beloved.'

'And so you are!' I say desperately.

'I spoke frankly to your brother and I shall afford you the same. You know all there is to know about me. I have let you into the most intimate places of my heart.'

I nod. There is a stone in my throat that is proving hard to swallow. She leans across the table and pats the back of my hand. It is a sisterly gesture, devoid of ardour.

'I hesitate to say this,' she continues, 'but I must, for it demands to be said. What, my dear Edie, have you given me in return?'

With every scrap of my being I want to say *everything*. But the word sticks and can't break free.

'I know next to nothing about you. From the first day of our acquaintance you have hidden half of yourself.'

I stare into my cup. Some tea-leaves have escaped the strainer and float on the surface.

'I have demeaned myself by asking Guy if he knows more, but you play your cards as close to your chest with him.'

'Guy is—'

She raises her hand. 'I have spread my dreams before you and waited for you to reciprocate. You have not. I catch glimpses into your soul. Just as I feel I am about to approach some vital truth, you withdraw. There is a need about you, Edie; it draws me in, only to thrust me away. I do not understand it and I am not sure you do, either.'

My heart swings like a clapper against the cage of my ribs. I bow my head miserably. She continues.

350

'I am intrigued by you. But I will not let this fascination wear a blindfold. You are a will-o'-the-wisp and if I continue to follow I will become lost. I cannot let myself be drawn further into this dance. I am tired of pursuit.'

'Do you think I do this on purpose, to hurt you?'

'No, I do not,' she replies, an aching sadness in her voice. 'You hurt yourself.'

'Help me,' I breathe.

'I have done all I can. I have trusted, loved, demonstrated openness. I have been patient. I can be so no longer. We can remain friends who shake hands and take tea, but an intimate connection – no. I wish it were not so. But it is.'

I cover my face with my hands. I can't bear to look at her, or have her look at me. 'Of all beings with whom I wish to share myself,' I croak. 'That woman is you.'

'Then why do you not? I want you in my life, Edie. But I can have no half-woman. I must have the whole.'

I hear our breathing: hers, calm and even; mine, gulping and shallow. I lower my hands and look at her. 'I want you, Abigail.'

'You do not. You want someone to hide in. I am not the answer to your emptiness. I am your equal. I will meet you halfway, on the bridge we build of our two souls, our two hearts. I cannot span that chasm on my own, nor shall I.'

I gaze at her. Never more desirable or out of reach. 'Can't you believe it is too much to tell you?'

'Not any longer.'

'I am – different,' I whisper. 'More than you can know, or understand.'

'I cannot understand? Yet you do not try me.'

'It is too difficult. Within me – part of me – dwell monsters.'

'And you consider me too feeble to face them? Edie, if you

351

can't trust me with the whole of you, then there is no more to be said. This grieves me more than you can know.'

'You have thrown down a gauntlet.'

'Perhaps I have. Whether or not you pick it up is up to you.'

She tilts her face aside, as if in search of inspiration. But she is merely checking the time by the clock over the till. A muscle in her cheek tightens under the force of powerful emotions and I glimpse the pain this has cost her.

'It is twelve o'clock. I have a meeting to attend.' She prises open the clasp of her purse, withdraws a florin and sets it between us.

'That's more than enough,' I say helplessly. 'We've only had tea.'

She does not respond, nor does her expression alter. She pushes back her chair.

'Wait.'

'What for, Edie? For you to speak to me truthfully?'

'Please, Abigail,' I beg. 'Give me a little time. I will. I promise.'

She pauses, gripping her bag in readiness to leave. 'It is a simple thing to find me when – if – you wish to meet me equal-hearted. I hope you do. Until then, goodbye.'

I watch her weave between the tables. A gentleman tips his hat and opens the door. She nods graciously and passes through into the morning sunshine. The clouds have peeled away. It is a beautiful January morning. All is well with the world. She shades her eyes, looks to the left and to the right, crosses Market Street and is swallowed by the crowd.

The newspaper spreads across the cloth. I lay my palm over the spot where she pressed her fingertips, and close my eyes.

'Sorry to startle you, miss,' says the waitress. 'Are you done here?' She eyes the florin longingly.

'Yes,' I stutter. 'Quite finished.'

352

She brings the change on a saucer. I stir the coins with my finger. Enough for a teacake. Two teacakes. With jam. I twist the newspaper into a tight roll and make my way to the door, pursued by the waitress.

'You've forgotten your change, miss!'

'It is quite all right.'

She beams. 'Thank you, miss!'

The trek to The Comet is a long one. I enter by the back gate to avoid fighting my way through the bonhomie of the public bar. Most of all, I do not want to go eye-to-eye with Ma and see that conquering smile as she reads the defeat printed upon my features.

I sit on my bed and stare at the wall, counting cracks in the plaster. The sound of lunchtime drinkers filters through the floorboards. I am a hundred miles from them, and more. I have spent my life surrounded by crowds and have as much in common with them as a blob of tar in a bucket of water.

The scales have fallen from my eyes. Gnome is not the harmless boy he pretended. I curse myself for an idiot. I should have expected it. He's been up to his destructive tricks all along and now he dares come between Abigail and myself. He is the cause of our disagreeable argument. That's all it is, I reason. A disagreement. One of those clouds blotting the sunshine of our affection. Like a cloud, this will pass over. Harmony will exist between us once again. All shall be well. All manner of things shall be well.

Despite my brave talk, I seethe with doubt.

None of this is my fault. It is his. It is Nana's for making me agree to sharing. It can no longer be countenanced. I groan. What, then, is the alternative? I shudder at the thought of a return to self-wounding to keep him away. Five years' worth of scars silver my flesh. What will my body look like after ten

353

years, fifteen? I've no one to turn to. If I tell Uncle Arthur, Ma will find out. As for Nana, she'll pontificate how I've brought it down on myself.

There is nothing I can do. The walls of my life press in as blankly as those of this room. I had such hopes, made such brave steps: employment, lodgings, friends. I experienced love and had it reciprocated. All of it dashed to pieces. Perhaps Ma was right all along: happiness is not for the likes of us. I am shackled to an empty future. No way out. Nothing but this family. I may as well cast off my foolish dreams of love, quit the Telegraph Office and resign myself to working behind the bar of The Comet. I may as well start now.

I regard my possessions, imagining Gnome's eye upon the cards and letters from Abigail. With a sinking certainty, I know he has read them all. I imagine the tip of his tongue running back and forth across his lips as his grubby fingers trace the words. I laid my heart before him, as plain as an account book. If only I'd laid my heart before Abigail so openly.

The door opens and my grandmother comes in.

'Come to gloat?' I say. 'Look at what your interference has brought me to.' I shake out the newspaper and thrust it under her nose. She reads it without taking it from my hand.

'He wouldn't—'

'Who else? Share with Gnome, you said. Find a middle way, you said. It is better that way, you said. He is uncontrollable. He will never change. I should never have listened to you.'

'I stand by every word, Edie. A balance is your only hope. Look at how bitter your mother—'

'Oh, don't start again with that old tune. At least Ma lets Arthur out once a month. When do you let your other half out, eh?'

She chuckles. 'You have no clue, have you?'

'Laugh if you want. I know enough to know you're a hypocrite. First in line to dole out advice, but I don't see you practising what you preach. I cannot recall one single, solitary instance when I've set eyes on – well, I don't even know his name.'

I expect her to snipe and sneer. Ma would. But this is not my mother.

'You cannot see what is before your very eyes. I expect nothing better from them.' She flutters her fingers at the world beyond the window. 'But you. For goodness' sake, can't you tell?'

'Tell what? What on earth are you on about? And will you forever stop smiling.'

'You are looking at your grandfather.'

'What? No I'm not,' I snort. 'Shut up with your nonsense.'

'It is anything but. This is what I mean by sharing.'

I stare at her: the whiskery chin, the broad features. 'You aren't my grandfather,' I say. 'You can't be. He'd wear trousers.'

'Good grief, Edie. What a stupid thing to say. I don't care what I wear as long as I am decently covered. A skirt is an eminently practical garment and I can't be doing with britches one day, petticoats the next. No one remarks on one more old biddy on the street. I'd rather pass unnoticed than be tarred and feathered.'

'I don't understand. Who are you at the moment?'

'I swear I shall box your ears if you don't stop asking ridiculous questions.'

'Please. Are you Nana or Grandfather?'

'I am me. We. Us. Both. Neither. All. Choose your word. I care not one jot.'

'At the same time? How . . .'

'This is my way. My balance. I hoped you might find yours as joyously.' She looks wistful.

'Why didn't you tell me?' I moan. 'I could have—'

'Because there's no fool like an old fool. I wanted you to find your way by example rather than instruction. Your mother nagged from noon to night and I wished to show a kinder face. I did wrong by you.'

'It's too late now. Gnome has ground any hope into dust.'

'Has he?'

How smoothly the accusation slips from my tongue, slithering out like a mouthful of blancmange. I am at a crossroads. I can continue to parrot a lifetime's worth of easy platitudes: *Gnome is angry, Gnome is hateful, Gnome is greedy, it's not my fault.* I know why Gnome is the way he is. How easily I've shrugged off any personal responsibility in the matter. I am perilously close to becoming my mother, with no desire to learn, to understand, to change.

'No,' I say, staring at my empty hands. 'I have managed that by myself. I was offered love and all I had to do was trust. I could not. I threw away my chance.'

'That Miss Hargreaves?' she asks. I nod. 'Do you trust her?'

'Yes. With all my heart.'

She grasps my shoulders. 'Don't you dare give up. It's too late for me and your ma, but not for you. If you've met a creature with the strength of character to love you, tell her.'

'I can't.'

Her eyes shine with a faraway look. 'Ask yourself: if she told you a secret about herself. Not something she'd done, but something she was. What would your answer be? There is your truth.'

'You make it sound easy.'

'I know it is not. What is the worst that might follow? That she does not believe you? That she thinks you deluded?'

'All of that.'

'It seems to me that if you don't tell her what you are, you will lose her. If you do, there is a small chance you will not. A small chance is better than none at all.' She stands, puffing with the effort, and points at the newspaper sprawled across my lap. 'Don't let it end like this.'

After she has gone, I stand before the mirror: head up, shoulders back. I have spent my life whining that I am hard done by, plagued with an incorrigible other half. We have both committed acts of cruelty against the other. Both of us frightened, angry, vengeful, at odds with our odd selves. I must hold myself to account for my part in the sorry mess we have made of our life.

I can avoid it no longer. I can't live on this tightrope for the rest of my days. I will breathe the air of the world's possibilities rather than sleepwalk through a half-dead existence. I will prove to my grandmother, to Abigail, to myself that I am worthy of love. I will face my terrors, before my courage fails. She may very well call me mad – for what other outcome can there be? – and send me packing. At least I will have tried.

I walk to Whalley Range in a turmoil and, all too soon, come to her door. I grip the sunflower door-knocker and crack it hard. A young woman opens up. After a momentary look of confusion, she gathers herself and asks for whom I am calling. Abigail appears at the foot of the stairs and rescues me.

'Thank you, Betty. Miss Latchford is expected.'

I blink. 'Am I?'

Abigail motions me indoors. I pause on the mat, afraid to enter. A grandfather clock thumps the seconds. I never knew the passage of time could be so deafening.

'Against my better judgement,' she says. 'I cannot snap my fingers and cease loving you merely because I ought.'

'Abigail. I have come to apologise. More than that. I am here to offer what you ask for. The truth.'

'I too owe you an apology,' she replies. 'It was unworthy of me to shout at you in the café.'

'On the contrary, you were quite fair.'

Betty flits back and forth across the hallway, pausing to dust a spotless umbrella stand. Abigail gathers her coat and hat and raises her voice a notch.

'It looks to be a fine afternoon for the time of year. Let us take a turn around the park before dusk sets in.'

I walk, stiff-legged, at Abigail's side. She does not touch me, nor I her, as if by brushing against each other the world might explode into a firework show. The park-keeper tips his cap as we pass through the gate.

'I'll be closing up in half an hour,' he says. 'Don't you ladies be getting locked in.'

We roam along an avenue of new elms, planted by a gardener who knew he would never see them grow to maturity. An act of faith and generosity for the enjoyment of future generations.

'These saplings are quite bare of leaves,' I remark, breaking the silence. 'They look rather lonely.'

Abigail gives me a crisp look. 'Have we come here to discuss the traits of deciduous trees?'

'No.'

'I thought not.'

A brace of swells give us the eye and I wait for disagreeable comments about two females walking unchaperoned. Something in Abigail's bearing makes them demur and they scuttle away with the mildest of salutations.

Conversation ceases. My mind tumbles as I search for words that might frame the impossibility that I am. My bravery falters. How can I watch her face – that beloved face – twist into repulsion? After a few moments, we find ourselves by the pleasure lake. I lean on the fence and look at my reflection.

With each breath of wind my features distort. One moment I look like Gnome; the next, Edie. All it takes is a trick of the light and there I am. There we are. How very ridiculous to say *me* and *him*. I drag my gaze upwards and face Abigail.

'Very well. It is time.'

She nods and takes a deep breath. 'I am listening,' she says, extending her hand. 'But let us be away from this awful place. It reminds me how easily hopes can be destroyed.'

I glance across the icy water and see the ruins of the Pavilion on the far side. 'Oh! I am sorry. I did not mean to bring us so close to…'

'It is no matter.'

I hold her gaze. If I am not to see her after this evening, and that seems likely, then I shall take my fill of her while I can. We proceed along the darkening avenue, arm in arm.

'I shall speak as plainly as I am able,' I say. 'You deserve the truth. If, afterwards, you wish to sever all connection, I shall understand. All I ask is that you keep my confidence.'

'Of course.'

'What I am about to say cannot be taken back. I conceal a secret about myself – not from you alone, but from the whole world – that could taint you with association and bring down shame upon your head.'

'What have you done?'

'It is not what I have done. It is what I am.'

'Oh,' she says, her face clearing. 'Are you ashamed of the passion we feel for each other? I am surrounded by women far more abandoned to physical pleasure than we two.' The heat of her glance strengthens my nerve. 'Indeed, I wish I could persuade you to abandon yourself further.'

I press my lips to her palm. 'So do I,' I whisper. 'It is not that, not at all. What if I am not all I seem?'

She cocks her head. 'I do not follow.'

'What if, one night, we held each other close and you discovered alien flesh? What if my body changed before your eyes?'

'I should still love you. These are wild speculations, Edie. You are affrighting yourself with imaginings.'

'This is not imagination. I wish it were. This is more than possible. It is true and, sooner or later, will happen.'

'Edie. By all that is holy, speak.'

I open my mouth, not sure what will emerge. 'My body is protean. Changeable. Stranger than the chameleon. Tiresian.'

'You are talking in riddles,' she says. 'Maybe it would help if you stopped being poetic.'

I blush. 'It is somewhat indelicate.'

She comes to a halt and looks me in the eye. 'No one is listening other than myself. Do not slip behind propriety, with me of all people. Out with it. Tell me, in plain words.'

'I am not a woman,' I say. The words have the weight of a cannon-shot in the tranquil park. Abigail stands so still I wonder if time has ground to a halt and we are suspended in some place outside of its forward movement. I take another breath. 'Nor am I a man. Not entirely.'

'Not entirely,' she repeats.

'Not all of the time, leastways. I shift back and forth. Female to male, male to female. There you have it.'

There is a pause. I wait for the trees to tear up their roots and crash to the ground, for the earth to open and belch fire. No such disaster takes place. Her lower lip sticks out a little, in that way it does when she is thinking.

'So,' she says. 'You exist between the sexes?'

It is part question, part statement. The words come as effortlessly as an observation that I come neither from Liverpool nor Birmingham, but a place between the two.

'I do,' I reply as simply. 'Gnome is not my brother.'

'Ah. Of course.'

'Two souls, one body. We take – turns. Night and day.'

'This is what you have hidden from me.'

'And the world.'

'I can see why. It is indeed difficult to comprehend.'

'I knew it.'

'Do not look so crestfallen. I said difficult, not impossible.'

'You *believe* me?'

'I've heard plenty of lies in my time,' she says dryly. 'This is too strange to be a fabrication. I do not believe you would invent something so outlandish when you could concoct a more reasonable tale of – I don't know – a child born out of wedlock, prostitution, forced marriage.'

I gawp at her. 'You are not disgusted?'

'As the Bard says, there are more things in heaven and in earth. I have female friends who are very like men; equally I know fellows who display all the habits of women.' She smiles. 'I have simply never met anyone who . . . vacillates. In truth, I am relieved.'

'Relieved?' I splutter. All those years of terror, stoked by Ma's admonishments never to let down my guard. A door creaks open in my whirling brain and a shaft of light breaks out.

'Yes. You have held yourself so distant that I feared some abominable duplicity. A number of my sisters warned me off, saying you were planted amongst us by private detectives employed by disapproving husbands, sent to spy on our meetings and beat us at our own game. It has happened in other cities.'

'Oh!'

'I even began to wonder if you had a husband somewhere, a hulking fellow who would dash my brains against the nearest lamp-post if he knew of our desires.'

'Oh,' I repeat, lacking a more articulate response.

'Do you not think I am relieved to find that you are different rather than dishonest?'

'I have been afraid, very much so.'

'That does not surprise me. I can see why you might hesitate to share such information. The world is both prurient and judgemental, particularly regarding issues of such an intimate nature. You must have lived in terror of discovery. You are courageous, Edie.'

'Or foolhardy.'

'I suppose that depends on the person revealed to.'

'I thought it would take longer to explain,' I say quietly. 'Yet here we are at the bandstand. We have walked barely two hundred yards.'

'It is always desirable to be in possession of the truth. It is as though, these past few months, I have been looking at you from a great way off. Come close.' She takes me in her arms, looks me up and down. It is the most delightful sensation. I am seen, truly seen, and accepted. 'Edie. You know my feelings for you. At least you should do by now.'

I am stunned by the intensity of her gaze. My heart thumps with the impossible rhythm *she believes me, she loves me.*

'Dearest Abigail,' I breathe. 'With you I am a better person.'

'How so?'

'It is not the whole truth when I say Gnome and I have taken turns. I have been selfish. I shut him out, Abigail. I found it in my power to suppress him and I wielded that power unfairly. No wonder he is angry.'

A pain in the pit of my stomach makes me double over.

'Dearest. I did not mean to upset you . . .'

I straighten up, gritting my teeth. 'No. I must say this. I've lived the lie that I have been on the side of the angels. He may have made terrible mistakes, but so have I. I can change. I shall change. I am sorry.'

'You are, aren't you?'

I cringe with shame that I should have felt years ago. Not shame about my family, but something far sharper. Shame at my lies, my selfishness, my wheedling excuses. I lurch against Abigail. My legs can no longer bear me up.

'Please, I must . . .' I moan.

She helps me to the nearest bench. Blood rushes in my ears.

'Edie, dearest. Can you walk to my house?'

'It will pass. A moment. I am simply overwhelmed. It is shock. Relief.' I try to breathe evenly. 'My entire life, I have lived in fear of this moment. Now it is here . . .' I laugh. 'I wonder why I was ever so afraid. Oh.'

The trees shimmer.

'Press your forehead to your knees,' says Abigail from a long way above me. 'It helps with such a fit. Dash it all,' she exclaims. 'I did not think to bring smelling salts.'

I obey. The roaring does not lessen, nor the nausea. I am halfway to losing sense of my separate self in the tornado boiling between my ears. My chest heaves. The front of my blouse sags as it finds less and less to fill it. I feel the unmistakeable quaking in my limbs. I shake my head: no. Our limbs. Not mine. I must change everything, down to the words I use.

Forgive me.

I don't know which of us says it. I slip from the safety of the bench and Abigail's arms, and down.

GNOME
JANUARY 1910

A pair of hands, firm about my shoulders. A voice, gentle with concern.

'Edie?' it says.

I fight past the thump, boom-boom commotion in my head. A gravel path presses its teeth into the back of my neck. My breath, tight-bound in a corset. Edie's corset. I haul myself to my knees, groaning with the stretching of flesh as I become man. I turn and see Abigail. A smile breaks on her face, more blinding than any sun. This is what love looks like, I tell myself. My heart judders.

'Oh,' she says. 'You're not . . .'

I throw my arm across my eyes. 'Don't look at me,' I wheeze. The banging between my ears grows louder. A steam hammer on an anvil. Abigail clasps my throat. Now she will throttle me. She pinches the buttons, undoes the collar. Breath dashes in. She helps me to my feet.

'Come with me,' she says, so low the hum communicates itself through my skin and into my gut. 'Both of you.'

There's a heartbeat. A breath.

'Both?' I hear my voice say *both*. I am sure it is my voice. I'd recognise it anywhere. My palms prickle with cold sweat. 'I don't know what you're talking about.'

'Edie has told me about you.'

'She's lying!' I cry. 'You can't possibly believe that nonsense!' My words hiccup to a stop. Her eyes flame with knowledge. I melt in the crucible of her fearsome understanding, that fire of love that burns but does not destroy. She raises an eyebrow.

'Indeed? Edie was here. Now she is not and you are.'

'No!' I no longer know whom I'm bellowing at: Edie, Abigail, myself. 'I've lost. She's won,' I moan. 'Let me go away.'

'I shall do no such thing.' She skewers me with her look, straight through to the back of my head and deeper, into that dank and dingy corner where I've booted my soul. I slam my eyelids shut, but it's no use. She sees what I am.

The twilight sickens. On the far side of the pleasure lake huddles the wreck of the Pavilion. I sniff charred timber, scorched tar-paper. The walls are blotched with a broth of mould. My stomach lurches at the memory.

'Mr Latchford. Gnome. You are not well. Please let us leave this place.'

'I'm not to be trusted! Look,' I say, pointing at the ruin. 'I did that. Everything I touch, I destroy.'

'You were angry, and stupid.'

'I am hateful. I am broken.'

'Stop this, I entreat you.'

'I tried to hurt you.' I twist my head. I mustn't look her in the eye. 'I would have . . .' I gulp. 'I'm a man. I can't be trusted.'

'There are innumerable men who wish to wreak that particular violence upon women.' She puts her arm around me. 'You are not one of them.'

I can't shake her off. I should be able to. My teeth knock like clouted skittles. 'Maybe I won't be able to help myself next time.'

'You did not harm me. More's the point, you could not.'

'How can you know that?'

'You and Edie are too closely interwoven to do me any harm.'

'That's what you think.'

'Yes, it is.'

'Wrong! Wrong!' I raise my hand to strike her, but am as impotent as yesterday evening. 'Let me prove how terrifying I am!' I cry. 'Let me hurt you!

'Stop this, now.'

My body sways, legs treacherous, disobedient. I slump to the ground. I curl my hands into fists, pound them against my ears.

'Let me have my anger,' I plead. I am swaying on a boat, lost upon the ocean. 'Don't take it away. It's all there is to me. It's all that's kept me going. Please. I'm nothing without it.'

'For God's sake!' She shakes me and my brains rattle. 'Away with this self-pity! Edie is sorry and so are you. It is possible to be repentant without the world coming to its end.'

I hang on to her skirt. If I let go I will drown. I plunge my face into its folds and weep. She is at my side, kneeling in the dirt.

'Come to me,' she murmurs. She cups my chin and turns my face to hers. A clutch of pigeons flap dirty wings. 'Yes,' she murmurs. 'Even now, Edie is with you. I can see her in your eyes. She does not want to lose you.'

'She does.' I wipe my nose on my sleeve and print it with a line of silver. 'You belong to Edie.'

'Don't you understand the first thing about love?' she says. 'If what Edie tells me is true – and I have no reason to doubt such an outlandish confession – then I am bound to love you, for you are part and parcel of her. She is part and parcel of you. How can I sever either of you from my life?'

366

'You might as well. Everyone else does.'

'What nonsense you talk,' she gasps. 'I'll say the same to you as I said to her. I belong to no one, neither man nor woman. I am not a thing to be fought or haggled over, like a piece of land.'

I blink. She said the same to Edie? No. It is not possible.

'I'm not worth the effort,' I sniff. Did I always sound so petulant? 'I don't want to be redeemed. I don't want to be whole. I'm filth.'

'Do you hate yourself so much that you would destroy yourself to prove it? Is love so terrifying?'

'Yes,' I whisper. A squeeze of air from a bellows. The fight pours out of me like beer from a staved-in barrel.

'For heaven's sake. It is time to get out of your gutter.' She takes my hand and with remarkable strength pulls me upright. Her eyes roar with fire. 'Be grateful for what you are not. Hell is not some afterlife. You are making one for yourself; making it now and forever. You do not want that.'

Something stirs, something new. It is as frightening as standing on a cliff edge, and as exhilarating.

'No, I don't,' I gulp.

She presses her mouth against mine. Edie rushes forward and tastes the fierce kiss. I surrender. This time she will find a way to keep me gone for good. I cannot blame her. I deserve it.

However, she does not shove me aside. We balance in that place of both and neither, that rope bridge strung between us I have not walked since childhood.

Gnome, says Edie, without speaking. *I have missed you. I have missed us.*

Water runs down my cheek, trickles into my ear. We weep. For the waste, the mess, the complete fist we've made of both our lives. When we could have—

'Stop it!' I cry, slapping hands over our ears. 'I can't do this, Edie. I can't live with myself. Get rid of me. I'm poison.'

I need you, Gnome. I'm not going back to that time.

'You're better off without me. Happier. You said so often enough.'

I was wrong. I'm not real without you. Something is missing; some spark.

'Edie. I – tried to hurt her.'

I know.

'You stopped me, didn't you?'

No. When it came to it, you stopped yourself.

'I was angry,' we say at the same time. With the speaking of the words the fury is gone, as if it was never there.

'I'm sorry.' We do not know who is speaking. It could be either. Or both.

I know.

'We have wasted—'

So much time, we say together.

'We were not so very different.'

We are *not so very different.*

'Will this be difficult?'

Yes. But we will be working together.

There is a silence, a long one.

'Edie?' says Abigail. 'Are you there?'

We open our eyes. Caw of a rook. Black spots waver in the treetops. Dusk sucks colour from the sky. Abigail is bending over us. Her expression uncreases from worry into relief.

'You're here,' she says. 'You went away.'

'Was I . . .' we stutter. It will take a while to sort out the *I* and the *we*. 'Was it a long time?'

'A few moments only. You fell. Let me . . .' She cradles our

368

shoulders, raising us from the bed of rotten leaves. 'Your clothes are wringing wet. The last thing you need to do is catch a chill. Come. We must talk. All three of us.'

She helps us to our feet. My head spins away and we stumble, but she is ready to catch us as we fall.

'You did not leave me here.'

'No,' she declares. 'I would not. It is not possible.'

With an elegance that makes me catch my breath, she bends and retrieves Edie's hat from a puddle. She surveys the bedraggled feathers before shrugging and placing it on our head. We make our way towards the gate.

'You are what you are,' she continues as we go. 'I said you should trust me, and I am a woman of my word.'

We can find neither words nor gestures to express our gratitude. We will need a lifetime.

'Look,' cries Abigail.

She points upwards, voice crackling with excitement. The winter sky is crisp with stars. A haze of light is rolling along the tops of the trees, like a scarf knitted of diamonds.

'A firework,' says Gnome.

'A comet,' corrects Edie.

'Is it Halley's?' asks Abigail.

'Too early. Not due till April.' In answer to her raised eyebrows, we remark, 'I have spent a lot of time in libraries.'

'A new one, then.'

We consider the orbits of wandering stars, the ages that pass. 'They are the opposite of new.'

We take her hand and she leads us out of the park as the keeper is closing the gates. We falter, unsure as a child taking its first steps. It could be the shooting star, or the alien yet familiar simultaneity of Gnome and Edie together. Perhaps it is the presence of Abigail: this jewel amongst women who

369

knows what we are, has witnessed our ugliness and persists in her belief that we may strive for beauty. We are her moon: half-hidden, half-known, changeable. Towards her we turn our face, bright and hopeful.

We slip through the maze of houses, talking of the lonely path of this comet in the frozen wastes beyond the earth; the countless aeons as it circles the universe; how we hope it will find us a more peaceable people when it returns. Words guide us, as sure as Ariadne's thread, to her driveway.

We take the few remaining steps to her door. She turns the handle and, together, we step inside.

ABIGAIL

I am an arrogant female. I have cosseted myself with the belief that I've dared all, done all, seen all this world has to offer. How often have I leaped into the fray, full of satisfaction at the sound of my own voice, the certainty of my arguments. I thought books furnished the answers to all possible questions; thought my lexicon inexhaustible.

How humbling to find my smug intellect challenged by so simple a thing as a pronoun: that *he* and *she* are not sufficient to encompass this new heaven, new earth. I have witnessed what I thought impossible: a woman make the journey into man, and return.

Lacking fresh words to describe my emotions, I shall do the best with those at my disposal: confusion, wonder, disbelief, fear. Yes, fear: that I should lose my Edie as she obeyed her body's imperative to emigrate from female to male. Fear I should not see her again.

That first time, I held her hand. Whether she was my anchor, or I hers, I know not. I watched her flesh transform into a twilight and sink, as day fades into evening. Second by second she dimmed. I waited for the moment when I could state with certainty: *She is gone and he is here.* However, just as it is not possible to point to the precise moment when day ends and night begins, so I cannot say for certain when she ceased being Edie and became Gnome.

How marvellous to be both and neither. How terrifying.

I am humbled by far more than my slippery grasp on syntax. I am in awe of their persistence, their grit, their will to survive against greater odds than we ordinary mortals can ever envisage.

They are my dearest loves. Infinitely precious, infinitely strange.

After experiencing them as two beings of such startling contrasts, my greatest surprise has been their similarity. They teach me how different we are not, none of us. Garb a woman in trousers, a man in a skirt and I dare say – comedic moments aside – far more would pass along a street unremarked than we would credit.

In their protean flesh they demonstrate how foolish are petty distinctions of masculine and feminine. How pointless to separate our selves into empty polarities of north and south. After all, at each extremity, there is nothing but lifeless ice. It is between that our earth spreads its wondrous glory: desert and jungle, tundra and taiga, mountain and ocean.

My schooldays are come round again. I am learning to guard against easy answers that have quicksand for a foundation. I am compelled to question: the greatest gift for which anyone could ask, and the most taxing.

There are a hundred stories to tell and a hundred ways to tell them.

We are learning to accept our contradictions. As time goes by, I am less and less certain with whom I wake, with whom I retire. Less and less does it matter. I thought my heart, given once, might not stretch to encompass two souls. Here is another matter in which I am a student. I am learning how elastic a thing the heart is. How far love can reach, of how much affection I am capable.

Perhaps I should not be so surprised. I love Mama, Papa, Guy, Mabel, any one of a multitude of friends, and that has never struck me as strange. Perhaps this is another of those falsehoods of convention, that we are only capable of loving one person. Perhaps the fire of love is infinite, inexhaustible, and can light a hundred lamps from one flame. Perhaps love is measured not by how much radiance it keeps to itself, but by how much it shines upon the world.

ACKNOWLEDGEMENTS

This is a work of fiction.

I am grateful to Manchester and all its glories, past and present. There is definitely something in the water, for it to be so steeped in radical history. I have been blessed with abundant resources upon which to draw. Far too many to enumerate, they include The Portico Library, The John Rylands Library, The People's History Museum, The Pankhurst Centre, Manchester Histories Festival, the local history publications produced by Neil Richardson in the 1980s and the copious archives held at Manchester Central Library, especially those relating to nineteenth century night-life. Thanks also to Brian Selby and Frank Rhodes for their invaluable work preserving the history of Belle Vue Zoological Gardens. A visit to the Nereid Temple in Room seventeen of the British Museum proved illuminating, and I heartily recommend one of the enjoyable Manchester Ship Canal cruises organized by Mersey Ferries. I wish I could say that doctors like Zambeco did not exist. They did, and chillingly, still do.

Thank you to Aly Fell, for everything. To Charlotte Robertson, who introduced me to the wonderful team at The Borough Press; especially Katie Espiner, Cassie Browne, Suzie Dooré, Charlotte Cray, Holly Ainley and Ann Bissell. Thank you too to my agent Anna Webber at United Agents who guided me on this journey. And a tip of the broad-brimmed hat to Jennifer Garside, seamstress extraordinaire, who pointed me in the direction of Miss Sanderson and the womanly art of parasol self-defence.